wHY
THINGS
FALL

Why Things Fall

Chris Else

TANDEM

First published in 1992 by
Tandem Press
2 Rugby Road, Birkenhead, Auckland 10
New Zealand

Copyright © 1992 Christopher Else

All rights reserved. No part of this publication may be reproduced, stored in a retrieval system or transmitted in any form or by any means electronic, mechanical, photocopying, recording or otherwise without the prior written permission of the publishers.

ISBN 0 908884 12 5

Production by Edsetera
Typeset by Typocrafters Ltd, Auckland
Printed by GP Print Ltd, Wellington, New Zealand

The publishers gratefully acknowledge the assistance of the Literary Committee of the QEII Arts Council.

*For
Patrick
and for
Jonathan*

Acknowledgements

To my partner, Barbara Neale, for her love and support and unerring professional advice.

To the QEII Arts Council for the grant that helped give me time to write this book.

Dinah Hawken's *Small Studies of Devotion*, an extract from which appears on page 189, is published by Victoria University Press, Wellington, 1991.

Several of the ideas in this book have their origin in Dr Marie-Louise von Franz's *Alchemy* (Inner City Books, Toronto, 1980). In particular, the extract from Walter Newton's notes on page 61 are quotations or close paraphrases from this work.

This book is a work of fiction. Any resemblance between the characters portrayed here and any actual human being is purely coincidental.

PART ONE
The Blackening
9

PART TWO
The Peacock's Tail
75

PART THREE
The Whitening
133

PART FOUR
The Reddening
189

Part One

THE BLACKENING

John-a-Nokes was driving a cart towards Croydon, and by the way, fell asleep therein. Meanetime a good fellow came by and stole away his two horses. John awakening and missing them said, 'Either I am John-a-Nokes or I am not John-a-Nokes. If I am John-a-Nokes, then I have lost two horses: and if I am not John-a-Nokes, then I have found a cart.

— Copley, *Wits, Fits, and Fancies* (1614)
quoted in *Brewer's Dictionary of Phrase and Fable*

1 The Creative

This is a story as true as any other. It is about a man who had two sons. He loved them both very much, but each one in a different way. The younger he loved as his flesh and blood, the hope for his future, but in the elder he saw a reflection of his own secret self. The elder boy was handsome, confident in his physical strength. He was kind and good-humoured and he had a lot of friends. He also had a problem. Often when he tried to communicate he would lose control of his words. He could manage the meanings, but the signs themselves, the sounds in the air, the marks that must be made on pieces of paper, were impossible to govern. This was especially true when he wanted to say something to his father, who had no such difficulty. The father was an engineer and a scientist. He had spent all his life searching for the secret of why things fall.

The son's failure with words made him very restless. Eventually, when he was twenty, he went away to another country. He found a job there and he met a young woman. She was tall and graceful. Her hair was gold and her eyes green. Sometimes in her company the words were no problem. The young man fell in love with her. He did not realise that the woman had a restlessness of her own. When she looked out of her window at the fascinations of her life, she often saw only a desert, a vast expanse of yellow-brown sand. She was drawn into this landscape. Someday, she knew, she would have to begin a journey into its heart.

The young man never understood her secret. To him, the woman's wild heart was a great freedom of the spirit. She was a bird that could soar through the air, swooping and diving like the meanings of the words he tried to catch with his clutching fingers. In fact, she could not fly. One of her wings was broken. Sometimes she hated him for his stupidity, for his failure to comprehend her. She railed at him and poured scorn on his weakness. He hated her in return when she was like this because he sensed her desperation, her inner struggle. Unless she could believe in herself, he was sure that he was lost.

One day they had an argument more vicious than usual. The woman was flippant, ironic, full of contempt. She was furious with her lover and with herself, afraid of the heat and the dry sand. The man was full of bursting anger, tormented by the words that buzzed like wasps in the air about him. Finally he kicked a small table, upsetting it and breaking a vase that held the flowers he had given her that morning. The woman screamed at him and stamped out, slamming the door behind her.

The man was calm then. He stood for a long time on the balcony of the apartment, looking down at the city, their life. After a while, he got a bottle of wine and a glass and started to drink. The evening sky was orange and blue and green. The green reminded him of the woman's eyes. The lights of the city winked at him from the streets below.

An hour later, he fell seven storeys to his death.

And these are the seven he fell through:
    first, his vanity
    second, his desire
    third, his father
    fourth, the woman with the broken wing
    fifth, the cloud of his words
    sixth, his love of all the world
    seventh, the soaring flight of his spirit.

When the young man's father heard of the accident, the news tore him apart. He could not move. Others had to help him and care for him. They gave instructions for his son's body to be brought back home and they attended to the funeral arrangements. They looked after the helpless father for a long time but gradually they grew tired of it. They had their own lives to lead, their own secrets to endure. At last, the man realised that although one of his sons was dead, he himself was still alive.

He went away into the country and rented an old farm on which there was a large barn. He bought tools and equipment and wood and iron and fabric. He began to build a hot air balloon. It was very large, over a hundred feet high when he inflated it, and round like a teardrop. The outside was blue and green like the earth, the inside blue-black like the sky at night. He built a gondola in which he could ride, and an engine to heat the air that would lift him off the ground.

When everything was ready, he carried the parts of the balloon out into a field and put it together. Then he started the engine. Gradually the balloon began to fill with hot air, wallowing and rolling like a monster cast up on a beach. Then it began to rise, growing rounder and rounder until it was tugging hard at the guy ropes that held it down. The man got into the gondola with the few things he needed and cast off. Slowly, silently, he rose up into the air. The balloon billowed out above his head like a gigantic roof.

The higher he went, the lighter he felt. It was as if the receding earth had less and less pull on him. He felt even lighter than the balloon and he clung tightly to the side of the gondola to stop himself floating off. He gazed upwards, past the engine into the blue-black interior above him. The burner roared. The balloon rose higher and higher. The man who had lost his son felt only his own weightlessness. At last he got tired of holding on. He let go and felt himself float upwards, past the engine with its glowing burner, high into the balloon itself.

Slowly he rolled like a rotating planet. In the dark blue darkness, he could see nothing but the flame of the engine at the hole through which he had come. It blazed orange like a burning sun. The man turned slowly. If it were not for that flame, he thought, I would have no point of reference. I would be lost in the void of heaven. But then, if it were not for the hole, I would not be here in the first place.

Gradually the flame got further and further away. The void grew darker. The man could not tell whether he was near the centre of the balloon or close to the inside of its painted skin. The midnight around him teemed with tiny spots of light, swarming like living things. He could no longer see the sun. It was merely one spot among millions.

If the darkness is light, he thought, then maybe I am on the outside after all. But if I am the light I project into the darkness, perhaps I am also the darkness as it is projected into me.

It was then that he heard the voice. It seemed to come from nowhere, all around him. He was a rational man and might have assumed that it was his own imagination except that he was no longer sure which was his imagination and which the inside of the balloon.

— The tale of the wraith stings like a red flash, said the voice. A whip, a bright slash, a weal across the face. You know the story of the wraith, don't you?

'No,' said the man out loud.

— A wraith is a double, a counterweight, a ghost. When a man or woman has a solid reality, the wraith is nothing. But if that person should become insubstantial, as for example when they are near death or asleep or at certain other times, the wraith floats gently into existence like a balloon in a blue sky. The lighter the person gets, the more real the wraith becomes.'

'Is that the secret of why things fall?' the man asked.

— No, said the wraith, that's gravity.

'I know all about gravity,' the man answered. 'It's the invention of Isaac Newton. It says falling is an illusion based on size. An apple dropping to the earth is logically no different from the earth dropping to the apple.'

— The sting of the wraith is red, like fire. It splits the mind from the body, the mask from the face. The wraith inhabits. It is within. It has no existence other than its non-existence. It is the dead-dead man. Once you are stung by the wraith you are already dead.

'Is there no cure?' asked the man.

— Yes, said the wraith. You must become everything you are not. You are the man who lost his son. That man built a balloon and he floated into the sky. He was so light that he floated into the balloon which became his world, his universe, his own head. The man could imagine anything he wished.

— He imagined, for example, that he was in the bowels of a ship, a great ship churning through a rough sea on a black night. Deep in the ship it was dark and hot. The solid thump of the engines boomed in the iron corridors. There was no light except for the fires from below, reflecting and flickering up the companionways.

— The man was afraid. The whole ship was in danger because somewhere down in the darkness of its bilges was an evil thing. It had tentacles like an octopus and it would strike at anyone who came near it with a crack like a whip and a red flash of high-voltage energy. Several people had been struck already. Some were energised themselves, crazy with the power of the creature. Others had become apathetic, staring with lifeless eyes and moving like zombies. The man had seen victims of both kinds and he knew they were all dead. Some were dead on the inside, some on the outside. The man knew that he had to find the monster and approach it without being stung. All he had to protect him was an iron bar and a pair of insulated gloves he had found in the electrician's locker.

— In the bowels of the ship the red glow of the fires gleamed dull on the iron walls. The rows of rivets stood out like the stitching of old scars. The man moved cautiously, looking to right and left. He did not need to be quiet because the noise and vibration from the engines drowned any sound he might have made.

— The monster was hiding in a narrow corridor. It came out at him with a rush, writhing over the metal floor. Its tentacles whipped at him but he parried the blows with his iron bar. The red

The Blackening

sparks cracked. Surges of electricity flowed through the iron. Even through his gloves the man could feel it growing hotter and hotter. It started to glow, first red, then orange, then yellow like burnished gold. The brighter it became, the feebler the monster grew. The slime of its tentacles sizzled as it struck the hot metal. Gradually it began to retreat, sliding backwards into the corridor. The man pursued it. He drove it before him with the heat of the bar. At last it was trapped against a bulkhead, writhing and cowering before him.

— "Don't hurt me!" a voice pleaded.

— "Why not? You've attacked enough people yourself," the man answered.

— "I was afraid," said the voice. "Many years ago, I wanted to be friendly, I wanted to love people but they hated me because I was ugly. They drove me out. Generation after generation of young men came to fight me. They wanted to prove their strength. Some of them beat me. I began to hide myself away more thoroughly. With each battle I became more and more afraid, but with each defeat I gained more and more power."

— The man held the glowing bar above his head to give himself more light and looked at the monster. All he could see was a gleaming mass, writhing and folding over itself like rubber, like a huge latex mask, torn off and flung into a corner, quivering and trembling. Then he saw that it really was a mask, a face furrowed with lines and wrinkles, a shapeless nose, a toothless mouth. It was the face of an old woman. His grandmother.

'Why his grandmother?' asked the man.

— The origin of his origin, the earth of his earth, the dust of his dust. She looked down upon him as he lay in his cot and smiled her toothless smile. She was his wisdom, his kindness, his unqualified love.

'Why did he attack her, then?'

— Haven't you been listening? the wraith demanded. When the heart is split from the head, the earth from the sky, then it is the time of the dead-dead man.

'Are you my heart?' asked the man.

— I am just a possibility, answered the wraith. Do you think or do you feel?

'I think I feel.'

— Thinking digs graves.

'Below ground there is less gravity.'

— A poor pun. Be careful when you stop a wraith laughing. Things are really serious then.

15

'Should I prefer an iron ship or the lightness of a balloon?' asked the man.
— What happens when a ship sinks?
'It fills with water.'
— And what happens when a balloon rises?
'It gets bigger.'
— And as it gets bigger and bigger the surface gets further and further away from the centre. So what happens to a floating speck if it rises more slowly than the balloon expands?
'It is lost forever,' said the man.
— Precisely, answered the wraith.
'So that is the secret of why things fall.'
— No, said the wraith, I don't think so.

2 The Receptive

Wairuru, February 1991

There was a woman walking up a hill. She was tall, big-boned, slow. Once, when she was younger and full of vigour, she could have covered this distance without a thought, but time had made her cumbersome, thickening her waist and hips, stiffening her knees, cramping her breath. She moved with a rolling gait, waddling from side to side. Her feet, in leather sandals, scuffed up the yellow dust of the path. She wore a big, battered straw hat to protect her from the sun, a loose-fitting blouse of faded lilac cotton, a long skirt, ragged at the hem, with a pale pattern of swirls and feathers and peacock eyes. In her right hand she carried a flax kit. The sky above was blue, the grass of the hillside a pale, dusty green. The path wound up the contours of the slope like a yellow snake.

As she moved she counted her steps under her breath. One, two, three, four. One, two, three, four. The woman believed in numbers but in a way peculiar to herself. She did not care about the rules of arithmetic, which could reduce the world to a column of figures. She was not a person for abstractions or analysis or logical calculation. She believed in the magic of the pure combinations of things. One was for unity and wholeness undivided. Two for dichotomy, separation, the beginning of consciousness. Three was the mystery, the combination, that which cannot be. Four was the power, the eternal principle of creation. Thus it was that she counted her steps; not to while away the time, not to drive herself forward to the end of the journey, but to reach an understanding, an insight into the meaning of the world. On some days she counted in twos, on others in threes, on others still in fours. It was not a choice she made. It simply happened, a natural event, like the turning tide or the wind over the hill.

One, two, three, four. Today it was four. It was good, it was what she needed, but it didn't make sense. Today, four disturbed her because she knew what she would find at the end of the path and she didn't want to know. She stood on the top of the slope and looked down at the house. It sat tucked into the side of the ridge, a red iron roof, a grey cedar wall with a row of windows. She tried to think of her own house with the cats on the verandah, the strings of herbs and garlic hanging in the kitchen, the kiln in the backyard still warm from the pots she had fired, but there was nothing behind her that was stronger than the power of four. She started to walk down.

The back door was unlocked. She opened it.

'Hello?'

There was no answer. She stepped into the kitchen and closed the door behind her. It was dark inside after the sunlight, cool. Red tiles of the floor, old black stove, the wooden table scrubbed to a pale, blond whiteness, the stainless-steel sinkbench. She could feel the colours as if they were solid things. It was all clean, tidy, exactly as she had left it the day before. She put the kit and her hat on the table and went into the living room. Light from the windows, in big slices, fixing the armchairs, the bookshelves, the filing cabinets, the desk. The house was so still that seeing had become alive in it.

'Walter?'

No answer. The bedroom door was open. Inside, it was dark again. A pale ghost of herself flickered in the mirror of the oak wardrobe. She crossed to the window, pulled back the heavy curtains, turned towards the bed. It was a big bed with brass ends, golden globes reflecting little curved images of the room. The man was lying on his back with the covers pulled up to his chest. He hadn't moved. He hadn't moved since yesterday. His head on the pillow was bald and shiny, yellowish like old ivory, mottled with brown freckles. His eyes were closed, the wrinkled lids a pale blue. Around his cheeks and jaw the stubble of his beard glinted like a dust of silver. His blue-striped pajamas were buttoned up to the soft flesh of his throat. The sight of him frightened her. She knew

without wanting to, resisting it but drawn to it at the same time, like the strength of the numbers. One, two, three, four.
'Eh, Walter!' She sighed and sat down on a chair beside him. 'You dead, then?'
Silence. Then there was a groan from the man. His lips parted and he began to make a coughing noise.
The woman stared at him, afraid for a moment but then surprised, relieved. 'You laughing at me, you bugger?' And she began to chuckle herself.
Walter opened his eyes. They were dark blue, the whites veined in a fine pink filigree. Slowly he turned his head and looked at her.
'You didn't get up, then?' she said.
'Couldn't.' His voice was husky, laboured.
She reached out and touched his clammy forehead, slid her fingers across it, stroked his temple. He was still looking at her from under her moving hand, eyes that seemed big, dark, right before her, but coming from so far away that she almost sobbed for pity at the distance.
'Eh, man, my man,' she said softly, stroking his cheek, the roughness, his neck, the hollow of his shoulder and across his chest. He did not move. Only the eyes kept looking at her. She took hold of the bedclothes, lifted them, pulled them up to his chin. The smell of shit wafted up to her, thin and sweet.
'You dirty bugger, you crapped yourself,' she said, jossing him, not wanting to let herself feel how weak he had become.
'Yes.'
'Let me . . .' She made to stand up.
'No,' he said. 'It's all right.'
'I should've stayed. Why didn't you let me stay?'
'It's all right.'
Suddenly the pity overwhelmed her, gushing up through her body. She began to cry. She went to turn away but found she couldn't and, instead, sat looking at him with the tears running down her face.
'It doesn't matter,' he said.
'Let me clean you up.'
'No. Waste of time, eh? Why waste it?'
He moved. His hand crept up, struggling to his shoulder, reached out, rolled and tumbled, fell into her lap. The fingers twitched. She held them in her own, stroked the wrinkled skin, the thick blue veins.
'I had a dream,' he said. The words he might have used on any morning they were together.

The Blackening

She sniffed.

'Blow your bloody nose,' he told her.

She pulled a handkerchief from the waistband of her skirt, blew her nose with a loud honk, and then at the sound of it, her foolishness, began to giggle.

'You still ordering me around, aren't you?' she said.

He smiled and closed his eyes.

'Tell me about the dream, then.'

He did not answer immediately. His eyelids twitched, eyeballs rolled to right and left.

'There was a battle. A big battle. We were all on horses, white. There were swords and noise and jang, jang, jang, like chords on a piano. My horse . . .' he paused, eyes rolling under his closed lids, breath in little heaves. His tongue came out and slithered over his lower lip. 'We were by ourselves. The horse was on the ground. It was dying. I looked out. We were on a plain. It was dark. Everything was dark except . . . There was a light on the horizon, a pale glow like dawn was coming.'

She stroked his hand. He did not need her to tell him what the dream meant.

'You're not going anywhere,' she said.

'No.'

They sat in silence for a long time. After a while she stopped looking down at his face, his closed eyes, the withered muscles of his shoulder and upper arm. She turned instead to the window and the green trees pressing close against it outside. The room was hot, but she did not notice the smell so much now. A trickle of sweat ran down between her breasts and over her belly. A little dark stain bloomed there in the faded cotton of her shirt. Her thighs were sticking together.

'What day is it?' he asked.

'Tuesday,' she told him. 'Twelfth of February.'

'Twelfth.' He was quiet for a while. 'That's seven, isn't it?'

'Yes. A three and two twos.'

'That's good.'

Seven was completion, ending, rest. She needed the four now but it wouldn't come to her.

'I want your hair,' he said.

She reached over her shoulder and lifted the long, grey plait that hung down her back like a thick rope. She swung it forward and the tufted end, tied with a strip of yellow ribbon, fell into her lap and bumped against his wrist. His fingers clutched at it.

'Do you want me to let it out?' she asked.

Why Things Fall

He didn't answer. She took off the ribbon but left the rest of the plait in place. He held it gently. She could just feel the weight of his fist pulling at her head.

'A bell rope,' he said.

'It made a tent for us sometimes.'

She stroked his arm, remembering. A blue and green balloon rose up over the crest of the hill. She remembered, too, the touch of his hands and how her insides melted.

'I never thought it would be so quick,' he said. 'In the end.'

A fly droned through the open door, circled the room, and began to fritter itself against the windowpane. The trees outside were dark, no more gold, flash, no more sun reflection.

'And how are the little ones? The baby?' he asked.

'Fine.'

'I was thinking about Michael before,' he said.

'Michael's dead.'

'Yes.'

'What about Paul?'

He didn't answer. She knew nothing of his sons beyond their names. His past was something he kept buried somewhere deep. On the rare occasions he talked about it, he spoke as if it belonged to someone else. Except that now, at last, she felt it was with them, in the room.

'There wasn't any point to it, really,' he said. 'It would've been all the same.'

He was quiet again. The fly droned over and circled her face. She flicked at it with her right hand. It came back immediately so she let it crawl on her, felt it tickle along her jaw and behind her ear.

'I'll tell you what, though,' he said.

She waited. The fly came back around her neck, across the base of her throat. Walter's breathing was slow. She could hear it now. A long intake, a pause, an exhalation, longer pause. She waited, hardly breathing herself, listening for the next indrawing of air, expecting it not to happen, but it did each time, except that it got softer, slowly, and softer so that after a while she could barely hear it, and then she knew that she could not. And then she realised that the last strength had left his fingers, that there was no longer a weight pulling at her hair. She felt his wrist and the pulse had gone. And she sat and waited.

3 Difficult Beginnings

Wairuru, March 1991

> EL DORADO
> MOTOR CAMP
> Kevin & Diane Kemp, Props
> Units Available
> Apply at Office

The sign was rusty, faded, pock-marked with the random strikes of stones. It stood out bright in the headlights. He slowed the car and brought it to a stop.

'This is it,' Anelise said. She yawned and he felt her stretch, the heels of her hands thrust down into the seat between her thighs.

He sat staring through the windscreen at the sign. The letters were orange, maybe, outlined in red on a yellow background. It was hard to tell because the headlights also had a yellowish tinge. El Dorado. I've got a business to run, he thought. I can do without stuff like this.

There was a little nick in the leather of the steering wheel between his hands, the carelessness of some negligent mechanic. He had noticed it a fortnight ago and it still irritated him; not only the imperfection itself but the fact that it was not quite at the top of the wheel, not quite centred in the symmetry of his driving grip. Ten to two. The precision, balance, tolerance. Necessary like clockwork.

'Are you all right?' Anelise asked.

'Of course!' he said, embarrassed that she had caught him out in his musing. 'Of course I'm all right!'

He eased the car forward, turned into the rutted, unsealed driveway. Stones popped under the tyres. The headlights smeared over bushes, flowerbeds. Ahead of them was a round stone, the size of a football, painted white, and above it the looming shape of a tree or bush sculpted into the form of a gigantic hen. A sign beside it pointed to the left, *Office*.

'My God!' Anelise said, gazing up at the hen as it slid past them.

He stopped outside a low, ranch-style building. There was a light inside, a pale glow through the ripple glass panels of the door and the white net curtains drawn across the windows. He turned off the motor and the headlights, got out, closed the door of the car behind him. The air was cool, a soft flutter against his bare arms. From somewhere he could hear the sound of the sea, the slow beat of waves. Above him, the sky was dark, high, moonless, alive with stars. He craned his neck, gazing upwards and felt a strange little twisting in his chest, a memory of something long ago. Stupidity, he thought, ridiculous. There was no need to get involved, no benefit. Get on with it. Get it over. Sort it out. With luck they could be back in Auckland for lunch on Sunday.

The office was about two metres square, split in half by a wooden counter. It had a grey carpet, threadbare, and faded wallpaper with a pattern of pale-blue tulips and a waterstain below the windowsill. There was a big poster advertising bus tours to Ninety-Mile Beach and Cape Reinga, and a glass case of ornaments: a mouse, a motor car, a little dressed-up doll, all made from bits of shell. On the counter stood a vase of red and yellow plastic roses and beside it a bell push, screwed to the wood, with a bright blue light under it. Sapphire. Blue corundum, alpha-alumina. The molecular structure, bonds, like a framework of jointed rods.

He covered the button with his thumb and squashed it down. A buzzer sounded beyond the open door behind the counter to the right. He stared at the flowers. The petals were thick and waxy, coated with a film of dust, and yet, from somewhere, he thought he caught a faint whiff of scent. Without thinking, he leaned forward, sniffed at the arrangement.

'Hi. They do look real, don't they?' There was a young woman standing in the doorway. She had long, blonde hair framing her face and she was wearing a red T-shirt with the words 'Save the Cow' printed in black across her breasts. Her skin was very brown, her eyes blue. She was smiling. White teeth.

'My name's . . .' He paused and cleared his throat. 'I'm Paul Newton. We have a booking.'

She shifted her weight from one leg to the other. Her hips rocked. The tight fabric of her denim shorts seemed to stretch with the movement. Her gaze wandered over Paul Newton's face and shoulders, his open-necked Francini shirt, back to his mouth. He recoiled as if she had touched him.

'We booked a motel unit,' he said. 'For two nights.'

'Oh, yes.' She stepped forward to the counter, and her chest, her message, seemed to thrust out even further towards him. The cotton clung to the curves of her breasts, the little knobs of her nipples. With her left hand she flipped through the pages of a hard-bound exercise book. There were columns ruled in red, smudged ballpoint. She looked down at the entries. Her hair slithered over the curve of her shoulder.

'For two nights,' he repeated.

The Blackening

'Oh, yes,' she smiled again. She turned the book round to face him and pointed to the empty spaces in the last two columns with a red-painted fingernail. 'If you'd be so kind as to sign the register?' Her voice was prissy and pretentious, wheedling him in a way that filled him with disgust. She was offering him a pen.

Paul signed his name, Paul Newton, and the address, 53 Kowhai Cres, Mission Bay, Auckland. I am here, he thought, by choice. My choice. Myself. Paul Newton, Company Director, specialist in the processing and refinement of precious metals. These people are irrelevant. They have no bearing on the matter.

The young woman flipped up part of the counter. In one hand she carried a key with a wooden tag, in the other a carton of milk. She stood beside him looking up into his face with an expression of deep feeling, sadness. Her eyes held the semblance of tears.

'I'm really sorry about your father,' she said.

Her sympathy, so naked, again like the touch of unwanted hands. He glanced away at the counter, the plastic roses, counted them. There were six, the scent from far away.

'He was a lovely old man,' she went on. 'I used to go up there and see him sometimes.'

'Oh?' And then he got a grip on it and pressed it down tight into a hard little pellet, a stone to be sorted, labelled, filed away. She was just an adolescent, a girl.

'It's so hard when people die. As if you lose part of yourself, your own life,' she went on.

'Yes.' He could look into her eyes now, knowing he had her under control. A teenager, no more. Like someone in one of the shops or the factory who depended on him for a living.

She smiled again, sadly, and gave a little shrug.

'Number twelve,' she said. 'It's down at the end. If you'll just follow me.' She stepped outside.

Paul got back into the car, turned on the lights, the motor. The young woman was walking on ahead. Her hips swayed, her buttocks rolled from side to side, the tight, blue, stone-washed denim, lit in every stitch, the frill of frayed cloth around her brown thighs.

Anelise laughed. 'Is that Diane? Or Kevin?'

'The local femme fatale,' he said.

She had turned to the right under a porch and was unlocking the door of the motel unit. They got out of the car and followed her inside.

There was a kitchen area, a sinkbench, stove, refrigerator, a bank of cupboards, a brown Formica table and two metal chairs with padded vinyl seats. Beyond was the main room, square, painted cream. It had a double bed, two more chairs, a coffee table with a rack for magazines underneath. The curtains were sun-bleached, faded red and yellow, half drawn over the ranch-sliders, and the carpet brown, with orange patterns in spoked circles, eyes perhaps, or wheels. On the wall above the bed hung a picture of a desert sunset with the silhouette of a big, three-fingered cactus sticking up into an orange sky.

'This is the bathroom,' the young woman announced. She was holding open a door to the right.

'Thank you,' Anelise said.

'That's a lovely blouse.' The girl moved towards them, smiling all her white teeth, nodding her approval. 'Is it silk?'

'Yes,' Anelise told her.

'Natural fibre. That's the best. Well, if you'll excuse me. Let us know if you want anything, won't you?' She drew herself up to her full height.

'Are you a vegetarian?' Anelise asked, indicating the T-shirt.

'Oh, no. That's just a joke.' She pulled at the garment, stretching it tighter, staring down at it. Then she laughed brightly, to show perhaps what a good joke it was. 'Good night, then.' At the door she turned and smiled again. 'Sleep well.' She gave a little graceful wave of her hand and was gone.

Anelise burst out laughing, doubled over, arms clutching her stomach.

Paul couldn't see what she found so funny. The girl was a slut, obviously, pushing her young, provocative body at anyone who came along, pouring her niceness like treacle, sticky, like a honey trap. She made his skin crawl, grubby, used, like the room with its edges scuffed, its colours garish, cheap attempts at richness. El Dorado. City of Gold. The gleam of yellow metal, wandering vein, like life in the dark rock. The heat of the earth. And the wheels in the carpet, spinning, going nowhere.

'No TV, no cupboards, and a rather small bed,' Anelise commented. 'Jolly little place, really.'

He knew her tone. It was cheerful, ironic, brittle, a defiant good humour hiding what he took to be her irritation and disappointment, a challenge to anyone who said she wasn't coping. It was a tone that often accused him at public functions, weather-bound airports, the corporate dinner parties she found so boring. Always it annoyed him.

'There doesn't seem to be a phone,' she said.

'We've got the mobile.'

A pause. He looked at her, her thin face, dark hair. Her mouth, as if she was about to smile.

'I didn't bring the mobile,' she said.

A stab of anger, then. A sense of black finality. Because he knew, he knew he'd asked her. The set of nested, interlocking lists which kept his mind in decent order had reference only to the simple request he had given her (he was sure he had given her) and his knowing, always that she would forget something.

'Never mind,' she said. 'There's still the one in the car.'

'What use is that when we're in here?'

'I can't see Theo wanting you for anything excessively urgent, can you?'

Her silly, patronising tone infuriated him. He clamped his jaws tight, crushing it down, forcing it back. She read his expression anyway.

'Darling,' she warned. 'Don't get peevish, please. I can't remember the mobile if you don't ask me.'

'I did ask you.'

'I don't remember.'

'Listen to me, listen to me. I can't organise things if you don't listen.' He hissed it at her, his voice rasping in his throat.

And then, as she looked at him, her expression changed. She became all softness, sympathy. There was sadness in her eyes, her feeling for him, as she saw or thought she saw his struggle, his emotion driving at him underneath, as if he were a tragic case, a grieving son. Her pity oozing at him like the blonde-haired girl's.

'Oh, love. I'm sorry,' she said.

And it did burst then, or almost, like a ruptured pipe, a jet of rage he couldn't stop, squirting bile forced out between his clenched teeth. Bitches, he thought. They're all bitches.

And he yelled at her. 'I do not need anyone to feel fucking sorry for me! Not you, not anyone else!'

She stared at him in shock, the whites of her eyes, and then defiance, her anger rising up to meet him.

'Fine!' she said. 'No problem!' She turned away, furious, slammed open the door. He heard her outside rattling her keys at the boot of the car.

It is not an issue, he told himself as his fists tightened harder. I will not let myself be affected by these women. I will not feel what I do not want to feel, grief for a man I haven't seen in thirty years, who means nothing to me, who abandoned his family, who . . . I hate him, he thought. I've hated him all this time. And the anger started to go then, draining away into a secret place, a fissure in the rock, and suddenly he felt weak and foolish.

Anelise came back, lugging her suitcase. She stood in the middle of the room looking for somewhere to put it. Then she dropped it, heaved it onto the floor against the wall. She went back out to the car. He followed her.

They stood side by side in the dark, facing into the boot. He gripped the lid to stop his hands from trembling. It was not her fault. Nor was it his. A strange place. An unknown situation. Rank disorder.

'Sorry,' he said, trying to show her that he meant it. And he did. The things they shared. For better or for worse.

She turned and looked at him. The bootlight cast a yellow glow over her face. Her eyes glinted. Then she sighed, let go, nodded.

'No,' she said. 'It's my fault.'

'I think we need a drink.'

'We sure do. There's some bourbon here somewhere.' Her hands clutching at the bags.

4 Inexperience

Anelise in white singlet and maroon shorts, Reeboks white with maroon flashes, her dark hair tied back in a pony tail. The morning air was cool and clear, the sky a flat blue-grey. Outside the motel unit, the grass was pale with dew. She set off down a narrow crazy-paving path, moving in a little trot, feeling the muscles in her calves and thighs begin to stretch. Variegated flax bushes crowded her ankles on both sides and dripped water on her feet. To her left was a mass of shrubs and small trees, to the right a wire fence and tennis court. On the other side of the court, beyond the grey-black asphalt, she could see the camping ground, the neat rows of tents in brown or white canvas with the cars scattered about among them.

The path led up onto the end of a long verandah. There was a row of windows curtained in white nylon net. The wooden boards creaked under her shoes. She slowed down to a walk again, striding out, breathing deep. Space, she thought. I need to open out. And move. I need to move. But then she stopped. An open doorway to her left, a big gloomy room, the smell of bacon cooking.

Down one side was a rank of electric stoves, each with a little bench next to it, and along the opposite wall, a like row of big porcelain sinks. In a line down the centre were three rectangular wooden tables with their tops scrubbed white. A woman was standing at one of the stoves in the far corner. She wore a shapeless cotton frock and her hair was tied back in a bun. The light from the windows beside her lit her face, her plump arms, her brown hair, the blue smoke rising from the frying pan. Further up the room, closer to the door where Anelise stood, a stumpy man in shorts and shirt was putting a dark green bin liner into a big plastic rubbish bin. There were two such bins, one at each end of the room. He lifted his head and saw her.

'Morning!' He stood up straight and began to waddle towards her, a big grin on his round face, a cap of shiny black hair, a red nose, red veins in his flabby cheeks. His belly hung over his waistband, cradled in the sling of his blue cotton shirt.

'Hello,' she said.

The woman at the stove was still intent on the bacon.

'Mrs Newton, isn't it?' He was smiling. Moist red lips and teeth with brown stains.

'Mr Kemp?' Anelise took a guess.

'Kevin,' he said. 'Kevin.'

'You run the place.'

He laughed and shook his head so the jowls quivered. 'Oh, run. Now there's a word. I'm a bit past running these days. I guess I get prodded along, though. That's what marriage is for, isn't it?' His voice was strong but with a faint asthmatic wheeze. A smoker's voice. And there was the smoker's smell about him and brown tar stains on the knuckles of his right hand. Brown eyes, dark and soft, with big pupils like a rabbit's.

'Mind you,' he went on, 'you look like you're ready for it. Running, that is.'

'Yes. All I need is a road.'

'Not much road around here. Left at the end of the drive you go back towards Dargaville. Turn right, you can go up the hill towards Makaras' or straight on to the beach. Not much choice really. Either way you meet yourself coming back. The road's a loop.'

'Thanks.' Anelise could feel the energy building in her body.

'If you go up the hill, you'll see Jane's place. It's about half a mile past the Makaras' back gate.'

'Jane?'

'Jane Shaw.'

'Oh, yes.' The letter. Paul holding it out to her as if it were something to dispose of.

'We were expecting you,' Kevin said. He looked at her, his confidential smile. He knew all about it. Everybody did, it seemed. The pause started to lengthen. Anelise tried to think of something to say to release herself from his moist mouth and swimming brown eyes. He was like a dog gazing at her, a spaniel waiting for a crumb of acknowledgement to reward its loyalty. She shivered, suddenly cold, and turned away.

'Anything we can do, you just let us know.' Kevin assured her.

'Thanks.' She walked to the end of the verandah, down onto the rough ground beside the drive, and began to run. Out in the road, she glanced left and then turned right, picking her way along the edge of the tar seal, gaining her rhythm, the footfall, thrust of leg reaching out. God, she needed this, the chance to go, to go and go and go and then forget. She needed ten k at least. Except that there wasn't time for anything so long with Paul asleep but waking up and feeling bad and looking grim and sulking for his breakfast.

The road divided. One branch curved to the right up a little rise. The other, more or less straight ahead, had a shop and a bigger building, white, with a rusted iron roof. She paused for a moment, jogging on the spot, looking up the slope, thinking of Jane Shaw and the letter. Dear Mr Newton. She ran on towards the shop. Its windows were plastered over on the inside with ads for ice-cream and frozen peas and soft-drink in bright, cold-beaded cans. It was closed. The building next door had a broken verandah and a sign, 'Wairuru Community Hall' in faded red letters. Big double doors, chained and padlocked.

Dear Mr Newton, You don't know me but I'm a friend of your father's. She hadn't been there when he read it, didn't know how he reacted, how much it really meant to him behind the control, the little shows of irritation. He behaved as if it were just another problem he had to deal with, like a crisis at the office stilled by his authority, his insistence on procedure. Even a calamity had to be handled according to the rules. She mocked it sometimes, this passion for order, but she knew, too, that it was the source of what she needed, what she valued in him; his dependability. There was a cost, though. Always a cost.

The sea was a roar, a slow, surging rumble up ahead. She could sense it already, see the whitening of the spray above the crest of the road between the pine trees, and feel the cool, the little change to damp against her skin. You don't know me but I'm a friend, a friend, a friend of your father's. The road dipped, a cutting through the dunes, the marram grass, and down towards the gap where the waves rolled in, a white, high, roaring noise, a foaming thunder in the cold grey water. Dear Mr Newton (and Mrs Newton). I don't know how to tell you this to make it easy but your father's dead. Paul with the letter in his hand, his face without expression. Dead. Like her own father and her mother, the little plane, high in the mountains, smashing through the trees. The blonde woman in the blue uniform explaining to her, holding her hand. A mouth of red lipstick, oh, so red. I don't know how to tell you this. I'm so sorry.

The sand was soft at first, impeding her, but the tide had turned and there was a damp, firm strip of brown closer to the water's edge. The beach stretched out in both directions, far into the distance. She headed north. On her right the dunes, the stand of pines. On her left the sea, the waves in long crashing lines, churning and fizzing up the sand towards her feet. There were people out there in the water, little figures, black and struggling with their black boards, crouching and balancing and tossed and hanging on, small and dark like demons in the white inferno. She wanted to stop and watch them but the rhythm of her run had taken hold. She skirted a log, a clump of drying kelp, and stretched her legs in a burst of speed. The wind tugged at her. Her hair was bouncing against her neck, her jaw on either side. I can run, she thought. I can still run like the old days. And, despite the effort of her body, she felt a stab of sadness, like a pain, the past, the long-gone possibilities. You don't know me. I don't know how to tell you. Sobbing breath, her lungs, her thighs, the muscles on the edge of weakness. And Paul. She would never have survived without him. I owe him this, she thought. I owe him the best I can give him now. Yours sincerely, Jane Shaw.

Slowing then to an easy stride, she thought about the woman, his father's friend, with the big blue handwriting. A letter about death which threw everything off balance. It was like a nudge in the shoulder, a spike through the foot. They didn't need this, she and Paul. They didn't need to know. Mr Newton and his wife, and the world they lived in, yours sincerely, Jane Shaw, friend, like a push from behind, like an ankle-tap. And she began to feel afraid. We were doing all right, she thought. It wasn't perfect. It wasn't much, maybe. But we were making the best of it.

In front of her was a creek, a river almost. Its channel cut across the beach, the swirling eddies, turbulence in set and quivering ridges. Her first impulse was to plunge into it, but she knew it was too deep and her wet feet, squelching socks and shoes with sand in them would only chafe her. So there was nothing she could do but turn around and head back, disappointed because it hadn't been anywhere near far enough, and fearful of Jane Shaw for bringing her here and despising herself for her fear, and Paul too, perhaps, for his blind belief in his own will, his refusal to see the danger even after all these years, and her weakness, her despair because she was dependent on him in a way she did not understand. Not for the money, nor the safety, nor the son they shared. It was as if his hard, cold, unrelenting precision somehow showed her the truth about herself. I don't like it, she thought. I don't like being this way. But how was she to be different?

Two of the surfers were coming out of the water. Black wetsuits, their boards under their arms. One was a young man, tall and lanky-limbed. The other smaller, a woman, wet hair straggling about her face. Anelise recognised her, the blonde girl from the night before. The same languid, easy walk, the body stressless, unencumbered. She turned and waved as Anelise strode past.

'Hi!' she called.

Anelise gestured in reply and ran on. Ahead of her the point at which she had to swerve and leave the beach and climb back up towards the road. Paul was waiting for her. Today they had to go and see his father's friend. She would have to watch Paul's self-control and face her fear without really knowing what she was afraid of. No, she thought, not yet. I need a little more. I must be allowed a little more. And suddenly the point of turning aside was past and she was running hard again with the breath sobbing in her chest, the pain of air, like sucking in the hot, cold fire, along the open sand. Stop me, she thought. Stop me, if you can.

5 Waiting

The sea breeze caught the surfboard on Linda's hip and twisted at her. She forced herself straight again and strode away from the damp-packed sand at the water's edge and into the dry, soft, grainy stuff that wriggled up between her toes. The sand wasn't brown or yellow exactly, more like a grey, a mushroom colour.

Craig had gone on ahead, up the beach towards the road. He had not looked back. Lost in his own little world, as usual. Where did he go when he disappeared into himself like that? What did he think about? She made no effort to catch him up. She enjoyed having him realise he had left her behind. He would feel awkward and guilty and worried that he had upset her. He wouldn't show it, of course. Instead of being sorry, he'd act sour, as if he was looking for an argument. She could always tell, though. The glint in his eyes that he thought was tough. She could always see the fear behind it.

Out of the water the wetsuit was already getting hot and she was glad of the breeze. It was drying her hair, fluttering it about her face, cooling her cheeks and her temples. It was stirring the tops of the pine trees too, but she couldn't hear them over the sound of the waves.

Mrs Newton was a good runner. Linda had seen quite a few lady joggers around the El Dorado. Most of them took little tiny steps or else they looked as if their knees were knocking together. Mrs Newton ran with a strong, straight stride, like a man almost. Linda wondered what she must look like herself, running. She had never really thought about it. She was one of the knock-kneed types, probably, with her legs flying round at the side like propellers. It was a bad move to do things you didn't look good at. No style. Mrs Newton had style. She had the money for it, of course, but it wasn't just that. There was something else, something to do with the way you felt about yourself.

Craig was standing waiting for her opposite the shop. He was leaning on his surfboard, trying to pretend he was Mr Cool. She put her head on one side and gave an extra bit of wiggle to her hips as she approached him. Through the floating screen of her hair, she could see him watching her. He didn't say anything, just fell into step beside her.

'You know who that was, don't you?' she said.

'Who?'

'That lady on the beach. Mrs Newton.'

'Mrs Who?'

'You remember old Walter? He was her husband's father. The one that died.'

'Her husband died?'

'Don't be thick!'

He was doing it deliberately, she knew. Trying to pretend that what she said wasn't important or that she was too stupid to explain it properly. Always trying to make himself look smart.

'They've got heaps of money,' she told him.

'How do you know?'

'It's obvious. You can tell by their clothes. And the car. It's a BMW. You should go and have a look at it.'

'I've seen BMWs before.'

'Not like this, you haven't. It's big. Huge. Silver-grey.'

He didn't answer. He wasn't about to be impressed with anything she was impressed with. Just because he lived in Hamilton, which he thought was such a bigshot place, he reckoned he knew everything. He was just boring, really. He liked her, he wanted her, he wanted her to like him, but he would never admit it to himself. So stupid.

'New Zealand's a dump, isn't it?' she said, trying to annoy him.

'It's all right.' But his voice and the glance he gave her told her she had got to him.

'And the people here are just clods. I mean, there's no sophistication, no style. It's incredibly boring.'

That one hurt. A frightened look in his brown eyes as if he knew she was talking about him. It made her want to laugh.

'I think I'll go somewhere big,' she went on.

'Like where?'

'London. Or New York. San Francisco.'

'Good surfing in California,' he said.

They crossed the road into the driveway. The stones were hard under her bare feet. She stepped aside into the softness of the grass.

'Who cares about surfing? That's for kids. I mean restaurants and theatre and music. Stuff like that. Cultural things.'

'Where'd you get the money?'

She didn't answer. It was just like him to try and pull everything down, make it all small and ordinary, as if he was scared of anything he didn't already know. For herself, she knew quite well how ignorant she was. She'd never been anywhere except for a few trips to Whangarei and twice to Auckland. All she knew about the world was from TV and magazines and talking to the campers at El Dorado. She wasn't scared, though. She wasn't scared of anything.

She put her surfboard down against the wall behind the house. Craig walked with her to the back door. He was hoping she would ask him in for breakfast after he'd got changed or, at least, that she'd want to fix a time to meet later. No, she thought. Not today.

'Bye!' She smiled at him and then quickly ducked inside, shutting the door behind her. She could see him through the lacy curtains, hesitating. Poor thing, she thought. Poor cloddish Craig. And she had to run away down the hall in case he heard her laughing at him.

Later, after she'd had a shower, she wrapped herself up in her big pink bathtowel and got herself an apple and a piece of cheese from the kitchen. Then she went into her room and lay face down on the bed. There was a window above her headboard and, propped with her elbows on the pillow, she could just look through it, peering between the bushes outside to where the motel units were. Number twelve was at the end, almost opposite. The curtains were drawn back but she couldn't see anything inside. She munched her apple and ate her cheese and thought about Mrs Newton running. It gave her a strange feeling. She knew that all kinds of people did all kinds of things, but part of her still didn't expect rich ladies to be so physical. Mrs Newton ran like a man. She had little breasts and you could see the muscles rippling in her arms and legs. Almost, Linda felt more of a woman herself. True, she liked surfing and sport, but she never wanted to be really good at it. Mrs Newton, she could tell, had something strong pushing her.

She chewed the last bits from the apple core and stood it on end on the windowsill. There was a movement in the unit opposite, a faint pale blur in the dark of the interior. She strained her eyes to make it out. Then, quickly, she scrambled across the room and grabbed the binoculars from the bottom of her cupboard. They were old and it was hard to get them out because the leather case had fiddly straps and buckles. She threw the case aside and plumped herself once more on the bed.

The window of the unit was a grey-brown blur. It grew bigger as she twisted the focus. Then suddenly it was clear. She could see the table and the chairs with clothes strewn on them, the kitchen with sunlight streaming through the little window, the bed with the covers pulled back. The door to the bathroom was open. There was sunlight there too, a yellow haze. Then a shadow, moving.

Mr Newton came out of the bathroom. He was naked. He had a little blue towel in one hand and was rubbing at his hair. His body was big, square, pink, his arms and legs long and thin, pink too at the shoulders and thighs but reddish, tanned shins and forearms. There was a fuzz of hair, golden-ginger, across his chest and down his limbs and belly, around his crotch, where the white tube of his penis hung pale. He turned and moved over to the bedside table, picked up his glasses. From the side his body seemed thicker and his legs skinny, with knobbly, jutting knees. His belly bulged and wrinkled into his chest as he bent forward. But then, standing up, he seemed big and powerful again, his face stern, sandy hair cropped short. Linda tried to draw him in closer but the focus started to go. He tossed the towel on the bed, walked over to a suitcase on the floor by the wall and crouched down, knees bent. The arch of his spine and buttocks gleamed pale, white, almost blue, like a boiled egg without its shell.

'Linda!' Her mother's voice. Linda wriggled, annoyed, pressed the binoculars closer into her eyes, stared.

Mr Newton stood up. He had a bundle of clothes in his hands. Slowly he walked back towards the bed. Then he stopped and turned, looked out, staring. It was as if he was looking straight down the binoculars into Linda's eyes. His face was still, serious, strange. He didn't seem sad or hurt or angry, although there was something of all three. Was it surprise then? A surprise that came from a sudden thought or realisation. He can't see me, Linda told herself. I'm sure he can't see me. And, as he continued to stare, she knew it was true. He had no sense of her presence. He was gazing backward somewhere deep into his own mind. Like Craig, she thought. Except that it was not like Craig at all. Because Craig always knew she was there somewhere, while Paul Newton couldn't care if she lived or died, and was staring at her, staring at her. And the more certain she was that he was not going to look away, the more frightened she became, as if she was gazing too hard at her own reflection in a mirror and had trapped herself, hypnotised, like a snake, and she could never get out.

There was a knocking at her door. 'Linda! Are you there?'

Quickly, she stuffed the binoculars under her pillow.

'Yes,' she yelled. 'I'm just getting dressed.'

6 Conflict

Behind the hedge there was an orchard: apples and peaches and nectarines. Some of the trees were still heavy with fruit; red and yellow globes among the thickly clustered leaves. The grass beneath them was strewn with windfalls. The drive curved up from the road in an S-shape to the front of the house. The old, cratered asphalt sprouted little tufts of weeds and was scattered with more windfalls. He stopped the car beside the steps and got out. Anelise followed. There was a sweet, rotten smell from the fallen fruit, and the hum of insects; wasps and fat blue flies. The house was painted brown with dark green trim, a big villa with six steps up to the verandah. The door beyond was open. He could see down the dark hall to another doorway at the far end, a rectangle of grey-white light. As he stood, hesitating, a figure appeared in the further doorway and came towards him. It was a woman, big in the hips, with a slow, rolling walk.

She came out onto the verandah and stood looking down at them. She was about sixty years old with a round, brown face and grey hair done up in a plait that hung down in front beside her left arm. She wore a faded T-shirt that might once have been blue, and a big tent of a skirt belling out over her hips and stomach. She seemed confused, uncertain. Then she smiled.

'Hello, Paul,' she said.

'Jane Shaw?'

She moved back a little, over to one side, gestured with her left hand. 'Please. Come in, eh?'

He was two steps up before he realised he had forgotten Anelise. He stopped, turned, almost fell, gritted his teeth with irritation. Do things properly, he told himself.

'This is my wife, Anelise,' he said.

'Hello.' Anelise came up the steps.

They mounted to the verandah. Jane Shaw reached out her hands to them. She was smiling, pulling a face. She looked as if she was going to cry. Anelise took her hands and Jane leaned forward and kissed her on the cheek. No, he thought, not that. It wasn't necessary. They were here to do a job, sort it out, get it over with.

He went into the house with the two women behind him. Down the hall. On either side there were doors ajar and rooms with drawn curtains; pale streaks of light and shadows, furniture and bottles and things he could not identify; a loom, was it? The whole place was full of smells, of herbs and spices, fruit and fermentation. The air was thick with it, a rich-ripe stew of essences of mellowness and juice and sweet decay. He could almost taste it, feel it like a condensation on his skin.

The door at the end led into a big kitchen. There were benches and cupboards around two walls, and shelves full of pots and pans and jars and earthenware crocks. The ceiling was hung with clumps of dried plants and strings of onions and garlic. There was an electric stove, a big, black, wood-burning range and two refrigerators. In the centre of the floor stood a huge table clustered about with ladderback chairs. Beyond it, along the whole back wall, a row of tall windows made of little square panes of glass. A view out into a bricked yard, sheds and a hillside in the distance.

There was a woman sitting at the table. She was in her mid twenties, with long, frizzy red hair, pale skin, almost white like flour, and green eyes. With her right hand she was holding up the hem of a blue T-shirt, exposing a full, round breast at which a small baby was sucking vigorously.

'This is my daughter Melissa,' Jane Shaw said.

Melissa smiled.

'And this is Paul and Anelise,' Jane continued. 'You know who Paul is, don't you?'

Melissa smiled again and looked tenderly down at the feeding baby.

'Is it a boy or a girl?' Anelise asked.

'A girl,' Melissa said. She had a soft voice, small and far away.

'She's lovely.'

The baby's pink little lips were working hard at the nipple. There was a tiny curved valley of blue-white milk between them and Melissa's breast. Paul turned away.

'Well,' Jane said, as if something was settled. 'I'll make some tea, eh?'

He pulled out a chair and sat down at the table. Anelise was still cooing over the baby.

'Thank you for your letter,' he said.

Jane took a battered kettle and filled it at the kitchen tap, pouring the water in through its spout. She put it on the stove and turned on the element. Then she came and sat down at the table, looked into Paul's face. He held her gaze, unflinching. She smiled sadly.

'Sorry I couldn't let you know about the funeral, eh?'

'That's quite all right.'

'I only found your address after it was all over. Among his things. Even then I wasn't sure it was right.'

'You explained in your letter. It's quite understandable.'

'It's good to see you, Paul.'

He smiled, nodded. He didn't need her sadness, her sympathy, her tearful eyes. There was some business to transact, an agenda of some kind. Nobody had to get upset. Their feelings were their own affair. No need to inflict them on anyone else.

'I'd like to get this thing sorted out as quickly as possible,' he said.

Anelise sat down in the chair beside his. He didn't look at her.

'Sure,' Jane nodded. 'That's fine.'

'I guess you want to talk about the estate.'

'I want to talk about whatever you want to talk about,' she said.

Not good enough. Sloppy, vague. There had to be a list, points of action, the details.

'The estate,' he said.

The kettle began to whistle. Jane stood up, made tea in a big, round earthenware pot, brought the pot and four mugs back to the table. The mugs were all different sizes, shapes, and colours.

'Walter left everything to my mother,' Melissa said in her faraway voice.

He was not surprised. He didn't flinch, or even look at her. Somehow he had known all along. They had got him here for no good reason. They were wasting his time. Anelise touched his arm. He pulled away from her.

'It didn't seem fair,' Jane said.

'It seems perfectly fair to me,' he told her. 'People have a right to leave their goods to whoever they choose. An inalienable right, I'd say.'

Jane poured the tea. It was red and smelled of spices, something like orange or lemon or raspberry. She handed out the mugs. Melissa reached out across the table and took hers. She had the baby on the other breast now.

'There's so much,' Jane said. 'I don't need it. There's the house. And all the books. And the money. Quite a lot of money. It seemed best to share.'

'I don't need his money,' Paul told her, laughing. But there was something sour there too.

'The papers. So many papers. Journals, letters, notebooks. Some of them might be important. I think there are patents. Things like that.'

'I'm afraid I don't have time to help you sort it out,' he told her. 'Perhaps you could hire someone.'

Jane stared at him. What did she want? He had a strange sensation, numbness in his skull. The light from the windows was so bright. Like water. Drown in water. Jane took a sip of tea.

'I thought maybe you might want the things that belong to you, eh?' she said at last, quietly.

'I don't understand,' he said. 'What could possibly belong to me?'

'I don't know. The past, maybe. Why don't you come up to the house and take a look?'

'Nothing in that house belongs to me. Nothing. It's yours. He left it to you. I don't need it. I never needed it before and I don't need it now.' He tried to laugh again but couldn't get it right. Precision, he thought. Make it work. The details, like the windows. There were eight little panes in a row across each one and ten rows down. Forty panes per window and eight windows altogether. Three hundred and twenty separate panes of glass. The brightness hurt his eyes.

Anelise touched his arm, burning, fire on his skin. He recoiled and turned on her, quickly, found her staring at him. Strange expression. Her eyes were brimming. She was appealing to him somehow, wanting him to say something, do something, help her. How on earth could he help her when he didn't know what was going on?

Then it was Melissa, her soft, high voice, hardly more than a whisper, a feather floating in the air. 'Why did you come here then?'

Why? He couldn't understand the question. What sense did it make? Why? It was obvious, wasn't it? The feeling in his head was suddenly stronger, like a steel band tightening round his brow, his temples, pressure growing, pain, no sense in it. The windows with the brightness in them, the three hundred and twenty panes, each one a shaft of grey-white light.

'I wanted to help,' he said. 'I wanted to assist in whatever way seemed appropriate. I felt I had a duty to get this business sorted out as quickly and efficiently as possible.'

'What business? What were you looking for?' Melissa's voice, a whisper. In his head. 'Did you think maybe he'd left you something? Did you think that maybe if he did that he would be asking you to forgive him? And maybe you could?' They were not accusations. They were simple questions, soft, like a child, like foolishness.

Suddenly he had had enough; the voice and the light, the pain in his head. He stood up. His chair scraped back. He was dizzy, staggering, but then upright and walking out, down the hall, the darkness, his footsteps echoing on the wooden floor.

He stopped at the top of the steps and stood staring out at the fruit trees. Breathe deeply, in, out, just keep breathing. Count the breaths. Count the trees. Six in each row . . .

'Paul, are you all right?' Anelise with her questions, stupid bloody questions. He had no time for this. At home there was a job to do, a business to run. He had to get away, safety somewhere, back into his own world, darkness, down below. The stumbling echoes.

'Paul?'

They insisted. They kept on insisting.

'No!' he said, and the word was like the first drop falling and the rest came down from nowhere. He was not even angry. It just poured like water in a torrent through the tunnel roof. 'Those stupid idiots, those bitches. Stupid little red-haired fucking bitch with that fat thing sucking at her fat white tit like a leech. She knows nothing!'

'Paul, please!'

'What right has she got to ask me why? Why? She doesn't know what it was like, what I went through. She wasn't there. She's a bimbo, an idiot. What right has she got to talk to me?'

'We can go, Paul. If you want to. Let's go now.'

And then he saw, he knew. His father here in this place and the woman with the red hair. Oh, God, the white pain of knowing how it was. She was his sister, wasn't she? His half-sister. And the baby was his niece. Oh, God, the nonsense of it, the craziness!

And Anelise knew too. He could see it in her face and she knew he knew and there was nothing he could do about it.

'Maybe it's too late,' she was saying. 'Maybe we'll just have to face it somehow.'

7 Collective Force

It was hot two o'clock and Linda, in her white bikini, skin slick with oil, was lying on a towel on the grass beside the tennis court. Donny and Craig and Sue and Douglas were watching her, or not watching, she supposed, but talking and fooling around, except that every time she looked out at them from the darkness of her sunglasses she could tell their eyes were on her, or little flicks of glances like feathers on her skin. They didn't go away and so, maybe, their reason for being there was to give her attention and watch her soaking up the heat and holding it deep in her body like an animal. A snake, maybe. Hot.

She liked the attention, of course she did, even if she wished they were older, more mature, like the men who stayed at the El Dorado who looked at her (and women too sometimes) in a way that made her smile inside. Tall, strong men, good-looking ones, or skinny ones, or fat, and men with wives and babies, kids of Linda's age herself and all their looks which sometimes they didn't want her to see (if they were shy, she supposed) but which she saw anyway and welcomed like the sun and soaked up, sweet. She felt good in the sun. She felt right. Even if the summer was nearly over and she didn't know what to do with her life.

'*Day and Night*,' Douglas said. 'You ever see that?'

They were talking about movies.

'Oh, man, that was amazing,' Donny agreed. 'It's about this dude that turns into a woman.'

'You mean with an operation and stuff?' Craig asked.

'Urgh, yuk!' Sue said.

'No. It's sort of like a werewolf story. In the day he works for this ritzy advertising agency and then, at night, he turns into this real class callgirl that screws all these rich dudes.'

'I reckon it's the other way around,' Douglas said. 'I reckon it's about this prostitute that turns into an ad man.'

Donny looked puzzled. 'What's the difference?'

Douglas shrugged.

'So what happens?' Sue asked.

'Well, one night he goes to this party and . . .'

'She,' Douglas said.

'What?'

'One night *she* goes to this party.'

'All right. One night she goes to this party and meets this guy she works with.'

'*He* works with.'

'Oh, for Christ's sake!' Donny said.

Douglas insisted. 'One night she goes to this party and meets this guy he works with.'

'That doesn't make sense,' Sue said.

'Dumb movie, eh?' Craig chuckled. 'Hey, Lind,' he called. 'Why doesn't your dad get a VCR for the TV room?'

Linda didn't answer. The front of her thighs felt sticky on the towel. She lifted her backside, wiggled her hips from side to side, and settled back down again. She was intrigued by the idea behind the film, the man inside the woman or the woman inside the man. What sort of man would she turn into at night? Someone big, someone powerful. And rich. She thought suddenly of Paul Newton.

'There's enough arguments about the TV without having videos as well,' Sue said.

'TV's crap,' Douglas announced.

'You watch it,' Donny said.

'Only 'cause there's nothing better to do.'

Linda rolled over slowly onto her back, felt the heat of the sun roll with her, across her side and over her belly. She propped herself up on her elbows and stared at the house, the long, low building, with its little square turret like a ventilator on a barn and the weather vane that never moved. Day and night, man and woman.

The Blackening

One turned into the other and back again. When did they sleep? Maybe they didn't. Or maybe the man was the woman's sleep and the other way round. Maybe they both just dreamed each other. Like if one was real, the other was a fantasy for that time. Like the man was looking all day for the woman, and the woman all night for the man, and neither of them realised they were both there all the time. Weird. She couldn't make sense of it. Searching for her own self in a man. In Craig? She laughed out loud.

'What's so funny, then?' Donny asked.

'Oh,' she said. 'I was just thinking about what a good time we're having.'

Douglas was scornful. 'Good time? You've got to be joking!'

'We could go down to French Lake,' Craig suggested.

'Naagh,' Donny said. 'Too late.'

'What about tomorrow, then? Hey, Lind, what say we go to French Lake tomorrow?'

'Not me,' she answered. 'I'm going up to Jane's. It's her birthday.'

'Who's Jane?' Sue asked.

'Jane Shaw. We always go up there on her birthday.'

'Where's she live?'

'On the Loop. Just past Makaras' road.'

'Oh,' Donny said. 'I know her. She's the witch.'

Linda laughed. 'Don't be thick!'

'I've been up there. Her place freaks me out, man. She's got this sheep's skull stuck up on a pole and there's little plate things with weird writing all over the place. In the flowerbeds and stuff. And she's always brewing things. Like spells.'

'She makes preserves,' Linda said. 'And wine.'

'How old are you, Donny, for Chrissake?' Craig demanded.

'She's going to shrivel you up, Donny!' Douglas wiggled his fingers in front of Donny's face and made a noise like a ghost or something.

'Who wants to go down to French Lake tomorrow?' Craig asked again. Everybody ignored him.

Sue was staring at Linda. 'Is it true about the sheep's skull?'

'Sure,' Donny said. 'Sure it's true.'

'I'm asking Linda.'

'It's true.'

'Why?'

'Why what?'

'Why is it there?'

'I don't know,' Linda said.

What sort of man did Jane turn into at night with a sheep's skull on a pole in the back garden? She shivered. Don't be stupid, she told herself. Then she thought, God, I'm sick of this place. I hate it. All the stupid things, the dumb people. Craig, who couldn't think of anything more exciting than French Lake. Donny and Douglas and Sue and everyone else who came and stayed, who were such boring people really. And her parents stuck here. Mother with her busy, busy, get things done. And her father. All he wanted was his beer and his smokes and his feet up in front of the telly. God, she thought, this isn't me. I want more than this. I want a car like Mr and Mrs Newton's and a real silk blouse and something to talk about and a man with money. I want a job of my own and a place in the world and eating out in restaurants and I want people to look at me, real people, to see me and show me and prove it to me. And I will, I will, I will. Oh, God, she thought. And the sun beating down, her sweat, her skin. I am my skin, she thought. I want to drink it all and soak it up, the whole world seeping through my skin so thirsty for it.

'*Eye of the Viper*,' Douglas said. 'You ever see that?'

'Oh, shit, man!' Donny shook his head. It was so great, so unbelievable.

8 Holding Together

Walter's house. A tiny place, unpainted cedar, built on a ledge in the side of the hill. There was a water tank at the back and a yard with sheds and an old chicken coop. The front windows looked down the valley towards the sea. A garden with trees and plots and flowerbeds. It was overgrown now, the weeds waist-high with nodding flowers and puffs of floating seeds.

Jane and Melissa waited in the yard while Paul went into the house. Anelise hesitated, not sure what he wanted her to do. Then she followed him. He was pale, subdued, passive; a mood she had seen him in before but never as marked as this. It worried her. Almost, she preferred his blind insistence on being businesslike, however bizarre that had seemed earlier in the day. Now he wandered slowly from room to room, looking around but seeming to take nothing in. He did not speak to her, did not even acknowledge her existence. Finally he stopped in the living room and stood staring out of the window. She felt helpless and angry with him that he was so unresponsive. If he needed her, he should say so. He should make things clear to her instead of leaving her hanging about like a forgotten child.

She looked around. There was a fireplace with two old armchairs, one on either side, and a worn rag rug on the floor between them. Bookshelves covered two walls, floor to ceiling, and there were other smaller shelves along the third wall beneath the front windows. In the middle of the room, facing the fireplace, stood a huge antique desk with an inlaid green-leather top. On it was an electric typewriter flanked by two boxes of blank paper, one with lines, the other without. Behind the desk was a swivel chair, red leather draped in a tattered sheepskin, and a pair of metal filing cabinets painted brown. A big wooden cupboard stood in the corner. Everything was neat and ordered; the books with their spines all aligned, the cupboard closed, the tops of the filing cabinets free of clutter. Meticulous, like Paul's study at home, like his office at work.

She went and stood on the hearthrug, looked up at the picture, a print in a thin black frame, above the mantelpiece. It was a mandala, she knew, but not like any she'd seen in museums or Buddhist temples, not Eastern. It had a big gold circle, like a wheel, against a blue background and eight little circles around it with pictures of people and strange, mythological animals. Inside the wheel was a square, red and gold with a thick border. Each side had a gap, the gates, maybe, in the four walls of a garden, and within the garden, in the centre, another circle, divided into eight segments like an orange and each one a different colour, radiating out of a bright white heart.

How old was it? The figures were European, medieval, like people from King Arthur or some other northern mythology. There was a king at the top and to his right a magician, an old man with a skull cap and a long white beard and a gown covered with stars and planets, the sun and the moon. In his hands he carried a glass ball. What did it mean? She turned her head, as if there was someone who could tell her the answer. Not Paul with his back to her. Instead she found herself looking down the room at the desk and the chair behind it and she realised, suddenly, that the man who had sat in the chair had lifted his head from his papers and gazed, musing, at the place where she stood, at the picture on the wall above the fireplace with its figures within figures and meanings within meanings. Almost, she could feel him there now, his heat, his smell. Almost, she knew, if she tried she would see him sitting there; chair swivelled a little to the right, leaning his elbow on the left arm, his head turned towards his left shoulder, eyes (were they blue?) lifted to the picture above her head. How could she know he would sit like that? Strange, a sudden fear, panic rising. Paul was still staring out of the window. She went to him, took his arm.

'Are you okay, darling?' she asked, trying to control the trembling in her voice, wanting to pull him away, out into the open air.

'Yes,' he said, as if he only half heard her.

'Come outside.'

He looked at her then, puzzled, as if it was an absurd suggestion. 'You go if you want,' he said.

And she did, almost running, feeling the fear behind her like a gun aimed at her back, feeling she was a coward to leave him. It was impossible, absurd, ridiculous, she had never experienced anything so silly before in her life.

Melissa and Jane were sitting on a long bench by the shed. The baby, Alice, lay curled up asleep in the shade on a rug at their feet. She had come up the hill in a sling on Melissa's back.

'Hi,' Anelise said, too loud, too cheerful. Like a schoolgirl, bouncy. She sat down beside them. Such a fool.

Melissa smiled.

'Everything okay?' Jane asked.

Yes, she wanted to say, it's fine, fine, fine. But somehow the words stuck. She could not pretend.

'I just had the strangest sensation,' she said. 'As if I could feel someone sitting in the chair behind the desk.'

'The old bugger!' Jane laughed.

'Walter?'

'What do you think?'

'I don't believe in ghosts,' Anelise said firmly.

'I don't care what you call it. Just as long as you know what you felt.'

'I had the same experience,' Melissa said. 'Alice and I came up here a couple of days ago. I was sitting in the living room feeding her when suddenly I just knew he was there in the other armchair, the one he always sat in, the one with its back to the window. I could almost hear him talking to me.'

'What did he say?' Anelise asked, and then felt stupid for asking.

Melissa blushed, pink stain in her white, white cheeks in the shade of her big hat. 'He complimented me on my breasts. He said I was made like a good mother.'

The Blackening

'As polite as that?' Jane asked.
'Well, not exactly.'
Jane laughed.
'I never met him,' Anelise said. 'I don't know anything about him. Paul never mentions him. All I know is that he left the family when Paul was sixteen. I think they must have hated him. Paul's mother . . .' She hesitated. Loyalty, confusion. The other two didn't speak. Melissa was looking at her with a wide-eyed, childlike expression. Such green eyes.

'She got rid of everything; books, pictures, house, furniture, car, even her own things like her clothes and jewellery, even things that she'd had from before they were married. She sold it all or burnt it or gave it away to charity. And she started again. From scratch. She's very proud of that. It's the only thing she ever says about it, how she got rid of everything that ever had any connection with her past.'

'She couldn't get rid of Paul,' Jane said.

'No.' The implication, the new angle on it, made her feel strange, to think how he had had to deal with such ruthlessness and how he was the only thing left from his mother's earlier life. Did that make him all the more precious? Or a remnant, a reject, like the ashes of the burnt family photographs. 'He had to chose. But really he didn't have any choice, did he?'

'Paul had a brother, eh?' Jane said. 'The one that died.'
'Yes. Michael.'
'Does his mother talk about him?'
'No. Well, not to me. Paul's mentioned him a couple of times. He was a good cricketer.'

Jane shook her head, sadly. 'Crazy, crazy people. How can the dead rest easy if nobody talks about them?'

And Anelise's dead, the broken bodies, coffins so shiny, red wood, warm, and the bright brass handles.

'Walter used to write to Paul, eh? Before he came here. And after for a while. Paul meant a lot to him.'

'What did he say about it?'
'Not much.' Jane grinned. 'Runs in the family, eh?'
'I think Paul hates his father,' Anelise said.
'Maybe.'
'How many children do you have?' Melissa asked.
'Just one. Andrew. He's fifteen. I'm not sure what he'd think of this. He's a child of the city really.' A night-owl, an intellectual, a clown. Sometimes he felt very strange to her, his mind like his hard, angular body, wriggling, restless, striving to no apparent purpose.

She missed him, though. Only a day away and she missed him.

Paul came out of the house and closed the door carefully behind him. He stood for a moment, looking up at the big water tank on its wooden frame. Then he walked over to where they were sitting. No sign of his feelings, his thoughts. No stress, no anxiety. It was all inside, it must be. Like the house, with its empty rooms and the ghost sitting in the chair behind the desk.

'Thank you,' he said.

'Any time,' Jane told him.

He seemed to hesitate, considering something. A frown flickered over his face.

'I'm not sure. Maybe, there's something I want. I'm just not sure.'

'Come up here again tomorrow,' Jane suggested. 'You could spend some time by yourself, eh?'

Paul nodded. 'Maybe. Yes, maybe I could.'

Anelise, looking at him, his empty eyes, haunted. Like her own grief, long gone, dead, so long ago. Was that what they shared? Was that what held them together? And she felt a surge of pity, of hope, of blinding love for him.

9 The Taming Power of the Small

The moon, today's moon, was in the last quarter. Mercury was moving into Pisces, bringing spontaneous communication. Today's number was five, the pentangle, the number of life, the striving between contending forces, the crucifixion. Five, today, was the rhythm in her feet. She plodded slowly down the hill. Ahead of her was Melissa, leading the way, with the baby on her back, and Paul, in a dream, with his eyes cast down. Anelise was behind her somewhere, following on, Jane couldn't see. Today was a five and tomorrow was six. Six was her birth number, and tomorrow was a six and her birthday, too. She would be sixty-one tomorrow. Six and one were seven. It would be a good day, then; all those sixes and a seven for completion. It would be a good day to die, like Walter on a seven. It would be a good day to begin again, too.

She looked at Paul's back, his bent head. The square of his shoulders, hips, his leg length, arms, the bulk of him was so familiar it made her weak and helpless, hopeless. Like the first time she'd seen him, this morning, on the steps of her house, and the shape of his face, the set of his eyes had knocked her back like a blow, like a tumbling back through the years. She was the same woman with the same feeling wrenching at her heart.

Paul was not his father, of course. Like the way he walked now would never have been Walter's way. Walter would've wanted the sun on his face. He would've wanted to look the sun in the eye, to bluff it out, to laugh at it, to open up his mouth and drink it down. A thirsty man, Walter, a thirsty, loud, objectionable man. Whereas Paul was bottled up and tight-arsed, and had never moved enough to make a decent sweat, poor bugger. Never had the courage to look at his own shit, that was his trouble. Jane sighed, feeling sad for the bowed shoulders. Then she sighed because of the pain in her knees. It was always worse going downhill, somehow. Not good enough for sixty-one. Her knees had got to last a long time yet. She would have to brew some elder tea to fix them.

At the bottom of the hill Melissa stopped and turned, tilted up her hat brim and looked back at them. Paul stopped too but didn't talk to her or look. He was apathetic, like a beaten dog, depressed. I'd like to get to him, Jane thought. I wish I could really talk to him. But that was her own need, she knew. She couldn't stand to see anything in pain. Paul was not to be pushed, though. He would come to her when the time was right.

'You okay, Ma?' Melissa asked.

Jane chuckled. 'I should be used to it by now. I've done it often enough.'

Anelise caught up with them. She took Paul's arm and gave it a squeeze. He hardly noticed so she let him go. It's tough on her, Jane thought. They're both at risk now.

Melissa was walking down towards the house, her long brisk stride, the rest of them following, three abreast. Anelise was at Jane's side, looking at her. Her eyes had a hurt expression.

'Is Melissa your only child?' she asked.

'God, no,' Jane laughed. 'I've got seven.'

'Seven? But Melissa's the youngest?'

'Yes,' Jane said. And she's Walter's, she wanted to add. The only one that's Walter's. But she held back, not knowing if Paul wanted to hear it even if he knew. Why shouldn't he know? He ought to know. But there was an instinct that made her keep quiet about it.

'Do you have many grandchildren?'

'Ten.'

'Do you see much of them?'

'A fair bit. They come and go, eh? Most of them'll be here tomorrow. There's probably a few down at the house right now. I want you two at my party, eh?' She glanced across at Paul but he didn't seem to have heard. Anelise, on the other hand, was taken with a sudden awkwardness.

'Oh, yes,' she said and then, 'What's that?' She was pointing to a big clump of bushes, green leaves and thick clusters of cream-green flowers like long, narrow trumpets. 'Is it Queen of the Night?'

'Yes,' Jane told her.

'You don't mind if I pick some, do you?'

'Help yourself.'

Anelise ran to the shrubs and broke off a stem thick with blossom.

'You remember this, Paul,' she said. 'Kate and Theo have it in their back garden. It smells absolutely fabulous at night.' She plunged her nose into the spray.

'Not much scent to it now,' Jane said.

Anelise offered the flowers to Paul. He leaned forward and sniffed at them.

'Yes,' he said, without much interest.

Cold as a fish, Jane thought. She wanted to tell him that his father had planted the bushes because they were the smell of lust, of passion, of the inward yearning of the soul for its own reflection, but there was no point in taunting him with stuff like that.

'I love the smell of it,' Anelise said. 'It drives me crazy.'

Paul looked at her, a queer, angry look. So there was passion in him somewhere, then. Ice, she thought. He's like a frozen river, white and calm, but deep down it's still moving, a little worm of water trickling on. And what happens when the sun gets to him at last? A torrent, maybe. An irresistible flood that could pour down and sweep him away. The idea of it made her suddenly afraid.

But then there was a noise ahead of them, a shout, a screech, and three of her grandchildren, Anne and James and little Kelsey, were bounding up the path towards them, leaping around Melissa and Alice and on again, yelling and waving their arms. Sam and Ace, her sons, and Ace's wife, Martine, were following behind. Ace had a bunch of red roses in his hand and he was grinning. Even from this distance she could see how big his grin was.

10 Conduct

Out of habit he got into the car on the driver's side. The other seat would have been more comfortable. The interior was hot. It stank of those flowers from yesterday, a sweet, heavy perfume, like swimming in it, warm. He left the door open, leaned over and opened the passenger door as well. Then he picked up the phone, dialled, waited. Kate answered.

'Hello?'

And immediately he had doubts about making this call.

'Kate. It's Paul.'

'Hi, Paul. How's it going? Are you all right?'

'I'm okay. Just fine.' He hesitated but it seemed he had to go through with it now. 'Is Theo there?'

'I'll get him for you. Hang on.'

He heard the clunk as she put the phone down. The little white table in their hallway. From somewhere, faintly, he could hear classical music. Theo indulging himself, savouring his pleasures. He was probably sitting on his terrace in a white bathrobe, sipping café au lait and reading the Sunday papers. On warm summer evenings that same terrace was awash with the smell that lingered in the car, the perfume flowing wave on wave, and Theo, with his head thrown back, drinking it through his nose. Ah! Abandonment. And Anelise said that it drove her crazy.

Hang up now, he thought. Immediately.

'Hello, Paul. How are you?' Theo's soft, cultivated voice, his trace of German accent.

'Sorry to spoil your Sunday morning, Theo.'

'Think nothing of it. How can I help?'

'I might have to stay on here another night. I'm not sure yet. There are still one or two things I have to get to.'

'Not a problem. Please. Don't rush it. Is there anything I should take care of for you tomorrow?'

Paul thought of his schedule with its fifteen-minute slots, the precise structure of his day, the measure of his control. Why was he wrecking it?

'Yes. I've got Alan Baxter from Ventura at eight thirty. He's basically coming to deliver the mining proposal but he'll probably want to go through it.'

'Eight-thirty? I can talk to him.'

'Good. Otherwise, I'm clear until three fifteen. Reports from the Hammond managers. Annette can reschedule those. I'll be back by three.'

'Take your time. Please.'

'Thanks, Theo.'

'You're welcome. I'll see you when I see you. Okay?'

They hung up. Paul sat staring straight ahead, at the blank wall of concrete blocks, the peeling yellow paint. Why had he done it? The lack of justification was almost worse than the decision itself. Strange, a strange state he was in. Ever since yesterday at Jane Shaw's he had been plagued by a feeling of indifference, as if the light had dazzled more than his eyes, his thinking blinded. Three hundred and twenty little panes of glass. The truth about Melissa. Then suddenly, just now, an idea had come to him, popped up out of nowhere, that he needed to stay and he'd acted on it, without thinking, against his will. Except that it couldn't be against his will, could it? 'One or two things he had to get to.' What things? Did he really want to go back up to that house today and be alone in it? He supposed he did. He supposed he would go. But he couldn't understand why. His needs felt as blank as the wall in front of him. He might be driving at it, full speed, towards a total wreck.

There was a movement to his right, a shadow.

'Hi.'

He turned, peered out. It was the girl with the blonde hair, the one he assumed was the Kemps' daughter. She was wearing a bikini, a flimsy white thing that tied with little bows at her back and hips, and a thin strap looped over the nape of her neck. She had white gym shoes on her feet and a smile on her face.

'Hello,' he said.

She lifted her right hand and rested it on top of the car door, shifted her weight to her left leg. Her body was brown, biscuit brown, fresh from the sun. He could almost feel the heat of it. Her yellow hair hung in silky strands to her right shoulder as she cocked her head to look down at him.

'Everything all right?'

'Fine, yes,' he told her.

'You leaving today, then?'

'I'm not sure. Maybe we'll need to stay another night.'

'No problem. We're not exactly booked out. Do you want me to write you in?'

'It might be a good idea.'

'Are you staying for Jane's party, then?'

No, he didn't want that.

'Everybody'll be there,' she went on. 'Neighbours and friends. Most of her kids and their kids. It's like a big event round here, like a festival.'

Kids? Like the ones he'd met yesterday and shaken hands with and nodded to. The Sams and the Aces. And the Melissas. Were there more Melissas with their red hair and white, white skin and pink-white babies? His sister in a way that bound him not just to the reminders of his own past but to the living person who was Jane Shaw, who knew, perhaps, a different story. How could he keep control of it?

'Nice car,' said the girl. Her warm brown belly had a navel dimpled in a convoluted little knot. Her breasts in the sling of her top were big, her cleavage chocolate dark against the biscuit brown, shining just a little. She was shining with a polish, oil. He should get rid of her, tell her to go away.

'Is it new?' she asked.

'A year old.'

'Big,' she said and ducked her head further to see inside. The cleavage, heat loomed closer to him. 'Must be nice to drive.'

'It's comfortable.'

'Do you ever pick up hitch-hikers?'

'No. Not really.'

She made a little noise, a sigh, a murmur. 'Sometimes . . . Sometimes I just want to get in someone's car, anyone's, and get the hell out of here. Doesn't matter where. Just somewhere real. Far away, you know?' She straightened up and looked, he guessed, somewhere into the distance, the journey she longed for, her somewhere real. Her right hand was still on the door, the left on the top of the car. Her belly, sleek and brown and hot, was no more than twenty centimetres from his face. Suddenly he had an impulse to lunge and grab her, rub his lips on her, lick her smooth, bare flesh. God, he thought, horrified, drawing back. I almost did that!

The girl ducked her head again and laughed. 'Silly, eh?' Then she caught sight of something, leaned forward, reached into the car beside his seat. She picked up a twig with cream-green flowers and small, pointed leaves, wilted now. Her nose in it, sniffing.

'I thought I could smell it,' she said. 'It's just about finished, though. I love this stuff. It makes me go all weak inside.' She tucked the spring into her cleavage, where it stood up, drooping over towards her chin. She breathed it in again. 'I wanted to plant some round here but Mum hates it. She says it makes her sick.' She laughed.

Paul stared at the concrete blocks. He was helpless. He could not move.

'Well,' she said, 'I better go and write you in, hadn't I? See you later. At Jane's maybe. Have fun.'

11 Peace

In the shade of the grapevine in the back yard, the baby Alice, wearing singlet and nappies, lay asleep in a bassinet under a veil of white muslin. The house was full of visitors and the bustle for the party underway. Anelise sat on a rug beside the bassinet and watched the baby sleeping, the chairs and tables carried out, the plates of food left under cloths to keep the flies off them. Relaxed. She was glad to be still. For the first time in days, it seemed, she was not gnawed by tension. Paul was up at Walter's place by himself. He was in a mood still, abstracted, uncertain, but there seemed to be nothing she could do about it. As far as she could tell, he wanted to be alone, to work things out without her help. He had booked another night at the El Dorado but had then insisted on packing everything up and stowing it all in the boot of the car. Maybe they would need to spend another night here. Maybe they would get away in time to go back. Anelise let him have his way. She didn't really care. Maybe she would stay here forever.

Just sitting, watching the baby sleeping. She had a feeling she was at the centre of herself somehow, as if little Alice, the youngest of Jane's grandchildren and so close to the beginning, was the symbol of everything that might be or might not, all the possibilities that could grow out of this one moment. Strange, she thought, the power babies have when they're such puny things. She looked down at the small, unconscious body, the closed eyes, the little fists curled up, and she felt the pull, the force that bound her to this helplessness and the fierce determination that went with the love she felt she could still give if she had the opportunity. Paul, in his own peculiar world, hardly noticing her, and Andrew, almost a man now, with his studied indifference to his need for her, and hers for him. She had given her life to them both, or more than twenty years of it. Andrew's education and Paul's career and nothing much for herself except her four years at university to get a degree that now seemed useless. But it was all right. It was the way she wanted it.

A girl in a blue gingham dress came around the corner of the house and ran towards her. She was about eight years old, thin, brown, dark-haired, arms and legs at unco-ordinated angles.

'Hello,' Anelise said.

The child peered into the bassinet.

'Oh,' she said, 'it's Alice. I thought it was your baby.'

'Isn't she beautiful?'

'I suppose so. My father says that all babies look like boiled rats.'

'Do you agree?'

The girl tilted her head to one side, considering. 'Not all of them perhaps.' And she bounded off, skipping in great leaps, with flailing arms.

Alice was beginning to stir. Her fists unclenched, fingers opening, clutching at the air. There was a farting noise. Her shoulders twitched. Her eyelids flickered.

She needs changing, Anelise thought. It's a long time since I've done it. And a little girl. How do you fold the nappies for a little girl? Alice snorted, coughed. Her big blue eyes stared up at Anelise. Then her mouth opened in a low, rasping cry.

There was a bag beside the bassinet. Anelise opened it and took out a fresh nappy. I can do this, she thought. Of course I can. She pulled aside the muslin tent. Alice was bawling now, arms and legs pumping, face screwed up in a tight, angry grimace. Anelise unpinned the nappy. It was soaked and squirted full of yellow shit. She wiped Alice as clean as she could and lifted the mess out of the bassinet.

Suddenly Melissa was there, crouching beside her. Anelise felt a surge of jealousy and disappointment that she would have to give up control of the baby at this moment. Melissa, however, made no move to take over. She merely sat on her haunches and watched, despite the yelling. Anelise cleaned Alice some more and rubbed ointment into the chapped skin creases at the top of her thighs. Then she folded a new nappy in the same manner as the old one and pinned it on.

'There!' she said, proud of herself, pleased that she had been allowed to finished.

Melissa picked Alice up and wrapped her in a cotton blanket. Then she sat down in a lotus position and put the baby to her breast.

'She's got good lungs,' Anelise said. 'I guess you heard her yelling.'

'No,' Melissa said, 'I can always tell when she's woken up.'

'How?'

'I can just tell. Even if I'm kilometres away I still know.'
'You must be psychic.'
'Yes,' Melissa said, as if it was an ordinary fact of life.
'Are you that way about other things?'
'If I want to be. My father gave me the idea.'
Her father, Paul's father, Andrew's grandfather. The connection was still a surprise, a strange feeling.
Melissa smiled. 'It's easy really. You just have to look inside yourself in the right way. After you've had a bit of practice, you can sort of keep an eye on it while you're busy with something else. I can tell fortunes too.'
'Really? What do you do? Palmistry or Tarot?'
'No. Jane's into that sort of stuff. Numerology, astrology. I just read faces.'
'Faces?'
'Yes. Would you like to try?'
A little wriggle of alarm. She was not sure she wanted to know herself any better. She was not sure she trusted this woman with her faraway voice and her calm inner confidence. She looked down at the feeding baby, a small, blind, unselfconscious thing with no knowledge, no fear.
'All right,' she said.
'Sit opposite me, then.'
Anelise shuffled herself across the rug and into position.
'Look at me,' Melissa said. 'You don't have to stare or anything. Just start by looking at me and then, after a while, you can close your eyes or shift them any way you like.'
Melissa's eyes were green, fringed with long, dark lashes. Green irises, flecked with radiating streaks of darker colour. They were not eyes even. They were strange stones, opals, something magical. The tension in Anelise's body began to give. The eyes wandered over her face in a slow circuit, with little flicks to the side or up or down and back again. She tried to follow them but it made her giddy. Then she was relaxing even more. She closed her eyes, let out a sigh.
'I feel you're a very determined person,' Melissa said. 'You like to set your course and throw yourself into things. And whatever you do, you like to do well. That's what matters to you most. Only . . .' A pause. 'Only you don't always feel you've achieved that. You do very well but you always think you could've done better.'
Yes, Anelise thought. Always.
'You're a physical person, too. Fit. You like sport and competition. You're very good at it.'
'I was. Quite good. Eight hundred, fifteen hundred metres.' Did

she say that or think it? The occasions, places, people, faces to her right somewhere. And the noise of the crowd and her own blood as she kicked out. God, she could still feel that sudden surge of will, that moment of triumph as her body responded, thrust her on and carried her, until the pain came, dragging, and on, through that too.

'And there's another thing,' Melissa said, 'another you. Tricking you, almost. It's as if once you've made your mind up over something, you're so determined that you can't change it yourself. Someone else has to do it for you so you have a special part of you, inside, like another person who you get to do the dirty work. It's like something growing. Like a chrysalis that stays the same until one day, suddenly, it opens up and a butterfly emerges, or a beetle, maybe.'

Jesus, she thought, I don't like this. I don't like this at all. But she didn't move. She kept her eyes closed, held her breath. Waited for the soft, caressing voice to go on.

'But don't worry. It's okay. Your inner self knows best. It'll look after you. Always. Listen to it. It takes you on, different stages, one to the next. You used to be a runner and then you changed into . . .'

'A wife,' Anelise said. 'And a mother.' And then, from nowhere, she was thinking of those foreign mountains and Coochy Creek, that little airport lounge and the blonde woman, the stewardess, holding her hand, and Paul, standing, looking at her, the first time she ever saw him, and the woman telling her again, as if she hadn't heard the first time, that her parents were dead.

'Pain,' Melissa said. 'There are some things between you and Paul.'

'No. Yes. I was thinking of the first time we met. He was so good to me. He did everything, held me together. I was a total stranger to him then. Except that he knew I was from the same country, of course. Because of the blazer. He recognised that. And he . . . I don't know why he did it. I'm not sure he does either.'

'And you're okay?'

'Yes, I'm okay.'

'You're happy?'

'Yes.'

'You're happy.' Melissa's voice, soft and secret, like her own deep-down belief, telling her, calming her.

'Yes. Except . . .' I shouldn't say this, she thought. It's so disloyal.

'You're not really close to each other,' Melissa said.

Jesus, she can see it! It's in my face!

'Physically,' Melissa said.
'Yes. But it doesn't really matter. It's all right. I've got used to it. I've stopped thinking it's my fault. Or Paul's. He just, well, he doesn't really like people to touch him. And I do sometimes, still. Touch him, I mean. And it annoys him. He doesn't say anything but I can tell it annoys him.'
'Don't worry. Be strong. You have all the strength you need.'
'I don't have to stop being a wife, do I?' Did she? She couldn't tell. It was such a strange idea. And how could she be sure of anything when she could change her mind without knowing she was doing it? Betrayal. Like the amazement she felt when she found herself thinking, I'm not an athlete any more. I'll never run another race. And knowing it was true. Would she do that to Paul? How could she?
'It's all your choice. Nobody forced you into any of it. Don't worry. If you can link your inner strength to your outer, you'll have everything.'
'I don't feel strong,' Anelise said. 'I used to, maybe. But not now.'
There was a touch, a light touch on her face, a feather across her cheek, Melissa's fingers. She opened her eyes.
'You're very beautiful,' Melissa said.
Oh, God, she thought and she felt suddenly as if she were melting, swiftly, flowing away, sucked up by the shrunken, dry, thirsty earth.

12 Standstill

Nothing to do but wait. He sat in the armchair with its back to the window, looked at the other armchair, listened to the silence. Something had compelled him to come back here and yet he could see no benefit. There was nothing in the house that he wanted, no thought or feeling that struck him as important. His father was dead and he didn't really care. Perhaps he was supposed to care. Perhaps that was the problem. Except that he had no time for psychology and he did not really believe there was any significance in his present state of mind. He was a little off colour, that was all, a bit disorientated. He wasn't hiding anything. There was nothing to be afraid of. He could remember his father quite clearly if he tried; a big man with red hair and a big laugh, a man who talked, told stories, made jokes. A man who walked out on his wife and son. An ordinary man, he supposed. The kind of man there were thousands of. He had lived in this house, died in it.

It's a ritual, he thought. Like a memorial service. I didn't go to the funeral so I have to come here and sit in this coffin because that is the law. There was no law that said you had to care about your parents, or about anything at all, but you had to do the right thing, follow the right formulae. That was how the world held together.

— I do not want to hear his name again, his mother said.

He could hear her clearly in his mind but he ignored her, stuck to his purpose. There were rules to follow. The observances, the observations. He would look through everything, go through it all deliberately and carefully, if that was required of him. One thing at a time.

He stood up. There was a picture over the mantelpiece. Symbolic, he supposed. A circle in the centre like a colour wheel, the spectrum. Except that the real spectrum had seven colours not eight. The extra one here, in the place between the red and the violet, was a deep purple, almost black.

— Rich old yachtie got buggered in Venice, his father said.

— Don't teach him things like that, Walter.

— It's a mnemonic. A simple aid to memory. Red, orange, yellow, green, blue . . .

— I know what a mnemonic is. And they don't have to be obscene.

The colours might be an eye, staring out from the centre of the square. And the square might represent logic. Except it had a hole in it on each side. A hole where the water ran out. Whichever way you turned it, the water would run out, like trying to keep it in your hands.

— Why won't it stay? It never stays.

A circle within a square within a circle and then a ring of smaller circles, all in a square that was the frame itself. There were eight small circles. Like the points of the compass. At the top, in the north, was the King on a throne. At the bottom, the Queen. To the right, Death in a monk's hood, with his scythe and hourglass. To the left, a jester in cap and bells. Between the King and Death was an old man, an alchemist maybe, with a long white beard and a skullcap on his head. Opposite him, between the Queen and the Jester, was a mermaid with golden hair sitting on a little island. On the other side of the Queen, in the south-east, was a miner with a

lamp and a pick, hacking at a rock face. In the north-west, between the Jester and the King, was a woman in a red dress. She had dark hair, braided up, and in her hands she carried a bowl of fire.
— Paul! said his mother. You ought to have more sense. You'll burn the house down. Promise me you won't do that again. Promise me you'll never fool with matches ever again.

The smell of paper, burning. When he wanted to be clean, like she did. Promise me. You fool. Opposite the Fool is Death.

He turned and looked at the chair he had been sitting in. The arms were worn and the seat sagging. The chair with its back to the window, with the light falling over the left shoulder. The other chair was in much better condition. Two chairs on opposite sides of the fireplace. The way it was back home, then.

His mother in her red dressing gown, on her knees before the grate. The yellow flames, the photographs like leaves, curling in the heat and bursting. Fire. Fire bursting out of the bodies, the faces. Bursting like Michael's face. Like the sun so hot. In the sky Michael fell through.

Michael with the bat in his hands, leaning forward into the stroke, the crisp hit, the red ball speeding over the grass. In Sydney, he joined a club and scored a hundred. His father read the letter and his eyes shone with pride. Yet Michael came home in a box and looked like someone else. His face. His mother wept for two days and then stopped. Crying did no one any good. She knew that. It wasn't going to bring Michael back. Life had to go on. You had to do the right thing. Rules, the details, make a list. The King rules in the north, opposite the Queen. Except that his father fell apart and drowned himself in whisky. And went away.

The woman with the fire and the braided hair. The mermaid on the rock. She must be cold and fishy, a fishy smell. Her golden hair, the golden sun. There was gold in the sea, gold in the sky, and gold in the earth. The gleam of gold in the dark rock two miles underground. They said it was haunted. Level six, Gallery J. A woman with a white shawl over her face and carrying a lamp. She always brought one or other of the miner's two worst enemies, fire and water. The floods through the tunnels or the flames flickering in the dark, the dull red glow along the passage ways.

That's stupid, he thought. It's fantasy, rubbish, nonsense. Like the books on the wall in front of him. There were rows of them. Two or three shelves were empty, but the rest were tightly packed with volumes of philosophy and poetry, psychology, theoretical physics, history, religion, magic, mathematics, and mysticism. All his father's fancies, theories, flights of speculation. At best such stuff was pointless, at worst it bred utter confusion and muddle. Better to have facts, and theories that were close to the facts, information that could make a difference in the world.

I think I like Chemistry best, he had said.

— You know what Rutherford thought of Chemistry, don't you? Besides, how can anyone descended from Isaac Newton possibly be a chemist?

We're not descended from Isaac Newton.

— Of course we are.

He never married.

— What difference does that make?

Anyway, Newton was an alchemist.

— That's not a chemist. Alchemists are interested in the secret of matter.

I thought they were interested in gold.

Something that made sense. Something he knew. You crushed the ore and ground it to a fine powder. You pulped it, then leached it in a series of agitation tanks with sodium or potassium cyanide to dissolve the gold. Then you added zinc, which combined with the cyanide and precipitated the gold out as a fine powder. You gave it an acid wash, to remove impurities, and then you melted it down. In some processes, you adsorbed the gold onto carbon and extracted it from the cyanide solution by electrolysis. Simple.

— Why on earth do you want to be a chemist. All they care about is recipes. Be a cook if you like recipes. At least that has the merit of pandering to people's sensuality.

Michael refused to be anything. He worked in a warehouse in Sydney. He wouldn't even be a famous cricketer.

The chair behind the desk creaked when he sat in it. He rested his elbow on the right arm, his cheek against his raised fist. The chair tilted with a little click and swivelled to the right. The sunlight, afternoon, was coming in through the window, whitening the furniture, the rug, the fireplace. Why is light so silent? he wondered.

— It doesn't move the air.

Why not?

— It's a form of radiation. It has no mass, in the normal sense of that word.

Why not?

— Because God made it that way, darling, his mother said. Now go to sleep.

— Let him ask questions. Why shouldn't he ask questions?

— Just as long as they're sensible.

— Sensible questions only have stupid answers.

— Please, Walter, don't confuse the boy.

On the King's right hand is the priestess with the bowl of fire; on his left, the alchemist with his crystal ball and his skullcap. The Queen, however, sits between the miner and the mermaid. It's rubbish. It makes no sense.

Where are you going?

— Sy-y-y-y-dney, Michael said.

Why?

— I have to ge-e-e-t away.

From Mum and Dad?

— Not ju-ust them.

You don't have a job.

— No. I'll get one.

You might not.

— I will. I want to go and do it. Tha-a-a-t's what this is about really.

It doesn't make sense to me.

— So-o-o-orry, Paul.

I wish you weren't going.

— Look, whe-e-en I'm there, whe-en I'm settled. You can come too. I mean, I'll get a flat. So-o-o-omewhere for you to stay.

When I'm older.

— Yes.

In a couple of years.

— Yes.

I wish you weren't going.

— So-o-o-orry, Paul.

Mum won't like it. She'll take it personally.

— I ca-a-an't help that. I ca-a-an't live my life for Mum and Dad.

'Michael,' he said out loud, suddenly, for no reason, and the word in the room in the air that the sunlight couldn't move was like an arrow falling, burning, and it hit somewhere soft, driving in and searing, spreading, dropping deeper, opening the flesh like a hot coal through snow.

He pulled at the drawer of one of the filing cabinets and it creaked out on its metal runners. Neatly packed folders labelled Correspondence, Clippings, Notes. He took out one and opened it and saw, for the first time in twenty years, his father's handwriting; the small, cursive script, precise and clear, with loops that were full, rounded, like ripe berries. It was so instantly familiar, so never thought of, like the smell of something. The shirt of a dead brother. His mother breathing at it and howling and throwing it from her,

her face twisted like a rubber mask as she ran from the room.

And there were pages of notes that made no sense. His father's mind.

> To see the symbolic aspect of the concrete
> — to spiritualise it.

> The body has to be spiritualised and the spirit has to be incarnated, both things must take place.

> The rock which is the water of life (Moses). The rock which is the well.

> p254

> The fire has to burn until the last unclean element is consumed.

> Thus,

> If you only follow your passion according to its indications it will never go too far, it will always lead to its own defeat.

The desk had eight drawers, four on each side. The top right contained a wooden tray with pens and pencils laid out neatly. In the second was a stapler, a two-hole punch, a roll of tape, a dish full of paperclips. The third was empty. The fourth contained an old brass picture frame lying face down. He picked it up and turned it over. It held a black and white print, faded over the years, showing a man and a woman and two boys. The man had his arm round the woman's shoulders. The boys, in front, were wearing shorts and long socks and lace-up shoes. Everyone was smiling at the camera. The smaller of the boys had no front teeth.

Remember, Paul, remember. His father and his mother and his big, older brother. And his father was smiling out of such a young face, and his mother with black tresses, beautiful and smiling, and the two boys, who were neat and standing straight and smiling. And the little one so happy, so unselfconscious that he didn't care if he had teeth or not, it was just so good to be there in that close, forever, far-off moment. Paul, he thought. And Mikey. And Mummy and Daddy. And Paul and Mikey. And Paul and Daddy, Mummy. Paul.

And the smell of the shirt and his father walking away down the path, the sunlight, with a pack on his back. And the pain, the tearing pain of it, the opening and opening, like a flower, a pit, a wound so huge, so impossible to bear he knew it would destroy him. Red. The red blood, fire, like a sea. The woman and the flames. The photographs were curling, letters, papers, black the ashes floating upwards, frills of incandescence, gone. The fire has to burn until the last unclean element is consumed. Burning through him. Lightness. Weightlessness. The black ash drifting, cooling. There was no more pain.

He stood up, walked down the room through the shafts of sunlight, yes. He stepped over the fender into the hearth and reached up to the picture above the mantelpiece, took it down from its hook. The King on his throne. The priestess in the red dress, the miner and the mermaid. The Jester in his cap and bells, the joke, the nonsense, fantasy, the black stupidity. He gripped the wooden frame of the picture and wrenched it apart. The glass fell into the tiled hearth, bright, like a sheet of ice, so clear. It smashed about his feet. Because Michael was gone. His father gone. The silent house. The sunlight, glass in glittering slivers, and the picture in his hands and the woman in the red dress reaching towards him with a bowl of fire. It was easy. He was free. Because the opposite of Death was the Fool, the madness come for its revenge.

13 Community

She sat in her chair, like the Queen, looking at the people in the yard: her children, her neighbours, her children's children. No one was taking much notice of her but she didn't mind that. It wasn't her job to entertain, not this time. She simply had to be there and get applauded because she was another year older. The food and the drink and the noise of their voices, the sun on her back, warm. The evening shadows were coming now, though, the day folding into itself, the earth on its way, rolling on, another round through space. She could see the moving planet in her mind and the image surprised her. It was not the kind of idea she was used to; more like something of Walter's, taking off on a flight into orbit and looking back down on the world from far away. She liked a low view for herself, close to the ground, a wide horizon. Flat-earther, he used to call her. If he is here, she thought. If he's still around, he'll be somewhere in the sky, with the sun, his element.

'You okay, Ma?' Sam hunkering down beside her chair. His narrow face, dark eyes.

She smiled. 'Yes. I was just thinking about Walter. Missing him a bit, that's all.'

The Blackening

'I know,' Sam said. 'I keep thinking of last year.'
'Yes.'
'Ace had a big argument with him. Remember that?'
'Ace always argued with him. He was the only one who would in the end.'
'Ace liked having him on,' Sam said.
'They had each other on.'
'You know what I miss most? His laugh. Couple of times today I've almost thought I heard it. That kind of shout he had. Like an explosion.' He was looking down at the ground, the red bricks, lichen filigree in pale green. She felt his strength pent up in him, his lean, brown body. Always moving like a restless child. His stillness now, his presence beside her, touched her in the old way. Love and sadness.
'Fire people,' she said. 'Him and Ace. They're both fire people. I was thinking about that before, too.'
'You mean their signs? I thought Walter was a Scorpio.'
'No, I mean the way they are, their main elements. Ace is fire and water. Walter's fire and air.' And I talk about them as if they were both still here and not just one of them, she thought.
'Fire and water are supposed to be incompatible,' Sam said.
'Not when they're properly balanced. Think of the sun and the rain. Wonderful when you get them right. Fire and water are mostly a problem for the earth-air people. That's because everybody really has all four elements. Two stand out and the other two are hidden away somewhere. What we each have to do is find the elements we don't use and get them all into balance. Earth-air people have to look for fire and water, but they don't know how to manage them. That's when it's dangerous.'
'So who's earth and air?' Sam asked.
'Well, you for one.' She laughed.
He looked at her, surprise in his face, and then he grinned. 'You're a crackpot, Ma.'
'And that's exactly what I'd expect earth and air to say.'
He laughed.
'I need some more wine,' she said, standing up.
'I'll get it.'
'No, you won't.'
They set off across the yard towards the knot of people round the table where the drinks were. Close beside him, she could feel his tension, something in him she was trying to understand. She reached out, touched his shoulder. His shirt warm from the sun.
'Are you okay?' she asked.

'Sure.' He looked at her, quickly. How sure was it then? 'The shop's a bit slow but we're surviving. Melissa's rugs are selling well. She's got a real talent, that one.'

No, she thought. I don't mean the business. And I shouldn't interfere. Except that I just can't keep quiet either.

'Take care, eh?' she said. 'You and Claire.'

He looked at her then but he didn't answer. Fire and water, maybe.

Kingi Makara and Kevin Kemp were leaning on the beer keg.

'Hey, Jane,' Kingi called, raising his glass. 'Happy Birthday, eh?'

'That's the third time today,' Sam said, 'at least.'

'Third time lucky,' Kingi laughed.

Jane took a bottle of her own apple wine from the ice bin on the table, poured herself some more. A sip from it, the soft, sweet smell of it. She went and stood next to Sam again. He put his arm around her shoulders. It was his way of showing that he was glad she cared about whatever his problem was.

Terry was there too and Kingi's brother, Joe, and Martine, Ace's wife. Kingi started into one of his yarns about how he and Terry had helped Walter build the road along the side of the back valley. Jane stood listening without really hearing the words. She was feeling for Sam and looking at Kingi and Joe and remembering the third brother, Tane, who had died in an accident, a flash fire in a boiler at Marsden Point. Nearly thirty years ago now. Tane was her daughter Hine's father.

I've had three men, she thought. Three husbands, more or less. And they're all dead. And now I've got three daughters and four sons. The apple smell, the apple taste.

They were laughing at Kingi's story.

'Hey, Linda!' Kevin called. 'Come over here, girl!' He beckoned with a sweep of his arm. Linda was talking to one of Terry's boys but she came anyway.

'Say Happy Birthday to Jane,' Kevin told her.

'I have already. Don't you remember?' She pulled a face to show how silly her poor old father was, pissed again. Kevin grinned at her, indulgent. He was proud of her, pleased with her, doting and admiring and terrified too of the power of her womanhood. And Linda knew it. She was smiling now at Sam and Jane. She was being her sweetest, most innocent self and, all the while, underneath, she had a secret sense, an instinct for the effect she had. This is water, this one, Jane thought, but she could not get a hold on what the second element was.

'Lovely party,' Linda said. 'It's really nice to see everybody again. And I'm glad you invited Mrs Newton. She's a lovely person.'

'Yes.'

'I guess Mr Newton's busy, is he?'

'I guess so,' Jane answered.

'And what sort of business does he do?' Her innocent eyes. What was she thinking? Jane wondered.

'He's got a company. They refine gold and silver or something like that. I think they run some jewellery stores too.'

'Jewellery? That's great. It must be nice to have them part of the family.'

Jane felt the sudden tension in Sam's arm. The idea of Paul upset him. He didn't like the notion that they had suddenly acquired this new connection, a relation almost, because of Melissa. Seven children, she thought. Seven's complete and the eighth just opens it up again. How could there be room for Paul, who was older than all the rest?

'Hey, Jane,' Kingi said. 'Where's our girl then, eh? Where's Hine?'

'Sydney.'

'She got herself a fella yet?' Kingi asked.

It was Sam who answered. 'Nagh. She's going to be a movie star. No time for fellas.'

Kingi laughed, his brows arched up over his puffy eyes. He loved to think how somebody from Wairuru, one of his family, could be in the movies, could be seen on his own TV screen.

There was a cheer from somewhere. Margaret was bringing out the cake. Sam moved away. Ace was there too. His announcement. The ceremony. Another year. Another hundred. Will I make it this time? Jane thought. Will I manage?

Linda touched her sleeve. 'I've been meaning to ask you,' she said, half in a whisper. 'That sheep's skull you've got on a pole by the compost heap, what's it for?'

'That? That's the Devil.'

'The Devil?' Linda gave a little wriggling shiver.

'I like to know where he is so I can keep an eye on him, eh?'

'We shouldn't believe in such silly things really, should we?'

'Why not? If you have God, you've got to have the Devil. Otherwise human beings are responsible for all the evil in the world and none of the good.'

'I don't understand things like that,' Linda told her. Yes, Jane thought, but you're not half as simple as you make out.

'Cake!' Somebody announced.

Why Things Fall

It was on the table, candles ablaze.

'Quiet please!' Ace with his arms raised.

The talking stopped. Ace smiled, his big lawyer's confidence, his voice. The candles fluttered behind him.

'Welcome, everyone, to Jane's sixty-first birthday. I know she won't mind me telling you how old she is, because she'll figure you know anyway. It's a long time since we all first got together on this day. I can't even remember how it became a regular thing with such a lot of people. But it's certainly something of an institution now. Especially when so many of us don't live here any more.'

And the dead, Jane thought. The dead we carry with us.

'I think the way we feel about Jane's birthday is shown by the big efforts people have made over the years to be here on the day itself. I hate to think of all the sickies it's been the cause of. Or all the varsity and polytech classes that've been wagged. We've taken our children out of school. We've driven half the night. We've hitchhiked and walked and come on bicycles. And this isn't just Jane's kids, either. I remember Joe had one or two adventures trying to get here one year.'

Joe laughing, nodding, shaking his head.

'We don't all of us make it, of course. Today, Hine's in Sydney working on a new film, and Dan and Julia and their kids are in London. I know they'll be thinking of us, though, all of them. Just as everybody's thinking of that other important person who isn't here. Walter.'

A little pause, a stillness, hush. Jane grinned to herself. You're wrong, boy, she thought. He's here all right.

'Because today isn't only about how old Jane is. It's about our family and our community. I don't know why Jane's birthday should have turned into something like this, but it has. So, to everyone here, to family and friends, let's celebrate in the way we've done for so many years now. Where are you, Ma?'

Jane stepped forward. Ace hugged her close. He moved aside, gesturing towards the cake. Sixty-one candles, burning, and she would blow them all out. She would have to. One day, she knew, her lungs would fail her. And what would that mean? What would it feel like? She would not have to struggle, of course. When the time came, they would all sense it beforehand and someone would help her and then it would be obvious without having to have it proved. She took a deep breath.

'One!' Ace shouted.

'Two!' shouted everyone.

Would it be this time?

'Three!' they roared, and she blew, blasting her breath over the burning surface of the cake. The flames went down in swathes. All of them, yes, all of them. She was gasping, dizzy, laughing.

'Another year!' Ace said, raising his glass.

'Another hundred!' They all shouted. And they started to sing 'Happy Birthday'.

Jane looked down at the smoking cake. Fire, she thought, fire. I have to wish. I wish . . . I wish . . . What was there to wish for?

14 Possession in Great Measure

It was quiet behind the sheds, quieter still because of the talking in the yard. The sun had gone down. The sky in the west was grey and orange, smoky over the sea. Linda could hear the waves in the distance, just, and the creaking of insects, crickets somewhere. She moved on carefully, bare feet, along the fence. Someone laughed loud behind her and she caught her breath. She was scared, she realised. So silly. But why not? Something was scary. Something inside her was making this happen and she didn't know why.

At the corner of the sheds she looked towards the compost bins; two open boxes made of wooden planks nearly as high as her breast. She could see it from here, on the other side. She stepped forward. There were hard little pebbles under her soles. The smell of the rotting compost came to her; sweet, strong, acid, rich. The first bin was full, dark. The second had pale vague shapes; of scraps, of vegetables, cabbage leaves and lettuce, rotten apples. She stepped on something squishy and her foot squirmed.

The skull on the pole was white in the gloom. There were two black holes where the eyes had been and a raggedness around the front of the snout. The horns, on each side, were darker, curved in a spiral round. It seemed to glow, the whiteness. There was no sound, nothing now, except for the empty eyes staring at her. She reached out her hand, watched it trembling on the end of her arm as the fingers spread towards the skull. The bone was dry and rough-smooth as she stroked it, the horn ribbed, polished, cold. A shiver ran up her arm and into her shoulders like an electric shock. It had her now. She tried to look away, to move her hand, but she was trapped. She wanted it to speak, to tell her what she had to do, but it did nothing except stare at her with eyes that grew blacker and bigger, like sucking holes.

'Please,' she said softly.

Silence. And then a voice or the words forming somewhere in her mind. Kiss me, it said. And she leaned forward towards it and held it gently on each side by the smooth horns and she bent her head and pressed her lips to the cold, white bone between its eyes.

For a moment there was nothing, no change, no surprise, and then she could smell something. It was faint, soft, sweet, a perfume floating in the air and she remembered the bushes, the Queen of the Night. It grew stronger slowly, like the tide coming up the river, and she closed her eyes and breathed it and it seemed to lift her up. She let go of the skull and turned after the scent. She began to move, a swimmer, out towards its source, her spirit rising, more buoyant, sick with the excitement.

The bushes were in front of her, a big clump, higher than her head. The leaves were dark and the flowers pale, glowing with the luminescence, magic of the smell. She moved towards them, into them, and the flowers and leaves were about her face and arms and the scent had filled her, filled her lungs and her brain, and she was lifting, lifting into the air. The twigs pulled at her shirt, her skin and then, suddenly, they gave way and she was standing in a space inside the bushes somehow, with the leaves all around and the flowers dangling up above her head and above, the stars in the night sky coming out now. She reached out her hands and touched the flowers, lifted them, pressed her face into clusters of them, breathed through her nose, her skin. She wanted more. She was aching, aching with it, and the perfume soaked into her, and the white skull on the pole stood in the distance somewhere, in a corner of her mind, watching her. She laughed at it, smiled, opened her mouth to gasp in more and the blossom blew its secrets at her, breathing on her, sticky on her skin. She pulled off her T-shirt and pressed herself into the flowers, bathed her shoulders, neck and breasts in them, felt her head and body fill with more aching, more lightness, more freedom, laughing at the skull on the pole, which was watching, wanting her, stuck, its anchor in the rot of the compost. Beginning, she thought, I am beginning. I am floating forever.

There was a noise. Shouting. She froze. Another shout from over by the house. Her heart was beating hard. She could hear it. And the bushes were alive, noise, rustling, shaking, quiver, leaves and flowers, tossing.

'What is it?' someone shouted.

Another voice, further away. Fire, did it say?

The Blackening

Running feet. Receding. A yell in the distance. The branches shook and there, suddenly, in front of her, in the secret centre of the bushes, was a man. Was it Him, staring at her? His eyes round behind his glasses. He was hot, she could feel it, he was so close, and her fear, her panic, wrenched and twisted in her belly like an animal. His staring eyes, white eyes in a darker face and his white teeth gleaming as he smiled a smile, a snarl, a moaning sound. His hands reached out to her. She couldn't move. And then he toppled forward. He was on his knees, clutching at her. His face pressed against her belly, hot and rough, his hair against her breasts, his fingers squeezing her. He smelt of fire, smoke, the heat of flames in his clothes. She struggled, tried to pull away. He gave a moan, a strange sound, sob, like pain and then she knew he was helpless. The scent of flowers started to come back and she breathed, stronger still. Again, and it was pouring into her and lifting her, her laughter. Yes! she thought.

His hands were fumbling at the button of her cut-off jeans. The zip gave way. He was pulling at them, face still pressed against her belly, lips hot, tongue like flame, its cold track up from her hip bone. She had her hands in his hair. It was short, bristly, hot. His skull hard, like a rock, beneath her fingers. She pushed, pushed him down and he moved slowly, his body folding, and she felt a strength, huge strength in her fingers, pushing down his head, and pulling him in, his hot rough face, pressing him between her thighs. The flowers breathing, scent like balm, like lotion, pouring down over her skin.

Noises. Noises still from far away.

'It's on fire,' someone shouted.

She felt it in her belly, rising. His hands were hard on her flesh like clamps, his tongue a hot thing. Fire. It's mine, she thought. My fire. I want it. I am queen of it. The ground beneath her back and the man with his hot body looming above her. Mine, she thought. I will take it all in. I will have it all. And a laugh rose in her throat, a low, strong laugh, which flapped and flickered like her own dark, unextinguishable flame.

15 Moderation

There were people on the hill, in the dark, running, walking, stumbling forward, lights of their torches swinging arcs across the ground. Anelise was in amongst them, weaving in and out and overtaking, stride by stride, not caring how the going was, the path rutted, twisted, but at least the shoes were right for it. Shouts about her, noise. There was a strange light, brownish, thin, like muddy water flowing, sloshing over the stones and grass, the feet and ankles of the people. She didn't look up to see where it came from, kept her eyes down on the track. Yells, and a low roaring noise and cracks and splinterings. The slope was flattening out and then a flash, a burst of yellow, roaring louder and the leaping sparks. The smell of burning. She stopped.

The valley was full of smoke and Walter's little house on the slope below her stood out in a misty brightness. Dark orange flames flickered in its windows and from one, the kitchen maybe, fire had broken through and was licking, slithering like fingers up the wall. The sparks rising. Men down there in the yard, their pulling, stumbling, down around the water tank at the back of the building, little figures in the leaping shadows.

Paul, she thought. Someone jostled her as she stood there staring, smoke catching at her breathing lungs. She stepped aside off the path. It was useless to go further. The house was done for and if Paul was in there still, he was dead surely. Except he wasn't there. She knew that somehow. He was gone, fled away, hiding in the dark. She thought of the books, the chairs, the desk, the mandala on the wall above the fireplace, and felt a twisting, tightening, deep inside her like a part of her was drying, shrivelling in the fire. Oh, Paul, she thought, what have you done? What have you done to yourself, to us, to all these people? There was smoke in her eyes, or tears, the bright flames blurring as they burst up higher and the valley leapt with huge, crazy shadows among the trees.

'Wow!' Standing beside her was a child, the little girl in the gingham dress. The light of the leaping flames flickered over her narrow face, her round, awestruck eyes. Slowly she lifted her hand, reaching out for someone. Anelise took it, held it. A billow of smoke rose, flapped into their faces. They coughed.

'You shouldn't be up here,' Anelise said. 'Come back to the house.'

She led the child away. The hill path was empty now. Down below, through the tears, she could see the lights of Jane's kitchen.

THE BLACKENING

She sniffed. 'What's your name, then?'
'Alexandra,' the girl said.
Talk, she thought, please. She didn't want to face it, to understand what it all meant.
'And what's your mummy's name?'
'Margaret.'
Ah, yes. 'And your daddy's Bill, right?'
'Yes.'
A pause.
'Why did Walter's house catch on fire?' the girl asked.
Why?
'I don't know, love. It happens sometimes.'
Why? What reason? At the precise moment when it was all offered to Paul, his past, his future, it had gone up in flames. And he had done it somehow, he must have done it. He had run away from himself.
'Why are you crying?' the girl asked.
Anelise sniffed. 'I got smoke in my eyes.'
'I got smoke in my eyes and I'm not crying.'
'I guess you've got tougher eyes, eh?'
The perfume of the bushes wafted to her, soured by the smoke. She turned and looked back up the hill. It was lit now by a glow, a pulsing light. The silhouettes of trees on the crest leaping, contracting.
'Mummy!' the girl called, letting go of Anelise's hand.
In front of them was a figure struggling up the slope.
'What are you doing? What are you doing?' Margaret, frantic, grabbing at the child, lifting her.
'Walter's place is on fire,' the girl said. 'It's burning and burning with huge flames.'
'Thanks for bringing her down.' Margaret's eyes, round, white, staring at her.
And suddenly Anelise knew that it was impossible. She couldn't stay and talk. She couldn't be here, facing this woman in the burning perfume smell with the fire leaping shadows on their faces.
'Excuse me,' she said. 'I have to get something.' And she ran. Fast. Down the rest of the slope, along the path beside the sheds, the yard, the house. Because it was not just Paul's chances that were burning but her own as well; the hopes and possibilities she hadn't even dared allow herself and hadn't yet begun to understand. For if he had not the strength to face himself, what hope was there for her?
The drive was full of cars. Their own, it was here somewhere,

there at the end. The key, the key, the key. It was in her bag inside the house. She would have to go in and get it, confront everyone, see the children kneeling on the chairs in the kitchen with their faces pressed to the window, gazing up at the glow at the top of the hill. But then she tried the door and it opened and she was inside behind the wheel with her head in her hands and the tears came again, flooding out of her this time, shaking her body and the dark light of the fire flickered in her mind and she could see Paul running, a shadow black against the flames.

'You fool,' she said. 'You stupid, bloody fool.' But which fool was it? Who? She couldn't tell.

The passenger door opened. He was there. Sweating, dirty, shirt undone. A black smudge on his forehead. No glasses.

'Drive,' he said.

'What the hell's going on, Paul?'

'Drive!' he yelled, his eyes glaring at her, full of hatred, spittle in his mouth.

'I don't have a fucking key!'

He reached into his pocket. There were big dark stains of mud, of grass on the knees of his trousers. He thrust the key at her. She started the car. There was no room, the driveway full, the other vehicles, a van, a truck.

'I can't get out,' she said.

'That way!' He jabbed his finger, arm out, hard towards a gap between the fruit trees.

She started, eased the big car forward, over the verge and into the soft grass, narrow way, between the trunks, the headlights lit up tangles of leaves and branches, coming at them, scraping up and over, screech of twigs along the roof and thump of fruit as it fell and rolled down over the bonnet, boot. And more trunks, moss coat, rocking, lurching, branches breaking, and a dip, a little ditch, a bump, the wheelspin, grip and they were free. They were on the drive's end, the wider slope that went down to the road. She turned left.

'Where to?' she asked.

'Home,' he said.

'Home?'

'Drive, for Christ's sake, woman!'

And the car sped forward, smooth on the smooth road, tarseal, down towards the beach, the fork with the shop and the old hall to the right. The El Dorado sign flashed up in the headlights. Smooth they went, the silence like a wall between them and the road reeling in and Anelise with the pain of something dying in her, like an unborn child.

After half an hour, she looked over at Paul. He was asleep.

16 Enthusiasm

Wairuru, December 1966

'Ma! Ma! Come and look at this!' Terry in the doorway with his dark hair, flopping in his eyes.

'What is it love?'

'A thing! A thing in the sky!' This from Sam. Margaret was there, too. And the twins. They were all crowding in, hanging back, beckoning her, their eyes wide, wonder, excitement, fear.

'It's a UFO,' Margaret said.

'Come on, Ma!' Terry, ordering her.

She stood up, scooped little Hine into her arms, moved towards the door. The kids were gone, out in the yard, leaping, yelling, pointing upwards. There, coming towards them from the south-east, was the thing, floating, green and blue against the sky. It was big, round, elongated, a huge tear-drop with a sort of cradle or box hanging underneath.

'It's a balloon, isn't it?' Ace asked her.

'Yes, I think so.'

'It's not a UFO,' Dan said. 'UFOs don't exist.' He took her hand, though, just in case.

The balloon was about half a mile away, somewhere towards the Makaras' place. It was hard to tell how high it was or what track it was on. It seemed to be heading towards the top of the hill. It'll crash, she thought. But then, if it didn't, it would soon be heading out to sea with the next landfall God knows how many miles away.

'Come on!' Terry, with a wave of his arm, was off, running, Margaret in pursuit and Sam trying to keep up with them. Jane followed with the twins and Hine. When she rounded the sheds, the three bigger children were already scrambling up the hillside. The balloon, to the right, was closer, larger, lower. It was getting thinner too, longer, more and more like a fat green sausage. The gondola or whatever it was seemed to be skimming over the ground, sweeping in. Was there someone in it? A dark figure? It disappeared behind the side of the hill but the green sausage kept on, driven by the wind, gradually hidden by the steepening slope.

The big kids were already at the top, standing watching. Jane and the younger ones toiled up towards them. Suddenly Margaret turned and came running back.

'It's crashed! It's crashed!' she was yelling, waving her arms, trying to keep her balance.

The balloon had landed halfway down the slope on the other side. It lay, like a huge bladder, empty, draped across the ground, the bushes, tangled in the branches of a small tree. The gondola had fallen on its side, pointing downhill. A man was struggling with the lines that attached it to the balloon. He was dressed in leather flying gear; boots, trousers, jacket, helmet. He untied a few of the lines and did something to a piece of machinery that was lying on the ground. Then he noticed Jane and the children watching.

'Hello!' he called, striding up the hill towards them, pulling off his helmet and his goggles. He had red hair and a bushy red beard. Ace and Dan and maybe Sam, too, moved closer to her.

'Are you all right?' Jane called. He looked all right.

'Fine.' He was close to them now.

'Can I have a ride?' Terry asked.

The man looked back down the slope at the balloon and laughed. 'I think it's flying days are done.'

'Where were you heading?' Jane asked.

'Oh, I don't know.' He turned and looked towards the sea, towards the valley, south towards the Makaras'. 'Wherever I get to. This place looks pretty good to me.'

Part Two

The Peacock's Tail

One is roasted in what one is.
— from *Alchemy*, Marie-Louise von Franz

17 Following

Extract from the Notebooks of Walter Newton, February 1969

THE CODEX MARCIANUS

1 Background

Written in Old Greek, dated 1st century AD. One of the earliest known alchemical texts.

Entitled 'From the Prophetess Isis to her son'

Isis had two brothers, Osiris and Set, the first of whom was also her husband. He was a great and beneficent ruler. Set was jealous of him and decided to kill him. He got hold of Osiris's measurements and made a fancy lead coffin, which he offered to anyone who it would fit. When Osiris got into it (only an Ancient Egyptian would be tempted by this macabre game), Set slammed the lid shut and sealed it. He then tossed the coffin into the Nile. After a time, it washed up against a tamarisk tree, which grew round it and covered it up.

Isis went looking for her husband's body but Set got wind of her intentions and found it first. He cut it into fourteen pieces and buried them in the marsh. Isis eventually found the pieces, reassembled them and brought Osiris back to life long enough to father a son, Horus, on her. (Alternatively, she found the vital bits and impregnated herself.) Osiris then became Ruler of the Land of the Dead (Paradise?).

When Horus was old enough to claim his birthright, Set opposed him on the grounds that he was illegitimate because of the odd manner of his conception. A struggle then raged between Horus and Set in which Horus finally triumphed and Osiris was avenged.

Horus, the hawk-headed god, the bringer of light and goodness and order, had two eyes, the sun and the moon. Set, too, was originally a sun god but he became the bringer of darkness and evil, the destructiveness of uncontrolled energy (cf. the Fall of Satan in *Paradise Lost*). Horus and Set were continually at war. In one battle,

Why Things Fall

Set stole one of Horus's eyes (the Moon) and Horus castrated Set.

Notes:

a) The lead coffin. Lead is the base material from which the alchemical work begins. It is also said to be evil, dangerous, possessed by devils. People who understand it are in danger of madness. The suffocation of Osiris is to be locked in the lead, to be locked in an unredeemed state, which, if it continues too long, is madness.
b) Horus is the son of a dead man. He is the sun and the moon, gold and silver. Thus, the birth of Horus is of itself an alchemical process. Out of the lead coffin comes the sun and the moon, embodied in the hawk (Eagle).
c) The battle between Horus and Set is the battle between Day and Night, Good and Evil. It is a battle for the soul of Man. Horus and Set succeed in dealing each other the blows that are uniquely painful to each, producing a blind hawk and emasculated passion. There must be another way than this to resolve the conflict.

2 The Codex

Isis addresses Horus. She tells him that while he was engaged in his battles with Set, she had gone to the city of Hermes. At a certain point in the conjunction of the heavens she was approached by an angel who had sexual designs on her. He was in a great hurry to have his way but she resisted him and told him that he could not have what he wanted unless he gave her the secrets of the gold and the silver. He replied that he couldn't do it but that a greater angel, a god, maybe, would come and would be able to solve the problem. She would know this angel because he would be carrying a bowl of shining water on his head.

At noon the next day, this new, greater angel arrived. He, too, was enamoured of Isis and wanted his way with her immediately. Again she resisted and eventually the angel showed her the bowl of shining water and made her swear an oath to tell no one except her son and her closest friend (Are these the same person?) so that 'you are me and I am you', he says. (i.e., the angel is Isis is Horus, maybe)

The oath she swore was by the four elements of Fire and Water and Air and Earth, by Heaven and Earth and Hell, and by various other mythical entities and objects, including, intriguingly, 'the three necessities, the whips and the sword'.

The Peacock's Tail

The angel then explains that the sower of barley can only harvest barley and the sower of wheat can only harvest wheat. Man produces man, lion produces lion and dog dog. Like produces like or, in the general formula of such texts, 'Nature enjoys nature, nature impregnates nature, nature overcomes nature.' This is the great secret. It is followed by statements of alchemical recipes for the production of the Philosopher's Stone, that magic transforming agent which will turn lead into gold and will make Man immortal.

Notes:

a) The great mystery is obtained from the gods by a female figure who does not submit. The first angel is pretty urgent in his sexual demands but when Isis asks him an intelligent question, he loses all his steam and goes away, meekly saying he'll send a better man tomorrow. The second angel is also forestalled. The text says nothing about him getting what he wants even after he has given Isis the secret. Important stuff here. Isis is the goddess of Earth, the female principle of matter. The angels are the bearers of knowledge, wisdom, consciousness, but the sexual coupling they want is merely that, a coupling, a combination. It does not signify anything other than itself. Isis wants knowledge and by the mere fact that she asks the question, she already has what she wants. She is already conscious. Her refusal to acquiesce to a merely physical union results in something new and different. Matter has become self-aware. Isis is the symbol of the (female?) principle of matter in which the (male?) principle of consciousness arises spontaneously. (Just as she impregnates herself with the genitals of Osiris and produces Horus.) Matter precedes mind and not the other way round.

b) Hence, the statement of the great mystery that seems so banal. Man produces man, lion lion, dog dog. This simply states that, on the one hand, we are limited by our physical beings. The crazy products of our inflated (male) egos can only lead to their own destruction. On the other hand, we are not merely physical. Man produces *man* not dog. It is as if, by recognising the limitations, we can somehow transcend them.

Nature enjoys nature, nature impregnates nature, nature overcomes nature.

Jane'll love this stuff.

18 Work on What Has Been Spoiled

Remuera, Auckland, January 1961

'Really, it ought to be possible,' his father was saying. 'There's no reason why they shouldn't make a decent wine in this country.' The bottle in his hand wavered, hovering over the little inverted bell of Michael's glass. Paul kept his eyes on the red-purple (blood, was it?) liquid as it gouted out. The bottle, long-necked, green, moved on, wavering more noticeably as it stretched for the other end of the table. His mother held her hand over her glass, a thin hand with narrow rounded nails and little knobs of knuckles.

'No,' she said. 'That's enough, thank you, Walter.'

Not enough for Walter, though. Now the meal was done, his father would drink on, laughing more, talking more loudly, coming out with more and more wonderful ideas. Unless they started to fight. They would probably fight, Paul decided. His mother had that pinched, disapproving look about her nose already, as if she was trying to filter each breath to keep the bacteria out.

His father was still talking about wine and the different parts of New Zealand that were good for growing grapes. The bottle had visited Sara now. Michael's girlfriend.

Paul held out his own glass.

'No, Walter, he's had enough,' his mother said sharply.

'Stop controlling him!' his father answered. 'He's fifteen. That's plenty old enough to decide for himself. And he can water it, like always.' His eyes, gazing at Paul, were moist with little red veins. His ginger brows lifted in round loops above them. His mouth had that set expression of being reasonable, always reasonable, but never quite meaning it either.

'Paul?' he asked with a little wag of his head to one side.

'Thanks.' A dollop in his glass. Paul added a dash of water from the jug.

'He has to learn to manage it,' his father said. 'How is he supposed to manage it if he doesn't have the experience?' He lifted his own glass, slurped at it, smacked his lips.

They'll fight, Paul thought. It's happening already.

He looked at Michael, who looked back at him. They both knew, they understood from the old days. This was why Michael had left, Paul was sure. He had had to get away. Now, he had a flat in Sydney. He was well dressed. He had a girlfriend with blonde hair and green eyes. At night he crept to her room and they did it.

The Peacock's Tail

Paul wondered if his parents knew. They must do. They weren't that stupid. But why, then, did his mother put up with such a sin in her house?

He sipped his wine. The sharp taste of the tannin and the fruit like big fat purple blobs.

Sara was wearing a white blouse, her slim, tanned throat rising from the V of the neck. In the V, beneath her brown skin, there were two little knobs of bone. They gleamed in the light like ivory. She was saying that she wanted to go to Greece.

'A sad sight,' his father told her.

'Oh, why?' she asked.

'All those ruins. Temples, statues, the rubble of the past. A country which invented the notion that thought was the way to beauty, that physical reality was a mere shadow of the world of ideas. Now there isn't an idea in the place that's worth ten drachma. It's a heap of rotting stone. Crumbling matter. Civilisation going backwards. Hellas through the looking glass.' He hung his head, sadly shaking it. But he gave Paul a wink to the side.

His mother let out one of her groans. 'Oh, no puns, please, Walter! We'll all get indigestion.'

'It's part of our heritage, though, isn't it?' Sara said. 'I think it's important.'

'Oh, certainly, yes.' His father was nodding. 'And there's a good lesson to be learned there too. You'll discover, for example, that most of the best sculpture from the Parthenon is in the British Museum. They're now called the Elgin Marbles after some aristocratic English ponce.'

'Really, Walter!'

'Greece has been stripped of anything movable. Mind you, they couldn't take away the wine. Or the olives. Now there's an interesting idea. The Importance of the Olive in the History of European Philosophy. An excellent thesis topic.'

Sara looked puzzled, polite. After two weeks, Paul had noticed, she still looked puzzled. Or was it worry? She seemed to feel that it was somehow her job to keep everyone happy.

His father chuckled. 'Yes, why not? Augustine could have done a lot worse. What better example of the argument from design? How could such a wondrous thing as the olive have come about by accident? Impossible. Therefore there has to be a God.' He had another bottle now and was winding the corkscrew down into the yellow cork. 'The olive and the grape, a major contribution to theology.' Pop, went the cork. A little glob of wine flew up, a gleam in the light, and fell in a red blot on the white tablecloth.

WHY THINGS FALL

'Do you believe in God?' Sara asked.

Oh, no, Paul thought. Not this one.

His mother, white-faced, pinched.

'Believe?' Walter said, pouring himself more wine. 'As the White Queen says, I sometimes believe as much as six impossible things before breakfast.'

'You're not really religious, then? You don't go to church?' Sara asked.

Walter shrugged. 'I take communion in daily life,' he said. 'Anyway, Elizabeth has enough religion for both of us.'

Sara nodded. She seemed to think it was a simple, ordinary conversation. Just a few questions she was curious about. Or was she doing it deliberately? Michael's head was starting to move as he sensed the disaster and struggled for a word to stop it.

'I'm never sure,' Sara said, innocently. 'If you want to be a Christian, do you have to go to church?'

'Obviously you do,' his mother answered. Her voice was low, controlled, the tension in it like a cold thing, sucking in the warmth.

'Elizabeth's right,' his father said. 'Absolutely. What's religion without observance?'

'I thought it was about morality,' Sara said.

'It's the same thing,' his mother told her.

'God bless us, woman! What an appalling notion!' His father laughed, drank, poured more wine, reaching out to the other glasses again. All he wanted was for everyone to have a good time, to talk and argue, to play with his ideas like bubbles, pretty things to blow and watch them float away. Except he couldn't stop. He never knew when to stop.

His mother was furious now, elbows drawn in close, her fingers in her lap beneath the table, twisting and knotting. He couldn't see them but he could sense the movement, the little shifts of agitation in her arms. She was waiting, he could tell, for the moment that would really offend her. It was her duty to be offended, her belief in herself, her justification. Just as it was his father's to annoy her without ever intending any harm. Michael was watching too, looking from one to the other. He was fighting for his words again. As always, the conversation wouldn't keep still long enough for him to grab hold of it.

'God's an appealing proposition,' his father went on, 'but I always suspect he's got scalped by Occam's Razor. Omit needless hypotheses.'

'Were you ever religious?' Sara asked.

'Certainly. And I was illiterate once too. When I was four.'

The Peacock's Tail

'Why did you stop believing?'

'Weakness!' His mother hissed in a tight-lipped, jaw-clenched voice. His father's eyes flashed up at her. His big fist clenched into a lump, a stone, but then, just as quickly, it relaxed again. He shrugged, smiled.

'I went to war and took to drink,' he said. 'In fact it was Greece that did it. The wine and the olives. The hot sun and the pagan ways. And the Nazis, of course. With their own special brand of paganism. But none of that explains it. Let's have no excuses. Elizabeth is absolutely and literally correct. It was weakness. Cowardice. I don't have the strength to believe or to not believe. I've lost my dignity, you see, my self-control. I was corrupted by obedience. That was the crux of the matter. I obeyed orders and I lost my self-respect. Elizabeth, on the other hand, uses obedience well. She sees appalling things happen every day; children dying of cancer and men and women going out of their minds. But she's a doctor. She follows her training. She prescribes poisons. She gives people up to be sliced into pieces by sharp knives. She does exactly what she's been told but it doesn't affect her. She keeps her dignity. That's the crucial thing. She believes she's doing good. And for that reason she keeps her faith.'

Sara could see now how it was; his mother's clenched fury and his father's feeling hurt, injured, fighting back because he did not quite know what he'd said, how he'd got here. She looked upset, surprised, as if she'd fallen into a trap or as if it was all her fault instead of the way it had always been as long as Paul could remember. His mother and his father squirting acid at each other. And it ate in, slowly, slowly. When you got acid on your fingers, the tips felt smooth, rubbing together, because the skin had been eaten away.

'But medicine's different from war, isn't it?' Sara asked, trying still, trying to make it better.

'People who play games with words can prove whatever they choose,' his mother told her. 'They can prove that blue is red on Mondays, Wednesdays and Fridays and green the other days of the week. All the colours of the rainbow, all the ideas that were ever invented. I do not happen to believe that cleverness is an end in itself, that's all.'

His father, hurt but laughing, leaning towards Sara, showing her his hand like a cradle, as if it had the answer in it. 'The problem is, you see, that my family had the chance to take a patent on the rainbow and missed the opportunity.'

'What do you mean?' Sara asked.

'Our illustrious ancestor, Sir Isaac Newton, and his experiments with the prism.'

Here was a chance to turn the talk. Paul pulled a face. 'Aw, Dad, we don't have to go through all that stuff again, do we?'

'It's your heritage, my child. Physics is in your blood. But then, no.' He flapped his hand, waving Paul away. 'You want to be a chemist, don't you?' He turned back to Sara. 'A heretic, a heretic. I have a son who's a heretic. "There are only two kinds of science: physics and stamp collecting." Do you know who said that?'

'No.' She shook her head.

'Ernest Rutherford, another relative of mine.'

'Really, I didn't know you were connected with him.'

'Rutherford's wife was one, Mary de Renzi Newton.'

'That's not a proper relationship,' Paul said, pushing harder. 'I don't know why you keep talking about that.'

'It's in the cells! It's in the blood! Flesh is destiny!' His father's finger wagging. His mother staring at the ceiling. Paul embarrassed at this flush of family pride but liking it somehow, wanting to push further, hit harder, like his nine-year-old self wrestling with his father on the back lawn.

Michael, too, joining in. His mouth gulping after the sounds. 'I-I-I-I-saac Newton wasn't married.'

'So?'

'I-I-If he had an affair with someone, the chi-i-i-ld wouldn't be ca-a-a-alled Newton, would it?'

'Affair? I doubt it was an affair.' His father grinning, fending off the blow. 'More like a knee trembler at the back of the cowshed. These were moral people, you know, religious people. They didn't allow themselves to enjoy their sin.'

'You're cheating!' Paul said triumphantly. 'You're dodging the issue!'

'What issue?'

'Michael's point. If he wasn't married, how come the child was called Newton. Why not Smith, or Jones, or Pitcaithly?'

'Pitcaithly? Good Lord! Why not Newton? Why not a cousin? Why not adoption by the family?'

'How do you know he didn't have a child?' Sara demanded, glaring at Michael.

'Becau-au-au-au-au . . .'

'Because all the history books say he didn't,' Paul told her.

'History?' His father laughing. 'Old man's fiction. Endless reinterpreting of things that can't be changed, like a reprobate trying to justify his sins.'

'Well then, how do you know he *did* have a child?' Sara insisting, turning on him.

'Because the family says so!' Paul told her, darting in. A little twist of joy, of triumph. 'Old man's fiction!'

His father stared at him, a pained look, then turning away, shaking his head. 'Children are so cruel,' he said.

His mother's voice, precise, a hiss. She didn't understand. She didn't see it. 'Do we have to have these ridiculous arguments? It's our last night together as a family.'

'Last?' his father raising his eyebrows.

'You know what I mean. Michael and Sara are leaving tomorrow.'

'Ah, tomorrow! Yes. Maybe we could get our friend Occam to look at that one too.'

19 Approach

Cambridge, England, March 1919

The boy Walter sat, like a good boy, watching the ladies talk. His mother was wearing her best church dress and a hat with flowers, not real flowers, some other kind. Lady R. had no hat. Her grey hair, drawn back tight into a bun at the back of her head, seemed to smooth away as if it was part of her face. Between them stood a tea trolley with china cups and saucers and a silver teapot and sugar bowl. In the bowl were little white cubes of sugar and a pair of silver tongs to pick them up with. On the lower level of the trolley was a plate with fresh-baked biscuits. The boy Walter had had two biscuits already and it was unlikely he would be offered a third. He looked round the room at the chairs, the sideboard, the carpet with its pattern of big dark flowers; red flowers like the ones on the china cups. The flowers on his mother's hat were blue.

A few feet from where he sat was a big armchair, brown leather, with leather buttons, the size of halfpennies. Beside it was a table and on the table a bowl of oranges. Five oranges, he had counted them. Lady R. had not offered him an orange. Nor had she offered any of the nuts that stood in another, smaller bowl on the same table. Walter wasn't hungry but eating would have been something to do. He was uncomfortable just sitting there. If he moved back in his chair, his feet wouldn't touch the floor. If he sat forward, his back started to hurt.

His mother and Lady R. were talking about people they knew. People back home in New Zealand who were related to Lady R. and to Walter's father. Walter didn't know any of their names.

He turned his head and looked out of the french windows into the garden. There was a green lawn and big trees, beds with bright spring flowers; daffodils. The yellow of the flowers was like gold growing in the garden, knobs of gold on dark green stalks. He thought of the story of Rumpelstiltskin, who had spun the straw into gold for the king's wife. The story had never seemed quite fair because the queen went back on her bargain when she refused to give Rumpelstiltskin her first-born child.

'Good afternoon!' The voice was so loud it made Walter jump. It belonged to a man who was just coming into the room, a big man with a big head and a bristly moustache. He was wearing a dark suit with a waistcoat that stretched tight across his chest and stomach. He shut the door behind him and strode across the carpet towards them.

'Ernest, this is Doris Newton, Frank's wife,' Lady R. said. 'Doris, this is my husband.'

The man took his mother's hand. 'Pleased to meet you. How's Frank getting on down in London? Everything working out?'

'Quite well really,' his mother said.

'Good, good.' The man sat down in the armchair beside the table. Somehow he seemed even bigger sitting down, with his knees spread and his big hands splayed upon them. They were the biggest hands Walter had ever seen.

'Tea, Ernest?' Lady R. asked.

'No thank you, dear.' He looked at Walter with eyes that were light, bright blue, direct, no-nonsense, but with the sort of look you didn't expect in an adult, a look of wanting to find out about you. 'Who's this, then?' he asked.

'My son, Walter. Walter, say hello to Sir Ernest.'

'Hello,' Walter said. He wondered if you had to say sir to people who were sirs.

The man smiled. 'I'm a famous scientist. Have you ever met a famous scientist before?'

'No,' Walter said.

'Come and shake hands, then!' He beckoned and held out a huge pink paw. Walter stood up and walked over to him. He offered his own hand and had it wrapped around with a quick grasp

THE PEACOCK'S TAIL

that surprised him it was so light and warm and gone before he knew it. There was a strong smell of tobacco about Sir Ernest and little brown burn marks on the front of his waistcoat.

'Now, Walter,' he said, 'you and I are related, you know that?'

'Yes, sir.'

'Good. It's an interesting thing about relations. There are always more of them than you think. How many people are there in England?'

'I don't know, sir.'

'Around thirty-five million. Now, how many parents does each of them have?'

'Two.'

'What's two times thirty-five?'

The way to do this was the two times table. Walter thought about it, trying to imagine the numbers written on the slate at school. 'Seventy,' he said, with more confidence than he felt.

'Good boy! So, thirty-five million people have seventy million parents. But twenty or thirty years ago, when those parents were younger, the population of England was only twenty-five million. So what happened to the missing forty-five million? Can you tell me that?'

Walter tried to think of a crowd and remembered the docks when he and his parents had come to England. Suddenly he had a vision of hundreds and hundreds of ships heading in the opposite direction.

'I think, perhaps, they went to New Zealand,' he said.

Sir Ernest laughed a big, loud laugh. 'Good try, my boy, but not correct. The trick, you see, is that most of the seventy million are actually each other! Relations, you see. The world is full of relations!'

This was too clever for Walter. He could not understand how forty-five million people could disappear just because you called them something else. Or how two people could become each other. He decided it would be safer if he asked the questions.

'My father says you split the atom.'

'Yes. That's right.'

'What's an atom?'

'Ah, well, now. Atoms are interesting little blighters. They're a bit like relations. They're everywhere. The whole world is made of atoms. The furniture, this chair, that teapot, you, me, your mother, Lady R. Different atoms put together in different ways make up everything there is. And they're small, yes. Very small. So small that if you had one for every grain of sand on the beach at Southend, you could fit them all into one of those teaspoons and still have room for another beach as well. Do you follow me?'

'Yes,' Walter said, not quite sure.

'Well, then . . .' Sir Ernest's arm reached out and his hand closed over one of the oranges in the bowl on the table beside him . . . 'there are two parts to an atom. One of them's called the nucleus, like this . . .' He propped the orange on the upraised fingertips of his left hand. 'The others are electrons.' In his right hand were three hazelnuts. He jiggled them around so that they rattled against each other and then wriggled one of them up between his thumb and forefinger. 'Now the electrons go round the nucleus like this.' He moved the nut in a big circle around the orange. 'They go very fast; faster than a bird or a bullet, faster than thinking even. Some atoms have a lot of electrons, a hundred or more, and they're all buzzing round the nucleus like wasps round a jam pot. See?'

The hazelnut was making big looping circles about the orange. Walter stared at it, fascinated. His mother was staring too. Only Lady R., with her cup and saucer hoisted up onto her lace bosom, had a peaceful look on her face like someone watching rain falling on a spring garden.

'Now,' Sir Ernest said, 'there's a couple of other tricks here.' He put the nuts back on the table and dug into the orange with the nail of his right thumb. The skin peeled back in a dangling flap. 'If we could look inside the nucleus, my guess is we'd find it was made up of different parts, stuck together somehow.' He pulled at the orange so that the segments under the skin started to separate. 'See? We think the number of parts in here has something to do with the number of electrons buzzing round the outside. The same number also tells us what sort of atom it is. You still following?'

Walter nodded.

'Good boy! Now what I did when I split the atom was, I took one of these fellows . . .' The peeled orange was back on the framework of his fingers. In his right hand he held a walnut. ' . . . and I fired an alpha particle at it . . .' The hand with the walnut zoomed in on the orange and tore off some of the segments. '. . . and smack, I knocked a chunk off it and turned it into something else.'

Walter looked at the orange with the chunk knocked off, which was still balanced on its fingertip cradle. If the number of parts was one kind of atom, then a different number of parts was another kind. Yes, he could see that. Like twelve pence made a shilling, and thirty pence made half a crown.

'I turned an oxygen atom into a nitrogen atom,' Sir Ernest said. 'Now, that's more or less what the old alchemists were trying to do, turning lead into gold. Although you'd need more than one atom to make it worth anything except scientifically.'

He held up the orange with the chunk knocked out. Was it the oxygen atom or the nitrogen atom? The lead or the gold? Walter wasn't sure. Turning straw into gold was what Rumpelstiltskin did when he wanted the queen's first-born. I'm the first-born, Walter thought.

'What d'you think of that, then?' Sir Ernest asked.

'I hope you're not expecting anyone to eat it,' Lady R. said. 'Not after you've been messing it about like that.'

Sir Ernest looked at Walter and winked. 'What do you say, my boy? How about a slice of nucleus?'

Walter nodded.

Sir Ernest pulled the segments apart and gave him some.

'Thank you,' he said, and he bit and sucked at the soft flesh, the juice. It was cool and sweet, like magic.

20 Contemplation

Auckland, May 1961

A narrow, two-storey building in pale blue stucco; three Gothic windows with geometric patterns in stained glass and an arched wooden door under the shelter of a tiled porch. Uncle Bernard rang the bell and they waited. Sara, shivering, pulled the hood of her duffel coat closer around her face like a cowl. Paul, in his school blazer, cap perched on his head, stood with his hands deep in the pockets of his grey flannel trousers. He felt calm or cold or not feeling anything. Like his father, who was staring at the blank blue wall. The door opened.

'Hello,' Uncle Bernard said. 'I'm Bernard Stringer, Mrs Newton's brother-in-law.'

'Ah, yes.' Mr Cheek was a small man with straight, dark hair and yellowish skin. His grey suit was carefully pressed, his shirt a crisp white, his tie plain, dark blue, almost black. He welcomed them with a wafting motion of his hand and stepped aside smoothly, as if he was on wheels.

'You've met the family, haven't you?' Bernard said. 'This is Sara. And Paul. And Michael's father.'

Why Things Fall

'Of course, of course.' Mr Cheek gave a little bow and beckoned once more, drawing them into the vestibule. The carpet was blue. The light from the stained glass windows made coloured patterns on the dark wood panels of the walls. To the left was an open door that seemed to lead into a chapel. Mr. Cheek gestured in the opposite direction.

'We have Michael in here.' He led them down a corridor to a small room. The same blue carpet. There were three upright chairs and a little wooden table with an ashtray and a Bible on it.

'He's in here.' Mr Cheek wafted his hand towards another door, closed, on the opposite side of the room. Then, he disappeared for a moment and came back with a fourth chair. 'Take as long as you like,' he said, and he was gone.

'What do you want to do, Walter?' Bernard asked.

'Yes,' Walter answered. 'Yes, all right.' He sat down.

Sara pushed back her hood and shook out her blonde hair. 'Maybe I could . . . Maybe Paul would like to come in with me. Would you, Paul?'

Paul nodded. 'Yes.' But he was scared, suddenly. The door, his brother.

Sara reached out and took his hand. Her touch was warm and soft. She led him to the closed door, turned the brass handle. It opened into a room like the one they had just left except that there was no furniture, only a trolley about three foot high with a coffin on it. She drew him towards it.

Michael was lying in the coffin. His eyes were closed, his hair neat, his lips firm, together, as if they were carved from some pale stone. He was wearing a blue sports coat and grey trousers, black shoes polished. His hands rested palm downwards on the outside of his thighs. The fingers were together but with a little gap between the thumb and the side of the first. He was clean, smart, immaculate, except for the huge black and yellow bruise down the right side of his face.

'Oh, God,' Sara said.

Paul stared. That's not Michael, he wanted to say. It isn't, it isn't. The face, with its eyelids precisely wrinkled, lashes like golden bristles. It wasn't real. It could have been anyone. But looking at the hands, he knew. They were unmistakable. The thumb with its broad, square nail, the fingers squared off, almost of equal length.

'Oh, they haven't done it right,' Sara said. 'He would have hated this. That's not the way he parted his hair. His tie's not done properly, look.'

Paul wanted to cry. He was crying, except that it was all inside, the blackness pouring down like endless drowning rain inside his head. He made a noise, a snort, a sob. Sara took his arm and squeezed it. She tried to lead him away but he resisted, his eyes still fixed on the body in the coffin, on the left ear, which he knew was Michael's ear, on the hairs that grew so clearly, so cleanly from the side of the scalp.

'He loved that jacket,' Sara said. 'He looks so stylish in it.'

On an impulse, Paul reached out his hand and touched the smooth plane of Michael's forehead. It was cold, so cold like a shock. He drew back quickly. He turned away.

In the other room, Uncle Bernard was smoking a cigarette. Walter was sitting with his elbows on his knees, hands dangling between them. He was staring at the floor. He lifted his head and looked up as Paul sat down. His face was white, sagging, eyes bloodshot. Sara came out of the room. Walter stood up.

'Do you want me to go in with you?' she asked him.

He shook his head, slowly. 'No,' he said. 'No.'

He moved to the open door, leaned against it for a moment, looking in. Then he stepped inside and closed it behind him.

'He's taking it hard,' Uncle Bernard said. 'Natural, I suppose.'

Sara took the chair next to Paul, reached out and squeezed his hand. Her fingers were tight, trembling.

'There's nothing you can say really, is there?' Bernard went on. 'No matter how much you feel, you can't say anything that'll make it any better.' He turned to look at her. 'You're from Australia, then?'

'Yes. When Walter and Elizabeth decided to fly Michael back, I knew I had to come too.'

Uncle Bernard nodded. 'We would've been here earlier ourselves but . . .' he shrugged. 'You know how it is. Better late than never, though, eh?'

'Yes.'

'Lucky for everyone you made that visit at Christmas.'

'Yes.'

'Doesn't seem five minutes since Elizabeth wrote and said you'd gone back and here you are here again.' He shook his head slowly, sadly.

'Yes. I wonder . . . Would it be all right if we were quiet for a bit?'

'Sure, sure, sure.' Bernard stubbed out the cigarette, folded his arms, and leaned back in his chair.

They sat in silence for a long time. Paul with the blank feeling, emptiness, as if the touch of Michael's skin, so cold, was like the flash of freezing through his own flesh. After a while he let go of Sara's hand, took out a handkerchief and blew his nose. It was a dirty handkerchief, crumpled, and there was a big inkstain in one corner, blue-black. He didn't put it away but screwed it up in his hands in his lap and stared at it. Cold, he thought. Absolute zero. -273.16 degrees centigrade. When everything stops, when all the atoms are frozen solid, when the Universe dies.

The door opened. His father came out and stood there. Sara went over to him. He gave a strange sort of twisted smile, acknowledging her. She put her arms round him, hugged him close. He started to cry. Slow silent tears running down his face.

'He loved you so much,' Sara said. 'So much, so much.'

'Yes.' His father sniffing, turning away, pulling out a handkerchief, wiping his eyes, his nose.

'Michael, Michael,' he said and then he gave a laugh. 'Terrible name for a kid with a stammer, eh? He could never say it. Always like it was being hauled out of him on a hook.'

'He was getting better,' Sara told him. 'He really was.'

'Oh, Michael, Michael. My sweet boy, my lovely boy.'

And Paul felt the terror of it opening and opening, like a black pit to swallow him and he curled forward in his chair with his face in his hands, rocking, rocking. Dead.

21 Biting Through

'I don't want to see him. It's not necessary. I know what dead people look like.' Elizabeth sat in her chair by the fireplace, her body rigid, hands trembling with agitation. With fear, Walter thought. Fear of her own visions. He wanted to go to her and give her comfort, but her sister May had already stepped in.

'Now, now, Elizabeth. Bernard was only trying to help.'

And Bernard looked crestfallen, full of injured innocence. 'I'm just passing on what Mr Cheek said. If anyone wants to see . . .'

'Thank you, dear. You've told us that already.' May leaning forward too, reaching out into the group to exert her control. She was younger than her sister, heavier. Clumsy in body and mind, Walter thought, but he could sense the same insistence on decent order, compulsory peace. Somehow, though, May got fat on the process, her secret gorging on the hidden things of life, whereas Elizabeth was starving away.

'... because of the funeral.' Bernard insisted on the end of his sentence.

'I'd like to go again tonight,' Sara said.

'Good. That's settled then.' May nodded. The subject was at an end. 'Now, what about a nice cup of tea?' She looked round the room, the offer in her face like a beaming searchlight.

No one answered. She stood up and went to make it anyway. Bernard followed her out to the kitchen.

'It's just not the way I want to remember him,' Elizabeth said. 'I want memories of life, not death.'

The bruise, like a stain. His skull in pieces, reassembled. Falling. Eighty feet in two and a quarter seconds. Speed at impact fifty miles an hour. Did he know? Did he understand?

'I don't think it looked like Michael,' Paul said.

'Of course not,' Elizabeth answered. 'How could it without a soul?'

'Maybe it's all a plot. Maybe they substituted somebody else instead.'

'Don't be silly, dear. That won't help either.' She thrust herself back into the chair. Her head banged, bounced against the upholstery with the force of the movement. She lifted her eyes and met Walter's stare for a moment. An expression of yearning, love, fear, anger, he could not tell which. And maybe there was no difference now. We are lost, he thought. It's already too late. He looked away, gazed at the empty hearth, the brick and iron, swept so clean.

'I brought a lot of Michael's stuff back with me,' Sara was saying. 'Maybe there's something you'd like.'

'What sort of stuff?' Elizabeth demanded.

'I'll get it.' She was on her feet, eager suddenly.

'I don't want much,' Elizabeth called after her. Then, almost to herself, 'I don't want clutter. Something small maybe.'

Silence. It was a buzzing silence, high-pitched, like a little, distant, elongated scream, like a shell falling. Thirty-two feet per second per second. Walter got up, went over to the cocktail cabinet, poured himself a whisky, water. He stood, sipping at it, looking out into the garden, the grey day, rain. There was no pain now. He didn't feel the pain, only the sense of something missing, like a part of his body torn away and the rest too numb to really know what had happened. Without a soul.

Sara came back with a big duffel bag made of navy-blue canvas, drawn tight at the top. It was Michael's bag. He had had it with him on his last visit. She sat down on the floor in the middle of the hearth rug almost at Elizabeth's feet and began pulling things out.

'When I decided I was going to come, I just grabbed whatever I could lay my hands on,' she said. There were books, photographs, ties, a couple of shirts, a camera, cufflinks, fountain pen, a wallet, batting gloves, a diary, wristwatch, socks, hairbrush, razor, a toy kangaroo with a baby in its pouch. A glass marble rolled over the carpet to Walter's feet. He bent down and picked it up. It was about an inch and a half in diameter and bright like crystal. When he held it to the light, it swam with shifting colours.

'It's a piece of Newton's glass,' he said.

Sara was watching him. 'Isaac Newton?'

'Yes. It's named after him.'

'I don't know where he got that. Keep it if you want it.'

He put the marble in his pocket.

'Take anything you want,' she said. She had laid the contents of the bag out on the floor and was sitting staring at them, touching them, adjusting them as if she was arranging a special display.

'Look at it all,' she said. 'I don't know why I brought so much.' And she started to cry, her head bowed, hands over her face, kneeling there with Michael's things like a barrier around her. And May standing in the doorway with the tea tray in her hands and Bernard holding the pot in its brown knitted cosy and Paul staring. Walter, helpless, with Sara's soft little sobs stabbing at him and the marble hard in his pocket.

'They're your things,' Elizabeth said. 'You keep them.'

'They're Michael's!' Sara answered, fiercely, looking up. 'He's still here. This is him. Here! You can still smell him.' She picked up one of the shirts and held it to her face. Then she thrust it out at arm's length.

Elizabeth took it. Her hand trembled as she lifted it, and then she had her nose among the folds and she was shaking. She gave a spasm, a scream, and threw the thing away from her as if it was alive and stood up, swaying, tottering to the door. May put the tray down on the sideboard and went after her.

The shirt was at Walter's feet. It was navy-blue, with black buttons. He picked it up. Soft cotton, pleated pockets with little flaps buttoned down. The weight of it in his hands, the touch against his cheeks and nose. He breathed it in, the odour, scent, familiar, hair cream, soap, and sweat, and lingering aftershave of male vanity, and somewhere, distant, fading, unmistakable, the always unforgotten smell of a young man, boy, a baby in his arms.

The Peacock's Tail

'Oh, God,' he said and held it out to Sara. She took it from him, her face pale, tear-streaked red eyes.

He went into the hall. Elizabeth was sobbing in her study with the door open. She was sitting at her desk with her head in her hands, May standing behind her and leaning over her, clucking, cooing, patting at her. He knelt on the floor beside her chair and put his arms around her. She turned to him but she was too stiff to draw in close.

'Oh, dear Lord!' she said. 'Oh, dear Lord!'

And her sobs, which were not tears exactly but the slow wrenching of her lungs, the dragging sound of each breath drawn into her. He held her bony shoulders, hand in her soft hair, stroking her, stroking, as she trembled like an arrow stuck home deep, and his own pain, wanting to fold her in it somehow so her hard, unyielding agony would melt and soothe them both.

'Dear Lord who taught us . . .' Her voice was a whisper against his neck. She swallowed, gasped for breath. 'Dear Lord who taught us . . .' A strange, heaving, wrenching, shudder. His hand on her back caressed the knobs of her spine beneath her dress.

'Dear Lord who taught us to serve thee as thou deservest, to give and not to count the cost, to fight and not to heed the wounds, to labour and not to ask for any reward save that of knowing . . . save that of knowing . . .' She lifted her head and stared at him, her round eyes, fear, her mouth, the little smudge of lipstick red, like blood against her death-white face. She closed her eyes. The lids trembled. Her voice came in a harsh, urgent, whisper. 'Dear Lord who taught us to serve thee as thou deservest, to give and not to count the cost. Help us, Lord! Help us! Our son, Michael, who is dead as your son died. He is with you now. His soul has gone back to you. You who are all soul, please. The soul of everything. Strengthen us, Lord, please. We don't want to give in to despair. We don't want such a Hell to take us. Lift up our souls so that we can keep going. Give us the support of your holy mind, Lord, the strength, the will to carry on.'

He watched her mouth moving, heard her words, the rising passion in them, and he felt only a sense of doom, as if the hope she pleaded for was being torn out of his own spirit, piece by piece, the beak of a great bird plucking at his wound. She was smiling, her eyes still closed, her face lifted, towards a light perhaps, or warmth, a gift from somewhere while the talons bit into him, cold and deep, and the meaning drained away, his purpose dying like a helpless animal.

And May was there, smiling down at them. 'Yes,' she said, 'yes. God is such a comfort at times like this.'

22 Grace

Raining still around the quiet house. Sara and Paul and Walter sat in the sun room. It had a red-tiled floor and cane furniture, big windows and french doors that looked out onto the back lawn and the sodden garden. On a table beside Walter's chair stood the glass water jug and the half-empty bottle of whisky. The drinking had numbed him enough to survive the visitors who had filled the house after the funeral, but now its effect was failing him. His body was still getting dull and numb, but his mind refused to go under. There was a patch of clarity, bright as a bubble, which stayed afloat somehow, a little gleaming raft of thought and pain, a clear white light. Of something still alive and self-aware, a tiny world in which a miniature of himself moved at the wrong end of the telescope.

He poured more whisky. The bottle chinked against the side of the glass. A slop from the jug, hand wavering but he kept it in focus, the crystal with its bright cuts, angles. And God saw the light, that it was good, and God divided the light from the darkness. Elizabeth, with her prayers, her comfort in the forms of words, she felt it, she felt it all, but she was a child before it. She threw herself on its mercy and therefore it would save her. He envied her that innocence and he feared it. There was no room in her world for the doubts he felt at the core of his being.

Sara and Paul were talking about Michael.

The whisky was pale brown, like the rusted water from a new boiler. He remembered the time in the works at Doncaster, the great engines, black and hot, with the wheels taller than his head, and his father shouting to him above the hiss of steam, wanting him to see, to understand the intricate connection of the rods, the hidden pistons in the hot, black cylinders. His father's pride. His own pride in his sons. It was the sin of fatherhood, the boast of knowing, the assumption of immortality, the little bright bubble, rising in the darkness, which saw itself as a whole world when it was really no more than a cavity in the solid blackness around it. Old Adam, Old Eve, the Original Sin, the choosing to be self-aware, the gift of consciousness to another being. The engine roared and steam engulfed them, smell of burning. He drank.

The Peacock's Tail

'He really loved Sydney, you know,' Sara was saying. 'He knew it better than I did, and I've lived there half my life.'

Paul nodding. 'He was always trying to find out about places. When we were kids he was into everything.'

'Yes.' Sara staring out at the rain. 'He had no fear.'

'He used to scare me sometimes,' Paul said.

Their earnestness, their desperation. The words like a spell to conjure something from the ground.

Sara staring out into the rain, the memory.

'Oh, God, I keep thinking, I keep thinking, why did I walk out like that? Why did we have that fight? Why didn't I come back sooner? God, you know, I keep thinking it's all my fault.'

'No,' Paul said.

'But, I mean, it's true, isn't it? If I'd come back half an hour earlier, it wouldn't have happened.' Her hands at her forehead, fingers in her hair, pushing, pushing it back. How could she cope with such a thing?

'People . . .' Walter struggled after the words. 'People are responsible for themselves. Even their accidents.'

'I know Michael,' Paul said.

'I mean why, though? Why? How? Why? Everyone today, here. They were all saying to me, all wanting to know. Even if they didn't actually ask it, I could see the question on their faces as soon as they found out who I was. I mean, I'm supposed to have the answer but I don't. I haven't the faintest idea. Not a clue.'

Walter stared at her. Something to tell her, a reassurance. A body tumbling through space. In Free Fall, Free Will. The apple in the garden, sin of Adam. Young Isaac Newton, in the year of the Last Great Plague, watching it fall, seeing it not as it was, the bruising of a soft fruit cast against the ground, but as the movement of two abstract bodies drawn together by the Law of Gravity; a force proportional to the inverse of the square of the distance between them. Simple mathematics. So the planets moved. And the apple hit the ground. And Michael died. And knowing made no difference.

'The only sense in it,' he said, 'is what we impose upon it. What sense did Michael try to give it? Did he fall or jump? Did he fall because he was careless or jump because he was desperate? There is a truth. It happened as it happened. But we will never know.'

'Michael wouldn't jump,' Paul said.

'No,' Sara agreed. 'No, he wouldn't.' The fear in her eyes. For if he jumped, aren't we the ones who pushed him?

'I can't imagine it, either,' Walter said. 'But the truth isn't really the issue. Survival, that's what matters. Your survival.'

'Mine?'

'And Paul's.'

'What about yours?'

'Of course.' He took another mouthful of whisky. Bubble rising, the evil of consciousness that knew no law. He felt Michael's hand in his own. A small, pale face. I have committed the sin of fatherhood, he thought, for which there is no forgiveness.

There was a noise behind them. Bernard came out of the house, a step down onto the tiled floor. He walked past them and stood looking out through the french windows.

'No much of a day,' he said.

'Sit down, Bernard,' Walter told him. 'Have a Scotch.'

'Thanks. Yes, I will.'

He had a glass in his hand. Did he bring it with him or pick it up somewhere? He poured himself a drink, waved the bottle at Sara and Paul. They shook their heads. In unison, like two children. What bullshit was I telling them? Walter wondered.

'Cheers,' Bernard said, raising his glass.

'And yours,' Walter answered.

'Are you all right?'

'I've been better.'

'For sure. For sure. It's like climbing a mountain, I reckon. You just get to the top of one hill and there's another one up ahead of you.' Bernard with his sad eyes, jowls like his canine namesake, faithful hound plodding in those mountains with a whisky bottle round his neck. And all of us buried in the avalanche.

'Hard on everybody,' he said. 'Especially the young people.' He turned to Sara. 'You all right?'

'Thanks, Bernard. I'm okay.'

'You've been through a lot, young lady. I admire you. It's a funny thing. I saw a lot of people die in the war. Young fellas of Michael's age. Younger even. But it never took me like this. I remember once, we were in Italy. Me and this mate of mine were fooling around. We thought we were safe. There wasn't supposed to be an enemy for miles. Anyway, I gave him a push and he staggered a bit over one way and there he was, jumping around and leaping about a bit, just fooling. And then he yelled something at me and right then, in the middle of what he was saying, a German sniper got him in the head. No reason. It took me years to get over that. But, somehow I don't know. It's not like life was cheap or anything, but you expected it. You were geared up for it. Now, with Michael. It's out of the blue, eh? It's like that bullet. Bang, and you're gone. Everybody gets it. I guess I'm not making much sense, am I?'

'You're doing okay,' Sara told him. 'Really.'

Walter, remembering. A cake of blood drying in the yellow dust. A mangled body, breath like a whisper of smoke. Onion, the soldier murmured. And he died. Was it onion? Why onion? End of it. A consciousness gone out for no reason, life ground up and crushed, the flesh subjected to the whim of an idea, a plan, a strategy, a falling shell. The fragile framework of Newton's equations.

The others were still talking, but gradually he ceased to hear them. Even when they spoke to him, he did not understand and gave them answers out of nowhere that meant nothing. He didn't even want the whisky any more, as if the activity of trying to drown himself cost too much effort. A stillness was settling on his mind, a balance, stasis, dark. There was the earth and there was the consciousness without substance, the life that made the yolk between the two. And the yolk was both a harness and a starting point, the living centre of the egg, golden yellow. Like daffodils in a spring garden. Onion. Was that it? He didn't care.

When, after an hour or so, he awoke for a few moments, he was alone and it was night and the rain was still falling outside and he thought of himself and his father and his father's father and the vanity of all male pride and striving and the absurd notion that a particular and living conjunction of atoms might have any significance and he did not think that he ever wanted to move again.

23 Splitting Apart

Trinity College, Cambridge, June 1691

The room was on the first floor to the right of the Great Gate. There were night-dark shadows over the shelves of books, the boxes, trunks of papers, dark wood, dark walls. The leaded windows, grey with condensation, filtered moonlight, gleaming on the round belly of an alembic, the curve of a bowl, a white ceramic mortar on the long bench. A smell of acid, sharp, and sulphur in the air. The big desk, papers, pool of yellow candlelight from a single flame, which stood unmoving like a drop of molten gold, half fallen. Silence.

WHY THINGS FALL

Staring. In the chair behind the desk, a man.

He was about fifty years old, with long grey hair flowing to the shoulders of his coat, a wide mouth, flat, protruding upper lip like a flange, a big, bony nose. His eyes were brown, bulbous, myopic, shining in the light of the candle with the fiercely concentrated focus of a burning glass. He had paused in his reading. The papers in his long fingers were covered in minute black handwriting, screeds of symbols, coded words, a Latin-English riddling of fact and magic. The covering note, in a different hand, read 'Ye Triale and Trew Progresse of ye Soule combininge ye Wisdome and ye Abounding Vertues of ye Sunne and ye Moone by Herbert Fleete of Driffield, Master'.

The sun, which was the gold which was the King's coin, and the moon, which was the woman and the waywardness of the flesh, were both on the man's mind. He had received two letters that day; one from his friend, the philosopher John Locke, the other from his cousin Esther. The first discussed a scheme to have him made Comptroller of the Mint. Lord and Lady Monmouth and Lord Halifax were all in favour of the proposal but, Locke warned, he should not give his hopes great rein because the King was still much inclined towards the Tories and consequently not easily disposed towards Whig preferments. The letter from his cousin he had not yet opened.

It was the thought of the coin that had distracted him, his eyes vague, staring into the blurred shadows. The place at the Mint had a salary of five or six hundred pounds a year. It was offered as a sinecure but, if he chose, he could make it otherwise, an occasion for service to his King and his Country. If he were to fail in his great quest for the secrets of the Ancient Wisdom, might he not take consolation in the duties of public office?

He rarely thought of failure. He had always been certain of his destiny, confident that the pressure that his mind could bring to bear would eventually crack open any problem. Yet there were moments, more frequent now than formerly, when he felt a worm of doubt wriggling beneath his conviction. He had solved the riddle of the planets, demonstrated their movements to the precision of a clock. He had explained the comets and the cause of the tides, but there were still some aspects of the universal explanation which evaded him. The complete theory of the moon, for example. Tugged at by the earth and the sun as she made her orbit, she was subject to endless shifts and little perturbations which he could not account for. Worse still was the mystery at the heart of his own invention, the force that was called Gravity and bound the spinning matter of so many worlds into the logic of his system. He had proved its existence but he could give no reason as to why it was so. It was somehow inherent in the stuff of Creation, a manifestation of the Will of God. He believed with all his soul that there was one single substance at the heart of all things. It was at the core of metals; gold and silver, iron and lead alike. It made the heat and light of the sun. It was the very principle of life which tugged at the muscles of a human body through its nerves. This, he was sure, was the cause of Gravity. He wanted nothing more in his life than to crack open the heart of matter and see this essence demonstrated beyond all doubt.

It was for this reason that he pored over the works of men like Herbert Fleete of Driffield who claimed they knew something of the secret. Fleete had taken certain crystals known as Star Regulus of Mars which were a combination of iron and antimony. He had added pure silver and common mercury and, through a process of sixteen distillations and subsequent washings, had produced another form of mercury, which could dissolve gold. That, at least, was what his manuscript seemed to say. The description of the chemical processes was obscure, fused with and overlaid by the Master's spiritual quest; his faith in God, his devotion to prayer and meditation, his life of sinless purity in pursuit of wisdom. The sun and the moon, the gold and the mercury, were symbols of his own transformation so that he became, it seemed, at one with them, and it was not the worldly power of wealth that he sought but the transfiguration that came from the power of knowledge.

In the darkness of the room, the silence, still night, the candle pure, unmoving, the man continued to stare. He did not doubt Herbert Fleete of Driffield. Rather, he feared that his story might be true. If the substance the alchemist had made was the true philosophical mercury, the active principle of the Universe, then it would reveal the corruption of all who touched it. It was the physical embodiment of pure spirit, and only someone without sin or stain could make it serve him.

The sun which was the gold which was the King's coin and the moon which was the mercury which was the quintessential truth. Why did Herbert Fleete not identify the mercury with its planet? Why did he think of it as the inconstant, subordinate and counter-mathematical moon? Mercury was the messenger of the gods. On his head he wore a winged helmet and in his hand there was a serpent writhing. The moon, on the other hand, was woman, Eve, the waywardness which first brought sin into the world. It was the unopened letter on the desk beside him. He could sense it there, suddenly, see it, without turning his head, at the edge of his sight. The handwriting on the outside was bold, vigorous.

> *I Newton*
> *Trinty Colege*
> *Cambrige*

He picked it up. With the edge of his thumb, he levered apart the sealing wax and unfolded the paper. The crackle of it sounded loud. The candle flickered.

> Der Cuzen,
>
> I rite to saie Walter is here at Woolsthorp. Hee comes downe from Oxford as fyne a yonge man that any one culd wishe for. It maie bee that yee doe not wishe to see hime so I rite to saie if yee tell mee if yee will come here I will sende him thence for ye tyme.
>
> Yr humble & obedent servint
>
> E Newton

He stood, felt the ache in his back and his knees from sitting so long. Slowly he moved away from the desk and the light towards the window. The dawn was coming, pale grey, beyond the glass. His eyes focused close on the little diamond panes bound tight by strips of lead. The condensation on the inside was like small beads. He could see them if he looked and focused even tighter on them. Each one a tiny, bright globule, a little optical system, with its reflections and its refractions. Each one from its special angle would fill with all the bright colours of the rising sun.

He thought of the woman and the child who was her claim on him, the one proof of his unworthiness. When she had first come to his home at Woolsthorpe, he had briefly imagined her to be the key to his quest, the embodiment of his determination to understand and conquer the world through his reason. She had brought with her papers full of knowledge about the process of transformation, and he had pored over them with her. Soon, though, he began to think that he was wrong. He began to believe that only the purity of his own heart and the drive of his own unaided strength could guarantee him success. God was of the spirit, before the world and apart from the world. Only a life purged of the corruption of worldly things could begin to approach him.

There were four steps. First came the blackening, the subjection to the principle of fire. Next was the bright spectrum, the iridescence of the peacock's tail, which he had already proved was the composition of true whiteness. Third came the whitening itself, the combination and purification, the moment when analysis became synthesis, the turning point, the forgiveness of sin. And if that sin could be forgiven, he could reach the final stage, the reddening, the triumph, the colour of blood and life and the god-like essence. Purged of the vileness of the flesh, he would be pure in mind. He would be reason transfigured.

And the sin was that one past moment, the woman, Eve, the temptress, moon, the quicksilver brightness, bead of perspiration on the window. Christ forgive me, he prayed. Dear Lord, forgive me.

And he was afraid.

24 The Turning Point

Auckland, August 1961

The rain in heavy drops was bouncing off the asphalt like bullets kicking into dirt. Sheets of water slicked in little ripples down the slopes and gurgled into the drains. Paul Newton and his classmate, Balcombe, stood in the entrance to the shelter shed watching.

'Boring,' Balcombe said, his nonchalant pose, leaning against the brick arch. His right leg was crossed over the left and propped on the toe of his shiny black shoe. Balcombe always managed to look neat, elegant, even in a school uniform that was half a size too small for him. He had a pale face, long, bony nose, hair smoothed back from his forehead in a shiny Brylcreemed cap.

Paul felt clumsy, lumpish beside him. He and Balcombe were not friends. They never saw each other outside school, and whenever they came together at moments like this it was as if it had happened by accident. Balcombe was so confident in his dealings with other people that he always seemed to be doing exactly what he and he alone wanted, as if he didn't care what anyone else thought. Paul envied him this self-assurance. He looked at Balcombe's brown eyes watching the rain and his lips, which were set in a delicate curve of discontent. He wanted to say something amusing, something that would create a moment that felt alive. Instead, he felt empty. He remembered the porch of the funeral parlour with the pale blue plaster wall.

Why Things Fall

Walsh bounced up to them, like a terrier dog with his short, blond, spiky hair and bow legs.

'Hey, did youse guys see the cricket on *Sportsroom* last night?'

'No,' Paul said.

'I know you wouldn't, Newton. You're a conchie. Swotting, I bet.'

'We don't have a TV,' Paul said.

'No?' Walsh grinning, pleased with himself.

'Stop skiting, Walsh,' Balcombe said.

'You've got a TV, haven't you, Balcombe?' Walsh's eyes were bright, blue, eager.

'Some people can't afford one,' Balcombe answered.

'But Newton can. His father's an inventor.' Walsh in triumph as if he had concluded a brilliant piece of logic. Paul was afraid, suddenly. He didn't want to talk about his father. Not here.

'An inventor?' Balcombe looked surprised. 'Of what?'

'Yes,' Walsh said. 'What's he invented?'

'Oh . . .'

His father's face, twisted, with the tears brimming in the creases of his cheeks.

'Probably just bullshit,' Walsh said. 'I thought Haynes was bullshitting when he told me about it.'

'Is he an inventor?' Balcombe asked.

'Yes. He's . . . he's got a few patents.' He thought of the factory in Panmure which his father owned, the men and women in dustcoats working at the benches, brass and plastic, boxes of components neatly labelled in the storeroom.

'Patents? That's like leather shoes, right?'

'Shut up, Walsh,' Balcombe told him.

Walsh grinned. Paul tried to think of something he could explain easily. The things the factory made were all too intricate.

'He invented a new kind of aileron,' he said.

'What's that when it's at home?'

'It's the flaps on a plane,' Balcombe said.

'What's new about it?' Walsh wanted to know.

'Its shape really, and its size in relation to the rest of the wing. People used to think that Dad's design could never work but he proved it could. He sold the idea to an American company. It has a lot of advantages, especially in small planes.'

'Hmm.' Balcombe was interested, impressed. Paul felt strange about it. The man who thought up the aileron was somehow not his father, not the person in the cane chair with the whisky bottle beside him.

'No, but the cricket was groovy,' Walsh said. 'The Aussies against the Poms at Old Trafford. Alan Davidson got seventy-seven not out. He smacked twenty in one over off this Pommie bowler.' Walsh swung an imaginary bat in a bandy-legged heave at a phantom ball.

Michael, Paul thought.

'How come you're no good at cricket, Newton?' Walsh was saying suddenly, like a worst fear.

'What?'

'Don't take after your brother, do you?'

'What are you on about, Walsh?' Balcombe said.

'Newton's brother holds the record for the highest score for the first eleven. A hundred and sixty-seven not out. Don't you know anything, Balcombe?'

'I've got more important things to think about,' Balcombe said, but he looked at Paul as if to say, Is this true? And the thought of Michael was a dread, a paralysis, the creeping cold.

'Why isn't he playing for Auckland?' Walsh demanded.

'He's in Sydney,' Paul said.

The present tense came out without him even thinking and then he was stuck with it, a lie it was too absurd to admit, which would give him nothing but the torture of embarrassment.

'Oh, shit,' Walsh said. 'He's not going to play for Australia, is he?'

Paul didn't answer.

'No,' Balcombe said, 'he wouldn't do that.'

'Clarrie Grimmett did,' Walsh told him.

The rain had stopped. Paul took the chance to break the conversation. He stepped out into the yard and started to walk up the hill towards the gym. He was surprised when Balcombe came with him, and Walsh too, tagging along. The sky was lighter and there was a sort of breathing, opening quality to the air with the dripping, gurgling of the water still in the downpipes and the drains. Some of the boys were already out in the fives courts. McLeod joined them and Paul was almost glad to see him. There would be a change of subject now, for sure. McLeod was only interested in sex.

'Hey, Balcombe,' McLeod said, 'you weren't at Peach's last week.'

'No. We went up North for the weekend.'

'You were missed,' McLeod said.

Balcombe didn't answer.

Peach's Academy of Ballroom Dance held classes for fifteen- and sixteen-year-olds every Friday. Paul had never been. He was too shy, too awkward. Somehow the thought of touching a young woman was too dangerous to contemplate.

Walsh was walking sideways, looking up at Balcombe and McLeod eagerly, waiting for the juicy bits.

'Poor Patty Hunter was looking all over for you,' McLeod said.

'Hunter? Spick Brown reckons he went out with her,' Walsh said. 'Reckons he pashed her for hours in the back of Wilkinson's car.'

'Piss off, Walsh,' McLeod said.

Walsh grinned. 'He reckons he got his finger up her.'

'Piss off, you little dork!' McLeod told him.

Walsh grinned some more but moved away a few paces, hanging around, waiting to come back.

'That cousin of Archer's was asking after you too,' McLeod went on. 'But she's a dog so she doesn't count.'

'She's all right,' Balcombe said. 'What's wrong with her?'

'All that metal crap on her teeth. How can you pash a girl with braces?'

'You don't look at the mantelpiece when you poke the fire!' Walsh said, grinning triumph, skipping away a yard or two and bouncing back.

'What about you, Newton? How's your sex life?' McLeod asked.

The inevitable question. Paul could see Walsh's little mocking eyes watching him like a hungry rat. There was Michael, dead. And his father, the inventor, who had no hope left.

'There's a chick lives in our street, next door to me in fact,' Paul said. The words felt strange as they formed not quite bidden in his mouth. 'She's pretty groovy.'

'Yer? What's her name?'

Could he say it? Could he follow through? He hardly knew the girl. She just lived next door and played with her dog on the back lawn in the summer sunshine. 'Bishop. Lorraine Bishop.'

'Bishop? Blonde? Goes to St Mary's?' McLeod's eyes were wide with surprise.

Paul nodded, appalled at himself, the perversion of reality.

'Wow, man, she's something!' McLeod said. 'She was at Peach's last year. Everybody was after her. Balcombe pashed her, though, didn't you, Balcombe?'

'Sure,' Balcombe said. He was looking at Paul with a strange sort of admiration, and Paul knew, immediately, that he was telling a lie. Balcombe had never touched Lorraine Bishop. Maybe he didn't even know her. Liars, all liars. The whole, lying world. And

Paul Newton, the biggest liar, with nothing to believe in, nobody. With a brother who was dead and would never play for Auckland, and a father who wasn't an inventor anymore, wasn't anything except a drunk, a pisshead, staring through the windows at the back garden, green grass, the trees in the rain.

'Bishop, the Blonde Bombshell,' McLeod said.

'What're her tits like? 'Walsh demanded. 'Big and squishy. I bet she's got big nipples. Ones you can chew, eh? Did you get her bra off?'

'Piss off, you greasy turd!' McLeod told him.

Walsh smirked, leapt away. His little grinning face was quivering with excitement, wanting to believe, wanting to rub himself in the fantasy. Dirty, disgusting.

Paul fixed his eyes on the wet asphalt black beneath his black shoes, the scrape of solid things, things that were real. The earth, dig down, dig down into the coal-black heart.

25 Innocence

One of the garage doors was open. Inside was the Daimler Dart, his father's car. Paul had stopped being surprised to see it there when he got home from school, but he still felt a sinking sense of hurt and apprehension at the mood he would find in the house. He swung his right leg over his bike and, with the left foot still on the pedal, scooted through the gate and up the path. Round the back there was a little lean-to with a corrugated-iron roof where he could park his machine. He took his Gladstone bag from the carrier over the back wheel and stood for a moment, looking at the garden, the pale winter sky. He felt cold, suddenly, but he did not want to go inside. Instead, he put the bag on the ground and wandered slowly down the path beside the lawn towards the back of the section.

There was a screen of bushes. Leaves brushed at his parka, his legs as he pushed past them. Behind them was a long, narrow space squashed up against the back fence. The incinerator, the compost bin, an old wooden wheelbarrow, and, in the far corner, a big silver-birch tree with its boughs forking up and its naked branches feathering into twigs and filaments, finer and finer, like antennae testing the sky. The remains of a crude wooden ladder leaned against the trunk and, above it, there was a platform of rotten black planks. A length of broomstick, which had once held a battle flag, stuck out from the platform at a low angle. He remembered the yelling, noise, excitement, triumph; himself up on the platform with his big brother, bold and resourceful, keeping the invading army at bay. He turned away.

To his right was the side fence; wooden palings about four foot high and covered with pale green moss. He stepped up to it and looked over into the Bishops' place. A big section with fancy flowerbeds and a wide, flat lawn. Until a couple of years ago it had belonged to old man Coster, who never went out and never talked to anyone and never gave back cricket balls. Now the Bishops. Lorraine, whom he had watched in secret and had now betrayed just so he could pretend he was something he was not.

A noise, high-pitched, yapping. The Bishops' little white dog came bouncing over the grass towards him. It leapt high up the fence and fell over onto its back, scrambled up and leapt again. A spiky, wire-haired thing with perked-up ears. Around its neck was a tartan collar. It reminded him of Walsh and he felt a sudden surge of hatred for its silliness. He leaned over and peered down at it. It cowered back, barking at him.

'Hello.' It was Lorraine. She was walking towards him, smiling, in her school uniform, her long blonde hair tied back in a ponytail. He didn't move. He could not, with his hands on top of the fence, his heart thumping and his belly churning over and over in fear, in guilt, in excitement. She picked up the dog. It wriggled around in her arms and licked her face. Its pedalling paws left brown streaks of dirt on the front of her blue tunic but she didn't seem to notice.

'Hi,' he managed. Her eyes were blue, looking at him, and the corners of her mouth were dimpled in a sly sort of amused and waiting look. His stomach twisted again.

'Fierce dog,' he said, surprised that there were any words he could find to say.

She laughed. 'Oh, yes. He scares everyone away. Don't you Binky?' She cuddled her cheek into the dog's muzzle. 'See, Binky, this is Paul. He's nice. He lives next door.' She held the dog up and Paul reached out his hand and scratched its head. He felt the warmth of Lorraine's face against the back of his fingers and the shock that she was real, solid, not just an idea he had but flesh and blood that could be touched. He drew back.

'You must be doing School Cert too,' she said.

'Yes.'

'What subjects?'

THE PEACOCK'S TAIL

'Maths, Physics, Chemistry, English, and French.'

'That's what I wanted to do but they wouldn't let me. I got stuck with Biology instead of Physics. How's it going?'

'All right. We've got our term exams in a couple of weeks.'

'Oh, we don't have any this term.'

A voice to their right, calling. 'Lorraine!' Mrs Bishop. Lorraine didn't move. For a second, a tiny moment, he found her eyes looking into his and there was something strange going on, a stillness, tension like a spring wound tight.

'I better go,' she said. She turned and bounded away. Her brown-stockinged legs and black brogue shoes leaping over the grass. He felt sick. His heart was pounding.

Inside the house it was warm. May, the home help, was starting on the evening meal.

'Hello, love.' She smiled at him, her face creasing up into her soft cheeks and wrinkling round her eyes. She was wearing a flowery apron over a brown skirt and a dark green knitted sweater. On her feet were the old blue carpet slippers that she left behind every night in the cupboard under the stairs with the vacuum cleaner.

He went over to the fridge, as he always did, opened it, peered into the white interior, the bottles, plates and frosty smell.

'I made you a sandwich, love,' May said. 'A bit of cold roast beef and pickle.' She gestured with the potato peeler towards a plate on the bench. Two thick slices of white bread cut across the middle.

Looking at it, he was not sure if he wanted it. His stomach knotted up. 'Thanks,' he said. He picked up one of the sandwiches and took a couple of bites.

Alice was watching him. She had a sort of misty look about her eyes. He knew what she was going to say.

'Well, you can't be too bad if you've still got an appetite.'

Yes. His mouth was too full to answer. He took the plate and wandered out down the hall towards the foot of the stairs. As he passed the dining room, he glanced sideways. Beyond the table and chairs, down on the lower level in the new sunroom, was a figure, sitting, hunched up dark against the glass.

The sight of his father gave him that same sick feeling again. The fear and anger. He wanted to run, hide in his room, be there in his own space, and not have thoughts of what other people needed, other people who were supposed to be stronger and more stable than himself. Yet there was something about the figure, its stillness, its sagging posture, that drew him to it, as if something of his father had collapsed in on itself and made a core of sullen, leaden density. He went into the dining room, down onto the red-tiled floor, stood there, hesitating.

'Hi, Dad.'

'G'day, son.'

Paul sat in a chair where he didn't have to look directly at his father. From the corner of his eye, he caught the bright flash of the whisky glass as it was lifted.

'You're home early,' he said.

Walter gave a laugh, a low chuckle with no humour in it. 'I wasn't being very effective,' he said, 'so I decided I was better off out of it.'

Yes, Paul thought, like always. This change in his father, the slackness, the giving-way, it was as if the cynical and subversive remarks, which were so daring after a few glasses of wine, weren't a game anymore but had come home to poison everything. Paul tried for another bite of his sandwich but it was a thick lump clotting his teeth, choking him. He struggled, swallowing, forcing it down, and gasped for breath. His father was staring out of the window at the green lawn and the grey sky.

'I loved him too, you know,' Paul said. And the words, from nowhere, were coming on a sudden flood of tears that he was desperately trying to hold back.

'God, Paul, I know you did!'

'I . . . I went down the garden and looked at the old fort we made and . . . Funny, I keep thinking how we used to play cricket.' The tears were okay. They were under control.

'Yes,' Walter said. 'You were a tough little critter. You used to bowl and bowl and bowl at him and he'd whack you all over the place.'

'It's a pity we never got to see him play for that club in Sydney. You know, when he made a hundred against that test bowler.'

'Yes.' Walter smiled.

'Do you believe in life after death?' Paul asked.

Walter didn't answer at first. He shifted himself in his chair and the cane gave out a slow creaking sound.

'I guess not,' he said, at last. 'I mean how can it be life if you can't eat and drink and make love and talk and do all the things you need a body for? And if you've got a body that works, how can you be dead?'

'But there might be something, mightn't there? Like radio waves or whatever. Energy, floating around.'

'Oh, sure.'

'Maybe that's what the soul is. A form of energy.'

The Peacock's Tail

'Maybe.'

Paul stared at the half-eaten sandwich on the plate in his lap. It didn't really matter what the soul was, Michael wasn't coming back. Walter reached out, with a little creak of cane, and poured himself more whisky.

'I was thinking. You know, Dad, I might take up cricket again this summer.'

'That's an idea.'

'I could be quite a useful off-spinner if I got in some practice.'

'Absolutely.'

There was a noise behind them. Paul turned. His mother was coming down the room.

'Hello,' she said brightly, smiling a bright smile. 'How are we all today, then?' Slowly, carefully, she was taking off her black leather gloves, pulling at the tips of the fingers one by one.

'We're okay,' Paul said.

'How's it going?' Walter asked.

'Ooof!' Elizabeth flapped her hands in a gesture of exasperation. 'Hopeless, hopeless. Everybody's hopeless.' She turned and looked at her son. 'Paul, your schoolbag's still out in the back yard. Go and fetch it, please.'

Paul pulled a face. 'Aww!' he complained, as he was meant to do.

'Go and fetch it!' Elizabeth insisted, leaning over him but smiling still. There was a look about her eyes, her mouth. Her narrow face, her dark hair with the streaks of grey, the little indentations in the bone at her temples. He felt a rush of love for her, her blue eyes looking down at him. And then he thought of Lorraine Bishop, with her dimpled smile that he was too scared to understand. A lurch in his stomach, a possibility impossible to imagine. His mother's face.

'Go on!' she said again.

26 The Taming Power of the Great

He was in his office at work when, suddenly, there was an earthquake. The room began to shake and things started to fall off the shelves and the desk. Then he was outside, looking at the building, and it wasn't the Panmure factory at all but a skyscraper and it was swaying and tossing like a tree in a gale. Broken glass and bricks were falling off as it slowly started to collapse. People were screaming. And then it seemed there was a big audience all laughing at the sight of the falling building. The screams grew louder. There were people inside trapped in the wreckage. The audience still thought it was very funny but, gradually, the agony drowned out the laughter and the laughing stopped.

Then he was standing on a chair on a chair, precariously. There was a woman with him. She had blond hair and was wearing a white dress. They were clinging together to stop from falling. Down below was a riverbed. A hole opened up beside a large rock and a young man came out. He began to splash around in the water. He was strong, slim, athletic, with very long golden blond hair hanging down his back. He was dressed in a white shirt and white trousers. Walter could not see his face, only the long sheaf of his blond hair as he bent over the water and the white clothes, dazzling white, with flecks of bright sunlight gold in the aura. He was the leader of a band of guerillas who had just wrecked the building. He was pleased because it had gone so well. 'I would have done an even better job if my girlfriend Elizabeth hadn't spilled the beans,' he said. Elizabeth was standing on the rock. She was thin and dark and wearing a dress of rich blue like ink.

Walter wobbled and the chairs he was standing on shook. The woman beside him fell. She landed feet first in the water and then struggled out, wading through the stream to the bank. Her clothes were wet and clinging to her. He was worried in case she had hurt herself because the river was so shallow. He jumped in after her and asked her if she was all right. She said yes and started to walk away from him. He followed, still worried. Perhaps she was hurt and was trying to pretend everything was fine.

Suddenly she turned round and came back towards him.

'I've found something,' she said. 'It scares me.'

'What is it?'

'Look! There!' She was pointing. 'It's even got something on its spine.'

In a mirror he caught a glimpse of the spine of a large book.

THE PEACOCK'S TAIL

There was a rustic or sylvan painting on the cover, and the part he could see was the head of a little imp. It winked at him. He put his arms round the woman and comforted her because she was scared.

He awoke. Eyes in the darkness staring out. The curtains, little seam of moonlight, silver. His eyes prickling with sleep. His brain had opened up, a cavern in his head, a cave, a blackness. He could hear his heart beating. Elizabeth in her own bed, sleeping. The curve of her hip. I'm afraid, he thought.

The imp winked at him and laughed. It had horns and a grin and it stood on one leg, a little brass thing on his grandmother's mantelpiece. The Lincoln Imp. He sensed the cave, looked into it. It was around him, in front of him, a solid thing like a black rock wall or a huge stone, a mountain, immovable. It was an emptiness that would swallow him like the maw of a great beast.

And then there was a room and an old man sitting beside a fire. He was working at a spinning wheel, his foot pumping on the treadle, and all the time he was talking about the first-born and Walter's situation, whether it was the past or the present. Then Michael was there. He was alive after all. He was three or four years old and lying in bed. He was crying. Walter sat on the bed and asked him what the matter was.

'I need a friend,' he said.

'I'll be your friend,' Walter told him.

But Michael began to change. His eyes bulged round like a doll's and his face had gone khaki green. There were square plates of flesh on his cheeks like the edges of a wing collar. His mouth kept opening and closing, trying to bite. It was full of sharp teeth. He looked part human and part insect. Walter was scared. He knew that if the creature bit him, he would die. He had his hands round its neck, holding it down, as it writhed and twisted, teeth gnashing.

The old man was still talking. He had his back turned so that he couldn't see what was going on. Walter kept trying to call out to him but there was no voice. Finally he managed a croak. The old man looked round.

'So that's the problem,' he said. 'We've been making a mistake.'

Suddenly Walter could speak. 'No!' he shouted at Michael. 'No!' Michael collapsed then, the energy gone out of him. 'You're dead, little fellow. You're dead,' Walter told him, almost crying. And Michael was lying there peacefully with his head on one side. He had become a tiny baby, bald-headed. His left ear was missing, as if it had been cut off. Where it should have been was a thin red slit or scar.

And Walter awake with the terror throbbing through him, his

tingling mind was a body, his body. Michael, Michael. I can't sleep, he thought. I don't want to sleep. I'm dead. No, you're dead. Yes. There are things I must do. The river. The cave. The fire where the pictures flicker in the coals. The wind blowing, mind folding inwards. Something jabbed at him. No, he said. I don't want to sleep. I've had enough. Let me be. The seam of silver in the dark curtains. The cold frost of the night outside, grass crisping white beneath bare feet. A woman's feet. I've had enough. I can't take any more. Let's be stupid. Let's be silly. It doesn't matter, does it?

He was inside, deep down. There was shelling somewhere in the distance. He was in a garden, or a zoo. He was carrying a child in his arms, a little girl. They came to a pond that was full of snakes. None of them could be seen because they were all under water and the surface was covered in a layer of foam. Walter stepped onto the moulded concrete rocks in the middle of the display. There were a lot of little snakes lying there unmoving. They were made of shit.

A young man chased by a young woman came running round a corner of a hedge. Walter greeted them, joking, friendly. The shelling had stopped. There was a great silence all around them. He knew that there was no one else in the world other than the people in this garden. He felt very powerful, strong. The young woman came to him. She was blonde and had blue eyes. He was full of passion for her. She was dressed in a white negligée but she had black stockings and suspenders. They began to make love on the ground, rolling over and over, on and on. He felt himself coming but still they did not stop. There was juice and come all over them, puddles of it in the dirt among the stones.

'Look,' he said. 'Look at this.'

She was laughing. Her eyes sparkled with joy.

27 The Corners of the Mouth

Woolsthorpe, Lincolnshire, September 1666

'Isaac! Isaac! Come quickly! Your Uncle Joshua is here! Here from London! The whole world is burning!' It was his half-sister Hannah, her little fists clenched in excitement, her cap awry, her bouncing, bright-eyed insistence goading him. Burning, he thought.

THE PEACOCK'S TAIL

'He's not my uncle,' he said. 'He's my father's cousin.'

'Charlotte's here too. And Esther. There's a great fire. It's all, all burned.'

He stood up, followed the girl as she ran before him into the house. He could smell the smell of apples from the orchard. The afternoon was warm. The hot sunlight on his back, seeping through his coat. Light and heat, he thought, they are the same. Is heat, perhaps, the light we cannot see? The eighth colour?

They were in the parlour, his family as he knew it; his mother, his half-brother, his two half-sisters. And his uncle also, who was not an uncle. And his not-uncle's daughters, the two of them side by side on the settle. They were fair, white skinned, dressed alike in white linen shirts and skirts of brown wool. Esther, the younger one, had her head bowed low but Charlotte looked up slyly at him as he came in. She had blue eyes. Joshua in his black preacher's garb; his shoes, his stockings, waistcoat, coat, his pale face, limbs like sticks. He was sitting on a high-backed wooden chair, leaning forward with his elbows on his knees.

'Isaac,' his mother said. 'Thank God!' She reached out a hand but he did not take it. He sat on a stool beside her. Her other children round her, Hannah and Benjamin and Mary, like a brood of chicks.

"Tis the destruction of Babylon!' Joshua said, his eyes flashing, blue like his daughter's. 'All along the Thames from the Tower to the Temple. The whole city burning. And the iron gates all melted. And the tallow and oil all burning on the river like a river of flame. "And she shall be utterly burned with fire: for strong is the Lord God who judgeth her."'

'Some say it was the French,' Charlotte said. 'Or the Dutch.'

'Be still, girl!'

'There's been a drought this seven month or more,' his mother said.

'Longer in London.' Charlotte told her. 'Scarce a drop of rain since October last. And a wind, such a wind. It drove the fire up into the City like a man running. I saw the pigeons burning as they flew around the eves.'

'Vengeance is mine, saith the Lord!'

'God bless us!' his mother said.

Isaac pondered the French and the Will of God. He looked at Joshua, spindle-legged, white-faced. There were pockets and droops of purple under his eyes like a man who had never slept. Esther still sat with her head bowed low. She was so pale, so white and still. Like the moon, he thought. A pink spot on each of her cheeks, blooming like two stains. Blushes. She knew he was looking at her but still she did not move.

'What would you, Uncle?' he asked.

'Tush!' his mother said, and flapped her hand.

'Nay, nay. 'Tis all one.' Joshua gave a tired smile. 'We have lost all our goods save those we could carry hither in the cart. I come to bring my children out of iniquity. 'Tis the destruction of Sodom and Gomorrah and we are brought forth safe by the Grace of God.'

'You're welcome,' Isaac's mother said. 'My husband Newton swore you would never suffer out of need if he had substance enough. So it shall be.'

'Is it truly the end of the world?' Hannah asked.

'Yes,' Benjamin told her, 'we have the plague and now we have the fire. Next will come the beast with seven heads and ten horns.'

'666 is the number of the beast,' said Mary. ''Tis the year, 1666.'

Hannah shivered and shrank closer to her mother.

The plague and the fire, the destruction of Babylon. He felt the dark heat of it gnawing at his mind, but he did not believe that the prophecies were being fulfilled. The destruction, when it came, would take place in one day and would be complete and utter like casting the millstone into the sea. And the beast would come before the destruction with the Great Whore riding on his back.

Joshua was falling asleep, his head lolling, the big sinew at the side of his neck stretched taut like a hangman's rope.

'If the French are coming, we must secure the house,' his mother said.

Later, in the evening, he stood at a window in the upper corridor looking out to the west. The sun was setting and the sky was dusty brick-red and orange and yellow. A strange light like water. He knew it must be the smoke from the great fire reflecting, refracting the sunlight in a peculiar way. The End of the World. If only it were so.

Something, someone beside him. He turned and found Esther standing there, like a ghost, looking out as he was. She was dressed in the same clothes as before, the white shirt, the looseness fastened at the neck and wrists. Her skin seemed paler than ever, and her body frail. She held her hands clasped in front of her below her waist, the fingers interlocked.

'How the sky is red!' she said.

''Tis the fire. The light from the sun is white but the smoke in the air divides it into colours. There are seven colours in a beam of sunlight.'

'Seven? Why seven?'

'As in a rainbow. I have proved it.'

She looked at him. Her eyes were green, glowing. And yet the light he saw them in was orange or red. He puzzled over it.

'Seven,' she said. 'Like the Deadly Sins.'

'And the days of the week. Or the seven planets.'

'How can the purity of whiteness be made of colours which are frivolous and worldly?'

''Tis so.'

She looked back out at the sky.

'There are more than eighty churches burned in the fire,' she said. 'My father says it is for the corruption of their clergy.'

'The Whore of Babylon is the Church of Rome. Not the Church of England.'

'He will leave me here,' she went on. 'He will go away to the north with my sister to preach. I shall be left to your mercy.'

'My mother said you could stay.'

'And you?'

'My father swore an oath.'

'And mine wishes to keep me innocent when I am corrupt already.'

'Corrupt?' he said.

Her eyes searching his. They were like torches, burning green like copper in a flame.

'In London,' she said, 'there was a man, a wise man of great skill and knowledge. He shared our lodgings. He was a chemist.'

'A chemist? What was his name?'

'Johannes Bridgeman. I helped him with his work.'

'You?' He did not doubt her. He was excited by the possibility she offered. Perhaps she knew something of importance.

'He called me his soror mystica,' she said. 'His mystical sister. Come, let me show you.'

She took his hand and he felt a tingling in his skin, his bone and muscle. She led him down the corridor to the little room where she was to sleep. She shut the door behind them and knelt down before a wooden chest. The key was on a ribbon around her neck and she looped it out of her shirt and fitted it to the lock.

'They thought I was a vain creature to carry so many clothes from the conflagration,' she said, lifting the lid. 'Such a big box for so foolish a child.'

It seemed as if it did indeed contain garments, but then she leaned forward and lifted out a snug-fitting tray. Beneath it, the body of the chest was filled with manuscripts, all tightly rolled and tied with strips of coloured ribbon. Quickly, trembling with anticipation, he knelt down beside her.

'And this is the work of Johannes?' he asked, reaching out, touching the parchment tubes lightly with his fingers as if they were the keys of a musical instrument.

'Yes.' She picked up a roll and untied it, offered it to him.

It was written in a small, clear hand in black ink. Latin. A treatise on the meaning of metals, their relationship to the planets. Mercury was quicksilver, Venus copper, Mars iron.

'The earth must pass through the fire and become liquid,' Esther said. 'It is turned into water. Then the water must pass through the fire and be turned into air. The air passes through the fire and becomes liquid fire itself, and when the fire passes through the fire, it is transformed into glorified earth.' Her voice soft, precise, as if the words were not just a description of the process but an incantation, part of a ritual.

He felt its power surge through him, a bolt of the energy that could turn lead into gold, water into wine, the corrupt flesh into the living body, resurrected, glorified.

'My father hopes that you will marry me,' Esther said. 'I know you will not.'

He looked at her kneeling beside him, her face unsmiling, pale, the colour of milk, the whiteness of the lamb, which was the rainbow.

'No,' he said. 'I will not. I will marry no one.'

'No one?'

'I serve God through the use of my reason, and for reason to be pure, it must be without sin.'

'And I have no reason for I am a woman and stupid. I am sin and corruption.' She spoke as if it were a simple fact.

'You have done naught,' he told her.

'The fire is burning,' she said. 'My father says it is the destruction of Sodom. I have read that story. In the same chapter, when Lot fled with his family and his wife was turned into a pillar of salt, he took his daughters up into the mountain. "And the firstborn said unto the younger, Our father is old, and there is not a man in the earth to come in unto us after the manner of all the earth. And they made their father drink wine that night and the firstborn went in and lay with her father and he perceived not when she lay down, nor when she arose."'

She paused. Staring into her eyes. He had ceased to breath.

'Was not that a sin?' she asked. 'Like unto the sins of Sodom?'

'No,' he said, 'no. For Lot knew nothing of it.'

'But his daughters knew. Why were they not consumed by fire? Or turned into pillars of salt?'

'Is this your sin?' he asked her.

'I have never lain with my father,' she said. 'But Johannes teaches that it is the earth that passes through the fire and becomes liquid. The purity of reason will give you nothing unless you begin with the corruption of the flesh.'

Her eyes like green knives. No, he wanted to tell her, no. It is not so. You are a tempter, a devil. You are Eve, corrupted, drawing me into disobedience. And yet the open chest before them was full of secrets, knowledge. Who knew what mysteries it might unlock?

Esther rose up on her knees, reached out and took his arm, gazed at him like a suppliant, tugging at him. Yet she did not seem to be weak or helpless. He felt, instead, the strength in her, the fierce determination of a spirit that would never yield.

'I will be your sinner,' she said. 'Let me stay here and I will take your sins freely to myself. Like Lot's daughters. You will know nothing that you do not choose to know.'

And he was burning. All through his body, flesh and blood afire with heat and light. It was a pain he could not bear and a power coursing through him, a godlike confidence in his own strength. For Esther and the secrets of Johannes Bridgeman were somehow inseparable, as if the manuscripts were no more than the coded descriptions of the spirit that already possessed her, the soul of a magician who could unlock the mysteries of God's mind.

And somewhere to the south the flames were raging through the great city.

28 Preponderance of the Great

Auckland, October 1961

Her name. Walter could not remember her name. Nor her face, a blurred image, her body insubstantial. She was all clouded, fogged over, pale shadow, a washed-out ghost, like the thoughts he could not form. Yet, he dreamt of her every night, every night the same. She came to him in the garden. Her blonde hair, her blue eyes. She was dressed in white and they made love on the ground, their passion endless, endless hunger. Even now, even here, in the cane chair, in the sunroom, in the cold morning, windows, tiles, the green of growing things outside, he still felt that desire. It washed through him like a tide and he was drowning in it, craving, lust without an object, without a body to be in and to drive, without a thing of any real solidity to batten onto. He was struggling to breathe, to get his consciousness above the water as if the next dunking, downward wave would drown him, dreaming still.

I am crazy, he thought. I can't help it. I can't stand it. This woman, this dream creature. I have to get hold of her, to make her be. She is blonde, remember that. She has blue eyes. Her skin is pale, like milk. Her hair, her long hair like spun gold is plaited in a thick rope down her back. She is gazing into the distance. There is a bloom of a blush or windburn on her cheeks. She is dressed in shorts and a khaki shirt. That's crazy, he thought. It makes no sense. But the words were solid, ideas to cling to, and he felt calmer with the notion of the strange woman. He did not lust after her now. She was a guide, wearing tramping boots, ready for the roughest kind of terrain. Yes, it was better. It was not a dream. He had control of it. There was nothing to fear.

He breathed out, a sigh. The windows, pale grey, gave onto the green garden. I have to stick with this, he thought. I have to follow it through. There is no other way. He closed his eyes and he was standing with the woman on the edge of a cutting. Below them was a road of yellow clay and, on the opposite side, a steep slide of rocks and dirt and gravel, like a waterfall but damned up solid. There were people coming down the slide, climbing slowly from rock to rock. He could hear them calling to each other in the thin, cold air.

The woman with the plait led him down into the cutting. They were going in the opposite direction to everyone else. Somehow they climbed the slide and then they were on a wide, flat plain with a river running across it. The woman headed off upstream. He followed her. He could not see her face, only the swing of her plait as it bumped against her shoulders. I can open my eyes, he thought, and all this will be gone. I'll be back in the real world. But he knew it was not so. There was no escape. He wasn't dreaming. He was crazy. There was nothing else.

In the distance, on the horizon, he could see two mountains, little peaks jutting into the sky. There, he thought, that's where I'm going. And immediately the peaks were closer, mountains rearing up, and there was a waterfall tumbling down between them and boulders all around. And he began to climb up through the boulders to the top of the waterfall, where he could see a cluster of dark green trees, and then he was under them, in a long tunnel with the trees overhead and the water flowing pale and rippling in the gloom. The woman was there somewhere, he could sense her, but she was different now. She was part of the darkness, the forest, and he knew he did not need her help as he went forward over the stones. The light at the far end of the valley grew bigger and brighter. There was a moment now when he could open his eyes and see the garden or he could stay here staring at the light, the white glow, the sunlight looming at the opening of the trees. He was getting closer to it. It is whatever I imagine it, he thought. Now.

Before him was a wide valley, opening to his right towards the sea. On the far side, climbing up into the blue sky, were hills of bare brown rock and on the valley floor a great city. It is the City of the Plain, he thought, and the woman's name is Belinda, which means snake, which is a creature of great wisdom and suppleness. How do I know such things? he wondered. The city was yellow, with spires and towers and red roofs, and there was a wall around it that had an arched gate with two turrets and people going in and out on foot, on horseback, in carts and carriages. He knew this place. He remembered it from somewhere in a dream, a story, another life. It compelled him. It was home. The end of his journey. Or the beginning.

And he was in the city and walking down an empty street. On either side were houses of yellow brick. The doors were open and there were boxes of red geraniums at the windows. Somehow he knew that the road was one of many, like the spokes of a wheel, that led to a circular space of bare yellow dust. In the centre of the space was a well. And he was standing there, looking down into it, and it was full of bright water, like a mirror, still and flat, reflecting only the dark sides of the well and the blue disc of the sky. He could not see any image of himself. I do not exist, he thought. I am not yet here.

He opened his eyes and found himself staring at the red tiles at his feet. They were glowing red, like blood. It's begun, he told himself, and I don't know how to stop it. Not now. I can't pretend any more. I have to see this through. For Michael's sake. For my own.

He smiled.

Elizabeth came down the three steps towards him.

'Walter?'

He looked at her, said nothing. He noticed how thin she was, how the lines of her face were etched in deep and her hands wrinkled, pale blue veins beneath the white skin. Have I done this to her? he wondered.

She sat down in one of the other chairs.

'You haven't spoken to me for two days,' she said. 'Not a word. You've hardly spoken to anyone for months.'

'No,' he answered. His voice sounded strange to him, loud and clumsy.

'Well,' she said, 'at last!'

She looked at him and her mouth twisted, angry, bitter, her fear of something that she saw in him. He tried to remember when it had been different, when he did not feel the same resentment, hopelessness and dread of what they might become to each other.

'I'm nearly fifty years old,' he said. 'I might live another thirty years, about ten thousand days. That's a lot. But it's not forever.'

She said nothing. He knew she was thinking about eternity, the damnation or redemption of the soul, her simple, literal, Sunday school belief in pictures that were so clear to her. Yes, he thought, perhaps I mean that too. The image of the blonde woman, curled and stretched, naked in his mind like a lover in a bed.

'I can't waste any more time,' he said.

'Good. I'm glad. I'm glad, at least, you've got some energy back.'

'I have to get away,' he said.

'For a holiday? Yes, that would be good for you.'

'No, not for a holiday. For life.'

'What do you mean?' She was puzzled, afraid, staring at him.

'I have to get away, get out of it, this existence. I'm dead, dying, crazy. It's killing me.' He felt the breathlessness coming again, the rising emotion, drowning passion, the strange feeling, sense of overwhelming power and purpose.

'Out of this life?' She echoed his words with a kind of horror and he thought of Michael dead. And Paul. The children they had shared. The loss of that. The loss of everything. The loss of half his being. But there was still the determination that he had to do something with the rest.

She gave a bitter laugh. 'You're going to leave me, aren't you?'

'No,' he said, 'no. That's not what I mean.' But what else did he mean? Wherever his journey took him, he could not imagine that she would want to share it. The mere fact that he did not know what the end was would be enough to stop her.

'What do you mean, then?'

'I'm . . . I'm not really sure. I guess I feel a destiny, a sense of something I need to do.'

'What?'

He could not answer. He had no faith in talk now. All that was gone. He did not want a rational discussion because the words would just drift away like smoke.

'Please,' she said. 'I want to understand. We used to love each other. I still love you, I know I do. But there's such a gulf between us. You're tempting me. You're trying to make me choose.'

'Between what?'

'You and my religion. And I can't. I won't. I need my faith. I need the authority, the sense of duty. I can't live in a structureless world of self-indulgence, fluttering like a butterfly after fantasies.'

'Why not? Isn't there a butterfly in you?' he asked her. 'A fantasy, like a dream you want to fulfil.'

She looked startled, wide-eyed. Her hand moved to her cheek as if he had struck her a blow. For a moment he thought she was going to burst into tears, but then she gave a strange, twisted smile.

'I knew you'd leave me one day,' she said. 'It was obvious. Your faithlessness. Why should you cling to me when you've abandoned God himself?'

'I'm sorry,' he said.

'I expect there's another woman, isn't there?'

'No,' he said, thinking of the shadow flesh of the dream.

'If you leave me, I shall never see you again, never talk to you, never think of you if I can help it.'

'Why?'

'Because I'll want to be quite sure in my own mind that you are wrong in what you're doing.'

'Because you're afraid I might be right?'

'You are not!' she hissed at him, her teeth clenched, fists, white-knuckled, knotted up with fury and determination.

29 The Abysmal

> Lead
> Soft, bluish-grey metal in Group IV of the Periodic Table.
> Symbol: Pb
> Atomic Number: 82
> Atomic Weight: 207.2
> Molecular Weight: 207.2
> Melting Point: 327.5°C.
> Specific Gravity: 11.35

> Occurs mainly as galena (lead sulphide). It is extracted by roasting the ore to convert it to an oxide and then smelting it with coke in a small blast furnace. Used in roofing, water pipes, ammunition, batteries, and as a radiation shield.
>
> Forms two series of salts: Valency of II (lead monoxide, PbO) and valency IV (lead dioxide, PbO_2). Also triplumbic tetroxide (red lead) Pb_3O_4.
>
> All lead salts are poisonous. Symptoms include colic, malaise, nervous paralysis, blindness and convulsions ultimately leading to death. The poison is cumulative.

His chemistry notes in the light from his desk lamp. Paul read the words again, his lips moving as he formed them in his mind. Their meaning was not fully clear to him but he was sure that if he could somehow learn the information, get it by heart, he would come to understand it completely. These were facts. Reliable, comforting. The way things were, the way they had to be. Chemistry had its laws that told you the manner, the order, and the proportion of all substances.

$$2Pb + O_2 = 2PbO$$

If you took twice the molecular weight of lead (414.4) and combined it with the molecular weight of oxygen (32), you got twice the molecular weight of lead monoxide (446.4). And it could be grams or pounds or tons or whole planets. If you were careful, if you did things the right way, everything would be all right. Like at the funeral. They had said the words, read the Bible, done what the order of service told them. Rules. To help get things back on the right track. Then they had driven Michael to the crematorium and he had gone through a pair of little sliding doors, like a camera shutter. Blue and yellow flames roaring in a brief burst round the coffin and it was gone, into the heart of the sun. The laws of combustion, quick and clean, but it was burning still in the back of his mind. It seemed a long time ago now. Did it really happen or was he just imagining it? Combustion, corrosion, and respiration were all examples of one fundamental process, oxidation. The chemistry of fire and rust and breathing lungs. Dying and living. White heat. Warm skin.

He thought of Lorraine Bishop and suddenly his blood was alive and crawling through his body. He had seen her several times recently, and twice they had stood and talked to each other for a few minutes over the fence. He had almost plucked up the courage to ask her out, but the reality of her somehow seemed to overwhelm

THE PEACOCK'S TAIL

him. When he pictured her in secret she was not a girl in a school uniform with a bloom to her cheeks and solid heat in her flesh, but a figure moving slowly, gracefully, in a white flowing gown that floated round her and clung to the soft contours of her body. She was cool and sinuous like a stream of sparkling water, and all the heat was in himself, his clotted blood, the thickening fire that stiffened in his loins. He would plunge himself into her and spend his heat in her pale serenity. No, he thought as the fantasy began to take its hold. It's sinful. I mustn't think like that.

He picked up a pen and drew the letter L in the margin of his notebook. Then another, bigger, more flowing in the centre of a loose sheet of paper. Another, and another bigger still. The L was a pound sign. For a pound weight of gold in the olden days. Or was it silver? The L for Lorraine, for longing, for loneliness. He reached out with his finger and drew the sign in the condensation on the windowpane.

Out there, in the dark, was the house she was in, the room. He leaned over the desk and rubbed a hole in the mist, peered through it out into the night. There were lights on upstairs next door but the pane was blurred with wet and he couldn't see clearly. He remembered the look in her eyes that set his heart thumping, blue eyes with pale white whites, and he knew, he knew what it meant, except he didn't, he couldn't, because he didn't believe it was possible she could even see him, let alone find him interesting. One of the lights was her room, maybe. The place where she woke and dressed, where she returned at night and did her homework and undressed once again, her body in the yellow light so pale, such roundedness, the soft balm for his hot and rigid flesh.

A little tapping sound at his door.

'Paul?' His mother. She poked her head into the room, smiling. 'Are you all right, darling?'

'Yes,' he said, confused.

'May I come in?'

'Sure.' By his elbow was the page with the L's on it. She closed the door behind her and came and sat on the bed. Quickly he shuffled his chemistry notes over incriminating symbols.

His mother looked at him, gave him a smile, one of her bright, brave smiles. She was holding her arms pressed in tight against her sides, hugging herself.

'I . . . I don't know what to do,' she said.

Her tone scared him. She was going to confess something to him, unburden herself. He did not want that. He didn't want to hear. She gave a little laugh.

'I've prayed and I've prayed and I've prayed,' she said, 'but it doesn't do any good. He's faithless now. Disloyal. He has no strength. No energy. Except for himself. Only himself. Selfish.' The word was full of bitterness and anger. Paul realised she must be talking about his father. He wanted to answer her, say something to show she was wrong, but he could think of nothing. Somewhere, yes, perhaps he agreed with her.

'It keeps coming to me. It keeps coming to me.' She bowed her head for a moment, covered her eyes with her hand. Thin fingers, shaking, little round nails. 'I keep thinking of Michael. And not really believing it could be true.'

'Yes,' he said, although he didn't know what she meant.

'I believe in sin. I believe the soul must be at one with God. And I believe in Hell because that's the way it is if you don't have Faith. A state of mind. If you don't have Faith, you live your life in doubt and torture and burning pain.'

The doors slid open like a camera shutter and the yellow flames roared with the voice of a beast. Michael was like his father. Neither of them believed in God. Hadn't she noticed? Or perhaps that's what she was saying. The faith to hold on, to survive. Strength and weakness.

'And I can't stop him, can I? It's like watching a patient die. There's a moment when the thing that kept you going, the faith, suddenly disappears and takes away all hope. Like water slipping through your fingers.' She stared at her hands. She was so small, thin, fragile-looking, but always with such an energy burning in her that it frightened him. Now he was scared for a different reason. He couldn't understand what troubled her, why she needed to talk to him this way.

'We somehow have to hang on,' he said, because it seemed to be what she was saying.

'Yes!' Her eyes bright, a triumph. Her lips pressed together in a thin, quivering line. He was terrified she was going to cry.

'Oh dear.' She sniffed, smiled, her lips still tight, gave a little laugh. 'I shouldn't burden you, should I? It's just that, well, I don't seem to have anyone left but you.' She stood up, came towards him, put her arms round him where he sat at his desk. 'My poor darling,' she said. 'My Paul.' She drew his head towards her against her body. And she was crying, he could feel the little shakes in her, and her heart he could hear as it beat beside his skull. Over the crook of her arm he could see the window and the clear space he had rubbed in the condensation and the L-shape like a pound sign with the water trickling down and blurring it like tears like a melting thing like the little hard lump of ice somewhere. Lorraine, he said to himself. But she was far away in her ice palace, cold and smiling at him with a beautiful frozen smile.

'It might not happen,' his mother was saying. 'It might not happen. I don't know. But, oh dear, my darling. You might be all I have left.'

30 The Clinging

Nothing. He wanted nothing. He wanted only to walk out into the street naked, like a new birth, new beginning. Instead he had to think of practical things like money and the legal issues; his shares in the company, his obligations to the people who worked with him, arrangements for Elizabeth and Paul, how best to make it clean and tidy, unencumbering. It was Saturday and he did not want to have to wait until Monday morning to get things done. He did not want to have to sit and think when he felt such energy and restlessness and purpose. He could not stay in the house. There was no reason to stay now.

He got an old tramping pack from the back of the garage and began to throw things into it; a shirt or two, some socks, underwear, a spare pair of corduroy trousers, heavy brown shoes. Then he stopped. What is this stuff? he thought. It's useless. I don't need any of it. The pack was dirty. It had left a dark smudge on the cream candlewick bedspread. He thought of his city in the sunlight, round and golden, and a sudden excitement gripped him. He could kneel at the well on the flat, grey paving stones around the rim and peer down, feel the cold draught of air coming upwards, smell the water. He could see himself, his dark reflection. He could be there. The pebble he dropped bounced and rattled off the damp curve of the wall, echoing, a splash and the blue image of the sky and the dark shape of his head shattered and rippled below him.

Paul was standing in the bedroom doorway with his arms by his sides, shoulders slumped, his mouth set, eyes behind his dark-rimmed glasses in an expression of puzzlement and hurt and anger, like a little child watching its parents fight.

'I'm sorry about this,' Walter said.

The boy didn't answer, didn't move.

Walter sat down on the bed and felt again the hopelessness of attempting to explain. He had tried once already and Paul had said nothing, just stared at him, and then suddenly walked away and shut himself in his room.

'I have to do this thing,' Walter said. 'I don't know why. You can come with me if you like.'

'How can I? I've got School Cert.'

The awful practicality of the answer was poignant, terrifying. 'Is that the only reason?'

'No.' Paul shook his head. 'No.'

'You don't have to choose between me and your mother.'

There was no reply.

'I'd stay if I could but . . . I just can't. I have to do this thing.' He felt himself pleading as if, somehow, sincerity would make up for a lack of explanation. Paul stared at him. Tell him the truth, Walter thought.

'I had a dream,' he said. 'It was like . . . Like a message from God.'

'A dream?'

'Yes. There was this garden and a woman and . . .' Her image tugged at him. He felt the desire, his lust for her begin to seep into him.

'A woman?'

'Yes. She was a sort of guide and she took me on a journey, along a river and up into some mountains. There was a forest full of dark trees with twisted trunks and then, at the end of it, a great city.' Bright in the sunlight, yellow like the sun itself. 'I feel it's somehow a sign that I have to go out and do something, find myself in some way.'

Paul said nothing.

'I guess that doesn't make much sense, does it?' And he felt, suddenly, the absurdity of it all, this running after a vision, but the compulsion still gripped him. He picked up the pack.

'I have to do it though.'

Paul shrugged. 'Do what you like.' He turned and walked away.

Walter took the pack down to the study, threw into it notebooks, pens and pencils, papers, passport, chequebook, a German bayonet, a copy of Kant's *Critique of Pure Reason*, *The Collected Poems of W. B. Yeats*. Out in the hall, he paused and called up the stairs. 'Paul!' He waited, but there was no answer. He was about to go up but then he saw them, Paul and Elizabeth, standing together by the living-room doorway.

'Well,' he said. 'I'm going now. I'll be in touch.'

THE PEACOCK'S TAIL

Her eyes, the hurt in them, the fear and the cold, hard fury. Paul's the same.

'I'll see you later, eh?' Walter said.

'No,' Elizabeth answered. 'You won't.'

He moved past them, slung the pack on his shoulder, and opened the front door.

'I suppose you know how ridiculous you look,' she called after him.

The air outside was cold, the sky blue, bright. He set off down the path towards the gate, his left hand hooked through the strap of the pack, his right in his trouser pocket, fingers smoothing the surface of the Newton's glass.

31 Influence

Auckland, January 1961

In the narrow bed, the grey darkness, he could feel her stillness, wakefulness.

'A-a-are you okay?' he asked her.

He felt her nod.

He propped himself up on one elbow and leaned over her. 'Wha-a-t's the matter?'

She turned in his arms. Warm air wafted up into his face.

'They don't like me, do they?'

'Who?'

'Your parents. They think I'm stupid.'

'No-o-o, they don't.'

'I was an idiot tonight.'

'No.' He hugged her close. 'Don't blame yourself for their problems.'

'Why do they fight like that? She's so disapproving and he . . . It's like he wants to annoy her. Like picking at a scab or something.'

'They've gro-o-own apart.'

'Was it the war that changed him? Like he said.'

'Maybe. He doesn't talk about any de-e-etails but something must have happened. They ga-ave him an MC.'

'God, it must have been awful. To do those things.'

'Yes.'

'It's sad, isn't it? To watch them like that. Like my parents. They don't fight, but then they don't talk to each other either.'

'Yes.'

'Is that why you came to Sydney?'

He thought about it but it didn't seem so simple. His need for freedom, his desire to cut himself off from his mother's morality and his father's pride. Would it be any different if they loved each other? They were quiet for a while. He let his head drop to the pillow and she turned over, snuggled back into him.

'I wish you could stay all night,' she said softly.

'Yes.'

'Do you think they know we sleep together? They must do.'

'My fa-a-ather might. My mother only sees what she's forced to.'

'Yes,' she said, 'she's like that, isn't she? She scares me stiff.'

'Ju-u-ust ignore her.'

She didn't answer. He stroked her thigh, her belly.

'Don't go. Stay the night,' she said, sleepily.

He felt her breathing slow. Her skin warm, soft. He thought of Paul in the next room, his neatness and determination, dogged, sticking to it. Paul wouldn't run away. He'd grit at it slowly, bit by bit, until it killed him. Maybe he was right. Maybe there was no escape for anybody. The sins of the fathers visited on the children even to the third and fourth generation. But if that was the case, no one was to blame. His parents, on the other side of the house, trapped in their bickering and their dependence on each other because of how their own parents had been. Was that all there was to look forward to? Separate beds, drunk at dinner, and a desperate faith in God.

Sara sleeping. He wondered if he loved her, if love was anything that could be depended on. Despite the fact that he needed her so much, he could not imagine them ever getting married or having children. It was as if they had them already, because they were still children themselves. He was her son and she his daughter. A boy and a girl. The perfect family. Like his parents, who were bound so close together that other people just got in the way. And nobody ever grew up, nobody ever really changed. People were like planets, drawn to each other, playing on each other in an endless system of attraction and repulsion, but without ever making contact, circling, circling for ever. Despite everything they did, they were all, in the end, alone, lost in the emptiness of space.

32 Duration

Extract from the Notebooks of Walter Newton, February, 1969

Compare how Isis got the Knowledge from the angels with the story of the Fall.

According to Genesis, God allowed Adam and Eve to eat of everything in the Garden of Eden except the Tree of Knowledge of Good and Evil. Isis had no such prohibition.

Eve was approached by a serpent rather than an angel. Both might be seen to be symbols of wisdom or enlightenment. The serpent, though, is of the earth and the angel of heaven.

The angel wanted sex with Isis, whereas the serpent's motives are not quite clear. Is it already evil? Is it intent on corrupting the innocent? According to Christian tradition (e.g., Milton), it had already been possessed by the Devil. Genesis only says it was 'more subtil than any beast of the field which the Lord God had made.'

Isis actively seeks knowledge. She negotiates with the angel in order to get it. Eve, on the other hand, is passive. The serpent persuades her to take the apple (or tricks her into it).

In Genesis, knowledge comes from eating a fruit, a physical act. It is, seemingly, spontaneously generated by this process (drug-induced?). In the Codex Marcianus, the knowledge is information that can be passed on.

Eve gives the knowledge to her husband and they are consequently thrown out of the garden. The emphasis is on what they lose. The knowledge they gain is a curse. Isis passes on the knowledge to her son and thereby confers a great blessing on subsequent generations.

The story of the Fall is about loss of innocence. The story of Isis is about the gaining of power.

Taken together, the two stories represent a single process; the development of an individual human being (and of the species also?). In order to gain the power and the independence of maturity, one must lose the innocence of childhood. In order to become a fully functioning adult, one must leave the safety of the family and establish the validity of one's own consciousness in the world. Why is it that Genesis takes such a jaundiced view of the process? Maybe because the world it portrays is dominated by consciousness (i.e.,

God). Mind, thus, precedes matter, instead of the other way round as in the Codex scenario. Note, also, that in Genesis, Eve is created out of Adam's body (i.e., Adam is created first), whereas in the Codex the natural order of a mother giving birth to a son applies.

When Adam and Eve acquire the Knowledge of Good and Evil, when they grow up, they begin to experience suffering.

God says to Eve, (Genesis 3) 'I will greatly multiply thy sorrow and thy conception; in sorrow thou shall bring forth thy children; and thy desire shall be to thy husband, and he shall rule over thee.

'And unto Adam he said, Because thou hast harkened unto the voice of thy wife, and hast eaten of the tree, of which I commanded thee saying, Thou shalt not eat of it: cursed is the ground for thy sake; in sorrow shalt thou eat of it all the days of thy life;

'Thorns also and thistles shall it bring forth to thee; and thou shalt eat the herb of the field;

'In the sweat of thy face shalt thou eat bread, till thou return to the ground; for out of it wast thou taken: for dust thou art and unto dust shalt thou return.'

All these ills are physical. The consciousness (ego/God) is saying, 'Matter, the body, is an evil. The result of this process (the Fall) is that I am chained to this accursed thing until I die. In fact, I will die *because* I am chained to it.'

The Isis story, on the other hand, is told from matter's point of view. Here, the knowledge/awareness/consciousness is a triumph, a crowning glory.

The question, therefore, remains.

> Which is it?
> Who am I?

Part Three

The Whitening

The clouds pass and the rain does its work and all individual beings flow into their forms.

— *I Ching*

33 Retreat

Auckland, March 1991

'So what do we do now?'
'Nothing.'
'Nothing? What about the fire?'
'What fire?'
'Oh, come on, Paul. You know what I'm talking about.'
'I don't know anything about a fire.'
'What about Jane and all those people?'
'What about them?'
'They might sue you.'
'Why?'
'Over the fire.'
'For God's sake, I told you. I had nothing to do with the fire.'
'You were the only one up at the house.'
'The fire must've started after I left. Anyway, who says I was the only one there?'
'All right. Why did we have to leave in such a hurry, then?'
'I wanted to.'
'This is ridiculous!'
'Look, we're never going to see those people again. We don't even have to think about it.'
'It isn't so simple.'
'Of course it is. I don't want to hear any more about it. I don't want to hear about them. I don't want to hear about a fire. It's finished. Over. Done with.'
'I left my bag up there.'
'What was in it?'
'My wallet. Lots of things.'
'Driver's licence. You can replace that. Money?'
'A bit. A hundred maybe.'
'Credit cards?'
'My Visa card.'
'Cancel it.'
'You'll have to cancel it. It's on the company account.'

'Okay. I'll cancel it. Anything else? Chequebook?'
'No. My keys, though.'
'Change the locks.'
'But . . . I mean, what if they contact us?'
'What about?'
'The fire. Or the bag, even.'
'They can talk to the lawyer.'
'You're mad.'

34 The Power of the Great

1 May 1991

It was Theo's occasion, his special event, ripe with boast and irony. He was dressed in a pale grey suit, blue shirt, his scarlet tie. His slender fingers played with the stem of a champagne flute, and his smile kept folding round his eyes and lining into his lean, tanned cheeks, his mouth with the black beard trimmed into a tracery around his jaw. He was smiling at them as they waited for him.

'Success!' he said, raising his glass.

'Success!' they echoed dutifully, and he laughed.

Paul sipped at the wine, the dry, golden, crinkling flavour of soft fruit. He thought, yes, why not? This is my moment too. I've worked for it. I have a right to it.

Theo leaned over the table towards him. 'Perhaps,' he said, 'we should make the special announcement to our shareholders.'

'Of course.'

'Announcement?' Kate was eager, laughing already. Her dark hair in waves. Her dress crimson silk.

'Attention, then!' Theo said. 'I am calling to order the Annual General Meeting and Celebration Lunch of the shareholders of The Bullion Centre, TBC Holdings, TBC Industries, and the John Hammond chain of jewellery stores.' He paused, grinning, teasing the women.

'So?' Kate said, on cue.

'Well, this is not yet official and I am jumping the guns on the accounting people but . . . our after-tax profit for the last year will be . . .' He glanced about him to see if anyone was in earshot and dropped his voice close to a whisper. '. . . in excess of five million dollars!'

'Bravo!' Kate cried and clapped her hands.

Anelise sipped at her champagne.

'And against such odds.' Theo shook his head with rueful delight at the dangers they had passed through.

Yes, Paul told himself. He was proud of their boldness and their achievement, even if he also felt it was due largely to Theo's nerve and entrepreneurial flair. His own contribution had been more mundane: sound basic management and the technical skill and experience to keep the refining and processing operations going. The future might be different, though. Since the night of the fire, he had felt full of energy and vigour, a new sense of confidence and a flowering of ideas and possibilities that often surprised him by their novelty. It had all paid off so well, better than anything he could have hoped for.

'And so,' Theo was saying, 'we deserve our celebration, I think.'

'You betcha,' Kate said.

'Therefore, we will drink champagne and have an excellent lunch and enjoy ourselves in the manner of the capitalists we are, and all on the day that is the traditional holiday of the working class.'

'You do like to rub it in, don't you, Theo?' Anelise said.

'Of course! It is my privilege, my right as an ex-revolutionary. For this I fought in the streets of Paris in '68!'

'A great year, '68,' Paul said.

'For revolution, yes. For champagne, '66 was much better.'

'And why were you in Paris in '68? Tell me again.' Anelise was teasing him, wanting him to expose himself with even greater extravagance. Theo would oblige, of course. Today he would go on and on as long as there was any encouragement.

'I was with my friend Cohn-Bendit. We were making revolution. The International Solidarity of the Working Class.'

'I thought you were students.'

'In those days, who cared? We were all mad in the heads. Crazy. It was quite absurd.'

'You were lucky you didn't get caught.'

'Of course.'

Kate turned to Paul, her black eyes. Her lips were red, moist, shining.

'And what were you doing in '68, Paul?'

'Studying chemistry.'

'See?' Theo said. 'Someone with sense. Where would we be now if Paul had not paid attention to important things? How can you make good with gold unless there is someone who understands the chemistry?'

Paul smiled.

'What about you, Anelise?' Kate asked.

'Me? In 1968? I was nursing a pulled muscle and trying to swallow my disappointment at not getting selected for the Mexico Olympics.'

'I was in love,' Kate said. 'I was always in love. Until I met Theo.'

'You didn't fall in love with Theo?'

'Oh, passionately. He was so romantic. Long dark hair to his shoulders, fire in his eyes, a wonderful accent. And me just a poor Kiwi girl trying to see Europe. What chance did I have?'

The waiter, tall like a crane, refilled their glasses. His gesture was a slow, smooth presentation, white-gloved hand extending from his black sleeve.

'And another,' Theo said, indicating the empty bottle. 'And then we will eat, maybe.'

'I'll be drunk,' Kate laughed.

'It is right for us to be drunk, the fat capitalists.'

'Fat?' Kate stretched herself upwards, pushing out her breasts, smoothing her belly with her red-nailed hands. 'I'm not fat. Anelise certainly isn't fat.'

'I'm fat,' Paul said.

'No! Darling!' Kate touched his arm. 'You're solid. Powerful. I like powerful men.'

He laughed. Drank. He felt good. He felt good at her touch, at the feeling of strength it gave him. A good day. The beginning of a great future. He felt as if a validation, confirmation, a new idea of himself was working through his body, his muscles, bone. He could feel the blood pumping in him. Like a lust. Anelise, with her new-cropped hair-cut, her slim, fit, sinew-taut frame alive, and her eyes as he remembered them, the little smile that fluttered round her mouth. He wanted her. It was good to feel such clear and unambiguous promptings from his body. It was very good. A beginning, he thought. A new beginning. New plans for the company. Expansion. Substance.

'So how come we are doing so well when the rest of the country is in trouble?' Anelise asked.

'Ssh!' Theo held his finger to his lip as if the answer was indelicate.

'Because they are so clever!' Kate said.

'Business is a sport, a skill. Like surfing. The economy goes up and down . . .' Theo's hand described the motion of a steep-pitched wave . . . 'and the skill is to stay afloat on it. Yes. This is a good analogue because the surfer must never go at the sea directly but always sideways.' The hand slithered along an imaginary wave-face. 'This is us!'

'You don't cheat, do you?' Anelise asked.

'Cheat? Ach!' Theo threw up his hands at such an absurd thought. 'How can you think such a thing? Even if I am a little risqué, maybe, you know that Paul is the pillar of integrity.'

'I love integrity,' Kate said. 'It makes a man so attractive. I love pillars too!'

Integrity. Paul felt Anelise looking at him but he avoided her eye. Then he was annoyed, self-conscious at his evasion. A flare of anger. Why should that spoil his lunch, his afternoon, his time of satisfaction? It was over and done with. Finished.

He picked up his glass and held it to the light, looked into the pale gold depths of the wine and the little bubbles that lifted in it. Gold, he thought. His endless fascination. Certainty and mass, solidity in shining chunks. He remembered the first time he had seen a good-sized nugget. Its roughness, weight, and the dull gleam of it were a revelation to him, as if for the first time he knew the meaning of value. The day's price in New York, for instance, would be \$US356 an ounce, but the money meant nothing to him compared to the solidity of one and a half cubic centimetres of glistening yellow metal.

'I'll give you a toast,' he said, raising his glass. 'Here's to gold!'

'Ah, yes, my friend,' Theo beamed.

'Gold!' Kate said. 'I love it.'

35 Progress

Anelise looked at the gold on her own hands, the wedding ring on her left, the dress ring made from an old half-sovereign on the right, the expanding strap of her gold watch, the solid twenty-two-carat bracelet on her right wrist. She did not like jewellery much. It irked her to be hung about with weight, with things of value. Paul couldn't understand her. He wanted her to display their wealth and had even hinted once or twice that she was failing in her duty as part-owner of John Hammond if she didn't deck herself out like a queen. She had tried to tell him that she didn't care about how beautiful the things were, and still less about their net worth. It was the meanings that came with them that mattered, the memories. Like the trip to India when Paul bought her the bracelet. Another life, their first trip away together after Andrew was born. And the wedding ring itself. She gripped it with the fingers of her right hand, squeezed it, turned it slowly, hard and smooth and round. It would be difficult to get it over the knob of her knuckle if she ever tried to take it off. Maybe they would have to cut it. Or cut off her finger. She lifted her hand to her earrings, the gold pendants Paul had brought back from Witwatersand, but instead she noticed, with a little shock, her lack of hair. She was still not used to the new style, her cropped, efficient look, which she had got on impulse in a sudden need to make herself feel purposeful and independent. Stupid, she thought now. It would take more than a haircut to get her mind straight.

Kate was looking at the menu while Theo grinned and chewed his tongue in his cheek somewhere, a secret joke. Paul, in his chairman of the board pose, sat with his fists on the table, solid, dependable. Since his father's death he had changed. He was warmer, more passionate. They had started to have sex again. Not often, but growing more frequent now. He was clumsy at it, and perfunctory, as if he wanted to get it over with as soon as possible, but at least something was happening, at least he was noticing her again. Her sense of relief as she lay there in the dark after he was done almost made up for the unfulfillment and the numbing sense of helplessness. Almost. The problem was that she was afraid too. Afraid of his new mood, his strange energy. Had he really set fire to his father's house? And if he had, how could the change in him be a positive thing? How could his new warmth and feeling arise from such an act of destruction and denial?

'Vol-au-vent,' Kate said. 'You know, whenever I read that I always think of farting chickens.' She giggled, drunk and silly but still managing to look beautiful, as always. Kate was a friend, like the sister Anelise had never had. They had known one another for fifteen years, helped each other raise their children. Could she tell Kate about Paul? It wouldn't be like their usual talk about their kids and their husbands. It felt bigger, more dangerous, a betrayal not just of Paul himself but of the whole four-fold relationship. Paul was bound to Theo, and Theo was bound to Kate. If Anelise did not keep the circle of loyalty closed, it might all fall apart for ever. Kate might turn against her. She could go to Theo, who might talk to Paul about it. She might totally refuse to listen. She was flirting with Paul again right now, leaning towards him, her red lips parted, eyes wide. Kate and Theo and Paul and Anelise, like birds in a row, on a golden perch, and each one held by a golden chain.

Anelise, self-conscious suddenly, glanced towards Theo, found him looking at her. He winked.

'It's been a long time since our first first of May,' she said.

'For sure.'

'I remember. I was pregnant with Andrew, and Kate was so worried because she was leaving Michelle with a babysitter for the first time.'

'Children, ach! They take our love and then they run away.'

'Yes.'

'Now, is that a good investment? Only a fool would make an investment like that.' He shrugged his shoulders to show what a fool he was.

'Maybe that's the point, Theo. To bring us back to reality.'

'Anelise, I want to say that it is one of the great privileges of my life to have met you.'

What? The words had come out of nowhere, just like another ordinary piece of conversation, but she had heard him right. He was looking at her straight, his dark eyes watching her to make sure she had heard and believed that what he said was the truth. Typical Theo, she thought. Trust him to see through me and say the right thing. But she was grateful too.

'Thank you,' she said.

He smiled, the impish-devil smile that meant he could go anywhere, do anything from here.

'And so we have fun, eh?' He laughed.

'You are a wicked man.'

'But of course. I am wicked beyond measure. It's part of my charm. They all say so.'

'They?'

'Except my enemies, of course.'

'Enemies.'

'Well, one must be especially charming to one's enemies. It makes it so much more exciting.'

'I don't have the least idea what you're talking about.'

'Neither do I.' He laughed again. His white teeth, throwing his head back, the sinews in his brown neck taut.

'What's the joke?' Kate asked, turning round to him.

'No, nothing. Just a little nonsense I thought.'

'And it will be bad for somebody,' Anelise said.

'No, really,' Theo protested. 'I am a nice chap. Harmless.' Theo turned to Paul and hunched his shoulders, hands spread to show the hopelessness of it.

Anelise laughed, looked at his lean, brown body, wondered if respect was what she wanted from him, remembered him in moments of frustration, anger, when something would not go right, when the world refused to bend itself to his will. And other times too. Like the day of the stock-market crash, Black Monday, when Theo and Kate arrived on their doorstep with a bottle of champagne, his laughter pure, his naked triumph wild like an animal. He had insisted that they all sell their shares, four million dollars worth, a fortnight before.

'You're wonderful, Theo,' Anelise said.

'Eat. We must eat,' he answered. He beckoned the waiter over to the table. 'Ladies, please. Decide.'

'Don't bully us,' Kate told him.

The waiter hovered for a moment and then retired again.

'I think I'll have the crayfish,' Anelise said, and suddenly Eliot's lines popped into her head.

'"I should have been a pair of ragged claws
Scuttling across the floors of silent seas."'

'Ah, yes,' Theo answered, grinning. 'I know that one.

'"Till human voices wake us, and we drown."'

'Oh, help, Paul,' Kate complained. 'Rescue me from these people.'

'Arty-farty wankers, pinko-liberal ex-revolutionary turncoats, former playcentre-committee English graduates, ex-Comparative Literature specialists cum neo-Marxist capitalists, reformed Labour Party supporters, *Metro* readers, retired athletes, greenies.'

'Paul! You're being quite funny,' Kate said, grinning at him.

'Am I?' Paul beamed in astonishment, pleasure, basking in her attention to him.

Theo laughed, clapped his hands. 'My friend, you are amazing. You are so ingénu. I love you.'

Yes, Anelise thought, that was probably true. And did they not all love each other? Love that bound them fast so that no one could escape. The shackles had been on for so long now that they hardly knew they were there, though their limbs were stretched and warped and pulled out of shape. Did it have to be so? I love Andrew, she thought. Maybe that means I'm going to cripple him. Keep him close, chain him with my attention, my dependency.

'My God,' Theo was saying. 'It is so wonderful. I love you all.' There were tears in his eyes, she could see.

36 Darkening of the Light

June 1991, Saturday afternoon

In a patch of watery winter sunlight, in the leather armchair by the window, Paul sat reading. His briefcase lay open on the floor beside him, the contents neat, the slots and pockets for his pen and pencil, calculator, diary, the papers clipped into their manilla folders, labelled with their topic and file number. In his hands was the Ventura Mining Proposal, RES913/4. His eyes behind his gold-rimmed spectacles were focused tight in concentration. He was not really thinking about the words as he read them, just letting them flow through him like a current that would generate the ideas he needed.

Ventura was a local consortium that wanted to establish a new gold and silver mine on the Coromandel Peninsula and they had been talking to TBC about refining the ore. One of their options was to float off a high-grade concentrate, which they proposed to sell to a third party for processing off-site. Paul had been interested but couldn't understand why they would want to sell rather than do the processing themselves. The option was, in any case, more expensive and less efficient than other methods. Its only merit was that it would eliminate or greatly reduce the on-site use of cyanide and thus help keep the environmentalists off their backs. After a couple of meetings Paul felt the consortium was not really serious about the approach and was just using it as an option to pretty up their environmental-impact report. At that point, though, Ventura had suddenly started talking about a different deal. They said they had become so impressed with Paul's approach to the refining business, and with the expertise of his people, that they wanted TBC to be part of the consortium and to contribute to ore processing no matter which method was finally adopted.

The most recent item in the file was a report from Baker Sleed Associates, who specialised in gathering information and would tackle anything from investigating companies to locating bad debtors. Paul had asked them to check out Ventura's connections and backing. They had found out nothing he did not already know. The consortium seemed to be what it claimed to be, no more, no less. All he had to do now was to decide on a course of action and talk it through with Theo.

Why then was he still hesitating, so confused and uncertain? Part of him, his new energetic self, wanted to seize the opportunity of expanding the company's operations and moving from ore-processing out into the wider arena of mining and extraction. The rest wanted to proceed in the old way, cautiously, step by small step, checking everything against the facts as he went along and minimising all the risks. He knew that six months ago he would not have considered a change as radical as the Ventura proposal and he would have been suspicious of the consortium's motives. Now he was not sure if his uncertainty was based on a realistic assessment of the situation, an intuitive sense that something was wrong, or simply lack of nerve.

He sat staring out the window at the lawn, the flowerbeds, the standard roses with their thinning crop of winter leaves and last tattered blooms. He had to decide but he could not. Like his father, then, in the cane chair whisky-watching as the rain fell. Darkness and the flicker of flames. It's all gone, he thought. There's nothing left now.

'Hail, O Wise One!'

He turned his head. Andrew was standing in the doorway. His thin face, blonde spiky hair, his tall, bony body all elbows, angles.

'Phone,' he said.

'Who is it?' Paul hated the phone when he was working at home.

'A woman. She wouldn't say. I told her you were busy with affairs of state but she said just to ask you. She said you'd know who it was and if you didn't you'd certainly want to.'

Woman? Kate? Ridiculous. Why should he think of Kate? And why would she play games like that? Andrew would surely recognise her voice, anyway. He took off his glasses and rubbed his eyes, looked up at his son, who was waiting curiously for the answer to the puzzle. Perhaps he should take the call in his study. No, more suspicious than ever. Damn, he thought. This is crazy. What am I scared of?

'Where's your mother?' he demanded.

'Gone for a run. Ten k today, she said.'

He got up and went down the hall to the kitchen, with Andrew at his heels. On the bench was an apple, a half-empty glass of milk and the telephone receiver lying on its side. He hesitated. Andrew took the apple and the glass and turned away, moved over towards the refrigerator.

Paul picked up the phone. I could just hang up, he thought. But he didn't. He didn't need to. The person on the other end had done it already. Andrew was watching him surreptitiously. He felt a sudden flare of annoyance, banged the receiver back onto the cradle.

'Were you having me on?'

''Pon my soul, Pater!' Andrew hand on heart, his eyes round with innocence.

'Well, whoever it was obviously couldn't wait.'

'Gott in Himmel, not even ze heavy breazing?'

'Don't fool around, please. It grates sometimes.'

'Sorry, Dad.' Andrew drained his glass, took a big bite out of the apple. 'Cuppa tea?' he mouthed around the pulp and juice.

'Thanks, son.' He sat at the breakfast bar, watched as Andrew busied with the kettle at the sink. 'What are you up to this afternoon, anyway?' he asked.

'Frightfully fiendish maths problems. Probabilities.'

'You mean what are the chances in a class of thirty-five pupils that two of them will have the same birthday?'

'No! That's easy. Kids' stuff. I mean like . . . and this one's not part of the homework, it's a dinky little number I thought up myself . . . you throw a dice and the first rule is whatever number you throw, you add that number to your score. So if you throw six, you add six. If you throw five, you add five and so on. The second rule is you go on until you throw a one, then you have to stop. Now, the question is, what's the probability of scoring more than thirty.'

'Search me,' Paul said. 'My permutations and combinations are pretty rusty these days.'

'Neat, though, eh? I mean, pretty stuff. Like the binomial theorem, I love the way all those coefficients just come tumbling out to a really weird-looking set of numbers. One, eight, twenty-eight, fifty-six, seventy. I mean, they sort of seem to make sense but not quite.'

'Yes.' The enthusiasm, excitement, energy. Andrew's face alive with the joy of the ideas. Paul felt a curious kind of envy for his son. Such fascination was something he might have had himself once. When was it?

'You know who discovered the binomial theorem; well, he didn't discover it but he really got it all out into the open.'

'No, who?'

'Isaac Newton, the family namesake.'

Oh, yes. The absurd myth of the famous ancestor. He could see what was coming. He could see it in Andrew's eyes.

'You sure we're not related to him?'

'Absolutely sure.'

Andrew stood there thinking, pulling his face around into strange, contorted grimaces. Then he shrugged.

'Pity,' he said. 'But I'll probably still go on bullshitting the guys at school, anyway.'

'Until someone reads a biography.'

'Sacrebleu! They'd never do that! Read? What are you thinking of?'

'Probabilities,' Paul said.

'That's exactly what I mean. I'm as safe as a mortgage.'

Paul laughed. 'Weren't you going to make me a cup of tea?' he asked.

'Sure. Certainement.' Andrew stood up, went to the sink bench, put a tea-bag into the cup, laid his hand on the kettle, and stopped. Frozen, he was staring out of the window, at the winter blue sky. When I was his age or a year older, Paul thought, my father left me.

'That's it!' Andrew said suddenly. 'Like Archimedes, "Eurhythmics!"'

'What?'

'The answer to the problem. One moment, please!' And he strode away.

Paul stared after him, his son, the joker, the genius taking extended maths classes to keep his mind busy. The heir to his hopes. If he had any left.

The phone rang.

He stood up, crossed the room, lifted the receiver.

'Hello.'

'Paul?' A woman, soft, breathy.

'Yes?'

'It's Linda.'

Linda.

'Hi,' he said.

'It's good to hear your voice. I hope you don't mind me calling you.'

'Well, no.'

'I'm in town, you see. In Auckland. I thought maybe we could meet.'

The smell, the heat of her, the scent of the flowers, the soft, warm fire, her skin, the sweet touch, her burning, all-enclosing body.

'No,' he said. 'No. I'm not sure that's such a great idea.'

'But I've got Anelise's bag. Maybe I should bring it over.'
'No!'
'It's a bit awkward, really. I mean, I only brought it because I knew I was coming down this way.'
'Okay,' he said. 'I'll meet you around lunch-time on Monday. No, Tuesday. Can you get to Parnell?'
'Yes, I think so.'
'There's an antique shop just at the top of Parnell Rise. It's called Pandora's Box. I'll see you there at twelve thirty. Is that all right?'
'Yes, I think so.'
'Good.'
'Thanks, Paul. It'll be really neat to see you again.'
Oh, God, he thought. Oh, please, dear God.
She hung up.

37 The Family

Sunday, Breakfast

Paul at the table with the paper, toast and coffee. Andrew on his second plate of muesli. Anelise watching them. Wondering. Feeling strange. The odd mood Paul was in, a sulking silence, drawn in tight. She wondered what had happened to upset him. She didn't want to ask because it might make him worse and, perhaps, she was afraid there mightn't be a reason. Just a change blowing in from nowhere, like a wind over the sea.

The paper rustled.

'Are you going to see your mother today?' she asked.

'Yes.' Quick and heavy, like a slap, his irritation with her. Didn't she know he went to see his mother every Sunday whenever he was in town? Of course, she did. Why was she asking stupid questions then?

'Do you want us to come?' she tried again.

Andrew looked shocked. He silently mouthed 'Oh, no!' at her and ducked as the paper rattled again.

'Not if you don't want to.'

Andrew wiped a phew of relief off his forehead. It was hard to suppress a smile. She turned away, thought of Elizabeth in her crippled darkness and knew that it was no joke to be like that, to end one's life in such a state. It was wrong to feel so little sympathy, herself and Andrew with his callousness, his young, unfeeling, egocentric . . .

A sudden heave and Paul was on his feet, chair scraping back, his face white, hard with tight-suppressed fury. He pounded the paper in half and in half again, a roll in his fist. He strode across the kitchen, smashed the roll down in the rubbish bin.

'Hey,' she shouted, 'I haven't read that yet.' But he was out through the door.

And in panic, despite her yell of protest, as if it was her fault somehow, as if she had done something to annoy him.

Andrew, wide-eyed in mock astonishment, crossed himself and hissed at her behind his hand, 'Ees a leetle dajerous round here, I seenk.'

The look on his face, the absurdity, cut suddenly across her fright.

'Don't be cheeky,' she said, but her impulse to laugh was so strong she had to stand up and leave the table to hide her expression from him. She walked across the kitchen towards the sink. The twisted newspaper like a grey club in the rubbish bin. She picked it up, unrolled it, spread it on the bench and smoothed out some of the creases with the flat of her hand.

Slowly, without thinking, she began to turn the pages. She was still caught up in her reaction to Paul's outburst, the infuriating sense that she was somehow to blame for it. How did she get into this pattern, this need to take responsibility for everything he felt? She wasn't his mother, for God's sake! But maybe she was, maybe that was what he wanted, someone, a woman, to tell him what to feel, to protect him from all harm, and reassure him that he was a good boy.

Oh, she thought, sweet Jesus, no! I don't need a naughty boy to bring up. I . . . In front of her, on page four, a picture with a headline 'Maori Actress Home for Movie' and beneath it the caption 'New Zealand actress Hine Shaw greeted at Auckland Airport by her brother Ace and sister Melissa. Miss Shaw, a star of the Australian TV series *Moonbreaker*, is back home to . . .'

Ace and Melissa and the sister she did not know were staring at her out of the paper. Melissa so pale, her delicate oval face, her frizzy hair. Ace, beaming, smug, awkward. Hine, between them, with a beautiful, self-confident smile. Anelise recognised her. From the TV perhaps, or the cinema, or maybe an advertisement somewhere. The kind of face that was striking and memorable, but not so different from so many others in the beauty business.

'What've you got?' Andrew was beside her, curious.
She did not know what to say.
'Was it the paper that annoyed Dad? The picture? Hey, that's what's-her-name, Hine Shaw, from *Moonbreaker*.'
'That's what it says.' Should she tell him more? Didn't he have a right to know? 'You remember when your Dad and I went up to Northland in March.'
'Sure.'
'Well, there was a woman there. She was a friend of your grandfather. Her name's Jane Shaw. These are three of her kids.' And Melissa's your auntie and you have a cousin called Alice and . . . but she couldn't say that. Enough already.
'Oddsbodkins! Wow! Really?'
Anelise turned away, went back to the table, poured herself some more coffee. She stood, looking out of the window with the cup in her hand. I shouldn't have said anything, she thought. I should have bit my tongue. She could feel Andrew approaching her. She knew what was coming now, his annoying, persistent, teenage logic. Why had she started this?
'That's weird,' he said. 'Why should Dad be so upset by the picture?'
'I don't know.'
'I mean what happened when you went up there?'
'Nothing much.'
'What did they do to him, these Shaw people? They must be real nasties.'
Something, his loyalty perhaps, brought tears to her eyes. And the sense, too, that maybe Paul didn't deserve such faith. But how could she think that?
'They're very nice actually,' she said.
'So, what gives then? Why doesn't he talk about it? Why doesn't he ever talk about his father?'
'You'd better ask him.'
'Oh, come on, Mum. You know I can't do that.'
No, he couldn't. And the fact that he couldn't, and knew he couldn't and the fact that she, too, knew that it was so, made her feel very strange. She put her arm round Andrew and hugged him to her. He bent, resisting, under her pull like a stiff branch.
'I guess your father has a problem,' she said. 'He just doesn't want to know about anything to do with your grandfather.'
'But *I* do! Why should I be deprived? I mean, it's neurotic, isn't it?'
Yes, she thought, it is. And even more so than I've dared to tell.

It's crazy, she thought. It's absolutely mad. And suddenly she didn't know whether to laugh or cry or run away. It was like a sin, an awful secret, hidden for years and now out in the open and everyone terrified and relieved not to be lying anymore.

'I mean, this is serious, Mum, isn't it?'

And she looked at him, her son, her lanky clown, her irony that kept her from examining herself too closely, and the tears started to come and she hugged him to her to hide them and couldn't stop them anyway until her shoulders shook and she knew he knew and she let go then and cried into his shoulder. This is awful, she thought. Unfair. I shouldn't be exposing him to this. He doesn't need this. He's got enough to cope with without me bleeding all over him.

Andrew patted her back and moved, pushed her away. He was looking at her with a twisted grimace, a funny, crushed, lop-sided grin.

'Ees a leetle vet round here, I seenk,' he said.

38 Opposition

'Hello, Mother.'
'Paul?'
'Of course.'
'Is that woman here?'
'Who?'
'The housekeeper. What's her name?'
'Mary? Don't call her "that woman". She's a qualified nurse. She's here to look after you.'
'Is she here?'
'She's in the kitchen.'
'Can't you find someone else?'
'Why? What's wrong with her?'
'I don't know. She annoys me. I don't like her voice and she can't read.'
'Of course she can read.'
'Not properly. She murders things. I ask her to read the Bible and it's like feeding it through a mincer.'
'She's not trained to read.'

'Well, she should be. Who else is there? I can't do it myself.'
'I'll speak to her.'
'It won't help her to read better.'
'I'll speak to her.'
'I try to use the talking books but it's not the same. I hate that American accent the man has. Americans always sound as if they own the Bible, as if they wrote it themselves. It depresses me.'
'I thought you liked that version.'
'I'm sick of it. I want the King James again.'
'I'll get you one. Next time I come.'
'It's no good, anyway. I can't operate the machine anymore. My hands are worse lately. A lot worse.'
'You should think about that operation.'
'Don't tell me about arthritis. I know about arthritis.'
'Sorry.'
'No, I should be sorry. I'm complaining again. It's frustrating, Paul. You know how frustrating it is? I've never been one to bemoan my lot, have I? I've put up with an awful lot in my life, you know that. I've put up with things that would embitter most people and I've always been cheerful and optimistic about it.'
'Yes.'
'I'm sorry. I hate to be this way.'
'That's all right.'
'Did Anelise and Andrew come?'
'No, not today.'
'Just as well. I don't want them to see me like this. I'm not always like this, am I? Complaining, criticising.'
'No.'
'It's not Christian to complain. "Let he who is without sin cast the first stone."'
'Yes.'
'I hope everything's all right with you.'
'Yes, it's all right. Everything's pretty much all right.'
'I hope so. I don't want to have to worry about you. Not at my age.'
'You don't have to. I'm fine.'
'Good.'
'Mother?'
'Yes.'
'There's maybe something I ought to tell you. My father's dead.'
'I don't want to hear that. I don't want to talk about that. You know what I think.'

'Sorry. I've known for a while. I wasn't going to tell you. It just slipped out.'

'I don't want to hear about it.'

'No. Of course not.'

'I have enough problems keeping myself going without thinking about things like that.'

'Yes. Have you been listening to the radio?'

'Sometimes. I'm finding it hard to control the stations. I have to call Mary when I need to change stations. I don't always like to. She's got a lot to do.'

'That's what she's here for, to look after you.'

'But I don't like to bother her.'

'Maybe we can get you another radio. Something easier to manage.'

'There's not much on, anyway.'

'Maybe I could read to you now. Would you like that?'

'Yes. Thank you.'

'What would you like?'

'One of the Psalms.'

'Which one?'

'Any one.'

'Here. Try this one.'

'"I will lift up mine eyes unto the hills, from whence cometh my help.

'My help cometh from the Lord which made heaven and earth.

'He will not suffer thy foot to be moved: he that keepeth thee will not slumber.

'Behold, he that keepeth Israel shall neither slumber nor sleep."'

'Dead, you said?'

'Yes.'

'Are you all right?'

'Yes.'

'Go on. Go on reading.'

39 Obstruction

She was there in the doorway, hesitating, her silhouette. She was wearing a short, tight skirt and high-heeled shoes. The light behind her shone in her blonde hair. She caught sight of him and came in, her heels clicking over the wooden floor.

'Hi,' she said. Her lips were red, white teeth. Her eyes blue. A short black-leather jacket and Anelise's bag over her shoulder.

'Hello.' He did not know what he thought about the bag. It unnerved him to see her wearing it. A theft, a presumption. He knew he ought to be angry but the emotion wasn't there.

She stood looking at him and smiling, her head on one side. Beneath the leather jacket was a red shirt, open at the throat, her neck smooth, pale creamy colour of her fading tan. He remembered the smell of her, the feel of her flesh in his hands.

'Well,' she said. 'What would you like to do? I mean, I can just give you the bag then go, if you like.'

Yes, he thought. Yes. I have to keep this down. I have to keep it under control this time.

'Or maybe we could get a cup of coffee somewhere.'

He paused. He tried to think it through.

'All right,' he said. 'There's a place just up the road.'

'Great.'

Outside, he was self-conscious, afraid that someone might see them together. She walked beside him, keeping pace with his stride, her thumb hooked into the strap of the bag. Every man they passed looked at her. At him.

'Auckland's amazing,' she said. 'You know, it's really scary to be in a place so big.'

'How did you get here?'

'On the bus. I was supposed to be going to stay with a friend of Mum's in Whangarei but I thought, what the hell, I'm sick of it up here. I mean, I haven't run away or anything. They know where I am.'

'Where are you staying?'

'With a mate of mine. Off Eden Terrace. Barking Street. She's in a flat.'

He held open the door of the coffee shop to let her in, caught the clean smell of her hair, the gold he wanted to get his fingers in. She went up to the counter, took a plate, selected a single fancy cake with dabs of chocolate and cream in whorls. She looked at him slyly, a little shrug, a grin. The food was laid out in glass-fronted shelves; sandwiches, rolls, croissants filled with ham and cheese and mayonnaise. The knot of excitement in his stomach made him feel sick.

Two coffees. He paid. They sat at a small table against the wall. She put the bag down between them, beside the ashtray and the sugar bowl and the salt and pepper. Then she picked up the cake and took a bite, a teeth-bared, delicate bite and mouth-moving little licks, her tongue out to get the cream, the flake of chocolate on her lower lip. She saw him watching her and laughed.

'I've got a job, you know. Well, I nearly have, I think.'

'Where's that?'

'In a shop. In Queen Street. It sells souvenirs and stuff like that. Amazing, eh? I mean, I never thought I'd get a job. I thought I'd have to go back.'

'Don't you want to go back?'

'No way. Not if I can help it. There's nothing up there. Why do you think all Jane's kids left? Oh, I'll go back for a visit maybe. One day. That'd be fun.'

Jane's kids. The hot sun, blue sky. The smell of fire.

'Just for a laugh,' he said.

'Yer,' she laughed. 'I'd love to roll up in a big flash car. Like yours. Hey, maybe you could take me!'

The thought, the presumption, was appalling, fascinating. The idea of having her alone, in his possession somehow, her body, her heat, his mouth and muscles, hands, to master and to enter her.

No! he told himself. It was a shout inside his head to drown out the other thoughts, to drag him away. He picked up his coffee, drank, but he couldn't control the little shake in his arm.

Linda was licking the last of the chocolate from the side of her finger. Long nails painted red, to match the lipstick, the shirt.

'I did something I shouldn't've, though,' she said, crinkling her nose. 'I used your money. I mean, Anelise's money. I hope you don't mind but I just didn't have enough to get started. I'll pay you back, honest. I start this job on Monday.'

Money? A hundred dollars or so. He stared at her, looking inside again for the anger he did not seem to feel.

'It's all right. Don't worry about it,' he said.

She reached out, touched his hand in gratitude. The shock of it ran squirming through him.

'And look, there's something else. I gave your name as a reference to this man at the shop. His name's Kennedy. He might ring you.'

'You should be careful about that sort of thing. It could backfire on you.'

'I know. But I was desperate. I really need this job. I had to do something. I thought it would be all right.' She paused, looked at him, her blue eyes clear. 'Is it?'

'I guess so.'

Fool, he thought. Idiot!

'You're wonderful!'

'Are there any more?'

'What?'

'Confessions.'

She laughed. What more could there be? The memory of something else.

'Linda,' he said, 'look. It's really nice to see you again, and I appreciate you bringing the bag back. I don't mind helping you either. The money and the reference, that's fine. But what happened before. That night. You know that's over, don't you?' He had said it. He'd done it. A sense of triumph, achievement, his command and growing mastery.

'Oh, of course it is,' she answered, her eyes wide. 'I know that. You've got Anelise and your son and all that stuff, eh? I'm okay. I'm great. You know, really I just wanted to say thank you.'

'Fine.' He reached out and took hold of the bag.

She looked at him, a quick flash of her eyes, and then stared down at her hands locked together at the edge of the table. Her hair fell forward against her cheeks. Long strands of golden yellow. Her parting neat, pink along the top of her skull. Was she crying? She won't get away with that, he told himself.

She lifted her head again. Her gaze moved over his face and up somewhere above his right shoulder. No tears. There was a shy little smile around her mouth. She looked at him again, blue eyes full of feeling, full of gratitude. It was gratitude. Or something else.

'That night,' she said. 'In those bushes, when you touched me. When we . . . That was incredible. Amazing. God!' She hunched up her shoulders and hugged her arms around herself, eyes closed, remembering, smiling to herself the feelings of it all.

'It taught me so much about myself,' she went on. 'I never knew I could feel anything so powerful. It changed me for ever. I want you to know that.'

He felt the burning, tingling of it in his arms, across his chest and belly, the wrench of it in his muscles, her soft compliance, smell of her, the heat and power, his self-control dissolving in drunkenness, in the raging of the fire and the flowers.

'It's . . . it's finished,' he told her. He was gripping the bag in his lap with both hands tight to hold himself still.

'Oh, Paul, sure. I know. I don't want anything. Really, I don't. I just want to say, well, like I said . . . thank you.'

He stood up. She followed suit.

Outside, a cold wind had sprung up. They huddled together in the doorway for a moment.

'You work round here?' she asked.

'Yes. That building across the street.'

'"TBC House",' she read. 'TBC, is that your company?'

'Yes.'

She shivered and zipped up her jacket.

'Maybe I can get you a taxi,' he said.

'No. Not to worry. Marlene said there were some fancy shops round here. I might take a look.'

'Okay.'

She stepped out onto the footpath and turned towards him. The wind blew her hair across her face.

'See you sometime.' She winked at him and turned away. He watched her as she walked up the street.

40 Deliverance

The ladies' changing room at Barrington's Gym. Cream tiles, mirrors, steam. The voices echoing from the hard walls, the hair-dryers screaming, the slam of a cubicle door. Kate was fixing her earrings, peering into the blurred mirror. Anelise, ready to go, stood watching her. The earrings were long, delicate constructions of jade and gold. Kate drew back, moved her head from side to side to judge the effect of the ornaments against her skin beneath the dark curve of her hair. So beautiful. Anelise stared at her own vague reflection, her skinny profile and boyish hair. Like a sparrow, she thought.

'Ach!' Kate said, as Theo might have done, and rubbed at the glass with a square of tissue. The image was not much clearer. 'I don't know why we come here. The facilities are much better at the Marquesite.' She took a little square of mirror and a lipstick from her make-up bag.

'Barrington's has better trainers,' Anelise answered.
'Trainers? Who needs trainers?'
'I thought we were here for the exercise.'
Kate gave a snort. It might have been a laugh if she had not been busy with her mouth. The little mirror held an image of her lips, pressed together, massaging each other gently.
'You may be here for exercise. For me, it's entertainment.'
'You mean the bodybuilders?'
Kate laughed. 'I know half of them are gay but who cares?'
She stood up, packed away her make-up and stored it in her sports bag.
'Coffee?' Anelise asked.
'Yes, but not here. It's execrable.' She pronounced the word with a French accent.
'Not even for the bodybuilders?'
'Don't be silly! Who wants to watch them with their clothes on, drinking coffee?'
They took the lift down to the car-park and stowed their gear in the boots of their cars. Kate looked suddenly normal without the blue nylon bag; her white silk blouse, long, grey-green woollen skirt and jacket, shoulder bag to match her calf-length boots of mid-brown leather. Anelise, in tracksuit and Reeboks, felt even more gauche beside her now.
They went to the Bistro across the street. A tiny place, panelled in dark wood, which served plunge coffee. The cups were china, ornate with roses and gold trim.
'So, what do you think about going public?' Kate asked.
'Public?'
'The share issue. Hasn't Paul talked to you yet?'
Confusion, panic. She didn't know if she should pretend she knew this thing or admit . . . admit what?
'No,' she said.
'He and Theo think we should list a slice of some of the TBC companies on the stock exchange. I don't really understand how it works, but Theo says we'll be able to raise several million dollars and start up something new.'
Anelise said nothing. This strange new notion, listing the company, when they'd always said they never would despite the supposed advantages. The pride of ownership, the two of them, Paul and Theo, building it all up from nothing and now, it seemed, only interested in the money or something new, or fascinated just by the idea of doing it because, well, it was something to do, after all. And Paul hadn't told her. He had been thinking and planning

such things and not discussing them, when he'd always mentioned decisions like that in the past, if only because it was the right thing to do, the proper procedure. He had changed again over the last few days, back to his old self before the fire but worse somehow, more withdrawn and hard, as if he had some deep fear or anger he was trying to hold down, pressing it down to keep it hidden. He had gone back to ignoring her, immersing himself in work in the weekends and evenings, shut away in his study or sitting in the upstairs lounge with his briefcase open on the floor beside his chair. His not talking to her about the share issue seemed another symptom of their failure, her failure to get through to him and help him.

'Is everything all right?' Kate asked.

Anelise, confused, afraid to speak because if she once began she might tell everything. Everything. She was not even sure how much that was. But her silence was a confession in itself.

'What's wrong?' Kate was concerned now.

'I . . . I'm just upset that Paul didn't discuss it with me.'

'No. Don't worry. Theo only told me last night. It's something new.'

'But why? Why do they want to do it?'

'I don't know. They're getting itchy feet, I think. They want to try something else, something different.'

Theo might want something different, but not Paul, surely. The end of the partnership. Kate didn't seem to see it but it was clear enough to Anelise what the result would be.

'You really are upset, aren't you?' Kate said.

'Yes. It's Paul, I suppose. Ever since we took that trip up north, he's been strange. First, he was bright and breezy, wonderful, like a new man, and now he's the exact opposite, angry, depressed, in a black mood all the time.'

'Is something bothering him?'

'I don't know. When his father died . . . Well, I thought maybe that was going to resolve some things, get him to face up to the past, come to terms with it. I guess it's worse than ever. He's got this huge blind spot. It scares me sometimes.'

'It's that mother of his. A real nasty bitch, that one.'

Anelise felt she should protest at the insult. It was wrong of her not to, not to want to. Let it go. She had probably said the same things herself, and might have done so still but for the thought of Elizabeth, helpless, afraid, faced with nothing but dying slowly in the dark.

'No man ever escapes his mother,' Kate said. 'They're always tied firmly to the apron strings. Even Theo. I'm sure he only became a revolutionary because his mother was a von something. And when that didn't work, he had to marry me and come to New Zealand to get away.'

'Is that why he married you?'

'There are always two explanations for everything. A high-flown romantic one and a down-to-earth cynical one. Both of them are usually true.'

Anelise was not sure if the remark was silly or profound. Whichever way, it seemed too clever for Kate to have come up with. Theo again. Can't we even think for ourselves anymore? she thought.

'There's something else,' she said. 'When we were up north. His father's house burnt down. I think Paul had something to do with it.'

'No!' Kate said, staring at her. 'That can't be right. Not Paul.'

'He was there about the time it happened. He was the only one there.'

'But it can't have been him. He's so stable, so solid, so careful about everything.'

And Anelise with a sudden feeling of despair. Kate was not going to believe her. There was no point in trying to explain. And did she even believe it herself? Wasn't it an absurd thing to contemplate?

'I guess you're right,' she said.

'Have you talked about it?' Kate asked.

'No, not really. He refuses to discuss it, just dismisses it out of hand.'

'Well, he would, wouldn't he? If he didn't do it and he thought you were blaming him.'

Anelise said nothing. Kate reached over the table and took her hand.

'If you're really, really worried, why don't you have it out with him? Make a scene. Scream and throw things until you're quite sure he's telling you the truth. That's what I'd do.'

Yes, Anelise thought, you would. And then she felt a strange sense of something wrong, as if Kate knew the truth but was refusing to admit it. She didn't want to be sitting there any more, listening to someone trying to smooth things over.

She looked at her watch. 'I've got to go.'

Kate squeezed her hand and gazed at her with eyes full of deep concern.

'Men are so stupid,' she said. 'You just have to humour them

Why Things Fall

and pretend everything they do is wise and sensible.'

They didn't talk much on the way back to the car-park. Kate got in behind the wheel of her red Fiat and rolled down the window.

'Don't worry,' she said. 'It'll all work out. I'm sure of it.' She smiled a sad little smile.

Anelise turned away and got into her own car. She sat staring through the windscreen as the red tail-lights of the Fiat disappeared up the exit ramp. She kept on staring. The concrete cavern, the yellow lights, the silent cars in angled rows. She felt frightened, helpless, trapped, a slow suffocation as if the air was going stale around her. And suddenly it seemed as if the building was moving, pressing down, settling itself to crush her underneath its weight. Get out, she thought. Get out now.

She started the engine, pulled back out of the spot, and then accelerated, a squeak of the tyres as she twisted out down the narrow way between the lines of cars and up the ramp into daylight. Breathing quickly, relief. I'm going mad, she thought. It's getting to me, all this stuff. She nosed the Honda out into the traffic, turned right and headed down Albert Street towards the waterfront.

She thought about Kate and felt cheated again and then the anger came and the embarrassment. Her best friend had refused to listen, had treated her secret fear like a nothing to be brushed aside. It was as if Kate was helpless to do anything, as if the real marriage was between Paul and Theo, so that their two wives, such weak, dependent creatures, had to subjugate all their own needs to the preservation of that relationship. Yet, if the partnership was so important, why did it seem that Theo wanted to break out on his own? Was he just trying to keep things sweet until the sale of the shares had gone through? Maybe he had seen the changes in Paul too, the stress, the tension. Maybe he didn't trust him anymore and had decided to get out before it was too late. No, she thought, that's unfair. Theo was a loyal friend, honourable, and far too clever to need to run away from Paul. It's my own fear, she thought. My own lack of trust.

Tamaki Drive through Okahu Bay and around the point. The wind was whipping spray off the water, white spatters of it over the windscreen. She felt a surge as the air tugged at the car, a push towards the centre of the road. A power to grab her, lift her, with her arms spread, up like a rag or a piece of paper, bird, a weightless thing, tossed high and far away.

Escape. She just wanted to get out. She had had enough. She'd stuck by Paul for more than twenty years and it was still the same as it had always been. No matter how open he was about some things, there was a silence between them. Maybe she was starting to believe it would never go away. She wanted to be free and, ironically, with the listing of the companies, she would have the chance. She would own shares she could sell whenever she felt like it. She knew it was disloyal to think that way, and she didn't really take it seriously, but at the same time part of her was insisting that she listen. I feel like a bomb, she thought. I'm a bomb, ticking. I don't know what's going to happen.

She turned the corner into Kowhai Crescent. The trees along the trimmed grass verge were hung with a ragged scattering of leaves. Winter. When the spring came they would be covered in blossom like thousands of golden moths clinging to their branches.

There was a car parked outside the house, a rusty yellow Datsun. She turned the Honda into the ramp off the street and stopped. The remote control for the gates was in the glovebox. She reached for it and took it out and, as she started to sit up again, a movement outside caught her eye. Someone was getting out of the other car, a woman, slim, with a frizz, a cloud of bright red hair about her skull. Melissa.

Anelise sat, staring. She was still leaning over the passenger seat with the remote in her hand. Melissa came towards her, bent down, peered at her through the window, smiled. Anelise reached out and pressed the window button. The glass slid down slowly.

'Hi,' she said.

'Hello.' Melissa's green eyes. She remembered. The voice. The words. But don't worry. It's okay. Your inner self knows best. It'll look after you. Always. Listen to it.

'How long have you been waiting?' Anelise asked.

'Oh, not long. Alice is asleep.' Melissa glanced over her shoulder towards the old car.

'I saw your picture in the paper. A couple of weeks ago.'

'That must be it, then.'

'What?'

'I knew there was some reason why I suddenly wanted to see you. I've been thinking about you a lot lately.'

'Well,' Anelise said, wondering what to do. 'Well. Would you like to come into the house?'

'If that's okay.'

'Oh, please. Oh, please, please do.' She felt a huge sense of relief and gratitude. Her eyes filled suddenly with tears. Oh, my God, she thought and sat up straight and pressed the remote control. The gates opened.

Why Things Fall

41 Decrease

11.45 a.m., Paul Newton's office in TBC House

A sixth-floor view over Parnell and the harbour, North Head in the distance and, to the right, further away, the cone of Rangitoto, dark against the grey winter sky. Paul at his desk with his back to the window. The room was light, with off-white walls and a beige carpet. Three screen prints of stylised landscapes in delicate dusty colours. A low, round coffee table and five easy chairs upholstered in pale blue. A bookcase with glass doors, a cabinet that held drink and glasses. The desk and a credenza. All the wood was rimu, gold.

Paul was going through his mail. It was a ritual he enjoyed, like the daily paper, a procedure to end the morning which opened up the possibilities of the afternoon gradually, without haste. Most of the letters were routine, the issues undemanding, but they absorbed him, soothed him, helped him focus on the world of solid things, removed the distractions, the noisy clutter at the back of his mind. Today there were reports from three of his managers, a monthly sales analysis of the John Hammond stores, several invoices and statements, a copy of the *Futures Bulletin*, and the usual assortment of junk mail offering training and advice and services and products of irresistible quality at bargain prices. He looked through the pile from top to bottom, without sorting it, taking each item in the order that it came, reading, making notes, signing his approval of payments and expenditure, putting aside the things that required more detailed attention, throwing the junk in the rubbish bin. As he worked, he sipped at the day's first cup of coffee. It would be cold before he had finished, a fact that somehow gave him an odd satisfaction, as if it proved how careful and thorough he had been.

The sales analysis looked encouraging. He left it for closer study later and picked up what seemed to be a free copy of a computer magazine. Something for Andrew, maybe. There was a bill for $23,000 for new laboratory equipment that he initialled for payment. And a company credit-card statement. The figure at the bottom was $4,237.44. He stared at it, for the moment not quite taking it in, and then his eyes began to register the items that made up the total:

Suzy's Shoes	657.90
The Flash Boutique	495.50
Hair Design	85.00
The Skin Store	743.00

There were more. It was Anelise's Visa card. He did not understand and then he realised that it was the card that had been in her lost bag, the bag that Linda had given back to him and which he had put without thinking in one of the drawers of his desk. It was the card he had forgotten to cancel. Quickly he leaned over, pulled out the bag and Anelise's wallet. Her driver's licence, her library card, a receipt from a parking building. He tipped the bag up and dumped the contents onto his blotter, the clank of keys, a lipstick rolled onto the floor, a ballpoint pen, the flop of a notebook with a bright-patterned cover.

Dear God, he thought. The little bitch has done me. He looked again at the statement. It was two weeks since the day he'd had coffee with Linda. The last six items on the statement had been bought that same day. They were from local stores. She had walked up the street away from him, the street where he worked. She had gone into all the little fashionable shops. She had forged Anelise's signature. She had racked up over a thousand dollars.

Slowly the realisation, the disbelief, gave way to a growing sense of the enormity, to a deep, ungovernable rage. His fists, his jaws clenched, muscles tightened in his fury. He hit the top of the desk so hard the pen and the keys jumped into the air. The police, he thought. I'll have her. I'll do the bitch. And then he thought, no. I can't give this away. I want her. I'll kill her. I'll do it myself. He was on his feet now, walking, across the room and back. His fists clenched tight and shaking up against his chest. He knew what to do. He could find her. He would find her.

At the desk, he pulled out the holder of business cards, flipped the clear plastic pockets over and back, over again. There. He dialled the number.

'Baker Sleed. Good morning,' the receptionist said. A practised sing-song tone.

'This is Paul Newton. Geoff Sleed, please.'

'Just one moment.'

He waited. There was a pain in his wrist from gripping the receiver so tight.

'Sleed here.' The voice was husky, rasping. He remembered the stink of tobacco smoke that hung around Sleed's person, and the tar stains on his fingers.

'Paul Newton from TBC.'

'Ah, Mr Newton. Good to hear your voice again.'

'I want you to find someone.'

'Yes.' A drawl, guarded, noncommittal.

'Her name's Linda Kemp. She's around eighteen. Lives in a flat off Eden Terrace somewhere. Barker Street. Something like that. She might be working in a souvenir store in Queen Street. Run by a man called Kennedy.'

'Okay.' Still looking for more.

Paul thought about it. Yes, of course. 'Her parents are Kevin and, I think, Diane Kemp. They run a motor camp in a little settlement called Wairuru. In Northland. The El Dorado Motor Camp.'

'El Do-ra-do.' Sleed was writing it down.

'That's about it. Do you handle things like this?' Intrigue. Grubby business, dirty little personal secrets.

'Sure. I can get someone to look into it for you. Any action?'

'I just want to know where she is.'

'Not a problem, Mr Newton. Leave it with us.'

He hung up.

The rage had gone now, subsided, settled into a cold, hard, clear determination. Like glass. Like a marble in which the colours smeared and merged, the flash of blue, the gold, the red. I want her, he thought. And I will have her. She will not do this to me.

He scooped up Anelise's bits and pieces from the desk and dumped them back in the bag, returned the bag to the drawer. He called the bank and cancelled the credit card. Then he turned, swung in his chair, and stared out of the window. The wind scudding cloud over the grey sky. Rain, he thought.

The door opened. It was Theo.

'Ah,' he said, stepping forward. 'You have a minute?'

'Sure.'

Theo came round and perched on the edge of the desk.

'Where are we with Ventura?' he asked.

'Our technical people are still talking to Baxter. I'll have a report by next Friday.'

'And you think we should still be going ahead?'

'At this stage, yes.' He was confident now, wasn't he? He had decided on good grounds. 'Our technology's fine. The financial involvement's not great considering the opportunity.'

'I'm wondering . . .' Theo folded his arms and looked out of the window into the distance. 'I agree with you on the specifics. It's the general question I have a problem with. There is a lot of fuss about this project. The green people don't like it.'

'That's always the case. Any mining venture's the same.'

'Sure. But . . . There may be big opposition in the next few months. Maybe it will get bigger still. Who knows? Maybe they will succeed in stopping the whole thing.'

'We just have to be careful. If we take it step by step, there's no risk beyond the normal costs of any development.' Paul was starting to feel defensive now, sensing a trick, a trap, a thing he'd missed.

'You know that. And I know that. But does the world? What happens with our share issue? I worry that maybe the market thinks we are taking risks, even if we don't.'

'It might see us as being aggressive and confident when everybody else is wimping out.'

'Maybe.' Theo looked at him and smiled. 'You know me. I don't like getting into bed with the big boys.' He chuckled to himself and hung his head, wagging it from side to side. Then he stopped, stiffened. Something on the floor had distracted him. He moved his foot, bent down, straightened up again. In his hand was the lipstick.

'Yours?' He was grinning.

Paul took it, confused for a moment. All he had to say was that it was Anelise's. But already the awkwardness had gone on too long. He opened the drawer of his desk and tossed the lipstick inside.

'We just have to be careful,' he said.

42 Increase

Alice was lying on her stomach on a rug in the middle of the floor. Her arms and legs worked in slow, jerky spasms as she tried to crawl. Her head up, eyes fixed forward on a distant goal.

'She's grown so much,' Anelise said, looking down at her. 'How old is she now?'

'She was born on Christmas Day,' Melissa answered.

'Is that good luck?'

'Her grandfather thought so. She's got the same birthday as Isaac Newton.'

'Really? Is she going to be a scientist too, then?'

'I doubt it. Science is a man's invention.'

Alice was succeeding, moving, a slow arc, half forward, half crabwise, her head shifting gradually left, her feet right. She gave out little grunts and snorts of effort as she worked her limbs.

'Does that make it bad?' Anelise asked.

'No, not bad. Just out of date, maybe.' Melissa smiled at her. It was an open, welcoming smile, full of possibility, as much or as little as Anelise cared to take. She felt again that same sense of relief and sadness that she had experienced outside as she sat in the car.

'I'm so glad you came,' she said. 'I . . . I can't really believe it, not after what happened.'

'I couldn't get you out of my mind. It's like you were calling out to me.'

Had she been? The thought was too strange to contemplate.

'How long have you been in Auckland?' she asked.

'About three weeks. We're staying at Sam's place.'

'When're you going back?'

'I'm not sure. I just came down to see Hine really, and then I thought, seeing I was going to be here, I'd take the chance to try to sell a few things as well. I don't like Auckland much, though.'

'How's Jane?'

'Fine.'

A pause. Anelise found she couldn't meet Melissa's eyes. She felt blank, helpless, trying hard to find something to say, anything, that would keep the conversation going and avoid the topic she feared most, the one she most wanted to talk about. Slowly the silence drew it out of her.

'That night. The fire. It was so awful. I felt so much had been destroyed.'

'Yes,' Melissa said.

'Not just Walter's things but me. My life. All burning. All gone up in smoke. I didn't realise it at the time, but I was really starting to think that if Paul could begin to make sense of things, I would too. I thought, maybe, we were going to start to get it right somehow. And then . . .'

'What happened?'

'I don't know. Paul won't talk about it.' She felt her tears begin to build again, a sense of hopelessness and loss. 'You must have hated us. All of you.'

'Not really. We were confused at first. We couldn't understand. And then when we found you'd gone we started to wonder if you, well, if Paul had anything to do with it. Terry was certain it was Paul's fault. He was furious. I think he would have really hurt him if he'd got the chance. The others wanted to find out for sure and then to get Ace to sue or claim for damages or something. It was Jane who stopped it.'

'Why?'

Alice had rolled over onto her back. She was gazing upward, wide-eyed, astonished, at the little chandelier in the centre of the ceiling. The bright crystals, the flashes, glints of colour.

'She said we didn't know that it was Paul's fault, and even if it was, it didn't matter. The house was his, his and mine, and he could do what he liked with it. That's what she said.'

'She didn't care?'

'Oh, yes! It was really bad for her. I've never seen her so upset. I think that's why Terry got so angry.'

The thought of Jane's distress struck deep, as if the idea of the family, Walter's second family, the happiness and the peace they seemed to have, was important to her. That's what I've lost, she thought. The chance to be part of all that.

'What about you?' she asked.

'Me? I felt as if Walter had died all over again. As if all my memories had been taken away.'

'Oh, God. I'm sorry.'

'But then I saw that was wrong. It was Paul who had no memories. I didn't need to share the house with him. It really was his.'

'And he burnt it,' she said, and for the first time she was sure that it was true. The last little doubt had gone, the tiny part of her that had tried to pretend it had all been a mistake, a coincidence, a freakish accident.

'Why?' she asked.

'Perhaps he believes that only physical things exist.'

Yes, Anelise thought, yes, he does.

'But I think with men, they never actually experience the physical world somehow. They're always operating with an idea of it. They always feel they can conquer it with their minds.'

'You think he was trying to burn Walter's ghost,' Anelise said.

'Yes.'

'God, that's awful. I know, I know you're right. I just don't want to believe it, that's all. Because I think that would mean he's mad. Or, if he's not mad, he's so totally different from me that he might as well be. And I'm mad too. Or hopeless. Or desperate. Because I've spent over twenty years in a relationship that has come to this.'

Melissa did not answer but just looked at her. The green eyes, like a cat's eyes, the stillness in them. The wildness, so calm. It was a sense of being in which twenty years was nothing. But I'm not like that, Anelise told herself. I've failed. And I'm trapped.

'Walter and his wife were married more than twenty years,' Melissa said.

Anelise laughed. 'And look where that got them!'

'You never knew my father.' She said it with a wistfulness, a longing for something that had been essential to her life.

Anelise thought of Elizabeth and Paul and the pain they had lived through. They hadn't invented it, the sense of loss and rejection and lovelessness. Was their suffering justified by the peace of mind Walter had achieved in the backblocks of Northland?

'You sound as if he was a saint,' she said.

'No.' Melissa laughed.

'But he wasn't just ordinary.'

'Oh, no. Extraordinary. Big. Extreme. He was never moderate in anything. Fire and air. Imagination and thinking. He had ideas all over the place. But somehow, though, he was a very centred person. He always seemed to know exactly where he was. It was as if he could move around the whole of life with his eyes closed without bumping into anything, just as if it was his own little house.'

'All burnt.'

'No! Everyone can learn to do that if they want to.'

'I never could,' Anelise told her.

'You especially. You're an athlete. You know what it's like to have your mind and your body in the same moment.'

Did she? Yes, perhaps, the limits of her strength, her endurance, what she knew to be her physical power. In those ways she had always had confidence. If only she could learn to feel her mind, her spirit in the same way.

Alice had rolled back onto her stomach now and had wormed her way towards the fireplace. Craning her neck, reaching out, she was cooing at the brass coal scuttle, the great golden bucket just out of her reach.

'When you're in action like that,' Melissa said, 'it's reality, it's in balance. You just have to find the same balance when you're not moving, when you're still and quiet and looking into yourself.'

'How?'

'Believe. You have to believe. It's like diving into the sea. Or the air. Maybe you need the air. You just have to believe that it will hold you up.'

'No,' Anelise said. 'I can't believe that. I'm scared of it.'

'Why?'

'My parents . . .' Were they really talking about the air in a literal sense? 'They were killed in a plane crash. I . . . well, I was sort of there.'

Melissa said nothing, looked at her, waited. Yes, Anelise wanted to talk about it but it had been a long time since she'd told anyone the story. She was not sure where the words would come from or what they would bring with them. 'It was 1970. I was in the New Zealand team that went to the Commonwealth Games in Edinburgh. My parents were in the States at the time. My father was a forestry scientist and he'd gone over there to study something or other. They were in northern California, so after the games, on the way back, I made an arrangement to stop off in LA and go up and meet them. It was a place called Coochy Creek. They were going to fly in there in the morning from somewhere further up north and wait for me. My flight was due in at two.' She felt a stiffening, a tension in her diaphragm as the story tugged at her, events in sequence that would end in pain. Would it be worse this time? Melissa didn't move, still watching her.

'So we took off and the flight was fine. Except that it was an hour late and when I got there, there was no one to meet me. I hung around for a while and then I went and enquired at one of the counters and they asked me a few questions about who I was looking for and then they said could I wait and they'd get back to me in a moment. All very polite and professional. And so I waited. And waited. And then, after a long while, someone came over to me, one of the staff. She had a blue uniform on and she sat down beside me and started to tell me and I knew before she even said it they were dead. In the mountains, in some mist somewhere, it was a tiny plane they were in and something went wrong with it, they think, or the pilot made a mistake and he came down the wrong valley and crashed. The people at the airport had been waiting, trying to confirm the news, trying to make sure. The mist had cleared in the morning and they'd sent up a helicopter and found the plane. They were waiting for someone to actually get to the crash site, which wasn't very far from a road up there, and some people had gone up and eventually they radioed back that everybody was dead. They tried to tell me it hadn't been confirmed yet, but they knew. And I knew.' She couldn't really understand why she was talking about it in such detail, going on about how she had found out, except that now she had begun she didn't want to stop. It had not been so bad this time, the fear, the hole that opened up and had always threatened to swallow her in the past. The words were making it real in the outside world, such ordinary words so that it had become an event like any other, just something which had happened to her, one thing which didn't have to mean she was crippled forever. Why had it taken so long?

'I was twenty-one,' she said, 'but I was a child really. I'd spent all my teenage years running. I hadn't even been to university then.

I put it off because I wanted to run. I had no boyfriends to speak of. I just wasn't interested. Paul, he was there at that airport. He'd been working in a mine up there and was waiting to come back to New Zealand. He held my hand, right there, while I grew up.' She sighed. 'Except maybe I didn't. Maybe nothing changed at all.'

'Paul couldn't change you,' Melissa said. 'Not by himself.'

No, she thought. It needs more than that. It needs magic. And suddenly she remembered the old man in the mandala in Walter's house, back then. The glass ball in his hands, the magic symbols on his clothes. And there was a feeling for that moment, the fear of the ghost, which was really no more than her fear of her own unknown self, and Melissa looking at her with those strange, uncompromising eyes.

43 Breakthrough

July 1991

'Hello.'
'Paul? It's Linda. Can you talk?'
'What do you mean, can I talk?'
'Is Anelise there?'
'Why shouldn't I be able to talk in my own home?'
'Don't get mad, Paul.'
'My God, why shouldn't I get mad?'
'You found out about the credit card, didn't you? I'm sorry about that.'
'You owe me four thousand dollars. I break people for less than that.'
'Sorry.'
'You're a criminal.'
'I know. Sorry.'
'What are you going to do about it?'
'Someone's following me.'
'I know someone's following you.'
'I popped in to see Mr Kennedy and he said a man had been asking questions about me.'
'He's working for me. I want to know where you are.'
'I don't like him. He scares me.'

'He's also costing me a lot of money, so if you want to get rid of him, all you have to do is tell me where you live.'
'I've moved.'
'Where?'
'Please, Paul.'
'Are you still working for Kennedy?'
'That was only temporary.'
'Where are you working?'
'I don't want to go to gaol, Paul.'
'Where do you live?'
'I love you.'
'What?'
'I love you. I can't help it.'
'Pull yourself together, Linda.'
'I tried not to. It was like I had to do it. Signing your name, her name. Anelise Newton. I thought I really was. I wanted to be. I wanted to be someone special. To belong to you like she does.'
'That doesn't make sense.'
'I'm scared, Paul.'
'Look, Linda, you're in no position to . . .'
'I love you. That was the reason, I promise. That night. Back home. I tried to pretend it was nothing, but I can't. I want you, Paul. I want you to do those things to me again. I know it's wrong and I know it can never mean anything, but I can't help it.'
'Stop it, please.'
'Don't you want me? I can't believe you don't want me a little.'
'That's not the point. I . . .'
'I just want to see you again.'
'No!'
'One more time. Just one more time.'
'Please, Linda.'
'I don't want to go to gaol.'
'You won't have to.'
'Promise you won't hurt me.'
'No, no I won't.'
'I want to see you.'
'No.'
'Please, Paul.'
'No.'
'When can I see you?'
'All right. Tomorrow. The Regent's. You know where that is?'
'Yes. What time?'
'Six. There's a bar called Cat Alley.'

'I love you.'
'You don't.'
'You'll see. Tomorrow.'

44 Coming to Meet

5.50 p.m., Cat Alley, The Regent's Hotel

The bar was shiny, slick, like coal and water. The black walls were dotted with small diamond-shaped mirrors in a geometric pattern. The tables and chairs and the stools at the bar had black tops and chrome legs, and the floor was covered in black and white tiles. Paul came in out of the cold and eased himself onto one of the stools. The barman, in a white shirt and red bow tie, was polishing glasses. He had dark hair, smoothed back, plastered to his skull and a narrow pencil-line of a moustache across his upper lip. Behind him, the glass and stainless-steel fittings gleamed, rows of bottles doubled in the mirror. He stepped forward, said nothing, nodded, smiling, raised his black eyebrows, inviting the order.

'A Manhattan,' Paul told him, 'with Jack Daniels.'

'Certainly, sir.'

Paul took off his trench coat, folded it in two and set it on the next stool. The only other people in the place were a young couple sitting at a table by the window and staring into each other's eyes. Outside, the dark, the streetlights, bustle of the city leaving work. Where was she? Five to six. She would be late. It would be in her nature to be late, to make an entrance.

The barman poured the stirred mixture over ice cubes, a dash of bitters, twist of yellow lemon peel. The glass, a bright inverted cone on a thin stalk. Paul handed over twenty dollars. The change came back on a red napkin in a white saucer. He left it there, lifted the glass, sipped at it.

In his pocket was the key to Room 4501 in the building above him. He wanted her alone. He wanted to get her out of this place into somewhere private, anonymous. He had a very clear view of this requirement, but he was not at all sure what would happen then. He needed to talk to her, of course. He needed to make her see how stupid this was and to figure out some way of getting reparation for what she'd stolen from him. He was not certain, though, how this should be done. Ever since the phone call his thoughts had been in confusion, rambling internal conversations with her, monologues in which he told her what could and could not be, what a scheming little bitch she was, how it made no sense, was impossible, absurd, fantastical, a joke. The words skeined round and knotted, twisted, tangles of writhing helplessness like seaweed in a swirling tide. He would know when he saw her, he decided. He would know then.

I love you, she had said. In the dark, on the hillside, he was running, stumbling down, away from the fire that was already up and glowing on the skyline behind him. There was someone down by the sheds. He caught the flicker of a shadow moving. Voices. Fire, they were calling. Come on. Beside him were the bushes, thick with the smell of blossom like a syrup. He forced his way into them.

The glass was empty. It was ten past six. At the far end of the bar was a young woman in a black-leather suit, her dark hair tied back from her face. She was smoking a cigarette and talking to the barman. Slim, her legs crossed, one foot on the chrome rail, the other swinging, twitching, twitch. The whisky was already mumbling his head. The woman had a red scarf round her throat. She took a long drag at the cigarette and hissed it all out, a grey-white plume, through her pursed red lips. The smoke, drifting, caught his nostrils. Twitch. The barman looked his way and Paul signalled for another drink. Same again.

The smoke. The fire had been hard to get started. The matches from the kitchen drawer were old, damp. And the paper too, although it caught well enough and flared up in a rippling orange tongue, went out again, smoking, when he tried to put more things on it. He got it at the third or fourth attempt. And it was blazing now. A heap of flame beside the desk, flickering up against the panels so the varnish bubbled. The brightness dancing in crazy shadows over the contents of the room.

Drink. He had to keep it under control, that was all. The cleansing fire. The molten gold. Her hair like molten gold. In the bushes, swamped by the drug of blossom, drowning. She was like a dark vision and her hair such white gold-silver, and the gleam of moonlight on her naked shoulder. Fire in his body, in the pit of him, the deep-down burning, hardening, the lust for her, the sickness, blazing in him. He steadied himself against the bar with one hand, picked up the glass with the other. Drank. The woman's dangling leg, the smooth round flesh of her calf, the round of silk. And the whisky was a numbness in the side of his face. Her foot in the black shoe. Twitch. It was six thirty. Not to drink too much. These things were strong and he had to make it clear to her. The warm and yielding softness of her breasts as he touched her. Drunk on blossom. The voices were calling out in the dark.

He flapped his fingers at the barman, dropped another twenty on the loose change, red napkin, white saucer. Where was she, little bitch? Making her big entrance. Sober to make sense. His slow burning. He could feel it in his groin. A bursting. Pressure like a cracking mould. Was it so simple, then? So simple all along. He just needed to fuck her. He would take his payment, money back by fucking her. And nothing, nothing that he was not owed. The sweet and nutty smell of her hot cunt. Drink. He sipped through pursed lips. Sucking in like the woman blew out smoke. Sucking in the fire that burned down even hotter. I got him, didn't I? he said to himself and smiled, a chuckle.

There were more people in the bar. Two young men, they were gay maybe. And a group of four, three men and a woman. Woman with blonde hair but she was not like Linda, not open-eyed and innocent seductive, with her fear and knowing to an ounce the power she had. Gold to the ounce. Today it was $US337.24. The dark-haired woman in the leather suit had swivelled on her seat, her legs spread now to face him in the tight wrapping of her skirt, her left foot on the rail, her right reaching downward, toe towards the floor. Her left elbow on the bar, another cigarette. The gap between her knees. By Christ, he thought, I got him, didn't I? I got him good for all the things he did to me. That second life of his, that secret airy-fairy world of Truth and Beauty, crap like that. Let's get the world cleaned out of bullshit. Burn the lot of it.

The blonde woman with the three guys. Was she watching him with her head on one side? To hell with it. To hell with her. To hell with all of them. His numb face, yawing in his head. I won't drink anymore of these things. Not used to them. Beer, I'll have a beer. Or a gin, maybe. Is the glass empty?

The barman was a bit slow in coming over. Red tie under his chin like someone had cut his throat. Paul ordered a gin and tonic, double. Had to say it twice. It was five to seven. Oh, God, she wasn't going to show. She had stood him up. To get away from him. He had scared her. She was too scared to meet him, run away. She was gone. His last hope. He stared at his watch, the bright gold second hand, its tick, tick, ticking. It wouldn't stop. The gin, in a squat glass, bright, sparkling. He drank from it, deep. His thirst to drown. I'll drown myself, he thought. Like Michael, diving into the air.

The blonde woman at the table, laughing, showing her white

teeth. Linda. Her mouth. Her tongue. Her lies. Her bullshit, bullshit. Fuck you, bitch! He was breathing hard and wanting to shout it loud. Tell all these stupid people. Smash their fucking faces in. He didn't care. He'd had enough. He didn't care about anything anymore. The old man, Walter, dead. I fixed him, he thought. I could be free. I could be free. If only I could forget all that stuff. The flames were leaping hungry at the bookcases. Fuck it, he thought. I don't care what happens now.

Another gin. It wasn't right the way the barman kept serving him. What were these people for if not to protect you from yourself? For all the barman knew, Paul might be planning to drive home. And wasn't he? He puzzled over it. The thought of Anelise and Andrew, their anxious eyes at the dinner table. Why couldn't they leave him alone? Stupid bitch would have to leave her bag behind. How else would any of this have started? How else would it all have come apart? No, he thought. I've had this stuff. I've had trying to control things. It can all explode. The lit fuse running to a powder keg. He stood at the top of the hill and looked back, saw the dark, dirty orange glow pulsing in the windows of the little house. A brighter flash. I want Linda, he thought. Dear God, have I become such a pathetic creature? Lord have mercy on my soul!

The woman in the leather with her legs apart was switching on her seat from side to side. He finished his drink. God, the time was? Nearly eight. Or was it seven. How long would they keep on serving him? This is a scientific experiment, he thought. I shall keep drinking until the barman says stop. I shall keep an inventory of my consumption and report him to the authorities, write a letter to the paper, complain to my MP. A person of influence. This isn't good enough.

Go home. His fingers were clumsy. The red napkin needed feeding again. The room looked blurred. There were more tables full. More stupid people. I will not go home, he thought. It's too late for that. The old man's dead and I have no choice anymore. I'm just tired. I've had enough. The gin and tonic was crooked in the glass. He drank, felt his stomach heave. Not used to it, drinking. Stomach empty. Please. I've had enough. I don't care. Carefully he stood up. The room lurched. He picked up his coat. Slowly, deliberately, he walked towards the door. The woman in leather was still switching on her seat. He stopped beside her. One hand on the bar. Surprised, she leaned back, turned away, her fear, revulsion. He tried to focus on it, stared at her. He wanted, wanted, wanted to say.

'Excuse me, sir.' It was the barman.

Paul stood up straight. 'Not a problem,' he said. 'Just tell her to keep her knees together.'

45 Gathering Together

Anelise awoke. The bed beside her was empty. The red digits of the clock gleamed at her in the darkness. It was six thirty-three. For a moment she did not really understand what the situation was and felt a strange sensation of comfort, well-being. Then she knew. Paul had not come home. A lurch of panic, dread, her heart thumping, but it somehow didn't drive her into action. She lay there, staring at the clock. It flicked another minute. I knew this would happen, she thought. I've been waiting for it. I have to decide what to do. But her purpose, her drive had disengaged itself. Her heartbeat slowed. She stared in front of her at the red numbers in the dark. I knew this would happen. Deep inside she felt the root of an ancient anger, something so distant she did not know where it came from or what it meant. It had not touched her mind or her muscles as yet, but it was stirring, growing. I should be worried, she thought. I should be afraid that something's happened to him. Long ago, it had happened long ago.

At seven fifteen, the radio came on, a burst of baroque music. The dawn had already greyed the seam of the curtains. She turned back the covers and got out of bed. Lights on. The room looked as it always did except that Paul wasn't there. She took a shower in the en suite, dried herself, put on her bra and panties, slacks, a cotton sweater and a pair of slip-on shoes. Then she sat down on the stool before her dressing-table mirror and turned on the hair-dryer. Her face, tilted towards the stream of hot air, stared back at her. It was long, narrow, the cheeks a little hollowed, mouth small, precise, eyes large and dark and steady, fixed on her. The short brown hair lifted, feathered to the dryer, lightening as the moisture left it. I'm forty-two years old, she thought. It's twenty-one years since I gave up athletics, since I met Paul. Half my life exactly.

On the way down the hall, she put her ear to Andrew's door to make sure he was awake. A pop song from his radio. How was she going to tell him? Explain? In the kitchen, she filled the kettle, plugged it in. Four slices of bread in the toaster. It was quarter to eight. She picked up the phone. Dialled.

Theo answered. 'Hello.'

'Hi, Theo. Paul didn't come home last night. I don't know where he is.' She was calm, controlled. She was surprised how calm she was.

Theo was taken off his guard.

'Would you know where I can contact him?' she asked.

'No. I've no idea. Have you called the police?'

'No, not yet.' Strange that she cared so little about Paul's safety.

'Are you all right?'

'Yes.'

'I'll come over. Half an hour,' Theo said.

The toast was done. She buttered it and left it on a plate on the breakfast bar. Marmalade from the refrigerator. Milk and cornflakes for Andrew. I've made too much toast, she thought. There's only two of us today. She boiled the kettle once again and poured the tea.

'Morning, Mater,' Andrew in the doorway. 'Phoebus has risen from his fiery bed.' Bleary-eyed and gawky in his school uniform.

'Have your breakfast,' she told him.

Perched on the stool. The cornflakes rustled out of the box. The white milk. She watched him. When do I say? she wondered. How?

'We've got a problem,' she said.

He froze, dramatically, spoon halfway to his mouth. He won't be able to laugh this off, she thought. What will it do to him?

'You're father didn't come home last night.'

He sagged. The spoon descended gently. He was staring at her.

'What's wrong?' he asked. 'Where is he?'

'I don't know. I'm sure he's all right. Theo's coming over. Maybe he knows something.'

Andrew turned back to his plate. Slowly the spoon rose again. He started to eat. Anelise went round the bar and put her arm round his shoulders. Hard, bony shoulders. She hugged him.

Theo arrived with Kate. He asked Anelise again if she'd called the police. When she said no, he did it himself, standing in the kitchen, hand on hip, his black patent-leather shoes gleaming. Kate bustling, wanting to be useful, bursting with questions that she was scared of asking in front of Andrew. Let him know, Anelise thought. He needs to know what this is about. She sat down at the bar next to him and drank her tea.

Theo was calling the hospital now.

'He's never done this before, has he?' Kate asked.

'Paul? Don't be ridiculous!' Which made her realise how strange it was, how strange that she knew it was going to happen.

'Maybe he's been kidnapped,' Andrew said.

'Oh, don't say that.' Kate looked scared.
'Or maybe he's stuck in a lift.'
Theo hung up, spread his hands to show no news. 'I'm sure there is nothing to worry about,' he said.
'What now?' Kate asked.
'I'll go to the office. There are some things I can do from there. You can stay here with Anelise, okay?'
'Yes, of course.'
'What about you, darling?' Anelise hugged her son again. 'Do you want to stay here or do you want to go to school? Whichever.'
Andrew looked at them all in turn, an assessment, a decision, a little nod.
'School,' he said. 'The show must go on.'
'Good man! I can give you a lift,' Theo told him.
Andrew slid off the stool and went out to his room.
'Anelise,' Theo said. 'I haven't yet made any formal report to the police. For now they will do nothing.'
'That's okay,' she answered.
Andrew came back and he and Theo left.
Kate made another cup of tea. She looked anxious, nervous, her hands with a little shake to them.
'Theo thinks there may be a woman,' she said.
'What?'
'He said he found a lipstick on the floor by Paul's desk, and Paul behaved in a peculiar way.'
'How peculiar?'
'Theo thought maybe he was guilty about something.'
Anelise did not believe it. Or, if she did, she was sure it was not the problem, not the issue. Tension in him, held tight, pressed down, pressure building like a huge boil. Had he found someone to tell his secrets to? Good, she thought, good. She felt a surge of anger. Except that it was not just anger. There was something else as well, an energy, a desire, a new purpose. No, she thought. I don't want to think about that yet.

46 Pushing Upward

He was conscious again, remembering, unremembering. His mind smeared, vague, like a dirty window, as if his brain was coated with a thick layer of muck that smoothed out all distinctions. His stomach heavy, rolling as he moved, while his cock, in defiance of his queasiness, was hard, erect, distended to the point of pain. He opened his eyes on the pale yellow light of the hotel room, pastel prints on the walls, the furniture of golden wood. It looks like the office, he thought. And turned away his mind from the idea of the real world, the duty, his responsibility. He remembered the bar, the woman in the leather skirt. He hadn't wanted her at the time, hadn't found her at all attractive, but now, it seemed, she was the focus of his lust, the target of the spear that grew from the pit of his belly. No, it was Linda. After he had left Cat Alley, he had gone looking for her, wandered up Queen Street in search of Kennedy's shop, his anger, frustration mounting. Another bar. He had been talking to someone, drunk. The yellow light of a naked bulb, the shade a flat plastic cone. After that he could not remember. Fuck it, he thought. Who cares? I've had enough of this. Enough. But what 'this' was, he could not say.

He sat up. His head swam, stomach lurched as the heaviness turned over. On his feet, a stagger, made it to the refrigerator. Drank two bottles of tomato juice. Cold. The air cold round his heated organ, which was still upright, wavering. Linda, he thought.

Eight thirty. He could not think of Sleed's number and had to look it up. A spasm of nausea. His finger shook as he pushed the buttons.

'Baker Sleed, good morning.' That perky sing-song, silly bitch.

'Is Geoff there yet?'

'Could I say who's calling please?'

'Paul Newton.'

'Just one moment.'

A silence. Paul's hand was still shaking. His clothes were scattered over the sofa and chair on the other side of the room. His shoes in the middle of the floor. He remembered, now, getting back to the hotel, the lift, the reeling corridor to the room.

'Sleed here.'

'Paul Newton.'

'Ah, Mr Newton. You're on my list of morning calls. We've found your subject. She's living in a flat in Herne Bay. 23B Marshall Street.'

'Hang on.' Paul scrabbled in the drawer next to the bed for a pen, a pad of hotel notepaper. Wrote down the address.

'Phone?' he asked.

Sleed gave the number, told him too that Linda was working at a place called The Boardroom, a men's fashion store. 'Chic', he called it. The address was an arcade off Queen Street. The telephone number for that too.

'Thanks,' Paul said.

'Glad to be of help.'

He did not even stop to think of what he was doing, dialled The Boardroom immediately. A young man with a soft, effete-sounding voice answered.

'Could I speak to Linda Kemp, please?'

'I'm afraid our staff don't accept personal calls, sir. Can I take a message?'

'For God's sake, this is her father. It's important.'

A hesitation, decision. 'One moment, please.'

He waited, listening, straining into the silence at the other end of the phone.

'Dad?' Her voice tiny and anxious.

'It's Paul.'

'God, you gave me a fright.'

'I want you.'

'Oh, no.'

'I know where you work and I know where you live and I want you.'

'All right. When?'

'Now.'

'Oh, God, I can't Paul. My job.'

'I'll get you another job.'

'No, please.'

'Tell them it's an emergency. Tell them you're sick. I'm in the Regent's Hotel. Room 4501. You got that?'

'Yes.'

'Now.'

'Yes.'

He hung up. He did not doubt that she would do as he said. He felt full of strength, a confidence that could bend the world to his will, and the small part of him that thought this conviction was audacious and absurd somehow added spice to his self-assurance.

He went into the bathroom and began his morning ritual. The shit, the shower, the shave, his teeth. Except that he had no toothbrush or shaving gear. He called room service. Certainly, sir. Then he got dressed except for his shoes, his tie, his jacket, which he draped over the back of a chair. His trench coat had a muddy stain on the right elbow. Had he dropped it or fallen over? He brushed at the mark ineffectually with his fingers and then hung the coat in the wardrobe.

His sudden burst of energy had stilled the queasiness in his stomach. He felt anticipation, eagerness. Maybe there was hunger in it too. Breakfast. The next step in the ritual. Should he call room service again? There were snacks in the cupboard over the refrigerator. He took a bag of mixed nuts, tore off the corner, dribbled some into his hand and scooped them into his mouth. He began to pace the room, over to the window, back to the bed, eating the nuts without thinking, driven by the growing, sickening excitement in his belly.

This is crazy, he thought. This is not good. But there was no power in the idea. He didn't care. He thought of work, the neat partitions of his day. The latest Ventura papers would be on his desk, the next steps to be taken. He wanted to be involved in that project, no matter what Theo said. His hunger battened on the idea of it and he remembered the mines he had known in Pokenaw and Coochy Creek, the excavators ripping at the earth, the shafts and tunnels, and the crushing, grinding, pulping slush of hot mud, poison, power, the heat and crackle of the current through the wires. The gleam of gold. He wanted it. He wanted it as he wanted Linda, and, for the first time, the sanctity of social order, decorum, morality meant nothing to him in comparison. His energy, the sense of his own power were just too big; swelling, bursting, erupting through the precisely woven fabric of his life. There was nothing he could do to stop it.

A discreet knock. Room service with the razor and toothbrush. He strode across the room, twisted at the knob and swung the door open.

She was dressed in a black suit; the jacket wide in the shoulders and narrow at the waist, a short, tight skirt. She had red high-heeled shoes, a red bag and matching earrings like red buttons. Her mouth red, her nails. Her white blouse was done up at the neck in a lacy frill. Her hair was layered like a golden mane, a look of contrived wildness.

'Hi,' she said. Her eyes, staring up at him, were huge, blue, fearful, determined.

'Come in.' He stepped aside, held open the door. She moved past him into the room. He stuck his head out into the corridor and saw the bellboy coming towards him holding a tray. He went out and took the tray, gave the bellboy a two-dollar tip.

'Thank you, sir.' Ardent.

Too much, Paul thought and felt pleased. He wanted to laugh. Release. The sudden sense that everything was within his grasp.

Back in the room, he closed the door behind him, put the tray on the shelf over the refrigerator. Linda was standing in the middle of the floor. She had taken off her shoes and her jacket and was unbuttoning her blouse. Little round pearly buttons between her red fingernails. He moved towards her, reached out to take hold of her.

'No,' she said, 'no. You have to look. Just look.' Her eyes the same, so big, fixed on his face, a challenge in them, the challenge of her fear. Her mouth unsmiling, expressionless. As if she was pushing her fear before her like a weapon to prove to him how strong she was, how much she needed, how far she would go for what she wanted.

He sat down in one of the armchairs.

The blouse undone. It gaped. The light through it in a white glow. Her white camisole, the sheen of it, like snow in the twilight. She unfastened her skirt at the left hip, pulled the hem of the blouse from the waistband, shucked her shoulders. Her arms slipped free of the sleeves as the blouse dropped to the floor. He twisted in his chair, staring at her, his lust for her rising, but he pressed down on it, tight. Not yet.

Her fingers were in the skirt, pushing at it. It came loose with a wriggle of her hips. She let it fall, stepped out of it, flapped it aside with the edge of her foot. Her movements were slow, deliberate but without flourish, without provocation, willing him to watch her as she watched him with her anxious eyes. There was laughter in his throat, a thrust, a crow of triumph but he held it back. Not yet.

Her pantyhose a snake's skin, sloughed, unclinging, her legs pale, creamy-white like ivory. Her red-nailed hands gripping the camisole, lifting it, peeling it, her arms reaching high above her head. Her gold hair lifting and falling in the light. She dropped the camisole and reached behind her for the catch of her brassiere, her left shoulder dipping, gleam, her breasts free, white, the brown nipples, belly smooth, the dimple of her navel like a little inverted mole. She was so pale, so golden, drops of red like blood, her golden hair, her soft cream flesh like the open earth but purified, transfigured. Mine, he thought. His power like a rock.

She bent, in profile, belly wrinkling, breasts in a pale, cupped curve, the arch of her spine, her legs in two slow, delicate steps. She walked to the bed with the panties dangling from her hand, dropped them to the floor, lay down, stretched herself, her legs crossed at the ankle. Her left hand to her side, dangling over the edge of the mattress, her right resting across her belly above the golden mound. Her eyes still watching him. A little smile on her red lips now, a twist of confidence.

He stood up.

'Now,' she said. 'It's my turn to look at you.'

47 Oppression

'So?' she asked.

Theo swirled the ice cubes in his Scotch, examined it closely. Kate, beside him on the sofa, had an anguished expression.

'Theo!' Anelise said, insisting. There was tension, worry, but underneath a strange, cool calm.

Theo cleared his throat. 'We have these people, an agency, that we use from time to time to track down information and the answers to, well, certain problems. They are very good. Most useful to us. I called them this morning to ask them to find where Paul was. It was a strange conversation. We got a little confused because it seems that Paul had called them himself last week wanting them to find someone for him.'

'Who?'

'A woman. It was a problem, my talk with them, because they thought perhaps that Paul's request was a private matter and they have their feelings about client confidence. Finally, though, I persuaded them that they should tell me. Paul, it seems, called them this morning too, and they told him where this woman was.'

'This morning?'

'Correct. They gave me her address and her employment. I called her work and they say someone has telephoned her just after she got there today. She told them her mother is sick and went running out and they've not seen her since. I think maybe this is just after Paul made his call to the agency. About eight thirty. I called her home and she has not been there since she went to work.'

A woman. The Other Woman. To admit herself despised, supplanted, sullied, scorned, betrayed. He had done this to her. He had humiliated her. He had not even had the decency to be honest with her, not the simple courtesy to tell her where he was.

She looked round the room, the furniture they had chosen together, the carpet, pictures, the house itself, which they had built here, tucked into the hill, the view down to the bay and the harbour. It seemed different, alien, as if the colour had all been leached out of it. A lightening, fading, like her own sense of weightlessness. There was nothing to hold her down. She would float away. Trusting in the air.

'It might be coincidence,' Kate said, but she did not seem to believe it.

I should be angry, Anelise thought. Let me be angry.

'It's not that important really,' Kate said. 'Probably just a stupid male menopause thing.' She gave a desperate, hopeful smile, as if she wanted Anelise to accept it this way, wanted her to share her own tolerance for male stupidity, male vanity, but knew too that Anelise would never be so forgiving.

'What's this woman's name?' Anelise asked.

'Linda Kemp.'

'What?'

'You know her?'

Anelise began to laugh, a burst of madness, violent release, the crazy, dumb, absurd, eccentric world, an irony like gas, like a drug, hallucination, everything distorted, wrenched beyond her understanding.

'Who . . .' Kate puzzled, smiling her wish to make it better. 'Who is this person?'

'An air-head, an idiot. The archetypal blonde bimbo.'

'There you are, then!' Kate laughed in relief. Because it was all right, wasn't it? Theo, too, a little grin, a shrug of his shoulders, man-of-the-world. So simple.

Not my world, Anelise thought, suddenly. A shudder of revulsion twitched at her and she stared at her two closest friends with a feeling of incomprehension. Strangers.

'Can anyone share the joke? Or do you have to pay?' It was Andrew in the doorway, his little wary grin, like a boxer's feint.

'Come in, darling. Come here.' Anelise beckoned him to the sofa, put her arm round him. How was she going to explain to him, the news, the laughter?

'Is it about Dad?' he asked.

'We have been talking about that.' She tried for the words but couldn't find them. For a moment she wanted to look at Theo, appeal to him for assistance, but she resisted.

'And?' Andrew asked.

'He's with someone else. A woman. We're not quite sure, but that's the way it looks,' she told him.

'Oh, yes,' he said, sarcastically. 'That's really funny.'

'I'm sorry, darling.'

'So what are you going to do?'

'I think I'm going to go away for a while.' The words came out from nowhere. Her decision. She had made it already.

'What about me?'

'What do you want to do?'

He didn't hesitate. 'I want to come with you.'

'What about school? I don't know where I'm going.' But she did know. She thought she knew. The old man with the glass ball.

'Don't be stupid, Mum!'

'You need to think about it. You need to talk it through,' Theo said. 'Not to be hasty.'

Enough thinking, enough, enough, enough. She hugged Andrew closer.

48 The Well

'Paul?'

'Yes.'

'I'm scared.'

'What of?'

'Everything.'

'Such as?'

'What are we going to do?'

'Fuck.'

'Don't use that word. I don't like it.'

'I like it. I love it. I love fucking you.'

'Please, Paul. Don't say that.'

'You like it. You do like it, don't you?'

'Yes.'

'Well, then.'

'Maybe I like it too much. You take me over. I think I'm going to disappear.'

'You won't disappear.'

'I didn't think I could want it so much or that, well, a man could either.'
'I've been saving up.'
'Don't you and Anelise . . .'
'No.'
'Poor you.'
'But I've got you now.'
'What about her?'
'Don't talk about her.'
'You're not going to leave her, are you?'
'No.'
'What's going to happen to me, then?'
'I'll look after you. You're mine now.'
'She isn't going to like that.'
'She'll have to.'
'What if she doesn't?'
'She'll get used to it.'
'I'm scared, Paul.'
'There's nothing to be scared about.'
'I get scared of you.'
'Me? Why? I won't hurt you.'
'I don't know why you want me.'
'You're my prize, my reward.'
'Are you glad you met me?'
'Yes.'
'What did you mean, before, when you said you'll look after me?'
'I'll get you a place to live. You can do it up the way you want. I'll give you some money, enough money, and you can do whatever you like with the place. You'd like that, wouldn't you?'
'Yes. I want it all to be white.'
'White?'
'Yes. It suits me. White and black. Will you pay the bills?'
'Sure.'
'Everything?'
'Don't worry, I can afford to look after you.'
'What about my job?'
'You won't need a job. I want you available.'
'You won't want me all the time. I'll get bored just waiting around.'
'You can think about all the things I'm going to do to you when we're together.'

The Whitening

'I do belong to you, don't I?'
'Yes. Do you mind?'
'No.'
'Do you like it?'
'Yes.'
'Tell me why you like it.'
'Because you're going to look after me. Because you make me feel like I'm in another world. A world full of pleasure. So much pleasure, I could die.'
'I want to fuck you again.'
'Yes.'
'Do you want it?'
'Yes.'
'Ask me, then.'
'No. Just do it.'

Part Four

THE REDDENING

Having broken the argument down and down
we have come to a place in the text — a clearing —
where a man and a woman have unexpectedly met.
We have been led to believe, remember, that one
will take advantage of the other, as we have been led
to believe that there is only one God.

— from *Small Stories of Devotion*, Dinah Hawken

49 Revolution

From the Journals of Walter Newton

10 February 1969

Here I am under true pretences

Walked today down the back road. The bush was fresh, dripping after the rain and in the sunlight there was an astonishing variety of little optical effects; the various greens of the leaves, the brightness of drops of water like tiny diamonds, the huge deep blue of the sky. It engendered in me a kind of stillness of the spirit and I looked at it all, just looked, without thinking or reasoning or analysis, and it occurred to me that I had *never really seen anything before*. I had never really seen anything without it somehow being contaminated by interference from my thinking. So I stopped it, the thinking, just locked it out, and for half an hour or so I wandered around taking in the world, sucking it in through my eyes as if they were drains, and the longer it went on, the more I felt a strange kind of exaltation, drawing me closer and closer to I know not what.

Isn't this the issue?

There are pleasures of the body. There are pleasures of the mind. There are pleasures of both body and mind. The trick is to know which is which.

Maybe bodily pleasures that get interrupted by the mind and processed through it are false pleasures because sensations the mind comments on are no longer sensations. They are already thoughts.

If I taste a good wine, I shouldn't tell myself how good it is or ask where it was made and how much it cost and when was the last time I had a wine like that or will I ever taste its like again and what's its name anyway? If I taste a good wine, I should taste it. Time enough for thinking when the wine is gone.

Try these for false pleasures.

Why Things Fall

1. I am eating my favourite food. I know I'm having a good time because it is my favourite food.

   I am eating my favourite food. I know I'm having a good time because it tastes the same as the last time I ate it.

2. Jane and I are screwing. I know I'm having a good time because we're screwing.

   Jane and I are screwing. Jane seems to be having a good time so I must be having a good time too.

   Jane and I are screwing. Therefore I must be a potent, sexual being. It is good to be a potent, sexual being. Therefore I'm having a good time.

3. I'm resting. I know I'm having a good time because I'm resting.

Maybe the way to the great truth is the avoidance of false pleasure. TWO WAYS, therefore:

1. Meditation. Shut out the senses and focus inwards on the dark centre.

2. Open up to the senses in a deliberate and disciplined way by shutting out the interference of thinking. Thus:
   Walking or sitting, focus on one sense or another or each in turn.
   Not thinking about what you see or hear but simply being aware of the sense.
   By resting in a state of balance with regard to the sense, by softly holding your attention as you might hold you breath, you achieve a new dimension to perception, an inner opening, as if the mind, instead of tightness and thinking and talking, becomes an entrance through which perceptions pour.

Dance without music flows from the body's centre.

What if I could live with the self-absorption of a dancer?

Style is being and being is doing and style is how it's done.

11 February 1969

The issue of the false pleasures, the issue of the two ways. The two ways are

The Reddening

The Way of the Mind
The Way of the Body

False pleasures are the mind interfering with the body.

There is one thing common to all human beings. We all have bodies. Therefore, we are all alive. Therefore, we will all die.

Excessive focus on the mind brings with it the fear of death. Hence, in Western civilisation, we are all busy pretending that we will not die.

But there's a catch. The more we succeed in avoiding a confrontation with our mortality, the more we are in danger of becoming out of touch with our bodies.

If we are to live, we must feed, clothe and shelter our bodies, but in our attempts to ignore death we blunt our awareness of these same bodies. Remember, too, that we experience other people through their bodies.

We exist in contradiction. In order to escape death we impoverish life.

We must learn to live in the contrary paradox. In order to live life to the full, we must first embrace our mortality.

The meaning of life is the meaning of death.

Ways of trying to ignore our mortality:

1. We simply do not think about it. We thus make the assumption that we are immortal until proven otherwise.
2. Sometimes we test our mortality by deliberately courting danger. When we succeed, we are confirmed in our faith.
3. We become obsessed with the idea of the body; its health, its care, its beauty, its fitness. As if, by forcing it to conform to an idea, we can idealise it and make it live forever.
4. We take comfort in the fact that our friends and relatives will remember us when we're gone.
5. We take comfort from the fact that we will leave something behind us by which we will be remembered.
6. We believe there is life after death.

I feel as if I have never known what it is to be alive, because thinking and consciousness have always been the centre of my existence. At the times when the physical reality forced its way to my attention, like the war, for example, I felt that it threatened my sanity, the way I was put together. I felt as if the closer the physical got, the more I somehow had to draw my consciousness away from it to prevent contamination. Retreat into unreality, therefore.

Think, on the other hand, of the Greek peasants. No retreat from the physical there. Not to idealise them, though. The threat for body-centred people is the power of ideas, the agents of change, the way in which the mind can force itself on the physical world. See them retreat into brutishness when that happens.

Isn't this the crucial question, therefore? The relationship between consciousness and the physical world. The balance. Isn't this the key to finding the Eternal City?

An interesting thought, though.

How do I *know* that I am not immortal?

50 The Cauldron

Wairuru, August 1991

Grey pallor of the sky, the still air, the rich winter green of the paddocks. Jane, in gumboots, heavy woollen skirt and knitted cardigan, trudged the old wheelbarrow from the vegetable plot to the compost bin. Her breath misted in the cold in little plumes. The wheel of the barrow gave a squeak with each turn. Once at the bin, she forked the compost into the metal tray. The rotted fibres parting, chocolate brown, and the pink and ruby threads of the earthworms, twisting. When the barrow was full she paused, rested on the fork, her breathing heavy. Take it easy, she thought. It'll be a long day. Because it's the right day for the garden, the best day. Time for feeding, time for sowing, with the moon around the first quarter and the weather just right to give the seedlings a start. Early as it was for the spring, she knew she could get away with things that otherwise might never stand the cold. The time, she thought. We must be ripe for the time.

On the pole beside the bins was the Devil, the ram's skull, chalky white. She grinned at it. The black hollow of its eye stared back at her. Its nasal passages sprouting slivers of rotting bone.

Hello, you old bugger, she thought to it. How's it going?

The skull didn't answer.

Got any advice for me today?

No, it said. Tell me something.

I feel good. I feel strong. I feel the world is going to burst into flower.

You've got to be joking!

Life, living. It's very simple.

Life? What's life? A fate worse than birth! the skull said.

It's being in harmony with the world.

Accepting your fate?

Destiny.

Necessity, that's what it is. Making a virtue of necessity.

The Joy of Necessity, that's it.

Necessity is the invention of mothers, said the skull.

Stupid bugger! she thought, and laughed out loud to it.

Then she bobbed down, bending at the knees to save her back, gripped the handles of the barrow, lifted, took the strain. For a moment she thought it was too heavy to move, but then the wheel turned, squeak, and the soggy pneumatic tyre began to roll down the path. Round the back of the sheds and out to the garden. There were winter cabbages in rows and the broad beans flowering. The bright green feathered tops of carrots and the thick trunks of the leeks. She began to spread the compost around the base of the plants, digging her hands into the rich brown muck and flaking it through her fingers as it dribbled out. The Joy of Necessity. Was that what Destiny meant?

'Yo, Jane!' Out on the paddock, a dark figure was coming towards her. Short, stocky. Kingi Makara. He had a shotgun under his right arm.

Jane straightened up, eased her back with the sides of her hands, and watched him as he climbed the stile over the wire fence. He was wearing a red and black checked Swanndri, brown trousers, white gumboots.

'Morning, Kingi. What brings you over here so early?' She knew, of course. He had a thirst for all the gossip of the district.

He waved the gun. 'Looking for something for the pot, eh?'

'No luck?'

'Going back, maybe.' He grinned at her. The two missing teeth in the side of his mouth. You should've seen the other fella, eh?

When he was young and wild. Like Tane, she thought. Except that Tane was cleverer somehow, or quicker. Never got himself beat up, even though in his deep-down self he was wilder, more angry than Kingi could ever be.

'This cloud going to lift?' She glanced up at the sky.

'Nagh. Tomorrow.'

'I reckon I'll start some pumpkins and tomatoes today.'

'Yeh?' He raised his eyebrows in surprise and then grinned again, the flesh in his brown cheeks creasing, bagging out under his eyes. 'We got a call from Hine.'

'You did? When?'

'Last night. She called up from some hotel in Wellington. That's good, eh? She remembers her Maori family. Aroha said before she visited that maybe she turned into a Pakeha. All those fancy Aussies she been hanging around with.'

'She's no Pakeha. Not in the way you mean.' Jane pictured her daughter chasing around Kingi's yard with his grandchildren. Her beautiful, elegant daughter. As wild inside as her father, maybe.

'Good, eh?' Kingi said. Then his expression changed, a look of mild interest that failed to hide the burning curiosity underneath. So, Jane thought. Now we come to it.

'Joe says you got a visitor,' Kingi offered.

'Two.'

He was waiting for more but she said nothing, teasing him just a little.

'He said it was that woman married Walter's boy.'

'Anelise, that's right. She's got her son with her. Andrew. They came back with Melissa. She and Paul are having a few problems and she wanted to get away for a while.'

'She all right?'

'Well, you know. She's pretty upset, eh? But she's all right.'

'I like her,' Kingi said. 'Not like her old man.' He shook his head and blew a little whistle through the gap in his teeth.

'Paul's got a lot to learn.'

'Yer. Like not to play with matches.' Kingi laughed. 'And to keep his hands off other people's kids.' And the laugh had turned a bit hollow.

So they all knew about Linda too.

'It's hard to know who might be to blame there,' she said. The strange conflict of her feelings. The girl was so young, with a head full of romantic nonsense, but she was also cunning and manipulative. And the man, who was Walter's son, so knowing in the world but such a fool in the turmoil of his middle age.

'Yer.' Kingi grinned. 'She's a cheeky little piece, eh?'

'And old enough to know what she's doing.'

'So? Are they shacked up together or what?'

'I doubt it. It's probably all over by now. But it's tough on Kevin and Diane. Especially Kevin. He really doted on that girl. And for her to more or less run away like that. And then this thing with Paul.'

Kingi nodded. 'How did he find out?'

'She wrote to him and told him. Like she was really proud of it.'

'Yer?'

'Hostages to fortune,' Jane said.

'What's that?'

'"Children make us hostages to fortune." Walter used to say that. It's a quote from somebody.'

'Yer, but that's kids, though, eh?'

'Kevin was up here the other day. He had a talk to Anelise. I'm not sure it did them much good.'

'Different ways of looking at it,' Kingi said.

And Kevin with his damp eyes, yearning eyes, and wanting to be told that it was all all right so there, there. But he knew deep down. He knew and understood in a way that Anelise did not quite yet. And there was so little anger in him. Nothing but his resignation.

'Yes,' she answered.

'And this boy? Is he okay?'

'He's a right little townie. Spends half his time in front of his computer. He likes Alice, though.'

'Alice?' Kingi laughed. 'She's a little beauty, that one.'

'Go down the house and say hello,' Jane suggested.

'No, not now, eh?' Feeling self-conscious, awkward. A coy little twist to his shoulders. 'I got to get something for the pot.' He grinned.

'Okay, then.'

'See ya.' He turned to go.

'Tell Aroha I'll come up and have a chat with her sometime soon.'

'Yer. See ya.'

He trudged away, his big boots through the tufts of grass. Once over the stile, he waved to her and headed off up the slope towards the south-east. He was an old man. They were both old. Hair gone grey and bodies thick around the middle. They had been neighbours, friends, relatives almost for nearly forty years. Now he had reached the top of the rise. His squat figure dark on the horizon.

In the empty grey sky above him was the point at which she had first seen the balloon. Twenty-five years ago. A quarter of a century. Eh, Walter. And then she grinned. It's time I stopped giving you the po-face, she thought.

51 The Arousing

And so he sat at his desk in the study. His body weary, drained for the moment of his lust for Linda, but his mind still whirling. A wakefulness he could not drown. On the blotter in front of him was a bottle of red wine, a glass. The wine was a deep purple-black in the green bottle. There was a bright star of light from the lamp on the sloping green shoulder, another star, brighter, in the bowl of the wineglass. The bottle and glass stood in a disc, an elliptical disc of light. Each cast a blunt, lumpy shadow. It was one, perhaps two in the morning and he had been home maybe an hour. Home to the empty house. Watching, as the garage door came up, to see if Anelise's car was there and angry with himself when it was not. Angry for hoping when he didn't want to hope. He had all he wanted. He was in control. The fact that he was not living with Linda proved it. He could spend evenings away from her two or three times a week, coming back just to be on his own. He could keep her separate, isolated, manageable. Couldn't Anelise see that?

He drained the wine from the glass, refilled it, drank some more. His head buzzing with fatigue and alcohol. The ellipse on the desk reminded him of something, but he could not think what. The drink, the wine had to do with death. Blood of Christ, in his mother's words. No, not that. He thought of Linda. Her red lips parted and her white teeth, gleam of saliva. She did things to him with her mouth, arousing him and sucking at him, draining him, and wanting more. And then, when he thought he had nothing left, she would try to prove that she could make him want her again. And she succeeded. He wanted her now. He could feel it stirring in him deep down. He could go back, have her again, make her scream with the pleasure he gave her, scream so loud he sometimes thought he'd hurt her. More, more, more. No, he thought. The wine. I have to get some sleep. It'll kill me, living like this. It can't go on, can it? I'm going to burn out soon. It'll be all gone, no desire, no more lusting for her. Empty, dry like a shrivelled fruit. Or dead of a heart attack. But what if it did kill him? Who said he wanted to live anyway?

Except for work. He had to keep on working. The plans for the share issue and the Ventura deal, which was almost ripe. He had persuaded Theo that they should join the project, not as full members of the consortium but as subcontractors handling ore-processing and refinement. So easy. So obvious. He was longing to get his hands on it, an urge, a drive, a hunger. His energy and power focused in it. It would have to work, and if it didn't, he would make it. Like Linda.

He stared into the bottle of whisky. Not whisky, no. Where did that come from? He never drank whisky, not Scotch, anyway. Hated it. Whisky was for the dead. Wine for the living. Drowning in life, in her soft flesh. Her voice whispering to him, whispering how wonderful he was. His pride, his new-found strength. He possessed her. She was his. He owned her. As he owned the world she lived in. And she wanted it that way. Only sometimes she was bored, her voice querulous, her face pained. *I get sick of television, Paul. I just sit here waiting for you to call. I've got nothing to do.* She had furnished the flat the way she wanted it. Her place. Her nest that he had paid for. Now she couldn't understand how jealous he was. Jealous of the time she spent on anything but him. She had talked him into letting her have a job, working mornings in a fashion boutique, but he hated even that. She might meet someone else. Men, younger than he was, who might understand her better. He was not sure how it would happen, but anything was possible. And there were times when she was late home and he wanted her at lunch-time and she was not available. It spoilt things, tainted it all, the perfection of it. *I need to do something, Paul. Otherwise I'd just eat and eat and get fat, and you wouldn't like that, would you?* She got whatever she wanted. She could always wheedle it out of him.

Her skin, smooth belly, breasts so round and soft. *You're so white,* he told her, *such a beautiful creamy white. Your tan's gone completely. Tans aren't fashionable,* she smiled at him. *The sun's very bad for your skin.* His hands stroking her side, her smooth white thighs. His fingers on the wineglass, cold and smooth and shining. Drank. The red blood in a slurp that dribbled down his chin. Soon, he thought. Soon, Linda. She was a presence in his head. She never left him. Pale. So clear.

But somehow he could never get a complete picture of her. She was close-up fragments, images huge in his mind. Her red mouth, hair like golden thread, her pink-brown nipple roused and prominent from his teasing teeth. And around these fantasies, beneath them in the dark, were all his secrets, magic, monsters, terrors that could rise up and consume him. Who was she? She was a monster herself. A thing in his head that he feared and hated. He entered her and he yearned. He yearned to break through into that darkness and dig down deep among all those secret things, but it was never possible. He was too weak. She contained him, held him in. He was blind in the tunnel of her, grubbing for the gold until his strength gave out. And finding nothing. Endless failure. Power flowing out of him like blood from a slashed heart. She had the power. She enclosed, enveloped, trapped him. She controlled him. In the real world of everyday, she was his toy, his vanity. But in the secret confines of his mind, he was her slave. He could only fall down and worship her, on his knees before her, his face pressed into the valley of her thighs as he breathed the female smell of her like a drug, an addiction that kept him in thrall. I'll die, he thought. There's no escape. His lust burning in him, aching muscle. I don't care, he told himself. Let me die.

52 The Mountain

From the Notebooks of Walter Newton

6/9/75

The guts of the answer is somewhere in the way we are made, the manner in which become who we are. A developmental issue, therefore.

Some propositions

1. In most societies, the biological mother of a child is also the environmental mother, the feeder, nurturer, prime care-giver, at least until the baby is weaned. This is normal (i.e., 'the norm').

2. The process of psycho-development for the child is one of dis-identification from its mother; the establishment of self-awareness, individuality, personal identity. The first step in this process is the moment of birth, the physical separation of mother and child. In the early months of its life, the baby learns

to distinguish itself from its mother. It becomes aware of itself as a separate being. It becomes conscious.

3 The beginnings of consciousness involve two things: first, the awareness that one's mother is not oneself and, second, that one has a body of one's own. To the consciousness, the body is a very tightly knit complex or pattern of experiences. Remember Melissa playing with her toes, the growing awareness that these strange phenomena are different sorts of objects from the beads or the peg doll. They are part of her.

4 Thus, the process of developing consciousness is based in the experience of the child. The process of physical maturation is different (but related, obviously). Jung says the development of consciousness is the prime task of the first half of life. It is essentially the development of a psychological strategy for dealing with the world. Which functions, which attitudes, which types of behaviour serve the child well? Which don't? Which experiences, which behaviour in others serve as models for imitation and emulation? The decisions begin at birth (before?) and go on, with more and more refinement, into adulthood.

5 Everything that is rejected or is less used as part of the strategy of consciousness becomes, to a greater or lesser degree, part of the unconscious. (Jung's view also?). Think of a computer. It is all present, all the hardware and software, but parts of it are used more frequently. Some of it, never at all. The choice depends partly on a natural tendency in the child and partly on its experience of the environment. The unconscious thus holds all the experiences and psychic functions that one has rejected. These include the experiences of oneself as a non-individual; the pre-conscious existence in which the child was part of its mother. The unconscious, therefore, holds *or is* the direct experience of oneself as a purely physical object.

6 The first important perception a parent has is of the baby's sex. From its earliest awakenings, therefore, the child is subject to sexual conditioning. The values and behaviour patterns that the parents try to inculcate may be more or less distorting depending on the child's natural predilections. Again, everything that is not encouraged to grow as part of the consciousness becomes part of the unconscious, including the understanding of one's sex. Thus, (Jung again) the soul of a woman is male, and the soul

of a man is female. (Thus, for example, the blonde woman of my dreams and the guide who took me to the imaginary city.)

7. There is a difference, though. The developmental task for the boy is to disidentify himself from his mother and to identify himself with male (father) figures in the world about him. This is a more radical and perhaps violent (although not necessarily more difficult) task than that of a girl, who must disidentify herself from her mother and identify with her at the same time. The males in the girl's world must be adjusted to rather than identified with.

8. Perhaps there is a difference in the quality of male and female consciousness in consequence of this. The girl's identification with her mother may help keep her in touch with the most elemental part of herself, the experience of herself as being part of the material world. For the boy, the disidentification may lead to a deeper rejection of his unconscious experience and a greater emphasis on the value (not the use) of consciousness. My own experience in this regard.

9. Thus, while the soul of a man is clearly female, it is not so inevitable that the soul of a woman is male. Perhaps, like the chromosomes, it a matter of XY and XX.

10. Maybe out of these ideas come the extremes of sexual stereotyping. On the one hand, the overweaning male ego, which has no clear view of reality. The man with an overblown consciousness thinks the world is always as he sees it and that it should conform to his idea of it. The final result of this is injustice, tyranny, and destruction. The woman, with an excessive emphasis on the physical, is the stupid, unthinking breeding machine.

Does any of this make sense? Think of Elizabeth. You could never accuse her of an underdeveloped consciousness. An insistence, in her, that the world conform to her ideas. And wasn't I following an idea when I left? Were we both examples of overweaning ego?

53 Development

Jane in the kitchen. The smell of baking bread. The kettle on the stove. A pot of half-made soup. She was slicing onions, pungent gas of them in her eyes and nose, the tears. She sniffed, wiped her eyes on the back of her wrist, which, of course, made them worse. Bugger onions, she thought. All my life they've got the better of me. The kettle started to sing. The big grey knife in her hand crunching through the last of the white and purple bulbs, the rings, through her tears, falling onto the chopping board.

The kettle stopped. Anelise, by the stove, had it in her hand. Jane looked at her blurred image, laughed. 'Shall I make some tea?' Anelise asked.

'Please.'

'What sort?'

'Mint. There's some over there, on the table.' Fresh twigs broken from the bush this morning. She carried the chopping board to the stove and scraped the onions into the soup pot. Sniff.

Anelise was looking at the mint twigs uncertainly.

'Pull a few leaves off and stick them in the pot,' Jane told her.

'I'm not used to fresh herbs.' Anelise laughed. 'I'm not much of a cook really.'

'Cook? Can't say you'll learn much from my cooking. Cordon noire, Walter used to call it.'

'That's not very nice.'

'One thing you could never accuse Walter of being was nice. He was a good cook, though.'

'The bread smells wonderful.' Anelise inhaled the scent of it, lifting her nose to take more of it in.

Jane sat down, easing herself into one of the wooden chairs at the table. As usual when she let herself relax, she felt the little aches in her joints. Still, she thought, once you stop, you're dead. Her father used to say that. Worked on himself till he was over ninety.

Anelise set the teapot and two mugs on the table, sat down opposite Jane.

'You don't talk much about your first husband,' she said.

'Brownie? He was my only husband. In the legal sense.' She remembered watching from the kitchen window as the horses came over the hill, Kingi riding one, Tane leading the other with the dead body across its back. 'It was a long time ago. Over thirty years. He wasn't a lucky man, Brownie.' Thin and slow. His sour face. Never smiling. 'I could never understand why I married him.'

'Why did you?' Anelise asked.

'I felt sorry for him, I suppose. I had a big brother that went away to the war. Mark, his name was. He got himself killed in Italy. Brownie was like him in a miserable sort of way. Well, you couldn't blame the poor bugger. He was a sensitive man, Brownie. He didn't take to fighting much.'

'Did he come from round here?'

'Not really. This place used to belong to his uncle. There was about three hundred acres. But Brownie used to come up here as a kid and he loved it. When his uncle died, there was no one else left to inherit.' Jane leaned over and poured the tea, the steaming water with its pale green tint. 'I only ever remember Brownie smiling twice in his life. Once was when I said I'd marry him and the other when he stood in that back yard out there for the first time and looked at his farm. 1957 that was. Three years later he was dead.'

'What happened?'

'Tractor rolled on him. Kingi and Tane found him and brought him back. Brownie's luck. He was never much of a farmer, anyway.' There was no pain left now. It was too long ago. And she had changed so much, she had become so much the person she was after Brownie's death, maybe even because of it, that there was nothing she could feel sad about. God, she thought, I wouldn't have liked to have nursed him in his old age. Poor bugger.

'It must have been terrible for you,' Anelise was saying. 'Left alone with young children.' There was a look on her face. Her anxiety. She was thinking, maybe, what it would be like to be alone.

'I thought it was the end of the world.' Herself in her appalled state of helplessness. She chuckled. 'The twins were about two, and then there were the three older ones. And I knew absolutely nothing about the way things worked. So bloody naive. If I hadn't been so naive, I might have given up.'

'How did you manage?'

'I had the widow's pension and some of Brownie's war pension. I sold most of the farm back to the Makaras and their people. Well, it belongs to them anyway. And they've been good neighbours.'

'I could never have done it,' Anelise said. Her fear growing.

'I guess I just liked kids, eh?'

'Well, you had two more.'

'Hine was a mistake. I never intended her. I mean, you would never have picked Tane as a father. He was too wild, too hungry. But he was a lovely man.' A twist in her belly now. A prickle of tears at the back of her eyes. 'A beautiful man,' she said.

'You had a beautiful daughter.'

God, yes. Sniff. She could not even pretend it was the onions.

'And Melissa?' Anelise asked. 'Was she a mistake?'

Jane laughed. 'Oh, no. She was a gift, eh?'

Anelise did not answer. She had gone somewhere, suddenly, lost in her own thoughts, her eyes wide, gazing out of the window at the yard, the fields, the green fields and the grey sky.

Jane stood up and opened the oven. A wave of heat wafted into her face. The loaves, three each on two trays, were done. She lifted them out one by one with the oven cloth and knocked them out of their tins onto the bench, set them on the wire rack to cool. Then she looked at the soup, which still needed more doing to it. She'd forgotten to finish it. Dreamy, she thought. Forgetting things.

Anelise was looking down at her hands.

'You okay?' Jane asked her.

'I should be getting back. I've been a burden on you long enough.'

'You're not a burden, girl. Don't be stupid!'

'There's Andrew's school. He missed three weeks of last term and now the holidays are nearly over too.'

'Sign him up for Correspondence School.'

Anelise looked at her. Hopeful. Wanting.

'You're not ready to go back yet, are you?' Jane asked. Nor's Andrew, she thought. Poor kid. Why pack him off to school when he needed attention and love and someone to help him figure out what he felt?

'No.' Anelise shook her head. She was close to tears. Not gratitude, not pain. It was relief. Something inside her, some set of rules that she'd not let have its hold for a while, had suddenly risen up and got her by the throat. She needed Jane to tell it to let go.

'Take it easy. It's not weak to look after yourself, is it?'

'No.'

'And Andrew's all right. He's a bright boy. There's plenty here for him to read.' She bent down, took half a pumpkin from the cupboard, began to trim it with the big knife. 'If he can't get an education from the books in this house, there must be something wrong with him.'

Anelise laughed, struggling back towards her good humour. 'Where did they all come from?'

'Walter's mostly.'

'But I thought Walter's . . .'

The fire. The ruin, the black ruin. The books still on their shelves some of them and burnt to a crisp.

'No,' Jane said. 'He never had enough room up at his place so he kept the ones he didn't want down here. Then, when he died, I swopped a lot of them round again.'

'Really?'

'The ones I wanted and his notebooks and journals.' Although, why? She sometimes wondered. All those words, endless words. Where had it got him, really? Dark green skin of the pumpkin, orange flesh.

'Oh, that's such a relief to me. You've no idea.'

Surprise. Jane turned. Anelise with a smile, her eyes shining.

'I thought you really had lost everything of his,' she said. 'I'm so glad you could save some of the important things.'

And for Jane, looking at her pleasure, a light dawning. 'You've been blaming yourself for all that, haven't you?'

Anelise surprised now. Her own realisation.

'You cut that out, now,' Jane said. 'You're responsible for yourself. Nobody else, you hear me?'

'Yes.'

'Good.'

54 The Marrying Maiden

Saturday, one thirty. He was waiting for her. He hated waiting for her. There was no point to it if he had to wait for her. The waiting proved — didn't it? — that his control was not complete, and if it was not complete, it was insecure. He might lose it altogether. Especially today. He wanted to take her out to lunch, to surprise her, make her feel happy. A celebration. The Ventura contract was signed. They were on the way. Linda wouldn't understand, wouldn't know what it meant. She had no real interest in his business beyond the fact that it paid her rent and her bills. She would enjoy being taken out, though, and he would look at her across the table and admire her and feel pleased with himself. She was one of the symbols of his success.

He stood, with a glass of chardonnay in his hand, looking round at the living room; the white furniture, the white rugs, the white silk roses in a glass vase. On the walls, the mounted photographs of exotic places; the Parthenon, the Taj Mahal, the Riviera. He wasn't often here alone and he realised he had never really looked at the place, the stuff he'd bought, without Linda there to interpret it. It was like a movie set, a reception area, a waiting room. The drapes were open. Through the net curtains he could look down on the street, the roof of the house next door. Straight down, four floors, was the alley, the wooden fence, a parked car. Michael.

If Michael had lived, he would have been over fifty now, with a wife and children perhaps, and a whole life behind him of being and doing. The world, Paul's world, would have been different. Maybe none of this would have happened. Maybe Paul would not be standing here now in the white, fluffy living room of his nineteen-year-old mistress waiting to celebrate the signing of a major contract while his estranged wife and son were hiding in a remote Northland settlement with a bunch of pseudo-relatives. What would Michael have thought? Would he have liked Anelise? Sided with her, maybe? Before he went to Sydney, he had always been like a part of Paul's mind, his knowledge of the world, the rules, and how to get things done the way he wanted. It was as if, when Michael died, all that was cut away and Paul was left without that part of himself, like a kid with a wooden leg who had to get on as best he could stumping and clunking where everybody else could run. Done all right for a cripple, though, he told himself.

'Ta-ra!' She flung the door open and her arms wide. She was wearing one of the boutique's creations, a black bodice with a thick, gold swirling pattern, a little gold frill of skirt and tight black pants like bicycle shorts, black shoes. Her legs were bare. Her lipstick red like her nails, her hair drawn back from her face into a bun. In her right hand she had a bottle of champagne.

'Celebration!' she cried, dancing into the room, twirling.

She knows, he thought. But how could she? He was not sure whether he was pleased or disappointed.

'Here, here. Open it.' She thrust the bottle into his hands and went into the kitchen. He peeled back the gold foil on the wine and released the wire cage. It was not vintage but it was genuine enough, had probably cost her forty-five dollars.

She was back with two champagne flutes and hopping from one foot to the other as he twisted the cork. The wine was well shaken by her eagerness. It went off with a bang, throwing the cork at the ceiling, and began to froth out over his fingers.

'Oo, oo, oo,' she cried, and fell on her knees, mouth open, tongue out to receive the foam. It poured over her face, her breast. Laughing.

He bent down, took the glasses from her, filled them from what was left in the bottle.

'What a waste!' She got to her feet, took one of the glasses from him. Her smile, her eyes, the kind of full, excited happiness she just gave out to everyone when it was in her.

'Here's to me!' she said, raising her glass.

Her? He sat down on the sofa.

She sipped the wine, grinned at him, teasing. 'Don't you want to know what we're celebrating?'

'Tell me,' he answered, wondering now, suspicious. Her joy, he saw, was too great to have been for him.

'My new job!' She bounced up and down, her elbows tucked into her sides. Then she hugged herself and shivered. 'With Antonio Picardy!' She laughed. And, then, when he did not ask her all about it, she went on to tell him anyway. 'He's one of Peter's biggest-selling labels. Fabulous, fabulous clothes. And he's been really excited about the number of garments I've sold of his. He's been into the shop several times and we've talked about ideas for things and he's actually tried some out and he thinks they're really good and now he wants me to work in his shop and run it and maybe I can have some input into his new collection.'

'Why?' He was confused, puzzled, unbelieving.

'Why what?'

'Why you?'

'Because I'm an excellent, excellent salesperson and I know about clothes. I have an instinct, Antonio says, a natural flair. And you know the best thing? Peter understands. We were all talking about it this morning. Peter says he'd be really, really sorry to lose me but, it's the chance of a lifetime and I'd be an absolute fool not to take it.'

'I don't like it,' he said. 'I've told you before. I don't like you working.'

'Oh, please, Paul. Don't start on about that again. I can't just spend my life being here for you, can I?'

'Why not?'

'It's boring, that's why. I'm a human being, not a doll or a budgie. I need to do things. I need a career.'

No, no, no, he wanted to tell her. It was like a scream in his head, like he was hanging on to something and his fingers, muscles, joints were crying out as it was ripped away.

She sighed and came and sat next to him on the sofa. 'I'm sorry I wasn't here for you today,' she said in a soft, placating tone. 'What would you like to do?'

She put her glass down on the table, snuggled into the crook of his arm. His anger squirmed in his chest. He wanted to pull away from her, push her off, but he could not.

'You're a very jealous man, aren't you?' she said, coaxing him. 'Were you always like that? Were you that way with Anelise? I bet you let her have a job.'

'Only when we were first married; we didn't have any money then.'

'And what happened after?'

'She had Andrew. And then she went to university and did a degree.'

'Weren't you jealous of all those handsome students?' He could feel the laughter in her, teasing him, and his anger twisted tighter. He was annoyed by her presumption, her probing after the meaning of his marriage. He was annoyed too because she was right. He had not been very possessive about Anelise. Did that mean he had never wanted her, never cared about her? He wanted her now. He wanted to be with her still. He simply refused to have her on the condition that he apologise and grovel and promise to be a good boy.

'Well,' she said, 'you wouldn't want me to have a baby, would you? And I'm too dumb for university. So.' She sighed, a soft, contented sound. 'I don't mind you being jealous. I like it really. It makes me feel you want me.' Her fingers, lightly, began to stroke the inside of his thigh. 'Maybe I could do something special for you. Just to make up for not being here.'

No, he thought. You're not going to get round me like that. But her stroking fingers were full of electricity, sensations through the fabric of his trousers. She was caressing his anger, his strength, focusing it to her own purpose.

'You don't really mind about the job, do you?' Her voice was almost a whisper. Her fingers were unfastening his belt.

Yes! he wanted to yell at her, but he was powerless. A shudder of revulsion swept through him. He hated her. His desire for her. His need. In the dark deep-down of his body the black, burning fire. Yet, despite himself, he turned his head, rubbed his face against the soft gold, the clean, silky smell of her hair. She was pulling out his shirt, unzipping his trousers, working her way through to his flesh. And he wanted her, bursting for her. The sweet, golden softness of her, her innocence. She was all in white, his princess.

'I hope not,' she said. 'I already told Antonio I'd take it.'

55 Abundance

It was cold down on the beach. A faint breeze from the sea and the waves roaring in their winter grey, white foam hissing up the sand. Anelise and Melissa walking side by side, towards the south. Andrew wandering, poking around in the flotsam, driftwood, banks of cast-up shells.

'I love this beach,' Anelise said. 'So wild. So few people.' She remembered the feeling when she first went for a run here, the opening up, the endlessness of the space before her. Now, looking back, it seemed like the beginning of something of her own and not just a need to deal with Paul's problems.

'I come here a lot,' Melissa said. 'I love the colours, especially when it's hot. It's all gold and white and blue and silver. Royal colours. Except for the plastic, that is. I used to come down here with my father when I was first pregnant with Alice. It was the last time he was really active.'

'What did he die of?'

'I don't know. Heart failure, the doctor said, but that doesn't mean anything. He wasn't well during last winter. He had a cold that lasted a long time. The first time I ever remember him getting anything like that. Then, a couple of days after Alice was born, he got really ill. For a while, he just stayed in the house. Then he stopped getting out of bed. He died about the middle of February. Jane and I think he just decided he'd had enough.'

'Why?'

'He was never sick. He didn't believe in it, he said. Well, that's not quite true. He had a theory about viruses. He thought they were basically just chemicals and that they only became alive with certain mental states.'

'You don't believe that, do you?'

'Yes. In a way, I do. Whenever I think I'm getting a cold, for instance, I say to myself, "No, I don't want that." And then there's a change in the basic way I feel and it doesn't happen.'

'Never?'

'Sometimes I don't actually mean it. But I always know when that is. It's like telling lies to myself.'

A strange notion. Kate had once taken her to a lecture on New Age philosophy that said similar things about mental powers. Anelise had been sceptical, and Paul even more scathing when she told him about it. She was tempted to believe Melissa now, though. Melissa, she felt, somehow knew.

The Reddening

There was a big log of driftwood ahead of them, silver white with dark, flaking bark. A crooked branch curving upwards that made her think of the arm of a swimmer churning through the sand. Like Paul, who always seemed to take the hardest course. Telling lies to himself.

'What's Linda like?' she asked.

Melissa looked at her and suddenly took her arm. A comforting squeeze.

'It's hard to say,' she answered. 'Silly. Clever. I think she's unformed. Maybe that's what she wants from Paul, something powerful to give shape to her life.'

Powerful? Paul? 'I'm not sure he's really powerful,' Anelise answered.

'He is in the public world. And maybe that's what Linda wants. She has no faith in her own inner reality so she wants someone else to dominate her. That's what being in love is, isn't it? Seeing the things in the other person that they can't see in themselves. Wanting those things.'

Love? Why love? And what did Melissa know about it anyway? At twenty-three, with no man in her life, no permanent relationship except, as far as Anelise could tell, a few months' liaison with Alice's father.

'I think a lot of people love like that,' Melissa went on. 'Their children, for example. What they want them to grow into. What they can't be themselves.'

'That's not good love,' Anelise said.

'Neither is Paul and Linda.'

'That's not love at all!'

'Oh, it is. I think it is.'

No, she didn't want to believe it. Love was fearful. The thought of love between those two made her so angry. Why should he have it? They have it? What right had they to take it all away from her?

'I don't feel loved,' she said. 'That's the worst thing about this. I don't feel loved at all. And in a strange sort of way I don't think he ever loved me. He never even saw me, really. I was just . . . a thing in his life.'

'An idea,' Melissa said.

'Idea?'

'When you are just an idea to someone it makes you feel like a thing.'

'Is that Walter again?'

'Yes.'

'He said some stupid bloody things!' Anelise said.

Melissa laughed, squeezed her arm, slid her hand down into the pocket of Anelise's jacket.

'He said a lot of bloody stupid things,' she said. Her hand in the pocket felt cold, delicate, gentle, cupping the backs of Anelise's fingers. She turned them to meet Melissa's grip and the two palms settled together.

'I love you,' Melissa said.

The words, like a shock, terrifying, electric. What was she to do with them? But I can say anything, she thought. Anything I want.

'How do you mean? Sexually?' A little tremor in her voice to make such a thought an open thing.

'What's sexually? It's all the same, isn't it? I love Alice sexually. I love her body. I love touching her. She makes me go all gooey inside.'

'I like men,' Anelise said. More firmly than she meant, maybe. 'I like men too.'

So strange. She was tense, waiting, as if every cell in her body was holding its breath. She looked down at her feet, their feet, moving together, her Reeboks and Melissa's home-made shoes of rough brown leather. The thin hand in her own, warm now. She wanted to ask Melissa what she meant, to explain. She needed to know, precisely. But she also knew she did not. This was enough.

'We should go back,' Melissa said, and they turned gradually in a wide circle, without losing hold of each other's hands.

The sun fell warm on their faces. About a hundred metres ahead of them a dark figure was standing, a twist, before the waves. Andrew. Throwing shells.

'It scares me when you say you love me,' Anelise said.

'Why? Because I'm a woman?'

'I don't know. Love always seems such a big thing, a heavy commitment, involvement. Complicated.' So much pain, she wanted to add.

'So much pain,' Melissa said, and it did not seem strange.

'Maybe it's you. Maybe you scare me.'

'Why?'

'You seem so wise. You're in such control of yourself. And yet you're so much younger than I am. I feel like I haven't lived somehow. And then I think, how can it be that you really find me interesting?'

Melissa laughed. 'We all love in others what they can't see in themselves.'

'And what's that? In me?'

'Your strength.'

212

'Strength?'
'I tell you often enough but you never believe me.'
'I want to.'
'You will. Remember when I read your face? I could see then how strong you are. Like steel.'
'I'm scared of that,' Anelise said. 'I don't like it. It doesn't seem human somehow.'
'No one's human on the deepest level. We're all animals down there.'
'I don't want to hurt anyone,' Anelise said.
Andrew was closer now. He bent down, picking over the shells at his feet, wandered forward a few paces. One he liked, it seemed. He stood up and drew back his arm, knees bent a little, leaning backwards. Then his arm flicked forward, forward and around, his body following, and the shell, a little white spinning thing, flashed out and down almost, rising, lost against the background of the white waves, and up, she saw it dark against the sky, spinning, curving, rising, coming back, until it fell behind him in a little kick of sand. She wanted to clap.
'That was a good one!' she called.
He turned and started to walk towards them.

56 The Wanderer

From the Journals of Walter Newton

840606

A sense today of the wholeness of things. Spent the night with Jane and she got at me about how I was allowed to stay at her place, while I never let her stay up at the cottage. Told her Mohammed had to come to the mountain and she hit me. I was right, though. I live in her world not she in mine. It is her centre that matters, herself at the centre. We made love and I didn't feel old.

Walked up the hill this morning on a warm winter day. Melissa came with me. I noticed how tall she was getting, long-limbed, coltish (if an adolescent girl can be coltish). She asked me if I'd ever been to Spain and I told her yes. She wanted to know what it was like, because it was the exact antipodes of New Zealand. So I told her what I remembered of Spain then, fifty-odd years ago, before the Civil War, and after a while she said she really loved the idea of how we were connected to other countries, how the ground we were standing on was part of the same earth as all the other people in the world were standing on. And suddenly I saw what an important insight that was.

'Yes,' I said, 'One world. We're only separate in our minds. Our bodies are part of everything, the world of matter.'

'Is my brain my mind?' she asked me.

I told her it was a tough question, one that philosophers had been debating for centuries.

'But our brains are part of the world of matter, aren't they?' she said. And I knew then that she was talking about God. It was as if a whole lot of things just clicked into place. Something like:

One world, the Great Circle, the Tao. The world is everything which is the case (Wittgenstein). Which means that everything that exists is part of this world and anything that is not part of this world does not exist. Which means that a dream is as real as a stone.

But we have to divide the one world into two categories: consciousness and matter. And consciousness means our ideas of things. The tree is not the same as our experience of the tree, our idea of the tree, the use of the tree, the meaning of the tree, or the word 'tree'. The reality of the tree is independent of anything in our consciousness.

And the great mistake of Christianity is to identify God with consciousness. This is a result of ego-centred male thinking and the reason why Western civilisation has been so successful scientifically and technologically, and also why it has got itself in such mess. The truth is the exact opposite. God is everything that is not consciousness, the endless undifferentiated (by thought) continuum of the universe and all the mysteries and powers it contains. And the most immediate and personal experience of God is simply your mind's experience of the unconscious, which is, ultimately, a physical thing; your brain.

I tried to explain it to Melissa as we walked up the hill, and she seemed to get the point in a way.

'That means,' she said, 'that if we just look inside our heads, if we look down, deep down, we'll know everything about everything. Because God will give it to us.'

'Yes,' I told her, 'I guess that's right.'

And I saw that if anyone was ever going to do anything with this stuff, it was Melissa, because all I had even now was just a mass of ideas. It didn't matter though. I was happy with that.

57 The Gentle

The path from the gate was lined with standard roses pruned into knobbly sticks. There were flowerbeds with bright chunks of polyanthus, daffodils in the corner by the steps. He mounted to the patio, the front door, rang the bell. A shadow stirred behind the frosted glass. The door opened.

'Oh, Mr Newton. Good morning.' The housekeeper, dumpy in her blue gingham dress and navy cardigan.

'Hello, Mary.' He stepped inside. 'How's everything?'

'Fine. We're fine. We're in the living room today. Taking a bit of sun.' She gestured towards the open door to her left.

His mother was sitting by the window. Small, thin. Pale face, silver hair tied back in a bun. Her narrow shoulders hunched. Her knotted hands with their folded, crippled fingers were on the arms of her chair, her elbows raised, as if she was about to stand up to greet her visitor.

'Paul?'

'Sit still, Mother.' He went over to her and kissed her cheek, soft and spongy. 'You're looking well.' He pulled a chair up beside her so he could hold her hand if she wished.

Mary was still in the doorway. 'Tea?' It was an exaggerated syllable, lifting high, and her eyebrows went with it.

'Yes, please,' he told her. Elizabeth said nothing.

'Dr Newton?' The same rising intonation.

'Yes,' Elizabeth told her. 'Thank you.'

A bob of the head and Mary went out, closing the door behind her.

Elizabeth gave a little shudder. 'The way that woman sounds, it's an offence to the ears. An abuse of the powers of speech.'

Why do you make her talk then? he wanted to ask. Instead he said, 'The garden's looking nice.'

'Yes. Cartwright's doing a good job with it, I suppose. I don't like the spring garden much. It's got no smell to speak of. How's Anelise?'

'Fine.' What else could he say?

'I haven't seen her for months. Why doesn't she come and see me anymore?'

'She's busy, I guess. At the moment she's away. She's gone away for a while.'

'Why?' A blunt accusation that he couldn't answer. The silence lengthened. 'Well,' she said, at last, 'I suppose it's your business.'

'Yes.' Relief that it was over.

'I don't want to know about it, then.'

'How are you feeling?' he asked, to change the subject.

'Fine. I'm fine. Mary would have told you that.'

'Yes. She did.'

'Well, she's right for once.' She turned her face to him, challenging him to deny her health. Her sightless eyes. Or perhaps she could see his shape, a vague blur with the sunlight falling on it. Her irises blue, pale, almost white, as if the colour had faded from them with their usefulness. If she does not see me, he thought, do I exist?

'As beautiful as ever,' he said.

The remark astonished her. He had never said such things to her before. Why did he say them now? He was not sure himself, except perhaps his gratitude for her not cross-examining him about Anelise.

'Don't talk nonsense!' But she was pleased, a tiny part of her, a little ghost of a smile, the spirit of a dead thing from the past, from so far back she could not remember. Holding her face up to him still, like a gift. The plane of her forehead drawn with faint lines arching over her brows. A thin, straight nose, the little bulb of the bridge shining like polished ivory. Her lips blue-pink, narrow, sweeping down from the double peak beneath her nostrils to the tucks where the deep folds of her cheeks ended. Lines. Vertical lines on her upper lip. Lines in loops beneath her eyes. A net of lines around the soft wattle of her throat. He had never looked at her before, he realised. Never, in his memory, had he seen her face.

A strange sensation, catch in his throat. His thoughts had gone, all business and purpose faded, voices silent, except for one small, distant murmur like something on another telephone line. He reached out and cupped his hand over the twisted pyramid of her knuckles. Her skin dry, rough at her fingers.

'Thank you,' she said softly. Her eyes filled suddenly with tears. He watched them form, well up and spill in a sudden bright fall from her pale lashes, down her cheek and round the curve of her chin. Her mouth twisted into a sad smile. She sniffed. Her right hand began to drag around her lap and into the side of the chair. A handkerchief, white, with lace edging. She gripped it in the flap of her fingers and held it up to her nose.

The door opened. Mary with the tea. She set it on a little table beside Paul's chair. There were two china cups, rich with decoration and gold leaf, a silver teapot and matching milk jug and sugar bowl, a plate with home-made biscuits. Mary, discreet, smiling, said nothing, laid out the things, bobbed her way out.

'Has she gone?' Elizabeth asked when the door had closed.
'Yes.'
'She's all right.'
'I know she is.'
'I vent my anger on her, you know.'
'Yes, I know. But she's paid for that too.'
'Not a nice job.'
'She seems happy enough.'

He leaned over, poured the tea, milk and sugar. The clink of the china, silver spoon seemed loud in the sunlit room. He held hers out to her.

'Can you manage the cup and saucer?' he asked.
'Yes. But wait till it cools a bit.'
'A biscuit?'
'What kind are they?'
'Chocolate, I think. They've got icing on them.'
'Mary's afghans. No, thanks.' A pause. 'She means well. I shouldn't get annoyed with her.'
'Don't worry about it.' He drank some tea. Through the window, on the patio, the wrought-iron table and chairs were bright-white in the sun.

'I just sit here, thinking, all day long,' Elizabeth went on. 'Trying to keep it all in order, trying to keep faith. I'm getting so that nothing else matters. I don't want to listen to the records or the radio. I don't want Mary to read to me. I just keep getting drawn back, drawn back into the same old questions.'

He waited, hardly breathing, wanting her to go on. Needing to hear the questions, fearing them.

Her face was turned to the window. She might have been looking out over the patio herself.

'Have I been so stupid?' she said. 'Have I wasted my life?'
The words were like needles sliding into his flesh, twisting.
'No,' he said. 'No.'
She didn't answer. Still staring at the bright world, the garden. The green of the trees along the front boundary.

'I'll have my tea now, please,' she said.

He held it out to her, guided her hands towards it. They opened to receive it, like two big claws, one clamping onto the saucer, the other on the delicate gold handle of the cup. She lifted the tea to her mouth, sipped at it through pursed lips.

'I think,' she said, 'that God made me blind because he knew I couldn't see. He made me blind in my old age so that I had no choice but to look inside myself. All the things I was afraid of. Now it doesn't matter anymore.'

And what about me? The voice inside him, thin, distant, but clear now. I've kept the faith too. I did it, did it all for you, for us. So you would love me.

'Poor Michael,' she said.

Michael, Michael, Michael, Michael. Part of me that died. I burned him as well, I burned them both. I was purged, we were purged. Clean. The fire has to burn until the last unclean element is consumed.

She cleared her throat, a little scraping sound, and he waited, listening, wanting.

'He didn't fall,' she said. 'It wasn't an accident. I know that now.'

Not true, not true. He could not bear it to be true, because if it was an act of will, then that was all that Michael's meaning led to. Not bad luck, not a random blow of fate, but a decision, a conclusion, a result.

Elizabeth went on, 'Walter knew it too. He always knew things like that.'

Her words, so soft, so calm, were like a rage in him, a swelling, churning turmoil, fire and storm and the earth heaving in his head. His father's name. She had uttered it. She had spoken his name as if it was an ordinary word. As if, after all this time, she had changed the whole meaning of her life. His life. So easily, so unconcernedly betraying him, their pact, the deal they had.

'Begin again. Begin again,' she said, so softly. 'How was it possible to begin again? I needed the miracle then. I needed the hand of Jesus to touch my eyes and make me see. Now it doesn't matter anymore. It's all the same now.' Her own hand, her left hand, was reaching out to him, wavering for him to touch her.

He could not move. Even if he had wanted to, there was no strength in his arm. He had no comfort for her. Her words had left him paralysed, helpless. He felt nothing, not anger, not hatred, not despair. The enormity of her admission took away all meaning, all possibility of reaction.

Her hand fell away, back to the arm of her chair.

'It's all right,' she said. 'It doesn't matter. You must look after yourself. You must be brave. Don't be like me. Don't be like me.'

58 The Joyous

Morning. Jane put on her dressing gown and slippers, drew the curtains at the big window. Grey. The mist outside pressing close against the glass. Her room. The wardrobe with the big oval mirror on the door, the Scotch chest, the double bed with its sagging mattress, shelves with the books she wanted to keep close. The pictures, photographs pinned to a board, interleaving, overlapping, layers of them, almost like the layers of the past. She had slept here for more than thirty years and it had gradually come to fit her perfectly, snug and comfortable, a cocoon, a second skin. She went out into the dark hall, down towards the kitchen, where the mist light glowed pale. She liked such times with the house close and quiet. The early-morning beginning.

Andrew was in the kitchen, fully dressed, cutting bread. He turned, startled, embarrassed, as she came in.

'Up early,' she said.

He grinned at her, sheepishly, looked down at the bread knife, the butter and honey on the bench.

'Eat, eat,' she told him and filled the kettle at the tap, put it on the stove. Then she sat down at the table.

'Couldn't sleep, eh?'

'I had a dream,' he said. He had the bread and honey on a plate. For a moment she thought he was going to rush away with it to his room, but then he hesitated, sat down too.

'A good dream?'

'Flying,' he said. 'I was flying, all over the place. I could go wherever I wanted. I woke up feeling really good.'

Gawky, awkward, his eyes behind his glasses dancing towards her and away again. He ripped into the bread with his teeth.

'You've had a lot of stuff weighing you down lately,' she said.

He glanced at her. He wouldn't want to talk about that. Careful of himself, private. Like his father but not so bad.

'Where do dreams come from, though?' he asked, between chews. 'What do you think?'

'I've got two theories. First, they're all part of a spirit world, like lost souls, waiting for someone to make them real. The second is that they're just your brain talking to itself. Take your pick.'

'The second,' he said. She knew he would.

'Well, the theory is that the brain keeps on churning out information even while you're asleep. It's the same sort of information that comes through your eyes and ears and fingers, except that when you're asleep your brain makes it up. Then it tries to interpret the information. And because there isn't any way it can check it against the real world, the brain can do what it likes. So it turns it into all sorts of odd experiences for you.'

He nodded. 'I think the brain's a computer, basically.'

'That's what I'm saying, isn't it? Dreams are when the computer runs by itself.'

'Mmm.' He was thinking about it, tasting it, a sweet idea along with the bread and honey.

The kettle started to sing. She got up, made herself a pot of tea, the morning mix of herbs from the tin on the windowsill.

'You don't believe that, though, do you?' Andrew asked.

'About the computer. Sure I do. Both theories are true. But I guess, by nature, I'm the wishy-washy-airy-fairy-mystical type.' She laughed, took the teapot back to the table.

'No,' he said. 'You're not wishy-washy. I don't think you believe in theories at all really. You believe in magic.'

Magic? He surprised her with his insight. Clever. He knew it. The look in his eyes as he watched her react to him. It was Walter's look.

'Do you want some tea?' she asked. 'Witch's brew?'

'Okay. Thanks.'

She brought two mugs to the table.

'You *do* believe in magic, though, don't you?' he insisted.

'I believe in numbers.'

'Mathematics? So do I.'

'I'm not sure we mean the same thing. Take the number one, for example. What's that?'

'Unity.'

'And two?'

'One plus one.'

'Two unities?'

'Yes, I suppose so.'

'How can you have two unities?'

'Urm.' He sat with his head cocked, eyes angled at her, mouth pulled into a little grin. Guarding his confidence, his conviction that he knew more than she did. Or did he? 'Is that a trick question?' he asked.

'Look at it this way. Unity is oneness, isn't it? It's the Whole, the completeness of everything. The Universe, if you like. How can you have two everythings?'

'So what's two?' He was intrigued now.

'You cut one in half, you get two.'

'So what's a half?'

'That's what you get when you cut unity into two.'

'Mmm. So that means all we ever have is fractions.'

'Isn't that so?' She picked up one of the mugs. 'What's this if not a bit of the world? On the other hand, you could look at it another way. You could say that one was the essence, the prime substance, the Philosopher's Stone. Then I could ask you what you would get when you cut one into two. And you'd say?'

He smiled, enjoying it. 'I'd say, "Half." And you'd say, "How can you have half of the essence?"'

'That's it.'

'So where does that leave mathematics?'

'Don't ask me. I think mathematicians are talking about something completely different. Ideas maybe.'

'That's good,' he said. 'I like that.' Sitting, smiling to himself, his head on one side. He was like a bird with his thin limbs, bright eyes. A bird in his dream, flying. The freedom of his thoughts floating everywhere, anywhere. Not caring how it had to be or what he was supposed to think.

'What's the Philosopher's Stone?' he asked.

'Ah.' She poured the tea, trying to find a way she could explain it. 'It's something the alchemists believe in. It's the essential substance, the thing from which everything is made. It's matter and spirit at the same time.'

'Like atomic particles. Matter and energy.'

'That's it. Your grandfather had an idea of it once. How did it go?' She thought back, remembering his face. His voice. The words beside her in the air as they lay in the dark and she listened with a growing sense of magic. Yes. It was.

'Well, imagine it's night, a pitch-black night. And away in the distance you see the Stone, like a star. It's made of pure, bright crystal, without a flaw or blemish, perfect, and it's so hard that nothing can scratch it, except another of its own kind. Now that's lucky because if it was ever to receive even the tiniest chip, it would explode into nothing, a cloud of drifting smoke.'

'How big is it?' he asked, eyes on her, caught up in her description.

'Hard to tell. Like a basketball maybe. Or a pea. Let's say it fits comfortably into the palm of your hand. But it's heavy, very heavy. As heavy as the darkness around it. None of that's really important, though. The big thing is the colour.'

'What colour?'

'Many colours. Thousands of colours. But only one at a time. It depends on the angle you look at it from. From one place it might be red, say, pure red. Now, if you go round it and look from the opposite side, the back, it's red from there too. From the top, though, it's blue, and from the bottom also. From right and left, it would be yellow.' She held out her left hand, fingers spread as if they were cradling a big grapefruit, and repeated the colours, pointing at the imaginary crystal with her finger. 'Front and back, red. Top and bottom, blue. Right and left, yellow. Now, that's just the beginning. Imagine that you are looking at the red and the crystal slowly turns towards the blue.' Andrew's eyes were fixed on the nest of her fingers, fascinated. Magic, she thought. Yes. 'The colour changes, see, from red to purple to blue and, if you keep going, it goes back to purple and to red again. Or say you looked at the yellow and the stone turns towards red. You'd see it go from yellow to orange, then to red and so on. Every direction produces a different pattern.'

'A spectrum. A different spectrum.'

'Yes. But the colour also depends on how far away you are. If you are looking at it from a great distance, it seems very dark, almost black, so that it disappears into the background. The closer you get to it, the lighter it becomes until, at a certain point, the colour is pure. Now, if you then go closer still, it keeps on getting lighter, paler, so that, in the end, when you get inside, at the very centre, there's nothing but a single point of pure white light.'

'So it has all the colours?'

'Not quite. There's no grey in the stone. It has all the colours between black and white.' She stopped.

He waited. Wanting more. She smiled at him. 'That's it.'

'Wow! That's amazing. Neat. I mean, mathematically. It's like co-ordinate geometry. Every colour has its own set of co-ordinates and, wow, its place in a spectrum is like a vector.' He was beaming at her. 'My grandfather invented that?'

'It was a dream, eh?'

'He dreamt it?'

'Yes. It was like some secret knowledge, the key to everything. It was a big deal for him.'

59 Dispersion

Sun on the water, the beach empty. Anelise sat with her back to a pine tree among the fallen needles. Below her the slope of yellow marram grass to the beach. The white of foam on the water, waves rolling in, the slow, beating rhythm. The sight of it and the sound had taken hold of her. The rising, turning crests, the falling rumble of it, mesmeric. It was in her mind somehow, her flesh and her bones, as if the sea was speaking to the water in her body, lulling it, soothing it, calling it back to itself. I have to decide, she thought. I can't stay here for ever. Yet, at that moment, it was hard to understand what the decision was. It seemed as difficult to leave her seat under the tree as it was to find a direction for the rest of her life. Or as easy maybe. The sun, warm on her face, floated slowly downwards into the sea. The evening and the morning of the sixth day. She remembered those words from somewhere. Why the sixth? The sixth week. The sixth month. The sixth year. The time of her becoming. So long. Over twenty years of marriage to a man who had everything. Except a soul. No, she thought, that's unfair. But was it? Wasn't that, in fact, her job, to be his sensitivity, his feeling self, his spontaneous utterance, while he tried to deny that any such part of him existed? Except that I'm not like that, she thought. But then she remembered what Melissa had said about wanting things from people and how they were not necessarily the things they saw in themselves. Maybe I'm all the spontaneity he can stand, she thought. After all, I did up and leave him in a matter of hours with only two suitcases, a box of books and Andrew's computer in the boot of the car. Spontaneous enough maybe. And if it is true that he married me for the parts of me I'm not aware of, then I ought to find out why he did it so I can know what they are.

Water. Maybe I like the water because I'm a water sign. Scorpio. Quiet and deep but with a sting in the tail, Kate said. Kate, who always sides with the men, who flirts with them all, who is faithful to Theo because he gives her the place in the world she thinks is her due. Come home, Kate had said over the phone. A woman has to give a little. And how can you deal with this silly blonde bitch if you don't come home and fight? I don't see the point in it, Anelise had said, when he doesn't even want to talk to me. Maybe he doesn't know what to say, Kate suggested. How about sorry for a start? But men never admit they're wrong, you know that. They're the most ridiculous creatures in the world.

He didn't even want to talk to her. They had spoken twice. The first time she had rung to tell him where she was. He had wanted to know mostly about Andrew's schooling and how he was going to keep up with his extended mathematics classes. He's getting extended life classes at the moment, she answered, wondering whether she was being sarcastic or serious. I want you back, he said. Why? she answered. What about your little blonde floozy? That's my affair, he said, and she thought, Is he joking? Is he really making a pun of it? Or is he so stupid he doesn't know what he's saying? Either way. Either way, she didn't know.

The second call was about the share issue. She had to sign some papers. She had to come home and do it. No, she said. Send them up here. You need a lawyer, he told her. What? For these papers or for another reason? These papers, he said. He sounded cold, icy fury, all suppressed and pressed down into his packed-tight anguish. Are you mad because I left? she asked. Or because I came here? Do what you like, he told her. You're a free agent. What do you want? she asked him. I want you back here with me. But he said it in such a way, a flat, monotonic voice, that she was afraid. Nothing had changed. Nothing would ever change. It had not changed with this crisis, nor with his father's death. It had not changed with the success of the business. It had not changed when Andrew was born. All through the years somehow, she had been waiting for it to be different and now it was too late. He had always been, forever would be, chained to his family, locked up in their world, the life back then. He was like his mother, never letting anything affect the rigid order of his life, suppressing anything he did not approve of, burning his past because he could not bear to take responsibility for it. Maybe he would burn his wife so he wouldn't have to take responsibility for her leaving him. Like a witch. Whereas it was he who had run off to Linda. Which made him just like his father, abandoning his wife and son. The son who worshipped him maybe, who was left in the clutches of a woman who would bind him tight, put him in the straitjacket of her religion, her principles, her strangulating moral rectitude. That's what Walter did. Well, yes. He found the meaning of life maybe. But he had a lot to answer for.

Wind. A little breeze coming up, stirring in the tree above her head. She shivered. I must go, she thought. But the sun was close to the horizon now beneath a drift of cloud, grey skein, underbelly tinted rose. The sea rolled in. The white foam had faded. Track of light, reflection back to the horizon, sky pale yellow, a tinge of green, the sun burning, orange. I'll go when it touches the water, she thought. That'll be the end. That's when I'll know. When they come together. Because she didn't have to do anything. It was not a decision about doing anything. It was a decision about being. If I am as I am, then the decisions will take care of themselves. She would make them without fret or anguish. Or not at all. Like Melissa, whom she loved and could say that without worrying about what it meant or what the consequences were or what she had to do about it. Because Melissa wasn't planning to do anything. She didn't want anything or didn't seem to. She just believed in her in a way that Anelise did not believe in herself. I used to believe in myself, she thought. When I was running, training seriously. I used to believe I could win. Was that what Paul had seen? The will to win. Maybe marriage had taken it away from her, sapped her of it. Or maybe it was something else. Not the will to win but the will to be. As if simply by enduring the heat of the fire, the inner self became stronger still. That was what Melissa saw, wasn't it?

And the sun, sinking, burning water, fire in the sky, she felt within herself a sudden blaze of light, her inner world on fire, melting and flooding through her, mind and body, feeling, thought, her need to take control, and she was nothing, she was invisible, she was a thing of glass, a mirror, striking back the sun's rays, meeting it with her eyes, her strength, a thing of glass, which blazed inside with all the colours, fusing, whitening, until she was filled with the sense of power, her life, her own red blood. Strong, she thought, yes. Like steel. And there was nothing to be afraid of.

And the sun touched the horizon and there was a sudden bright flash of light like a beacon in the sky.

60 Limitation

'What's this? Pilau?'
'Yes,' Kate said.
'It's nice.'
'Yes. I like this recipe.'
'More wine?' Theo holding out the bottle, smiling.

Why Things Fall

'Thanks.' The golden-yellow chardonnay into this glass. Paul sipped at it, nodded, yes.

They ate. Theo and Kate strangely quiet. Did they have a plan for who was going to speak first? he wondered. Should he help them out?

'It's a while since we had a meal together,' he offered.

'Yes.' Kate gave a tight little grin. They were all thinking of happier times, of course. Of the person who was missing. Of the peculiar events that had intervened to disturb their lives. I'm responsible, Paul thought, but he felt strangely distant from it. Their diffidence and their concern seemed odd, unnecessary. He felt, somehow, that he did not quite understand what was going on. Perhaps he should try and get it over with.

'Have you heard from Anelise?' he asked.

Kate looked at him. Her serious, dark eyes. Beautiful Kate. He could want her too, if he let himself.

'Yes. We've talked on the phone a couple of times,' she answered.

'Is she all right?'

'I think so.' Kate hesitated. Did she have a message to convey?

'It's really none of our business, of course.' Theo with a discreet shrug of his shoulders.

'But it is, though, really, isn't it?' Kate said, suddenly. 'It is the business, for one thing, and, well, we've all been friends for so long.'

'Yes,' Paul said. Sipped his wine. Waited. He was anxious. Something was going to happen but he was not sure what. He couldn't understand why Theo was being so circumspect, and Kate so serious. Yes, it was a big deal, of course it was, but there was no need for them to behave like undertakers. Kate reached out and laid her hand on the side of his wrist.

'Have *you* talked to her?' she asked. Her fingers light. The rings glinting. Gold chain bracelet looped over the thin bones, brown skin.

'I called her. She called me. We haven't really got past first base,' he said. Anelise had been a small and distant voice, calm, cold, clear. He knew that determination in her and knew now that he was not going to yield to it. We are too alike, he thought. In that way, at least.

'Is there anything we can do?' Kate asked. 'Anything?'

'I don't think so.'

'Poor Paul! It must be hell for you!' she said.

Sympathy? For him? A surprise, a little shock, to feel that

anyone could see him that way. He smiled.

'And thank you for the pilau,' he said. And ate, looking from one to the other of them in the awkwardness. Yes, he thought, they are genuinely my friends. And I need them. And he felt very calm and glad of their company and their interest in him. It was simple. Clear.

'So what is to be done?' Theo asked

'Anelise and I must reach an understanding, I suppose. I expect she's very angry with me.'

'Of course she is,' Kate said.

'But then I'm behaving in what everyone considers to be a very silly manner.'

'No, no.' Theo tut-tutting to show that no one really thought it was silly at all. 'We understand these things. An attractive young woman . . .'

'Oh, but she's nothing,' Paul said, and at that moment he believed it. Linda, a silly girl. Frivolous, naive, dependent on him. She was a nuisance, a drain on his time and energy. Suddenly he felt a great distance from her. He was in control again, godlike, powerful. He could almost laugh at how ridiculous he had been.

'An infatuation,' Kate said, smiling at him.

'Yes. Crazy really.'

'You must explain it to Anelise. She'll understand. I know she will.'

Linda waiting for him in that ridiculous flat with the white-vinyl lounge suite and the fluffy rugs. Poor kid, he thought. I really have been stupid with her. The least I can do is keep on paying her rent for a while. It was strange, so strange, his new view of her. As if he had turned over a beautiful carpet and suddenly seen all the seams and the joins and the ugliness that held it all together.

'It is a big relief to have you talk like this,' Theo said. 'I think, you know, you really have not been yourself for some time.' He was smiling too, a big grin. 'Welcome back.'

And where had he been? On what far journey? The memory of his lust like a distant fire. That fire.

He smiled. Nodded.

'Yes,' he said.

After dinner, Theo brought out a bottle of port, a celebration. They sat round the open fire and laughed and talked about old times. Only a little difficulty, complication because of Anelise's absence. Theo smoked a cigar and they stared for a while into the fire. There was more port, more coffee.

'There is another thing we must talk about,' Theo said suddenly. A catch in his throat. He coughed gently. Kate was sitting very still, her thumb and forefinger gripped tight, white-knuckled on her coffee cup. Paul alert and puzzled, waiting.

'I have been thinking lately about the future,' Theo went on, 'and I have to decide for myself. We will have a new company with a new structure, board of directors, managers we must consider. I know we have talked a little about this, but I do not know how comfortable I am in those arrangements.' He paused, twirled the glass of port in his fingers. The light winked deep in the ruby red.

Paul said nothing. He knew what was coming but he didn't believe it. If Theo had wanted this, he must have known, he must have known all along, so why had they even started?

'I think,' Theo continued, 'that I wish only for a place on the board for the new company and not for any involvement with the management.'

'Why?' Paul demanded.

'We have twelve million shares on offer for a dollar fifty. The brokers say that is no problem. We are already over fifty percent subscribed. So for Kate and I there is a realisation of nine million. Also, I think, with a little luck, we will come into the market around a dollar eighty. That values our remaining shareholding at around twenty million.'

'You're not telling me you're going to sell out, are you?'

'No, no. Not so stupid. That would ruin everything. But maybe in the future, a little by little.'

'You want out.'

'No, no, not at all.' Theo shaking his head. You're lying, Paul thought, and he could tell as much by Kate's attitude as by the tone of Theo's voice. Head bowed, elbows pressed into her sides. The cup of coffee. She was staring into it as if it held the offer of escape.

'What the hell's going on, Theo? I don't understand,' Paul said.

Theo hunched his shoulders, spread his hands, all innocence. 'Nothing. It is no big deal. I just want to let you know that I have thought and that my interest for the future will be for Kate and I to do something on our own. I just want to tell you that we must consider the question of the management for TBC. I will not be there and . . .' He paused, looking for the right words.

'And what?'

'Maybe you should consider for yourself your own involvement.'

'Are you saying you want me out too?'

'No, my God, I want you in. We have a disaster otherwise. But

I think maybe you should look to some help.'

'So I can't run it on my own, is that it?'

Theo, smiling, little shrug of his shoulders. Sorry, sorry, Paul, but it is so, is it not? Theo has to be replaced because Paul is too stupid, too dull, too unpredictable on current performance to do the job on his own. And if Paul doesn't agree, then Theo may fight him in the boardroom or perhaps just sell out everything as quickly as the market will allow.

'It will be okay,' Theo said. 'We must be friends, you know.'

It was ten thirty when he left. He had swallowed his anger, suppressed his impulse to walk out and stayed for a final glass of port, an awkward truce, Theo's toast to the future. They shook hands at the door. Kate kissed him goodbye. Her warm, soft lips on his. Her fingers on his upper arm. He paused by the car and looked up at them as they stood together on the balcony. Then he got in behind the wheel and backed out into the street.

Betrayal. Theo with his smile and shrug, his acceptance of Paul's inadequacy as if it were a fact of life. The truth, was it the truth? Because if it was, then the damage was more hurtful, more deep than ever. When things were said out loud, they exposed you on the inside to yourself, such stark simplicity, how your best friend saw you. And your father, like a grey ghost, stood at the bottom of the stairs with a pack on his shoulder, calling upwards. Paul! And Paul beside his mother down the hall, watching. And the fire in the grate, the burning photographs, her silence. Never, never speak his name to me again. And their pact, broken at a whim because she tired of it, grown old, and Theo with his shrug, so simple, wanting out, and Paul standing naked, stripped of his illusions, hating, hating his innermost secret weakness. They all saw how weak he was. How he had nothing now but Linda and that inner vision of her, that gold-white princess, cold as death. And all his sense of power was slipping away, like melting crystals, water into dark and sticky, stinking mud. He was exactly like his father, exactly. Abandoned everything for an idea, a dream he could not explain or understand. And a wife now who hated him, who wanted nothing more to do with him for the breaking of her faith. A slow, black tide of self-disgust seeped through him and, with it, the return of his desire, the hot dark blood in his belly, his rising flesh, like a mocking thing. As if the more he loathed it, the more it grew, engorged, hard, unendurable.

The lights were on in the flat. He got out of the car, slammed the door, walked, ran, stumbled across the road to the entrance of the block. His lust was an agony, restricting him. Release. Relief from it. He did not know what he would do when he got upstairs. His key in the lock. The lift. He waited, bending forward to ease the pain. The lift stopped, doors opened. Inside, he pushed the button for the fourth floor. Looked at himself in the mirror on the wall as he ascended. His short-cropped hair, his cheeks drawn, staring eyes behind his gold-rimmed spectacles. Someone strange. Someone he hated. The corridor to the brown door with the glass bead of a spy-hole. His key in the lock. He was inside, pacing, staggering from room to room. All the lights were on but she was not there.

He turned away, walked through to the kitchen, took a bottle of red wine from the rack in the cupboard. Any bottle. Did it matter? Opened it, a glass. To Michael, he thought, toasting the window. And drank. The Blood of Christ. The Blood of All the World. The Blood of Linda.

Where was she? There was a fashion magazine open on the white sofa, a glass of fruit juice, almost empty, on the coffee table. In the bedroom, the sliding door of the wardrobe was open. Her clothes on hangers pressed in tight, her shoes in neat rows on the floor beneath. There was a blouse on the bed, a white blouse, her virginal look as she glanced up when he came through the door while she sat on her sofa in her virginal setting. Had she changed to go out? He lifted the blouse to his face sniffed it, faint scent of her. His flesh had subsided now but it stirred again at her odour, glow, the fire deep down. He let the blouse fall to the bed and stood, staring at its crumpled form. Then he reached out and, with one hand, straightened it, smoothed it, opened it up so that the arms were outstretched on either side. Another gulp of wine. The glass in his hand. He held it out, tilted it. The liquid swung toward the rim, quivered, slopped. The gout of purple dribbling down the outside, cold over his fingers, falling. Splat, splat, splat. Exploding stains across the blouse. The left breast, ribcage, belly to the right hip. Ripped her open. He looked down at it.

'Paul?' She was there in the doorway, staring at him. Had she seen?

'I spilt some wine,' he said. 'I'm sorry.'

Her eyes widened as she saw the blouse. 'Oh, God!' She lunged forward, grabbed it, held it up. 'Oh, God, that's silk. What am I going to do? I can't soak it.' She crumpled the blouse in her hands, red nails. 'And look at that.' Pointing. There were stains on the duvet. 'How am I going to get that out?' She began to pull at the duvet cover, looking for the place it opened.

'Leave it,' he said, and walked past her. He got the wine from the kitchen, took it into the living room, sat on the sofa. Drank some more.

'Leave it!' he shouted.

She appeared then in the doorway. She was wearing jeans, tight jeans, black boots, a red shirt. A black-leather jacket was draped over the back of the sofa beside him.

'Come here,' he said. 'Sit down.'

She obeyed him, perching herself on the edge of one of the armchairs, watching him.

'Where have you been?'

'I got bored, waiting for you. I called Antonio. He was home, doing nothing. We just went out for a drink, that's all. I thought you weren't coming tonight.'

Antonio, the grateful employer. He had already given her a raise and a company car.

'Where did you go?' he demanded.

'The Gluepot. There was a great band.'

He believed her. It was all innocent. Of course he believed her. Except that he could not bear the thought of her existing in anyone else's world. Keep cool, he told himself, keep calm.

'Take it easy,' he told her. 'Get yourself a glass. Have some wine.'

She was tense, trembling, but she managed a little grin. She stood up. He watched her walk away, the shape of her in the jeans. I need her tonight, he thought. I'm going to enjoy her tonight.

She came back, sat down in the same chair. He poured wine for her. She smiled, looked at him. Something about her. Awkwardness.

'So. You had a good time.' he said.

'Yes. Antonio's so funny. He was saying all these crazy things about the people there. I was laughing so much it really hurt.'

'I don't like you going out with other men.'

'He's my boss.'

'He's still a man.'

'Oh, for God's sake, Paul. He's gay. I thought you knew that.'

Gay or not, he did not care. Another being had sat with her, listened to her words, made her laugh, smiled at her smile. How could that be when she did not exist except in his head, when she was nothing but a reflection of his own dream?

'I still don't see why you have to go out with him.'

'He's my boss. It's good for my career. It's good for me to be seen with him.'

'Fuck your career! I don't want you working. I told you before,

I can look after you.'

'All right,' she said. 'Marry me.' Her determination, jaw set, challenge. Her eyes hard, staring at him, full. He did not know what to say, the scream in his head somewhere. She took his silence for an answer. 'See? You don't want me really, do you? Not in any permanent way. I'm just something for you to play with, have a good time with. You don't really care what happens to me in the end. Just so long as I'm here when you want me now. One day you'll get bored with me and drop me. Just like that.'

No. The rage, the boiling rage, coming up with the pain. He could not hold it, all, all coming apart.

'No!' he yelled, and smashed the wine glass on the edge of the table. Glass and liquid spattered over the surface. She winced but stayed where she was. 'I own you,' he hissed through clenched throat, his voice rasping. 'I own you.'

'Sorry, Paul.'

'I own everything here, everything in this room.' He swept it wide with his arm.

'Except me,' she said.

'You bitch!' He made a grab for her but she stepped out of his way and he fell across the table. There was a stab of pain in his left hand.

'Piss off, Paul!' she said. 'You can do what you like. You can kill me if you like. But you'll never own me. Deep inside me, I'm mine and I always have been. Always.'

His hand was bleeding, blood dripping into the puddle of wine, the bright slivers of glass reflecting red. The piece in his hand was a sharp edged chunk, gleaming like an embedded gem. He picked at it with his fingernail and it came free. Blood welled out, dripped onto the table, the white carpet. He wiped the cut on the front of his shirt.

'Here,' she said, 'I'll get you a plaster.'

She went into the bedroom.

He stood up. The room was moving, swaying. He stared at his hand, the V-shaped flap of flesh and the blood welling up, trickling down the inside of his wrist and collecting along the edge of his watchstrap, brimming, slop, onto the cuff of his shirt.

Linda in the bedroom doorway with a box of plasters, opening the paper wrapping.

'Here,' she was saying. She came towards him. He held out his hand like a child and she stuck the plaster over the cut.

'You'd better get that looked at,' she said.

'Bitch!'

Her eyes flashed back at him.

'Get fucked!' she yelled, stepping back, away from him. Her jacket from the sofa. Her bag. She turned. 'Have a good time,' she said. 'Wreck the place if you like. I'm sick of it anyway.'

He made a lunge for her and almost fell, but she was flinging back the door and out in the hall. The lift closing, the whine of the motor.

He took a step, staggered. He was across the room at the window. He gripped the net curtains, yanked at them with both hands. They ripped away from the runner and fell about him. The window, open it. He swung it wide and was leaning out, his face in the air, staring down the four floors to the alley, the giddying spin of the space around him. There she was, below, walking, her hair bright in the streetlight. She did not look up. She got into the car. The air was cold, open, free, the suck of it. He tried to see. She was driving away. He leaned out further, saw the ground below, the heave inside his head, his catapulting thoughts. She had gone, then. Over. Michael. Michael. Yes. Now.

'Go!' he screamed, his breath ripping out of him. And the ground below, down there, the huge suck of force about his shoulders, hands, gripping, slipping. The earth, hard dark, the black smash of unconsciousness, buried forever. Michael. Yes. A wrench. And panic. Michael falling. He could see Michael falling, body free, and himself held back. He was teetering, slipping, fighting for his balance with the windowsill across his guts. And Michael falling, writhing free. His own fingers clutching at the metal frame, the air about his face, the treacherous air was sucking at him, sucking like a great mouth, dragging him out, his frantic muscles wresting, twisting. And Michael's wheeling helplessness was smashed into the ground head first. No. God. No.

He had the frame held tight, his arms hard, holding, balance. He was drawing back. His feet touched the floor. He was inside, falling, slumped against the wall, and the relief was pounding through him, heaving lumps of air ripping into his chest. He threw up over the white carpet.

61 Inner Truth

From the Journals of Walter Newton

851112

My seventy-fourth birthday. I sat in the sun at the front of the house and looked down the valley to the sea. I felt warm and snug and still like a cat, and I wondered if that was when the peace would come, when the brain finally stopped.

It's nineteen years since I first came here, twenty-four since I left Elizabeth and Paul. Trying to make sense of it.

I keep thinking of the circle of the *I Ching* with its sixty-four points, an eightfold combination of the yin and yang, female and male, earth and heaven. When we divide and count the yarrow sticks, we choose one of those points and are given the distilled wisdom of centuries associated with it. But do we interpret the oracle? Or do we ask the oracle to interpret us? What we have in that moment is the random confrontation of our current state of mind and an element of ancient wisdom. It is not all chance, nor is it all human will. It is not all nonsense, nor is it completely sense.

I sit here at my desk, with a room full of sunlight, staring at the mandala above the fireplace. The circle with the eight symbols, the square within it, the inner circle in the centre with the eight colours.

The symbols

```
                    King
            Priestess    Alchemist
        The Fool                Death
            Mermaid      Miner
                   Queen
```

The four cardinal points

> The King and Queen, which are Mind and Matter
>   in the right balance
> The Fool and Death, which are Mind without Matter
>   and Matter without Mind

and between them the four elements

> Priestess — Fire (Imagination)
> Alchemist — Air (Thought)
> Mermaid — Water (Feeling)
> Miner — Earth (Physical Sensations)

And in the eight points of this compass are all the directions a human life can take, at first outwards, away into the world, but eventually returning, for the circle represents the wholeness of being and the square within it is the walls of the Eternal City, the inner city of the self, teeming with its inhabitants, its memories, its ghosts. It has four gates, one for each direction, each element, and all of them lead into the heart, the eye, the stone that is the smallest point of concrete whiteness and, at the same time, the infinity of colours that is our experience of the whole world. This heart is somehow the essence of what it is to be alive, to be nothing and everything, to be the blind endurance of rock and the ephemeral power of living thought. And yet, what is it, this stone, but the core of Matter in us, the truth and the reality, our physical being? It is the stuff the world is made of and it is alive. And it shines. And it sings. It sings to the glory of the whole world.

62 Preponderance of the Small

Such an afternoon when it was still winter, when there had been so much rain the day before. They sat in the yard in the deck chairs, Jane and Melissa and Anelise, with Alice asleep on a mattress in the shade of a big umbrella. Sun warm, windless. The sky blue and high, looking upwards it was an endless blue. Jane, in the depths of it, a feeling for the seasons coming, spring growth, summer fruit, the heat in her bones. A different world from a year ago but the same. The same Earth turning, force of life thrusting up through the ground. The force was in each separate shoot, each living leaf. But was it the shoot that mattered, ultimately, the individual life, or just the existence of the force itself? Philosophy, she thought. The mist of words. She had often argued with Walter about it, with him saying that without words there was no clarity, and her knowing that the words obscured everything somehow, like clouds across the blue sky.

'I'm going to go back soon,' Anelise said. 'Maybe in a day or two.' Her voice was calm, confident. Jane could see that she knew this time. A strength in her.

'When you're ready,' Jane said. She looked at Melissa, who was hiding beneath the rim of her big straw hat. The moon child, silver, with her blood-red hair. Maybe Melissa would go too.

'I'll sort everything out,' Anelise said. 'And then I'll know what I'm going to do. I'm not in a hurry.' She looked up at the sky, the twin reflections of the sun in her dark glasses.

'Come back whenever you like,' Jane said. 'You're welcome here any time. And Andrew too. I like that boy. He's bright but he's not stupid, eh?' Bright like a light in the dark he was afraid of. All fearful. All of them afraid of the dark. Of their own true selves.

Anelise smiled. 'It's been good for him here. He's more at ease than I've ever seen him. Not trying so hard to entertain everyone. He's even got quite useful.'

'He's like his grandfather,' Jane said. 'More like his grandfather than he is like his father maybe.'

'I don't want him to be like anyone,' Anelise said.

'Especially not them, eh?' Jane laughed. Anelise looked at her. What were the eyes behind the glasses saying? She was annoyed? Puzzled? Ah, Jane, thought, we all worship Walter here, don't we?

'Walter was a clever bugger,' Jane said. 'He could understand anything you put in front of him. Even himself. I never knew anyone so good at understanding himself. But what's understanding, when all's said and done? Another book on the shelf? Another lecture in the air? It's living that counts.'

'Wasn't Walter good at living?'

'He was willing to learn.' Jane laughed.

Melissa got out of her chair and crouched down beside Alice, lifted the sleeping baby into her arms.

'I think I'll go for a walk,' she said. 'I think I need to go and see Walter's place.' She moved off towards the house.

Anelise looked after her, went as if to get out of her chair.

'Stay here,' Jane told her.

'Did you upset her?'

'Maybe.'

Anelise still watching as Melissa mounted the steps to the back door.

'It won't hurt her,' Jane said.

Anelise relaxed, sat back in the chair, the sun on her face again.

'Melissa's like the air,' Jane said. 'Like breathing the air on top of a high mountain. So pure it hurts your lungs.'

'We get on well together,' Anelise said.

'I know. You're good for each other. Maybe she should go to Auckland with you.'

The suggestion took Anelise by surprise, the tension in her shoulders, neck. The glasses staring at Jane.

'What would you do?' she asked.

'Me?' Jane laughed. 'I'm fine. Nobody needs to worry about me.'

'You could come too.'

'What for?'

'There might be more to do.'

'Oh, no. I never need to go looking for life. It just comes dropping out of the sky.'

'Like a bird?'

'A balloon.'

63 After the End

The house was dark after the sunlight. She walked quickly down the hall to Andrew's room. He was sitting there in front of his computer, staring at the screen.

'So there you are,' she said. 'Why don't you come outside?'

'No, Mum. Wait.'

Should she tell him? She grinned at the thought, the shock he was going to get. 'There's a surprise for you.'

'Just wait a minute.' He flapped his hand impatiently and then typed something, pressed another key, stared. 'Holy guacamole!' he yelled, his fingers still pressing buttons. 'It works!'

She stepped round to where she could see the screen. In the centre was a disc, bright orange. As she watched, it gradually turned a khaki colour and then moved into a vibrant blue. Andrew's fingers shifted on the keyboard and the blue became purple.

'That's pretty,' she said.

'It's brilliant!' he corrected her. 'Say I'm brilliant.'

'You're brilliant, darling. What is it?'

'It's the Philosopher's Stone. Where's Jane? I must show Jane.'

64 Before the End

Even when he found the road, he was not quite sure. It was not marked on the map and the only clue he had was that it was somewhere on the stretch before the stream. He slowed the car to a crawl for the last kilometre and scanned the verge for a track or a pathway leading off to the left. There was only one, rutted and paved with grey-brown metal. He drove on past it and then came back again. Stopped. Thought about it. His head was aching, beat of blood behind his right temple, and his stomach churned from fear and the wine he had drunk last night to try to blot it out. The cut in his hand was still sore beneath the strips of plaster. He stared at the road. There was no way to be certain it was the right one, but there was no other offering and if he did not try it, he would have had a four-hour drive, with a hangover, for nothing.

He eased the car forward, conscious of how peculiar it would look, a car like this in such a place. The surface was good, clear of plants where the grip mattered and the ruts not too deep. The road curved around the side of a little hill. There was bush on both sides. Then, after a hundred metres or so, it dipped and the vegetation on his right thinned. He could see a valley, steep-sided, full of ferns and trees. The stream must be at the bottom. The car bumped forward. The road snaked along the valley wall. Stupid, he thought. He could get stuck here. How the hell was he going to back out along a track like this? In places it was no wider than the car, leaves and branches brushing against the roof and the windows on either side. Maybe on some of the bends, where the road looped into the cliff, it was wide enough to turn in, but . . . Stupid. His hands gripped tight on the wheel and he fixed his eyes on the way ahead, the arch of trees above, the shafts of light breaking through the green, bumping, shifting. He had to do this thing. He had to. The idea had come to him like a certainty as he sat on the floor in Linda's apartment. He had to go back because there was nothing left. He had to go back to that one point and prove that he had had no choice, that it could not have been different.

The road was wider now, the bush thinner. To his right, the valley was full of sunlight, the trees in colours from almost yellow to dark, glossy green, the heads of the pongas spread like hands reaching upwards. The sky, when he caught a glimpse of it, was a deep blue. The colours of the valley and the patterns of light in the leaves around him were alive, shifting, the teeming combinations of a few simple elements, bewildering and mutinous. The blue, the green, the gold.

A bend. In front of him, a dark mass. He hit the brake but too slow, slammed in, threw him against the seat belt, head jerked forward, back. The car stalled. It was a slip and he was bumper-deep in it. A slew of brown dirt, rocks, the curling roots of a ripped-out tree, a slump across the road. In the centre it was a metre high. There was a little ripple, shower of stones and dirt skittering on the slide and pattering against the metal of the front mudguards. It was moving, by God. In a sudden panic, he twisted the ignition key. The engine didn't fire. Again. This time yes. He ripped the selector into reverse and backed away around the corner, further still until he felt the slope of the hillside ease. He stopped, breathed deep. The pain throbbed in his head. His hand was bleeding again, red ooze through the little pores of the plaster. Think, he told himself. Go back. He looked at the odometer. He had figured that the road was around six kilometres and he had driven almost five. He could get there on foot from here and then come back. It was three o'clock. Enough time if he wanted to, providing he could cross the slip.

He got out of the car and examined it. Dirt in the grille, a scratch or two maybe. Nothing much. He walked back along the road and round the bend. The slip was about three metres wide, and fresh, loose. Slowly he stepped out onto it and his city shoes sank down through the surface ankle-deep. He twisted, arms flailing. There was a flash of deep-green valley to his right, and then behind him as he wrenched himself round to face the slope, hands grabbing at the dirt. Okay. Slowly, not daring to look down, he moved crab-wise. Pebbles, soil tumbled around his wrists and ankles. He grabbed the uprooted tree but it, too, shifted. A few more steps. Easier. He was across. His shoes were full. He took them off and emptied them, felt the damp soak up through his socks. Ahead of him, the road curved on, another loop against the hillside. Silence.

Such silence. He could hear his own footfall as he walked. Sometimes there was the sound of a bird or a crack, creak from the vegetation, but in the windless valley nothing seemed to move. He strained his ears for the noise of the stream but there was nothing. Alone. The air was warm. He breathed it, the smell of last night's rain maybe, the percolating rot of the leaf mould. Growing things. He had never liked being in the open in this sort of place. The bush had always made him uneasy. It was living but senseless, a reflection of the blind processes in himself over which he had no control. Now, though, the solitude and the quietness produced not anxiety but a growing feeling of anticipation, excitement even. He was here because he had to be. To prove a point, to demonstrate that none of it could have been anything other than the way it was. Otherwise . . . Otherwise . . . He did not know. But he would know. He would know when he got there, because he was not afraid of it anymore, because there was nothing left to pretend about. His mother's truth abandoned and Theo seeing him for what he was and fearing his limitations, and Linda, like the last absurdity, his strength and power, like a booby trap, a doll blown up in his hands. I've got nothing left, he thought. Nothing left except this one last chance. He was walking quicker now, his stride longer, head cleared, excitement mounting. Quicker still. Almost he broke into a run.

Ahead of him was a clearing. The valley widened, the deep bed of the stream veering away to the right towards the sea. On the left-hand side, where he was walking, the slope of the hill had become more gentle, flattening out into a shelf. The road stopped here. There was a corrugated-iron shed with a pair of big wooden doors, painted green and fastened with a chain and padlock. He went up to the window, smear of dirt and cobwebs, and cupped his hands against the glass, peering between them into the gloom. Inside, there was a Land Rover and what looked like a big metal box or cradle, open at the top and bent and twisted as if it had been bashed by something heavy. Around the rim was a layer of padding and a series of loops to which ropes might be attached. Behind it, a big heap of dirty blue and green canvas or some other such material had been roughly folded and stuffed into the corner.

He turned away and went on down the path that led from the shed around a stand of trees. Overgrown. Lush grass and weeds flapped at his ankles. He kept his eyes on the curve of the path, the way ahead. He was not so eager now. He was afraid of what was coming, what it might do to him.

The first thing he saw was the water tank. Blackened, rusted. Its wooden stand had burnt away and it had slumped down, leaning over, twisted out of shape. There was a section of wall left on that side of the house, and another, making an angle with it, which still had some shelves attached to it and a window with the glass in place. The rest had collapsed. The iron of the roof, with its red, blistered paint, had fallen into the floor except for one angled sheet, which was propped on the edge of an enamel bathtub with claw feet.

He stood at a distance, in the shelter of the trees, staring at the wreck, the blackened charcoal, the rusted metal, shards of glass shining in the reflected rays of the sun. Was it what he expected? He could not tell. He had no feelings for the scene at all. It was just an assemblage of shapes and colours, a ruin that should have been pulled down completely because it was dangerous. Had he killed the ghost after all, then? What would he do if there was nothing here to find?

He stepped forward, walked across the clearing. Crunch of wood and glass under his feet. The weeds were already growing up through the debris. He was standing now where the front of the house used to be, with the view that was once to be had from the living-room window. Before him, the valley with the cleft where the stream was, a V cut in the horizon where it funnelled out of the hills. He could see the sea through there, a dark blue against the lighter sky. Like liquid in a cocktail glass. The old man standing here with the wind stirring his white hair. What did he look like old? Was he frail or strong? Could he see the view like this? Smell the air? He had had this life, this place. He had died here. And then it was too late for me, Paul thought. I left it too late. And so did he. The letters he sent me when I was young and I never answered. He should have known I didn't mean that. He should have known I wanted to, somehow, somewhere. And he felt a strange surge of anger, sadness welling up inside him. Tears. He was crying softly and it felt like the first time ever. The sobs shaking at him and the valley, sky, the sea, all blurred with the bright liquid. There were no ghosts here. There never had been. The possibilities had died with the old man.

He took off his glasses and dried his eyes on his shirt sleeve, turned back towards the house. It was a good site for a place, with the sun all day, the view, enough flat land for a fair-sized garden. He stepped forward onto a sheet of iron, which creaked and lifted. Over to his right, in among the weeds and the soot-black mess, there was a flash, a bright blue light. He moved towards it, trying to keep it in view. A piece of broken glass, maybe. No. He probed in the ashes with his fingers and pulled it out, a glass sphere, a marble. He polished it against his shirt and it came up smooth and bright. Tough to have survived the fire. A glint to it, a flash of light like a gem. He lifted it to his eye and it rippled with colour. He held it out again towards the sky in the south-west, but something else caught his attention, a movement near the top of the ridge from where the path wound down through the trees. There was someone there. A woman in a long floral skirt and a yellow shirt, coming down the path. He stood his ground, waited, watched her progress. She had a bundle on her back. She came towards him across the clearing. Pale skin, red hair.

'Hello, Paul,' Melissa said. 'I knew you would be here.'
'Knew?'
'I was thinking about Walter and then I felt someone else was here as well. Then I knew it was you. You came in the back way.'
'Yes. Stupid, really. My car's stuck somewhere down the road there.' He glanced over his shoulder towards the valley.
'I'm glad you're here,' Melissa said. Her eyes fixed on him. Green eyes, impossible to escape. She is Walter's child, he thought. My sister.
'You came to meet me?' he asked.
'Yes.'
'Thank you.'
The bundle on her back stirred. A head lifted, clad in a white hat. Two big blue eyes stared at him over her shoulder.
'Do you want to come back down to the house?' Melissa asked.
'Are Anelise and Andrew there?'
'Yes.'
'All right, then,' he said, feeling suddenly scared.
Melissa smiled.
'It's a mess,' he said, turning away, gesturing over the ruin.
'Yes. I guess we'll have to rebuild it.' He stared at her, not understanding, wondering who she meant. Her eyes, so green.
'Did you find what you were looking for?' she asked.
'Only this.' He held out the marble.
'Ah, yes,' she said. 'Newton's glass.' And then, 'Ouch!' as Alice yanked suddenly at her hair.